A SPY FOR THE REDEEMER

THE OWEN ARCHER SERIES
BOOK SEVEN

CANDACE
ROBB

DIVERSIONBOOKS

The Owen Archer Series
The Apothecary Rose
The Lady Chapel
The Nun's Tale
The King's Bishop
The Riddle of St. Leonards
A Gift of Sanctuary
The Guilt of Innocents
A Vigil of Spies

The Margaret Kerr Series
A Trust Betrayed
The Fire in the Flint
A Cruel Courtship

Diversion Books
A Division of Diversion Publishing Corp.
443 Park Avenue South, Suite 1008
New York, New York 10016
www.DiversionBooks.com

For more information, email info@diversionbooks.com

First Diversion Books edition July 2015.
Print ISBN: 978-1-68230-107-4
eBook ISBN: 978-1-62681-981-8

ACKNOWLEDGEMENTS

For devoting their time and sharing their knowledge throughout the imagining and writing of this book I thank Lynne Drew, Kate Elton, Sara Ann Freed, Joyce Gibb, Jeremy Goldberg, Fiona Kelleghan, Evan Marshall, Nona Rees, Compton Reeves, Charlie Robb, Patrick Walsh, the staff of the National Library of Wales in Aberystwyth, and my colleagues on the Internet discussion lists Mediev-l, Chaucer, and Medfem. Any mistakes are surely my own.

ACKNOWLEDGEMENTS

For devoting their time and sharing their knowledge throughout the imagining and writing of this book I thank Lynne Drew, Kate Elton, Sara Ann Freed, Joyce Gibb, Jeremy Goldberg, Fiona Kelleghan, Evan Marshall, Nona Rees, Compton Reeves, Charlie Robb, Patrick Walsh, the staff of the National Library of Wales in Aberystwyth, and my colleagues on the Internet discussion lists Mediev-l, Chaucer, and Medfem. Any mistakes are surely my own.

GLOSSARY

archdeacon: as was (and is) customary, the archdeacons of St David's were appointed by the bishop and carried out most of his duties; however, because the Bishop of St David's was the lord of the March, his archdeacons were men of considerable power

certes: certainly, to be sure (middle English)

demesne lands: The land immediately attached to a mansion, and held along with it for practical or pleasurable use; the park, chase, home-farm, etc.

houppelande: men's attire; a flowing gown, often floor-length and slit up to thigh level to ease walking, but sometimes knee-length; sleeves large and open

jongleur: a minstrel who sang, juggled, tumbled

Lady Chapel: a chapel dedicated to the Blessed Virgin Mary, usually situated at the east end of the church

liege lord: the superior to whom one owes allegiance and service

leman: mistress

Marches/Marcher Lords: the borders of the kingdom and the lords to whom the King granted jurisdiction over them

mazer: a large wooden cup or bowl, often highly decorated

minster: a large church or cathedral; the Cathedral of St. Peter in York is referred to as York Minster

no fors: does not matter (middle English)

scrip: a small bag, wallet, or satchel

seneschal: in the household of a sovereign or great noble the official who administers justice and controls domestic arrangements

solar: private room on upper level of house

summoner: an assistant to an archdeacon who cited people to the archbishop's or bishop's consistory court, which was held once a month. The court was staffed by the bishop's officials and lawyers and had jurisdiction over the diocesan clergy and the morals, wills and marriages of the laity. Also called an 'apparitor'.

tabard: a loose upper garment without sleeves

vicar: as a modern vicar is the deputy of the rector, so a vicar choral was a cleric in holy orders acting as the deputy of a canon attached to the cathedral; for a modest annual salary the vicar choral performed his canon's duties, attending the various services of the church and singing the liturgy

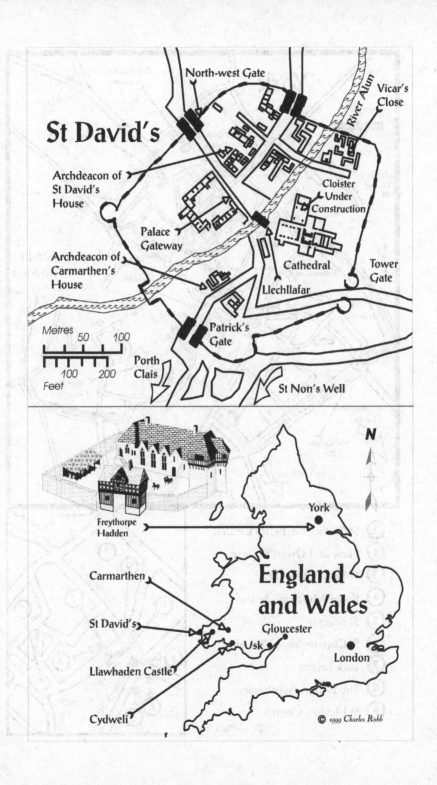

St David's

North-west Gate

River Alun

Vicar's Close

Archdeacon of St David's House

Cloister Under Construction

Palace Gateway

Archdeacon of Carmarthen's House

Cathedral

Tower Gate

Llechllafar

Patrick's Gate

Metres 50 100

100 200

Feet

Porth Clais

St Non's Well

Freythorpe Hadden

York

England and Wales

Carmarthen

St David's

Gloucester

Usk

London

Llawhaden Castle

Cydweli

N

© 1999 Charles Robb

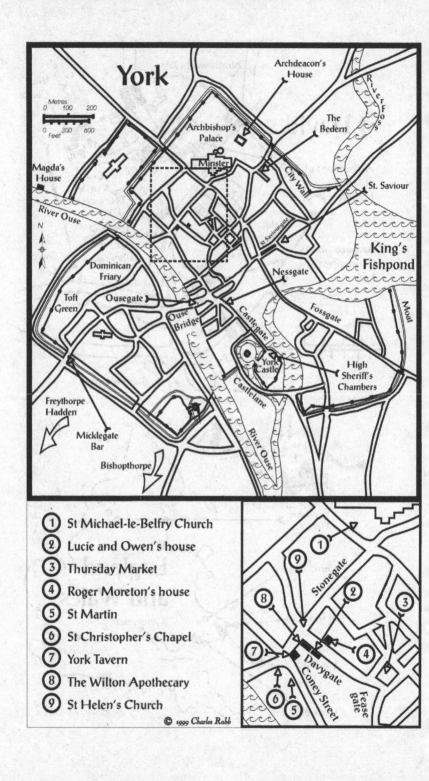

York

Metres 0 100 200
Feet 0 300 600

Archdeacon's House

Archbishop's Palace

The Bedern

Minster

Magda's House

City Wall

St. Saviour

River Ouse

N

St Saviourgate

King's Fishpond

Dominican Friary

Nessgate

Toft Green

Ousegate

Fossgate

Ouse Bridge

Castlegate

Moat

York Castle

High Sheriff's Chambers

Freythorpe Hadden

Castlelane

Micklegate Bar

River Ouse

Bishopthorpe

① St Michael-le-Belfry Church
② Lucie and Owen's house
③ Thursday Market
④ Roger Moreton's house
⑤ St Martin
⑥ St Christopher's Chapel
⑦ York Tavern
⑧ The Wilton Apothecary
⑨ St Helen's Church

© 1999 Charles Robb

Stonegate

Davygate

Coney Street

Feasegate

PROLOGUE

CANDACE ROBB

A shaft of early morning sun shone on the effigy, enlivening the cloth carved to drape gracefully over the stone torso. Ranulf de Hutton thought if he stared long enough the stone folds would lift and fall with the statue's breath, so real did it look in this light. God had blessed his fellow mason Cynog with enviable talent. But Ranulf had as much skill if not more. Why had he not been chosen to work on the tomb?

He was the senior mason working on the cloister walk and chapel at St David's Cathedral, always the first mason chosen for decorative work. Why had he not been granted the honour of fashioning this tomb? The English knight had died while on pilgrimage, after being blessed with a vision at St Non's holy well. Cynog did not deserve the honour of working on such a man's tomb. This past year he had been slow in his work, distracted by repairs to a wall in an archdeacon's cellar that should have been assigned to an apprentice, ever late returning from his visits to his parents' farm outside the city.

As he was this morning. Already the apprentices and journeymen worked in the stonemasons' lodge, smoothing, chipping, the stone dust spiralling in shafts of sunlight from the open sides. But no Cynog. Ranulf regarded the tomb. The face had not yet been brought out of the stone, nor arms and hands. Still so much to do. He ran his hand over the rough stone from which would grow the face, remembering the old knight's cheekbones, his gentle smile.

'What say you. Does it please?'

Ranulf turned round with a gasp. 'Cynog!'

The tardy mason's tunic was crusted with mud on one side and his boots were caked with mud. It had rained yesterday, well into the evening. 'You slept without the walls of the city?' Ranulf asked.

'In the wood, aye. Rolled off my cloak and look at the damage.' Cynog brushed the tunic with his long-fingered, delicate hands. The hands of an artist he had, as well as the eyes, deep wells of soft brown, seeming ever wide with wonder. Though this past year they had taken on a melancholic cast.

Ranulf's envy dulled, replaced by relief to see his friend back before the Master discovered his absence. 'You have come in good time, no matter. And what of Glynis? Did she meet you at the city gates Saturday evening as promised?'

Cynog lowered his head. 'She came, aye. Only to tell me she would not make the journey with me.' He swung his fist sideways, hitting a lodge pole. 'The mariner cannot love her as I do. I sacrificed my honour for her. She is my life!'

Ranulf had thought the young woman's recent friendliness merely a tease. 'She walked away from you in the autumn, my friend. It is now late spring. How can you still hope?' And yet, against all reason this, too, Ranulf envied. He had never been so besotted with a woman as Cynog was with Glynis. He could only imagine the passion. To be so alive. 'But you lost no honour by her leaving you. Do not think it.'

Cynog ran his fingers over the unfinished tomb. 'There are already many pilgrims at the cathedral door,' he said, changing the subject, another irritating habit of late. 'I thought you hoped to repair the font before they entered?' The flood of pilgrims during the day made work in the public parts of the church difficult.

'Oh, aye, I must do that, yes.' Ranulf picked up his sack of tools, tied it round his waist. 'Cover yourself with an apron. No need to provoke the Master Mason.' He grasped Cynog's shoulder. 'Work on the face today. You cannot think of her, or your pain, while freeing Sir Robert's face from the stone. And who knows, the holy knight may intercede for you, or ask the Queen of Heaven to do so.'

'Make Glynis love me?'

'Nay, friend, heal your heart.'

1

TOO LONG AWAY

On a May day that hinted at summer, such a day on which the people of York rejoiced in opening their doors to the warm, fresh air and found excuses to walk along the river in the sunshine, or to walk out on to the Strays to check on their grazing animals, Lucie Wilton and her adopted son, Jasper, were shut up in the apothecary, staring down at the mound of dried herbs a customer had just returned. The tension between the apothecary and her young apprentice seemed to suck out the air. Jasper's cat scratched at the closed shutter, begging to be released.

Jasper glanced over at Crowder and began to move towards the shutter. Lucie grabbed his hand. 'Crowder must wait. You are too easily distracted, that is the problem. If you kept your mind on your work rather than on the intentions of friendly neighbours, you would not have made such a mistake.'

Jasper yanked his hand from Lucie's and pushed his straight, sand-coloured hair from his forehead with an impatient gesture. 'Peppercorns for nasturtium seeds. It is a mistake anyone might make.' His tone was insolent.

Lucie resisted the urge to slap him. 'Any fool can tell the difference between the two, in scent as well as hardness. I cannot think how you made such an error. Look at me when I speak to you.'

Jasper met her gaze, then dropped his eyes, hunching his shoulders. 'It will not happen again.'

'It should never have happened at all. An apothecary cannot make mistakes. Have I not told you that if you are at all uncertain—'

'I thought I was pouring from the correct jar.'

'Because you were thinking of something other than the task before you. Taking down the wrong jar—you know what is in each jar. You clean them. You fill them.'

'I swear it will never happen again.'

'If it happened once…'

'I swear!' Jasper shouted.

Sweet heaven, if only Owen were here. Since Jasper's twelfth birthday he had increasingly withdrawn from Lucie, at the same time growing closer to her husband, Owen Archer. Though Owen disciplined the boy more often than Lucie did, Jasper seemed to respect his criticism while thinking hers unfair. 'If Owen—,' she began, but finished with just a shake of her head.

Jasper clenched his fists, jutted out his chin. His colour was high. 'If the captain were here, what would he say about Roger Moreton?'

'Jasper!'

'Or your mistake–' He stopped, dropped his gaze.

'Alice Baker's jaundice,' Lucie said quietly. 'Is that what you were about to mention?'

Though the boy's straight blond locks fell over his face, Lucie could see how he blushed. 'I meant—'

'Best to say no more.' Lucie needed no one to help feed her sense of guilt over the woman's condition.

Someone knocked on the door. Worried that Maria de Skipwith had already spoken of the boy's error, Lucie picked up the parchment full of herbs and handed it to Jasper. 'Take this into the workroom and pick out the peppercorns.'

Jasper looked down at the mix in horror. 'How can I find them all?'

'It is not to give Mistress Skipwith,' Lucie said. 'It is to fix in your mind the look, the taste, the scent, the feel of a peppercorn.'

Jasper hunched his shoulders and shuffled off to the workroom. Crowder followed close on his heels.

Lucie approached the door, wishing she would find on the other side a messenger with news of Owen, announcing his return. In late January her husband had headed south to join Geoffrey Chaucer on a mission into Wales for the Duke of Lancaster. Lucie's aged father, Sir Robert D'Arby, had accompanied Owen, wishing to go on pilgrimage to St David's in thanks for God's sparing the family from the recent pestilence. None of the company from York had yet returned. This was the longest Owen had been away since they had wed. Lucie had not anticipated the difficulties such a prolonged absence would cause. And that Jasper would be most difficult of all—that had been an unpleasant surprise.

Lucie swore under her breath as she found the door locked. She had not wanted a customer to hear her chastise Jasper. But the shut shop might itself cause rumours. Mistress Skipwith had said she understood, Jasper was merely an apprentice and there was no harm done, just some sneezing, she would tell no one, the lad would never do it again. But tongues wagged despite the best intentions.

A monk stood without, in the black robes of a Benedictine, his head bowed beneath his cowl.

'*Benedicte*,' said Lucie.

The monk raised his head. It was Brother Michaelo, secretary to the Archbishop of York and her father's companion in pilgrimage. What did it mean, that he appeared alone? The monk's patrician face was drawn, his eyes sad. *Dear God, please let Owen be well.* 'Brother Michaelo. I did not know you had returned.' Lucie stepped aside, welcoming him into the shop.

'*Benedicte*, Mistress Wilton.' The monk bowed as he entered the room.

Lucie glanced out into the street before she closed the door. 'You are alone.'

'I am.' Michaelo drew a stack of letters from his scrip. 'Captain Archer entrusted these to me.'

'My husband is well?'

A nod. 'I left him well.'

Deo gratias. 'God bless you for bringing them,' Lucie said, though her heart was heavy as she took the letters. 'My husband is yet in Wales, then?'

'By now the captain had hoped to depart for home. God willing, he should be home before Corpus Christi.'

A month. Still so long to wait. But she had managed this long. 'And my father?' When they had departed, Sir Robert D'Arby had not been in the best of health.

Brother Michaelo lowered his eyes and crossed himself.

'Father,' Lucie whispered. She had thought herself prepared for this. 'When?'

'On the third day of Passiontide, Mistress Wilton.'

More than a month ago. Lucie, too, crossed herself. She began to shiver. When had the room grown so cold?

'I am sorry to bring you such news,' said Michaelo, taking her arm, helping her to a bench.

It should not be a shock, Lucie thought as she heard Michaelo slip behind the counter, pour water from the jug. He sat beside her, held a cup until she was calm enough to take it.

'I should not have encouraged him,' Lucie said. 'He had not recovered and it was so cold when they rode out, then such a wet spring.' Sir Robert had caught a chill the previous summer. Despite his sister's devoted nursing he had never quite recovered. A recurring cough and hoarseness had been particularly troublesome.

'You could not have foreseen the weather, Mistress Wilton.' The monk drew a scented cloth from his sleeve. 'Sir Robert found the journey difficult.' Michaelo dabbed at his eyes. 'But he never complained.'

'Is it for my father, those tears?' Was it possible the self-absorbed Michaelo had been moved by Sir Robert's death?

Michaelo raised his eyes. 'I have walked in wretchedness all the way from Wales—selfishly, pitying myself for the loss of my friend. For your father was joyous in death and welcomed his release.' Michaelo's voice rode the waves of his emotions. 'After you have read the letters, I shall tell you of your father's last days. You might find comfort in hearing of them. Come to me when you are ready. I shall be with Jehannes, Archdeacon of York.' He rose. 'Should I send for someone?'

'Jasper is near.'

'You are very pale.'

His sympathy brought tears to her eyes. 'I shall come to you at Jehannes's house as soon as possible—tomorrow, if I am able.' The archbishop's secretary bowed, turned and departed silently.

If I am able. Lucie moved to a stool behind the counter. Alice Baker and her jaundice, Maria de Skipwith and Jasper's mistake, Jasper's distrust of Roger Moreton. And now she had lost her father. Her eyes burned. Sweet *Jesu*, but she was tired.

She needed a shoulder to lean on. Someone to comfort her as she wept for her father. She needed Owen. But he was not here. Her instinct was to go to see her kind neighbour, Roger Moreton, but the foolish Jasper had decided Roger was wooing her. He could not see that Roger was kind to everyone, not just Lucie.

Her father was gone. She must go to Freythorpe Hadden and break the news to Phillippa, her father's sister and long-time housekeeper. Could she close the shop for a few days? Would Alice Baker start rumours about Lucie's incompetence while she was not here to defend herself? Alice's jaundice was not Lucie's fault—most people would know that. For most of her married life Alice had complained of sleeplessness and fluttering of the heart. It seemed hardly a week went by that she was not in the shop buying new ingredients for the remedies she prepared herself. Lucie guessed that it was the skullcap purchased most recently that, mixed with something else on Alice's crowded shelves, had caused an overabundance of the wrong humours and turned her skin and eyes yellow, her urine a peaty brown. The midwife Magda Digby had agreed with Lucie—skullcap and valerian should not be mixed. Magda had prescribed an infusion of dandelion root and vervain. Lucie had mixed it for Alice, but who knew whether the woman was drinking it? And what she had added to it.

Sir Robert was dead. Lucie noticed the letters in her hands. She had forgotten what she held. Ink and parchment. She wanted *Owen* here, not his letters.

'Who was it?' Jasper stood over her, turning his head this way and that to see what she had in her lap.

'Brother Michaelo.' Lucie noticed that the boy's nose was red and his eyes watery. He would remember the punishment. 'Did you find all the peppercorns?'

'Made me sneeze.' He wiped his nose.

'Good. It did the same to Mistress Skipwith. You did your best?'

He nodded. 'What did *he* want?'

Jasper despised Brother Michaelo. The archbishop's secretary had once threatened the life of someone the boy had loved dearly, Brother Wulfstan, the old infirmarian of St Mary's Abbey.

'Brother Michaelo brought letters from Owen,' said Lucie. 'And—news of my father's death.'

'Sir Robert?' Jasper whispered. He crossed himself. 'May God grant him peace.'

Lucie crossed herself, too.

Contrite, Jasper said, 'Go, read the letters. I can manage the shop.'

Lucie pressed his hand, glad of the truce, however fleeting. 'I *should* read these and think about what to do. You can find me in the garden if you have need.'

He gave her a lopsided grin. 'If Mistress Skipwith has told anyone of my mistake, there will be little to do.'

'She said she would not speak of it.'

As Lucie rose, Jasper said, 'I am sorry about her. It will not happen again. I swear.'

Lucie nodded, squeezed his hand again. He was young, bound to make mistakes. Perhaps she was too hard on him. But the guild would not tolerate more serious errors. Even this would have been punishable. 'Now mix the correct herbs and spices for Mistress Skipwith. When we close the shop, you can take it to her. There will of course be no charge. And you would be wise to thank her. She might have spoken to the guild master and had you in the pillory.'

The apothecary's garden behind the shop had been the masterwork of Lucie's first husband, Nicholas Wilton. It held not only the herbs one might expect in such a garden but also many exotic plants grown from seeds Nicholas had collected. Lucie chose a spot amidst the roses, near Nicholas's grave, well away from the noise of the children at play. But it was not of her first husband she thought as she stared down at the letters. She thought of Owen and his misgivings about Sir Robert making the pilgrimage to St David's. Owen had pointed out the hardships of such a journey, to the farthest west of Wales, even for a young, healthy man. They must depart while winter still froze their breath. Could she not see how dangerous it would be for Sir Robert, almost four score and in uncertain health, to attempt such a journey? Lucie had known Owen's arguments were sound. But when she faced her father, saw the yearning in his eyes, she could not forbid it. And in truth, had she the right? All Sir Robert had wished was to reach St David's. Lucie realised with a pang that she did not know whether he had reached the holy city. Brother Michaelo had said that Sir Robert had passed away in peace. Surely that meant he had completed the pilgrimage? It was this, the question unasked, that at last loosed a flood of tears. Lucie let them come. She did not even notice Kate, the serving maid, until she spoke.

'I saw Brother Michaelo,' Kate said, standing over Lucie, holding out a cup of ale. 'He looked so solemn. And then I saw you weeping. I pray that nothing has happened to Captain Archer.'

Lucie took the cup. 'It is Sir Robert. The chill took him at last.'

'Oh, I am sorry, Mistress. He was a good man.' The young woman shifted feet. 'Are those letters from the captain?' Kate had boundless admiration for the literate.

'They are.'

'Will he be home soon?'

'Brother Michaelo says the captain hopes to be home by Corpus Christi.'

Kate made a face. 'Still so long. But it is good to have his letters?'

'It is, Kate. I was going to read them now.'

'Oh, to be sure. I must return to my duties.'

'You will not tell your sister about Sir Robert in front of the children?'

Kate's older sister, Tildy, was with Gwenllian and Hugh near the kitchen door. 'Oh, no, Mistress Lucie. It is for you to tell them. I shall not even tell my sister.'

Lucie sighed as she watched Kate hurry away. Why did everything seem so difficult of late? When had she last laughed?

Roger Moreton had made her laugh last night, at supper—until Jasper insulted him. The boy's animosity was misplaced. It was true that Roger was a widower. His wife had died in childbirth—a stillbirth—the previous autumn. But his wealth and good reputation made him the hope of all parents of marriageable young women. Who would be his next wife was a topic of much excited conjecture in the city. Roger had no need to woo a married woman.

Lucie looked down at the letters in her hands. Where to begin? She untied the string that held them together. Owen had marked on each the place and date of writing so she might read them in order, and so follow his journey. In the first letter he mentioned Sir Robert's cough, his dizziness. The river crossings had been difficult in the early spring, from the border country to Carreg Cennen. There was much in the letter about Owen's mixed feelings upon returning to his own country, but Lucie skimmed to find news of her father. Owen wrote of constant bickering between Brother Michaelo and Sir Robert, good-humoured on the monk's part. A later letter mentioned Brother Michaelo's tender nursing of her father. The monk perplexed Lucie—in the time she had known him he had metamorphosed from a self-serving sybarite to a trusted servant of the Archbishop of York. Practical changes, she had thought, still self-serving. But this tenderness towards her father—this was change of a deeper sort. God had watched over Sir Robert, to grant him such a companion on his final earthly journey. In the last letter, Lucie at last found the news that calmed her. Not only had her father reached St David's, but he had been granted a vision at St Non's Well, a vision that had given him the absolution he had sought over many pilgrimages. Sir Robert had died in peace, a happy man. Thanks be to God.

For a long while Lucie sat, head bowed, the pile of letters in her lap, remembering her father. Melisende, her ageing cat, curled up at her feet. Faintly Lucie heard her children's voices.

The church bells chiming Nones woke Lucie from her reverie. She must return to the shop. Gathering up the letters, she took them to the workroom, tucked them on a shelf that had once held wooden dishes and spoons when Lucie and Nicholas, and later Owen, had lived in this house behind the shop. It was Sir Robert who had given them the fine house across the garden. He had tried hard to make up for his earlier neglect. Lucie hoped her father had known, in the end, how much she had loved him.

Jasper raised his head as Lucie entered the shop. 'Does the captain say when he might return?'

'In his last letter he said he hoped to be home within the month. That was over a month ago.' She nodded towards the package he was wrapping. 'Is that for Mistress Skipwith?'

'Do you want to check it?'

'I should.'

Jasper unwrapped it. Lucie poked about with a mixing stick, found nothing amiss and handed it back to Jasper.

'By the time she has cooked this in lard it will be useless anyway,' Jasper said glumly as he refolded the parchment and placed it on the counter.

'She believes that it helps her sleep. A little on the temples.'

Jasper hung his head.

Lucie hated seeing him like this. 'I shall close the shop while I am at Freythorpe Hadden. I must tell Phillippa of her brother's death.'

'I could go to Freythorpe.'

'You will stay here. It needs a woman's delicacy. And I need you to see to the stores, and the garden.'

'But the roads—'

'Take the remedy to Mistress Skipwith!'

Jasper grabbed the package.

'And hurry back. We have much to do.'

• • •

As Lucie walked out on to Davygate the next morning, a hooded figure stepped out of the shadow cast by the jettied upper storey.

'Have you found the counterpoison for my jaundice?' Alice Baker asked.

Lucie felt her blood rise to her face, her heart pound. It was not her nature to enjoy confrontations. 'I told you what I thought caused it and what you must do to undo it.' She repeated the advice, hoping this time Alice would hear it. 'An infusion of vervain and dandelion root. Nothing more. Then fast for two days, drinking only water, eating nothing. After that, eat moderately and take no medicines.'

'You have found no counterpoison.' A statement, made an accusation by her tone.

'That regimen *is* the remedy. I believe you mixed valerian with skullcap.'

'Have a care, Lucie Wilton. I could ruin you.'

Ungrateful wretch, Lucie thought. But she merely said, 'I cannot believe you wish to do that, Alice.'

Lucie glanced up at the sound of a door opening and shutting across the street.

'May God go with you, Mistress Baker, Mistress Wilton.' Roger Moreton smiled as he crossed the street from his house. Another man followed in his wake. Lucie mirrored Roger's smile—how did he manage to be there when she needed him?

'Master Moreton.' Alice Baker simpered, then remembered herself and turned so that her jaundiced face was in shadow.

Roger was a handsome man, clear-featured and solidly built. He always seemed delighted with life, his eyes twinkling, his colour high.

'Can you believe it?' said Roger rather breathlessly. 'Just as I mentioned your name, I turned, and there you were. Is it not so, Harold?'

'Quite so.'

'God go with you, gentlemen, Mistress Wilton.' Alice hurried off.

Lucie had paid no attention to Roger's companion. Now she looked up into the stranger's eyes. Sweet heaven but they were remarkably blue. He gave her an oddly formal bow.

'You spoke of me?' she asked Roger.

'I lied. But that terrible woman. She will insist on blaming you for her foolishness.'

'It is difficult to accept that one is a fool,' Lucie said. 'But I thank you. And you,' she said to the stranger.

He in turn glanced uncertainly at Roger.

'Forgive my discourtesy,' Roger said hurriedly. 'Mistress Wilton, this is Harold Galfrey. He is to be my household steward when I move to St Saviour.' Although he lived alone, Roger had recently purchased a large house in another parish in the city. It had increased the frenzy of the rumours regarding his choice for the next Mistress Moreton.

Lucie would not have guessed the man to be a steward. With his tanned skin and sun-bleached hair he did not seem one who spent his days inside, organising a household. Neither was his physique that of such a man. However, his attire was appropriate for a household steward. His clothes had been chosen with an eye to cut and fabric, and yet in such muted colours they would offend no one or call attention to him. 'You are fortunate to find yourself in Master Moreton's household,' she said.

'I am indeed, Mistress Wilton,' said Harold.

'I must be going now. I have much to do before I leave for the country.' She needed time to talk to Brother Michaelo as well as arrange for a Requiem Mass for her father. And though she had shut the shop, she hoped Jasper might catch up with replenishing the stores—so there was much to discuss. 'Thank you for rescuing me. God's blessing on your day.'

'Leave for the country?' said Roger. 'What takes you to the country?'

Lucie had no one to blame but herself for mentioning the journey, for knowing Roger, he would wish to hear everything and then offer assistance. 'I received word yesterday of my father's death, while on pilgrimage in Wales. I must go to Freythorpe Hadden to tell my aunt.'

'God rest his soul,' Roger said. 'I must do something. I shall accompany you.'

'You are kind. But I shall stay several days. You cannot leave your business so long.'

He nodded, frowning. 'But you need an escort.' He brightened. 'Harold is idle until I am in the new house. He shall escort you.' Roger looked pleased with his inspiration.

Harold looked perplexed.

Lucie had no time to argue. 'Thank you, Master Moreton. I shall consider your offer.'

2

PRAYERS UNANSWERED

High on a cliff that hung over the white-capped sea, threading along a path through a bowl-shaped meadow ringed by low, ancient stones in the midst of which stood a small chapel, pilgrims braced themselves against windswept rain. Heads bowed against the storm, soggy cloaks wrapped tightly about them, they waited for their turn at a stone-roofed well that formed the lowest spot in the bowl. One by one the bedraggled pilgrims knelt there, cupping their hands to drink the water or pour it over some sore or malformation, and prayed to St Non for healing. Then they hurried to the chapel for a prayerful respite from the tempest.

Owen Archer watched as a departing pilgrim stumbled on the low, slippery standing stones at the edge of the meadow. Another stooped to help him. The fallen pilgrim shook his head as he rose, expressing his embarrassment, no doubt. Owen thought it odd that the man brushed off his rain-heavy clothes. If he was as cold and wet as Owen—and how could he not be?—he could not possibly notice any added moisture from the wet grass.

Owen fought the arrogant notion that the Almighty had staged this tempest for him, to chide him for thinking he might dip his hand in St Non's Well, say a prayer and so easily regain the sight in his left eye, like the blind Movi who held St David under the water at his baptism. But was it not a sign of his faith that he would seek out the water that had cured many pilgrims with eye ailments? God would surely choose another way to teach him humility.

Owen's journey to St Non's Well was ill timed, that was certain.

He had conceived the plan yesterday, while rejoicing in the stretch of warm, sunny weather that had dried the puddles in the roads and allowed his small company to make good progress from Cydweli Castle. His three companions had been making wagers about how many days the same journey had taken their comrades, Jared and Sam, who had departed Cydweli two weeks earlier in a drenching rain that had continued for several days. The two were to arrange passage for Owen's company on a ship out of Porth Clais, St David's harbour. A ship set for England.

In case Jared and Sam had met with quick success, Owen had stopped at St Non's Well on his way to St David's. In truth, he had little hope for a miracle. He had never doubted God's hand in his partial blinding. *That* had been his hardest lesson in humility. He had taken much pride in his skill with the bow and in his judgement of men. He had been wrong about the Breton jongleur whose leman had blinded him. His own pride had robbed him of his skill and his confidence in his judgement in one slash of a knife. He could think of nothing he had done in the intervening years to earn reparation for his past sins, unless it was his service to the archbishop. Perhaps he should have complained less, practised more humility. But who was he to think he could predict God's judgement?

The rain had begun as the company approached St Non's. But as it might be Owen's last chance to visit the well, he persisted. He had dismounted, handed his reins to Iolo, and directed him, Tom and Edmund to ride on into the city. Owen would continue on foot, a proper pilgrim. The rain had been but a drizzle then.

Still, this was a most holy well. It had sprung from the ground to mark the site on which Non gave birth to David, who became the greatest saint of Wales—his coming had been foretold by St Patrick. St David had been born out here, in this meadow, in the midst of a terrible tempest that shielded his mother from the clutches of Sant, the arrogant tyrant who had raped her. Owen could not remember whether the legend told that Sant wished to claim the boy or whether he still lusted after the mother. In the pain of her labour, Non clutched a stone, which ever after carried the imprint of her hands. The stone, now in two pieces, was buried beneath the chapel.

Was it a good omen that Owen had come to the well in a tempest? Had it been such a day when his father-in-law was blessed with a vision in the holy waters?

Owen found it difficult to keep his mind on St David and St Non. He wondered how his men fared in the city. Had the three found Jared and Sam? Did a ship even now lying at anchor in Porth Clais await them? That would be good news indeed. Owen needed only enough time to inspect the tomb he had commissioned for his father-in-law in St David's Cathedral and to attend the burial service.

He was not the only one eager to return to England. Tom and Edmund had talked of little else on the journey from Cydweli. Owen had never heard York so praised.

Iolo, the fourth member of their company, had been quiet on the journey. He was Welsh and would remain here in Wales. He had joined Owen's company in February at Lancaster's castle of Kenilworth, where he had been sent by Adam de Houghton, Bishop of St David's, the previous autumn. The young man had seemed overjoyed to find a company travelling west. Owen would miss Iolo, who had an uncanny ability to appear when Owen had need of him. He was a good fighter and true to his word.

As if conjured by Owen's thoughts, Iolo stood before him. A murmur rose from the folk behind Owen, who thought this newcomer was pushing ahead. 'Peace,' Iolo called to them in Welsh. 'I am come to see my captain and wait on him on his return to the city.' As Iolo turned back to Owen he shook rain off his cloak.

'You might be dry and warm had you obeyed my order to wait at the palace,' Owen said.

'Something does not feel right, Captain. I thought you might need me.'

Owen knew Iolo well enough to accept his explanation. 'You found Sam and Jared?'

'Aye. They have bad news. The stonecutter Cynog has hanged himself.'

Owen bowed his head and crossed himself, though he also

muttered a curse. Cynog was the stonemason he had hired to carve Sir Robert's tomb.

An elderly pilgrim admonished Owen for cursing in this holy place.

'And Sir Robert's tomb is unfinished, no doubt,' Owen growled with a dark glance at the pilgrim who had chastised him.

'I do not know how far Cynog had got,' said Iolo. 'Forgive me. I did not mean to draw you from your prayer. The tale can wait.' He bowed his head.

Nine pilgrims still ahead of Owen, his dripping clothes creating puddles beneath him and, after all, he might have waited for a dry day—who knew how quickly he would find another mason. He might be in St David's for some time. Owen moved forward one man. Water trickled down his back. He hunched forward. The gesture reminded him of Cynog.

Of whom he should be thinking. Cynog, a gentle man with a God-given gift for turning cold stone into things of beauty. Owen remembered wondering whether Cynog sensed the soul of the stone, if that was how he made it come alive. Hanged himself. There were men whose deaths were little mourned, men who had made little difference while on this mortal soil. Not Cynog. Many would mourn him. Those who had witnessed his gift. What could have caused him such despair he committed a sin that damned his soul to the fires of hell for all eternity?

At last it was Owen's chance to descend to the stone-roofed well. He knelt, prayed for his soul and those of his family. And for Cynog's soul. Then, after removing the leather patch from his left eye, Owen scooped up the clear, icy water in his already cold hands and pressed it to the puckered lid.

Tom, Sam, Jared and Edmund all gazed on Owen's patch with disappointment when he and Iolo entered the great hall of the bishop's palace.

'I was unworthy of a miracle,' he said simply. 'Get me some ale and move away from that fire. I am soaked through. And nothing to show for all that.'

When Owen had slaked his thirst and warmed his belly with the ale, he felt ready to hear about Cynog's death.

'They found Cynog at dawn, four days ago, hanging from an oak among the graves,' Jared said. Tall, gaunt, with brown, wildly curling hair, Jared was the gossip of the group.

'What could have happened to drive such a man to hang himself?' Owen wondered aloud.

'Some say his lady found another,' Jared said.

'There are many say he did not kill himself,' soft-spoken Sam chimed in. 'In truth, most say it.' He kept his gaze from Jared as he spoke.

Owen turned his other side towards the fire and nodded to the shy man. 'Why do they say that?'

'The knot on the tree was a mariner's knot,' said Sam. 'Cynog was no seaman.'

Iolo snorted. 'We are near the sea. Many round here know how to tie such a knot. I do.'

'Such a wonder you are,' Jared muttered.

Iolo's devotion to Owen had not gone unnoticed by the others in the company. Nor had the conversations in Welsh, which they could not understand. Owen had meant for Iolo to accompany Jared to St David's, so that the negotiations for sea passage could be conducted in Welsh, if necessary. But it had not been worth the aggravation.

Jared thrust his face close to Iolo's. 'If you are so—'

Owen quit the fire to pull Jared away. 'We are speaking of a man's death. If he died by his own hand, he is now burning in hellfire. Think on that.' Owen turned to Sam. 'Was Cynog working on Sir Robert's tomb when it happened?'

'He had much of it finished,' said Sam. 'But he awaited you to advise him on the face and hands.'

What had happened? Owen had confounded himself by lingering in Cydweli. 'So I shall need to find another stone carver. How soon does our ship sail?'

'Soon,' said Jared. 'Captain Siencyn awaits news of your arrival.'

Passage home. So near and yet—how could he face Lucie if he did not stay to see to the completion of her father's tomb? Owen sank down on a stool by the fire. 'God is not smiling on me this day.' It was a day for penitence.

Owen had tarried at Cydweli Castle to await an expected party from the convent at Usk, hoping that his sister, Gwenllian, would be among them. He had not seen her since he left Wales twenty years before. Eagerly he had watched the arrival of the party, rushing down from the tower to greet them in the outer court. Behind the priest stood a tall, freckle-faced nun, beaming, waiting for him to notice her. As Owen met her eyes, she stretched out her arms and hurried towards him.

'God is merciful,' Sister Gwenllian had cried as she embraced him.

'Gwen.'

Later, they had found time to talk.

It filled Owen with joy to look on her. His brother Morgan was so frail. Not Gwen. Her wide smile displayed a full set of healthy teeth, her skin was unblemished, her walk straight and unhampered, her embrace as bone-crushing as ever. 'You look happy, Gwen.'

'Sister Gwenllian, I remind you.' She laughed. 'You are surprised? Did you think I had been sent off to the nunnery against my will?'

In truth, he had. She had always seemed the sort to marry and fill a house with freckle-faced children. 'Morgan said only that you were there. So it was your choice to devote your life to God?'

'To live a comfortable life in a convent, truth be told. My devotion to God came later.'

'And is the convent comfortable?'

'Not so much as I had imagined, but it is a good life. It suits me. And what of you, brother? What of your poor eye? Can you see nothing from it? Was it an enemy arrow? Or a brawl over a beauty?' She laughed. 'Oh dear, of course it is the question all ask you.' She looked him up and down. 'Lancaster's livery and a Norman beard—you are a Welshman only in your language.'

'In my heart, too.'

'It is good to be back?'

'I am so glad to see you well, Gwen. And happy.'

There had been much talk in the following days. Owen enjoyed Gwen's tales of the family he had left behind so long ago. And she plied him with questions about his life since he went off to be an archer in the old duke's service.

He had thought it a worthwhile delay. Now he cursed himself for it. He prayed that at least Brother Michaelo had reached York with the letters Owen had written. But how had Lucie received the news? Would she close the shop and allow herself time to mourn her father? He prayed that the letters had found her well. And the children.

A servant stood at the edge of the group with the air of someone waiting to be noticed. Owen asked his business.

The young man begged Owen's pardon for interrupting, but he had been sent by Archdeacon Rokelyn. 'My lord the Archdeacon of St David's invites Captain Archer to sup with him.'

Rokelyn was second in command to the bishop in this holy city. Owen doubted the archdeacon craved his company. What now?

'I shall attend him,' Owen replied evenly. The lad should not get a red ear for the message he brought.

3

FREYTHORPE HADDEN

In the end, Roger Moreton's new steward did accompany Lucie to her father's manor. York was abuzz with tales of outlaws on the roads and Lucie had to agree that though Harold Galfrey was not trained as a soldier he looked sufficiently strong to be threatening. His presence reassured Tildy, Lucie's nursemaid, never a willing traveller, but determined to help Lucie during this difficult time. Lucie had confided to Tildy that she feared Phillippa might collapse at the news—though her aunt had always been a robust woman, she was getting on in years and had been devoted to her brother. Tildy could be trusted to keep the household at Freythorpe together while Lucie saw to her aunt. The company riding out from York also included Brother Michaelo, who had kindly offered to tell Phillippa all that he had told Lucie. His offer required neither sacrifice nor permission from the archbishop for he would easily continue on from Freythorpe Hadden to Bishopthorpe, where Archbishop Thoresby was in residence.

It was a beautiful spring day. Lucie wished she might enjoy this ride, this brief moment in the midst of all her duties. There would be tears enough at Freythorpe. But she had awakened with a yearning to see her father once more so that she might tell him how much she had enjoyed his company in his last years. She had told him so on his departure, but she wondered whether she had said enough. She lifted her head to the sun, shining round puffs of cloud. A gentle breeze set the spring leaves trembling against the blue and white sky. The meadows were already blooming. Labourers sang in the fields.

'God's blessing is on this day,' she said.

'God is certainly smiling on the land,' Harold said beside her.

Lucie started. She had not noticed he rode so close. 'Do you fear I shall fall off my mount?'

He had a hesitant smile, as if uncertain it was appropriate to a steward. 'In faith, Mistress Wilton, you seemed so lost in thought I feared you paid little heed to keeping your seat.'

'Do I look like an inexperienced rider?'

'Not at all. Forgive me.'

They rode in silence for a while.

'I am the one who should apologise,' Lucie said. 'I was steeling myself against the task before me. It will be difficult for my aunt.'

'Made more difficult by a stranger in your midst.'

'You must not think of it. You are here at my request, and I am grateful.'

'I was thrust upon you.'

'I am quite capable of refusing Master Moreton.'

Harold smiled with more assurance. Lucie fell back into her thoughts of her aunt. Phillippa had been widowed within a few years of her marriage. She had come to Freythorpe Hadden at the invitation of her brother, who was then unmarried and needed someone to represent him at the manor he rarely visited. Phillippa had been straight-backed and strong, with her feet squarely on the ground and a determination to order the world around her to her liking. As far as Lucie knew, Phillippa had nothing from her marriage. Sir Robert had mentioned his sister's husband only once that Lucie could recall, referring to him as a man too fond of his ale. Phillippa's only child had died in the same year as her husband. But God had looked after her. When Sir Robert brought Lucie's mother to Freythorpe Hadden, Amélie had no wish to wrest control from Phillippa. For forty-five years Phillippa had ruled the manor. And if she wished, and was able, Lucie thought to leave it that way. She had no intention of giving up her apothecary or her house in the city to live at Freythorpe, and her son Hugh, heir to the property, was but a baby.

Indeed, Lucie hoped her aunt would choose to continue acting as mistress of Freythorpe. It would be difficult to find another she could trust so completely. But Lucie would accept whatever decision her aunt made. She had much to thank Phillippa for, including her life in York. Phillippa had encouraged Lucie's marriage to the apothecary Nicholas Wilton, believing that the wife of a respected member of a York guild, trained to assist her husband in the shop, would have a more secure widowhood than would the wife of a knight, which would more properly have been Lucie's lot.

Wrapped in melancholy, Lucie watched Harold ride forward, bend close to speak to Tildy. He was a thoughtful man. Roger Moreton had chosen wisely.

Shortly before the company passed on to the demesne lands, Brother Michaelo asked whether Lucie needed to rest and refresh herself. She declined, eager to reach the manor house.

Brother Michaelo glanced over at Harold. 'What do you know of that man?'

'No more than that Roger Moreton has hired him as household steward on the recommendation of John Gisburne.'

'John Gisburne? The man who believes a man should be judged by his deeds, not his family connections? So he has seen this man at work?'

Gisburne was a member of the class of rich merchants in York trying to wrest the governance of the city from the old ruling families. It was proving to be a long struggle. Thirteen years ago Gisburne's election to bailiff had been overturned by the the mayor, John Langton, a member of the old families. The animosity between the two groups grew, occasionally spilling out into the streets, often ending in violence. With each outburst the two sides became more rigid in their positions. Gisburne's party preached that a man should be judged by what he did, not by whom he knew or to whom he was related, for obvious reasons. 'I assume that John Gisburne lives by his professed creed,' Lucie said.

Michaelo looked doubtful. 'For all his talk of the common man, Gisburne prefers to dine with nobles and influential clerics. He hopes to be mayor, you know.'

'I had heard.'

'Let us pray that he does judge men by their deeds. For once it would be useful.'

'You find something in Harold Galfrey to distrust?'

'It is perhaps a petty complaint—but he does not look like a steward. I should have taken him for a soldier.'

'All the better for our purposes.'

'You are right, of course. But watch him on your return to the city, when I am not with you.'

'Did my father ask you to watch over me?'

'He would have wished me to voice my concern.'

'I am grateful. But I assure you that Master Moreton's opinion is to be trusted.'

'Forgive me, I did not mean to cast doubt on Roger Moreton's judgement.'

By the time the company reached the gatehouse of Freythorpe Hadden the steward, Daimon, had been alerted and stood ready to challenge or receive the four. The relief on his young, barely bearded face alarmed Lucie.

'You expect trouble?'

He mentioned recent trouble at a nearby farm—a band of outlaws, a theft, injuries.

'*Deus juva me,*' Michaelo muttered, crossing himself.

'I might not be so wary,' said Daimon, 'but that two days ago some workers in the field spied a man in a tree, watching the hall. He took flight when he knew himself discovered. Had a fast horse tethered near. Aye, I do expect trouble, Mistress Wilton.' Daimon's pleasant face did not lend itself to a threatening look, but he was well-muscled and held the sword in his hand with an air of fierce assurance. He would do, Lucie thought. He had grown quite like his father, Adam, Sir Robert's former sergeant and late in life the steward of the manor. Trouble had usually backed away from Adam.

'You are fortunate to have such alert men watching out for you, Mistress Wilton,' Harold said.

Daimon glanced at Harold, nodded curtly.

'They do say there have been more outlaw bands since the pestilence,' Tildy said.

Daimon gave Tildy a little bow. 'It was not wise, riding out with such trouble about. But you are welcome to Freythorpe, Mistress Matilda.' He smiled up at her.

'So,' Brother Michaelo muttered, seeing how it stood between Tildy and Daimon.

Lucie might have echoed him, but she held her tongue as the young steward turned to her. 'Mistress Wilton, please come within and give your aunt good cheer.'

When Tildy dismounted in the yard before the house, Daimon motioned her to step aside. His eyes on the ground, his voice too soft to overhear, he spoke urgently to the young woman. Tildy, also keeping her head down, shook it once. Lucie watched with interest, wondering what precisely had transpired between them the previous summer when Tildy had been sent to the manor with Gwenllian and Hugh for safety during the pestilence. As Tildy moved away from Daimon, Lucie noticed that another pair of eyes followed her. Well, and why should Harold not find her pleasing to look at? Tildy had huge brown eyes, a high forehead, rosebud lips and skin the colour of the ivory rose in Lucie's garden. For a young woman of twenty years who had been born in poverty, she was remarkable in having all her teeth and, but for a wine-red birthmark that spread across her left cheek, a perfect complexion. But Daimon need not glower at Harold as he did when he saw the direction of the stranger's gaze— Tildy had not blushed so prettily when Harold leaned towards her as she did when Daimon was near.

Lucie took herself over to the young steward. 'I bring sad tidings, Daimon. Is my aunt well enough to hear them?'

Daimon coloured. 'Dame Phillippa is well enough to keep the servants busy,' he said. He lowered his voice. 'I would speak with you later, Mistress Wilton. At your pleasure.'

'I thought you might wish a word,' Lucie said, and headed for the house, taking Tildy by the elbow and propelling her forward.

By the time Lucie's party entered the hall, the servants had set up a trestle table near the fire. Flagons of ale and wine, and a cold repast were brought in for the travellers. Lucie looked round for her aunt.

'I shall fetch the mistress,' a maid said, bobbing a curtsy.

'No,' said Lucie, 'it is best that I speak with her alone.' The maid directed her to a screened area in the far corner of the hall.

'She no longer sleeps up in the solar?'

'No, Mistress,' the young woman said.

Lucie paused halfway across the hall, noticing a rent in the tapestry on the far wall, repaired with the open, ineffectual stitches of a child just learning to sew. The tear extended an arm's length from the side of the tapestry inward. 'What has happened here?' she said to herself.

At her elbow, Daimon said quietly, 'I should warn you, Mistress, Dame Phillippa has not been herself of late.'

'She tore it? Or repaired it?'

'Both, I think.'

Such clumsy stitches? And on Phillippa's favourite tapestry, one of the few items left from her dowry.

The alcove had once held her parents' bed, before the hearth had replaced the fire circle and a fireplace was possible up in the solar. It was a large space, enclosed by carved wood screens. Lucie tapped on the screen nearest the heavy curtain that served as a door. 'Aunt? It is Lucie.'

A little cry, then a shuffling. Lucie pushed back the curtain. Phillippa was already there, one arm stretched out to embrace her niece. 'My dearest child!'

'Aunt Phillippa.' Lucie was startled by her aunt's bony shoulders. She stepped back, saw how her aunt's gown hung loosely upon her tall frame. And she leaned upon a stick. 'You are unwell. I did not know.'

'Always eager to try your remedies on me, child.' Phillippa patted Lucie's hand. 'But I do not believe that you have a remedy for old age, eh? Is my brother with you?'

Lucie shook her head.

Phillippa's smile faded. 'Tell me,' she whispered.

Lucie looked round. The space was lit by two oil lamps on either side of Phillippa's large bed. At the foot was a chest and in a corner of the screens a bench. Lucie drew her aunt down on to the latter and told her Owen's account of Sir Robert's passing.

Crossing herself with a trembling hand, Phillippa sighed as if weary.

'Brother Michaelo is here,' said Lucie. 'He was with father to the end. He has offered to tell you all you wish to know about father's journey, and his passing.'

Phillippa dropped her gaze to her hands, which rested limply in her lap. 'So many years on pilgrimage,' she said sadly. 'Well, it is how he wished to die.' She was weeping now, silently, her head bowed.

Tildy appeared in the doorway with a cup of wine. At Lucie's nod she pressed it into Phillippa's hands. The elderly woman lifted the cup, but paused with it halfway to her lips, set it back down.

'Father had a vision at St Non's Well,' Lucie said. 'He saw my mother and she smiled on him.'

Phillippa put aside the untouched cup and drew a cloth from her sleeve, blotted her eyes. 'So long a pilgrim. I am grateful that God at last granted Robert's wish. Would that I might go on pilgrimage.' Lucie was about to ask what favour Phillippa wished from such a pilgrimage, but her aunt suddenly said, 'I should like to talk with Brother Michaelo.'

'You do not need to rest a while?'

'That is what I should be asking you, my dear one,' Phillippa said. She handed Lucie the cup. 'I am certain that you need this more than I do.'

Lucie was tired. And thirsty. She accepted the cup gladly.

'Your father did not expect to return,' said Phillippa. 'It was forgetful of me to ask if he accompanied you.' She reached for the stick. Lucie supported her as she rose. 'Apoplexy,' Phillippa added. 'I have seen it in others. Not so bad as some, God be thanked, but it has me leaning on this stick, as you see.'

She walked slowly, pushing the left leg forward rather than

lifting it, refusing Lucie's arm in support.

When they joined the other travellers in the hall, Lucie introduced Harold Galfrey. Phillippa welcomed him, then turned to Brother Michaelo and invited him to join her and Lucie by the fire. As soon as the three were seated, Phillippa asked, 'Did my dear Robert suffer long?'

Gently, Michaelo told her of Sir Robert's last days. Phillippa listened quietly, asking a question here and there. Lucie thought her oddly calm. But when the monk's tale was finished, Phillippa said in such a low voice Lucie almost did not hear her over the crackling of the fire and the bustle of the servants, 'What am I to do without him? Where shall I go?' Phillippa looked old, frail, frightened.

Lucie put her arm around her aunt. 'This is your home. But you are also welcome to stay with me in York. For as long as you wish.'

There was no reply. Phillippa did not weep. She stiffly accepted her niece's embrace, but kept her own hands in her lap. When Lucie drew away, Phillippa sat quite still, staring off into the fire.

Lucie awakened in a dark, unfamiliar room. Softly, someone whispered. Lucie sat up and gradually remembered she was sleeping in the alcove with her Aunt Phillippa and Tildy, all in the large bed, Lucie in the middle.

'Mistress,' Tildy whispered beside her, 'it is your aunt. She mutters in her sleep. Last summer she paced, also.' 'Gwenllian said her great aunt had walking dreams.'

'What is she whispering?'

'I never could hear—the floorboards creaked too much up there. But some of the servants were talking this evening, said she speaks to her dead husband, Douglas Sutton.'

'Shall I wake her?' Lucie asked.

'Ma always said that folk should never wake a sleepwalker. Oft times they die being torn from the world of dreams.'

Lucie doubted that, but she decided against waking her aunt.

And tomorrow night she thought she might move up to the solar. She had not wished to leave her aunt alone after giving her such sad news. But it seemed her presence offered no comfort.

Phillippa had said the weakness came on her suddenly, just after Sir Robert departed. 'Why did she not send word to me she was ill?'

'She is a proud woman,' Tildy said.

Lucie already knew she could do little but comfort her aunt. Nicholas, Lucie's first husband, had also been struck suddenly with apoplexy. He had suffered terrible headaches with it. But God seemed at least to have spared Phillippa the headaches. It was the hardest thing to bear, watching a loved one suffer and being unable to help them.

In the morning, remembering Tildy's comment about the servants talking, Lucie sought a quiet word with Daimon. 'My aunt is causing gossip among the servants?'

Daimon shifted his weight, frowned. 'I do not like to say it, Mistress, but Dame Phillippa has been queer of late. Muttering to herself, refusing to eat, fixing her eyes on a spot in the air, as if she sees something we cannot see.'

'Tildy knew she paced and whispered to herself at night, but the rest of it—did it come on with her illness?'

Daimon nodded.

'This muttering? Can you understand any of it?'

'Not myself, no. But cook says she talks to a man named Douglas and sometimes calls him husband.' Daimon lifted his shoulders, dropped them, shook his head. 'My mother talked much the same in her sickness, but to a sister who was long dead.'

'Does her behaviour bother the household?'

'We worry for her, is all. She is a firm mistress, but fair.'

'Do you think she *sees* him?'

Daimon looked down at his hands. 'She speaks to him, Mistress. Whether she sees him I cannot say.'

'Thank you, Daimon.'

He shifted to the other foot. 'Mistress Wilton, I must explain my conduct in the yard when you arrived.'

'I have wondered what is between you and Tildy.'

'I would marry her. But she will not have me.'

'Truly?' But what of Tildy's blushes? And the warmth in her voice when she spoke to him?

'She says that your children are too young. And her family too far away. And she is not good enough for a steward's wife.'

Too many arguments. They might all give Tildy pause, but could they turn a young woman against her heart? Lucie guessed the truth was something else entirely.

'Are you certain that you love her?'

'I am, Mistress. I think of no one else. Truly.'

Daimon looked so sad Lucie believed him. 'Would you like me to talk to her? Reassure her that she is free to follow her heart?'

'No, Mistress, though I thank you for being willing. But she might take it wrong, think you encourage my suit. I do not think Tildy would be happy unless she came of her own accord.'

The poor young man walked away with an air of doom. Lucie watched him cross the yard to the stables. There must be something she might say to Tildy.

'Your steward has worried you?' Harold said at her side.

'God have mercy,' Lucie said, almost jumping out of her skin. 'You have a way of stealing up too silently.'

'It stands me in good stead when I wish to catch a servant misbehaving.'

She turned to look at him, not liking the sound of that. She believed that if she treated servants fairly, she could trust them. 'Brother Michaelo says you walked about at dawn. Did you visit a tenant? Do you know someone here?'

Harold shook his head. 'I enjoy a morning walk. Did Daimon give you bad news?'

'No. Nothing like that. Merely a heart broken that might be mended, with care.'

'Ah. Are you to lose your nursemaid?'

'Perhaps not. She has refused him.'

'Her heart is sworn to another?'

'I do not know. I thought it plain she loved Daimon.'

'She teases him, perhaps?'

'That is not her nature. No, something is amiss. I must discover her reason—discreetly. You must say nothing to anyone.'

Harold bowed, another of his oddly formal gestures. 'I shall say nothing.'

'You are a good man, Harold. Master Moreton is fortunate.'

Late in the afternoon, when the shadows were lengthening and a pleasant breeze stirred the trees, Lucie wandered out into the garden. She found Phillippa sitting on a bench at the entrance to the yew maze. It was strange to see her aunt so idle. Lucie joined her.

'Come to York for Father's Requiem Mass at the minster, Aunt, and stay with me for a time.'

Phillippa did not answer at once, though she took Lucie's hand and squeezed it. 'You have heard about the stranger watching the hall?' Phillippa suddenly asked.

'Daimon told me. He thinks we were fools to ride out with such bold thieves about.'

'It was once far worse. When Robert the Bruce used the North to try to force our king to give up Scotland. Scots everywhere. And Frenchmen, they did say, eager to use our enemies to weaken us.'

'Did your Douglas fight the Scots?'

Phillippa shifted on the bench, turning so that she might see Lucie's face. In the clear light Lucie saw how like crinkled parchment was her aunt's skin. Her eyes had always been deep-set, but now they appeared sunken. 'Why do you ask about Douglas Sutton?'

Because he is on my mind, Lucie thought. 'You never spoke much of him. I was curious. With the Scots burning the countryside. Did you not live farther north then, in the Dales?'

Phillippa studied Lucie's face a moment longer, then dropped her gaze to her idle hands. 'I grow old, Lucie, my dearest. I grow useless. You would find me a burden in your busy household.'

'Not at all. Kate has much to learn and Tildy is busy with the children.'

'Perhaps…'

Lucie took her aunt's hands, turned them palms up. 'Still calloused. I do not think you are useless.' She kissed her aunt on the cheek, then rose. 'Do not stay out too long. Already the evening chills the shadows.'

4

THE ARCHDEACON'S WILL

Owen shrugged out into the early evening. He paused on the great porch of the Bishop's Palace, surprised by the hastening gloom. He had expected a soft grey sky, some lingering daylight. But although the storm had quieted to a drizzle, the rain-heavy clouds crouched close to the horizon, ready to snag on the towers of the palace or the cathedral and loose a flood in the valley. The world smelled of damp wool, damp stone, mud, mildew and moss. It suited Owen's mood.

The gatekeeper came over. 'Captain, the house of the Archdeacon of St David's—'

'—is just without the gate,' Owen growled. Needlessly. The man meant to be helpful.

'Aye. Then you know the way.' The gatekeeper stepped back into his corner.

'Forgive my discourtesy,' said Owen. The man was Welsh, had spoken in his own tongue. No doubt that was why he was but a gatekeeper, not an archdeacon. Or archbishop. 'I had a long ride and a thorough soak. I thought to rest easy by the fire tonight with my comrades.'

'Archdeacon Rokelyn is sure to feed you well,' said the gatekeeper with a kindly smile.

Fatten him up for a favour. Oh, aye. The English were good at that. If Owain Lawgoch, great-nephew of Llywelyn the Last, arrived on this soil to wrest the country from English control, would this Welsh gatekeeper support him? Throw off his livery and fight on the side of his people? Or was he too comfortable on this grand porch, ordering the wealthy pilgrims about, eating the bishop's food? Would he worry he might wind up back in a turf-roofed hut sleeping with his sheep if he backed the prince of the Welsh?

Owen's boots squished through the muddy yard. His dry clothes did not keep his flesh from the memory of its drenching earlier in the day. Pulling his cloak close about him, he hunched into the misty wind. He had not far to go, a matter of yards, but his cloak and the neck and shoulders of his tunic were damp by the time he rapped on the great oak door to the house of Adam Rokelyn, Archdeacon of St David's. A servant opened the door, bowed Owen in. A Welsh servant, Owen guessed. He tested him with the language. The servant replied in kind, looking pleased, ushered Owen to a chair in the hall near a hot, smoky fire, poured him a cup of wine. At least he could get warm again. Not drunk, however. There was too much he must remember not to say. A pity. The plummy wine slid silkily down his throat.

Voices came from behind a tapestry-covered doorway near Owen. Thinking it might be to his benefit to hear the matter discussed, he moved his chair closer.

'You are not the law here.'

'In the absence of the bishop, I am. Go tend your flock in Carmarthen. And take your weasel Simon with you.'

'Who are you to speak to me in such wise?' Now, as the voice boomed in outrage, Owen identified the speaker—William Baldwin, Archdeacon of Carmarthen.

'Hush, for pity's sake. I am expecting a guest.' That must be Archdeacon Rokelyn.

Baldwin heeded the warning and lowered his voice to a murmur. Rokelyn did likewise.

Not wishing to be caught listening, Owen did not draw closer. But the argument interested him. Even more so than in York, the archdeacons here were politically powerful. This was not only an important ecclesiastical city, it was a city in which the Church ruled completely. Bishop Houghton *was* the law. And in his absence, the archdeacons ruled. Owen would guess Rokelyn was correct to consider himself the bishop's second in command, being the archdeacon of the area, as Baldwin was the bishop's second in command in Carmarthen.

'*Benedicte*, Captain Archer.' Rokelyn stood in the doorway, holding the tapestry aside for Baldwin. Rokelyn was a heavy-set man, with an unremarkable face save for its complete lack of hair—neither lashes nor brows, nor crown above. Something in his countenance made him look a man devoid of guile. Owen knew it to be a false impression—though he did not know Rokelyn well, he did know that a guileless man did not become Archdeacon of St David's.

Baldwin slipped past Rokelyn, nodded to Owen. 'I trust you accomplished your task in Cydweli, Captain Archer?' His deep voice was tempered now. He was Rokelyn's opposite, olive-skinned, with a wealth of dark hair.

They exchanged courtesies, then Baldwin excused himself and departed. Owen was not surprised after what he had overheard.

'They tell me you were at St Non's Well today,' said Rokelyn, still with his pleasant smile.

Had he spies at the well? Or was it mere gossip? Owen decided that he, too, could play the jolly innocent. 'I was. And had I been judged worthy, I might stand before you tonight without a patch. As you see, I was not so blessed.'

Rokelyn made a pitying face, then brightened. 'They say you shoot straight and true, even with the loss of your eye. Perhaps St Non saw no need to intercede for you.'

'In faith, I had little hope for it. But it seemed foolish not to try.'

Rokelyn gestured to Owen to sit by the fire. Two heavily carved, straight-backed chairs with arms had been angled half facing one another, half facing the fire. Embroidered cushions softened them. A table with the wine stood between. Rokelyn settled into one of the chairs with a contented sigh. 'We shall dine in a while. I thought first we might share this excellent wine. Talk of easy matters. About your family. Did you find them well?'

'A sister and a brother, aye. The rest are with God.'

The archdeacon expressed sympathy, spoke of God's will being mysterious, then went on to explore many other topics, while Owen fought a dangerous drowsiness brought on by the day's long ride, the sudden warmth and the wine, and the earlier tankards of ale at the palace. He was grateful when a servant called them to a table laden with food. Even better, Owen was seated well away from the fire. Soon a draft had chilled his still damp boots. It was enough to keep him awake and alert.

But it was not until the wafers and sugared nuts and fruits were set on the table that Rokelyn at last came round to his purpose. 'You have heard that a stonemason was murdered?'

Owen almost choked on a sugared almond. 'Murdered? I heard one hanged himself.'

'Cynog,' Rokelyn said. 'Was he not working on a tomb for your wife's father?'

If he knew to ask that question he knew the answer. Owen took a few of the wafers, sat back in his chair. He must appear unruffled, though he did not like the direction of this conversation. 'He was. Which is why my men thought to tell me of his death.' Rokelyn had dipped a cloth in his wine and now dabbed at the crystallised sugar on his chin and upper lip. Owen let one of the thin, crisp cakes dissolve in his mouth, then remarked, 'Now I must find another stonemason to complete the work.'

Rokelyn wiped his hands, put aside the cloth. 'You chose the best stonemason in St David's.'

'Aye. I shall not find the likes of him twice, I think.' Owen swallowed another wafer. 'Murdered, you say?' He shook his head.

'Who recommended Cynog to you?'

What was this? Was this, too, a question to which the archdeacon already knew the answer? Owen hoped not. 'I cannot recall. Was it you?' He was not about to volunteer that it was Martin Wirthir, an old friend whose allegiance changed as it pleased him. Martin was presently a spy in the service of King Charles of France, who was supporting the cause of Owain Lawgoch, the would-be redeemer of the Welsh.

'Let me ask you another way,' said the archdeacon. 'Why Cynog?'

'Is there a reason I should not have chosen Cynog?'

'Someone hanged him, Captain. One does not hang somebody for personal reasons. When a man is hanged, it is done to set an example, give a warning—do this and you, too, will be so punished. Who was using Cynog as an example, and why? What had he done?'

'What indeed,' Owen said. 'I liked Cynog. Admired his work. I would never have imagined such a death for him.'

'Would it surprise you if I were to tell you that this afternoon the guards apprehended Cynog's murderer? That he is confined in the bishop's gaol?'

'Surprised? Yes, and interested. What does he have to say for himself?'

'He claims that he is innocent. *That* I do not believe. But that he is perhaps ignorant…' Rokelyn wagged his head. 'It is possible. In truth, I think of him not as a murderer, but an executioner. And the executioner is rarely, if ever, the one with the purpose.'

Owen liked neither the archdeacon's expression nor his tone. Rokelyn was baiting him. 'You have given this much thought.' Rokelyn nodded. 'Still,' Owen said, 'it is difficult for me to imagine why someone would have cause either to murder or execute Cynog. Perhaps because all I knew of the man was his fine work with stone.' Which was quite true. Martin Wirthir had said nothing about Cynog except that he might create a tomb worthy of Sir Robert.

The archdeacon watched Owen through half-closed lids. 'Piers the Mariner, the man we are holding, is the brother of Captain Siencyn, the man with whom you sail shortly.'

So that was the connection. 'It has been a day of unpleasant news for me.'

'News.' Rokelyn sniffed. 'I wonder.'

'Oh?'

The archdeacon tilted his head to one side. 'A man working for you is murdered by the kinsman of a man with whom you have business. From where I sit, you look as if you are squarely in the middle of all this.' His tone was matter-of-fact, not in the least emotional or even judgemental.

'If you are implying that I had anything to do with all this, I remind you that I have been in Cydweli on my king's business.'

'Two of your men were here in the city,' Rokelyn said reasonably.

'Of what are you accusing me?' Owen asked, quitting the game.

Rokelyn leaned forward, opening his eyes fully. 'Cynog supported Owain Lawgoch. Did you know that?'

'Cynog?' Owen had not known, but he might have guessed. 'And you think he was executed because of that?'

'I want you to find out.'

'You must forgive me, but I cannot. I have been too long from home and my duties for Archbishop Thoresby. I must find someone to complete Sir Robert's tomb, see him buried beneath it, and then take ship for England.'

'You are suddenly eager for home. Why?'

'It is not sudden.'

'I say that it is.' Rokelyn snapped his fingers. Two palace guards entered the room. Sweet *Jesu*, this archdeacon thought to bully him into co-operating? Owen stood up. The men moved towards him, fingering the daggers on their belts. Owen took a step towards them, but stopped there. What was he thinking? He was outnumbered. Oh, he might enjoy bringing one of them down, but in the end he would be the one lying there, bruised and humiliated. With age came a certain level-headedness. He would resist Rokelyn in more subtle ways. Raising his hands, palms forward, Owen laughed and shook his head, resumed his seat. The guards began to back away.

'Stay a moment,' Rokelyn said to them. 'I do not trust this humour.'

'I laugh at myself,' said Owen. 'It is so long ago now that I was a soldier, and yet so easily I forget.'

'Help me willingly or you will become quite intimate with Piers, the accused. Which will it be, Captain?'

'Truth be told, you do not seem to need me. If Cynog supported Owain Lawgoch as you say, is it not obvious that this Piers the Mariner executed him for treason against the King of England?'

Rokelyn flushed crimson. 'This is not a game, Captain. If you refuse to assist me, I shall have every reason to suspect you to be in league with the people behind Cynog's death. Folk would not find it difficult to believe.'

They would if they knew Owen's feelings about Owain Lawgoch's cause. 'Why would I hire him and then have him put to death before he completed his task?' Owen put up a hand to stop Rokelyn's reply. 'I play no game with you, nor have I said I would not assist you. But tell me this—if Cynog was Owain Lawgoch's man, and you are the King's man, why should you care why he was murdered? You have one less traitor hiding in your city.'

'No one has a right to bring justice in this city but the bishop of St David's, or those of us who act on his behalf. I do not care whose side Cynog was on. I want the person who believes he can take the law into his own hands in this city. He must be stopped.'

'You are right, of course.' Tomorrow Owen could think about a way round this. Meanwhile, he would put Rokelyn to work. 'If I agree to assist you, will you find me a stonemason to complete the tomb?'

'I shall.'

'And if I miss Siencyn's sailing, you will find me passage—comfortable passage—to England?'

'When you have satisfied me. If you do.'

Owen ignored the last remark. 'Then we are agreed. And now I must leave while I still have the strength to walk back to the palace. It has been a long and wearying day.' He rose.

'Do not try to leave the city,' Rokelyn warned.

'And how might I do that? Swim?' Owen bowed low, then headed for the door. As he passed the guards, they began to follow. Owen turned suddenly, his small eating knife in his hand. 'No. We have an agreement only so long as I do not have escorts.' He enjoyed the surprise on their faces. Such a small knife was nothing to fear and they would quickly discount it. But it was cheering to have given them pause.

'Let him go,' Rokelyn barked.

Owen expected the archdeacon to order the guards to follow him once he was outside. He bade the Welsh servant a goodnight in his own tongue and stepped out into a cold, wind-driven rain. It quickly woke him from his heavy-lidded, swollen-headed state. Blinking rapidly, he pulled his hood over his head and leaned into the storm. Then paused. Beneath the dripping eaves, he sensed more than saw a familiar shadow to his right. 'Quiet,' he whispered, joining Iolo, 'we are followed.'

They were out of the lantern light when the first guard appeared, squinting into the wet night. The man looked this way and that, muttering to himself. Owen could not hear him above the wind and the rain.

'How many?' Iolo whispered.

'Two.'

The second one appeared, quickly understood that they had lost their man. The two began to argue.

'Shall we fall upon them?' Iolo asked.

'To what purpose? Let us rather fall behind them.'

It was late and most of the guests lodged in the great hall were already settling in for the night. Owen and Iolo shrugged out of their wet cloaks and picked their way to the fire circle in the centre of the room to spread out the cloaks and dry out a bit before finding their pallets. Folk made room for them, whether because of their dripping condition or their grim faces, Owen could not guess. Sam must have been watching for them. He picked his way through the drowsy crowd, bearing a full wineskin.

Iolo grabbed it and drank greedily. His wet tunic hung unevenly and his leggings sagged at the ankles. His thinning hair looked even thinner slicked back, making his bony face and pale eyes almost sinister. Just how long had he stood beneath those eaves, Owen wondered. He shook his head when Iolo handed him the skin. 'I have had my fill of that for one night. Some feverfew in warm water would suit me better.'

Sam slumped with disappointment. 'I do not know where I might find such a drink.'

'The water is all I need,' said Owen. When Sam had gone off in search of water, Owen turned to Iolo. 'You were foolish to follow me this evening—you must have a care not to hurt your chances for a post in this city.'

'I have other plans for my future. You can use a shadow. I am coming to York with you.'

'When did you decide this?'

'Today. Though it has been much on my mind.'

'Ah. York is no paradise. The city is crowded and stinks of man and beast. Bitter cold in winter.'

'I have been to London. It cannot be worse than that.'

'Colder.'

Iolo looked unimpressed.

'Iolo, you honour me with your offer. But you are young. You can make a life for yourself here, in your own country.'

'I am decided.'

How had Owen inspired such loyalty in the young man? For young he was, despite the chiselled planes of his face and his well-honed skills. 'In York you would always be a stranger, as I am. If nothing else, our manner of speech sets us apart. I know. And so I warn you.'

'I have been among the English,' Iolo reminded him. 'I know what it is like.'

'But it was only for a time. You always knew that. Look how quickly you stepped forward for our mission, eager for the chance to come home. What happened?'

'I found an honourable man to serve.'

Fortunate man, to think so. And a great burden to Owen to prove so. 'But you wished to return to Wales.'

'I was under orders from the bishop to return at my first opportunity, though not before making note of all I could about the duke's household.'

Iolo could do well in the service of the ambitious Adam de Houghton. Owen had no doubt that this bishopric was not the loftiest position Houghton would attain. 'Did he wish you to continue in his service?'

'If it so pleased me.' Iolo raked phantom hair back with a long-fingered hand.

'And you would give this up to serve me?'

'I would. And gladly. You need me. I wish to serve you.'

Owen could certainly use him here. And sometimes in York, when Thoresby involved him in troublesome business. But most times he lived a quiet life, helping Lucie in the apothecary, overseeing repairs at the archbishop's palace of Bishopthorpe, finding things to occupy the time of the archbishop's retainers. What would Owen do with Iolo? Would Thoresby accept him as one of his retainers? If not, Owen was not grand enough to have a squire. What would Lucie think?

And then there was the matter of Iolo's bloodlust. The young man had a taste for violence. Owen had discovered quickly that he needed to be quite clear that he wished his victims to live.

'Much of my time at home is dull.'

'I should keep your retainers in line.'

No doubt. And in constant rebellion. What would Alfred think, to be unseated from his role as Owen's second in command? 'What of this Owain Lawgoch? Now he's a man could use someone like you. If I were free to take up arms for him, I would.'

Iolo's pale eyes searched Owen's face. 'In truth? I should think if you felt that way you would find the means to do so.'

'You are young and free. I have responsibilities.'

'Fighting for our rightful prince would be a proud legacy for your children.'

'If we won.'

Iolo shook his head. 'Spoken like a shopkeeper and clerk of the archbishop. I never thought to hear such a thing from you.'

Nor had Owen ever thought to say such a thing. Had his love for Lucie and his children unmanned him?

5

SIX HORSEMEN

The bells of York Minster thundered overhead as Lucie knelt in the nave, head bowed, trying to hear the ceremony in the choir. The bells and the screen made it difficult. And her own weeping. Why had they taken her father's body to the high altar, from which she was barred? And Jasper—what was he doing in there?

'He is taking his vows, of course,' her father said.

Lucie turned, found her father sitting beside her. He wore his shroud like a hooded gown. 'But you are dead. You are lying in the coffin by the high altar.'

Sir Robert took her hand. His was cold and dry. 'I heard you weeping. I wanted to comfort you. It is a good thing, your adopted son taking his vows. Why do you not share his joy?'

'He did not tell me. And why today?'

'He hopes to join Owen in St David's. He will accompany me.'

'St David's. You died in St David's.'

Sir Robert nodded. 'Just so.'

'You cannot be here. And why would Jasper go there? I do not understand.'

'Jasper did not think you would mind. You have Roger Moreton.'

'That is not true!' Lucie shouted, waking herself.

She sat up, clammy with sweat, shivering as the blanket fell from her and her damp skin met the chilly morning air. Or was it the dream that made her shiver? Talking to her father's corpse—had that been a dream, or a vision? Had she made Jasper so unhappy that he would take vows? Or had it nothing to do with his mistake, her

52

reprimand, his suspicions about Roger? Had she not been listening to Jasper? Did he truly wish to take vows? He was so difficult these days, so quick to accuse her of prying when she asked what he was thinking, where he had gone. Lucie knelt on the cold floor and prayed for understanding.

Later, when she had dressed herself, she remembered her father's last words in the dream. Roger Moreton. Now that, surely, was the stuff of dreams, not a vision. Still, her father's presence had felt so real. And what of St David's? Was Owen not to return from there?

Still shivering from the dream, Lucie hurried towards the hearth, joining her aunt, who sat at a small trestle table set near the fire.

Lucie crouched down by the fire, warming her hands. 'Have you been up long?' she asked.

Phillippa did not reply.

'She is far away, Mistress,' Tildy said, setting a bowl of broth on the table. 'Daimon says this happens often. Come, warm yourself with this.'

Phillippa's eyes seemed unfocused. Her hands were limp in her lap. She smiled slightly, as if amused.

Tildy withdrew.

Lucie sipped her broth and waited. At last, disturbed by her aunt's unwavering stare, she called her aunt's name.

Phillippa blinked, slowly brought her attention to Lucie. 'I hope my restlessness did not keep you from sleep last night.' She seemed unaware that Lucie had sat there for some time. She chatted on, telling Lucie she had resolved to return to York with her on the morrow, to attend the Requiem Mass for Sir Robert and then stay a while in York. 'Until I feel more at peace.'

'I am glad.'

'But I worry how the servants will behave with no mistress of the household. Would you allow Tildy to stay and take care of things?'

'Tildy? Stay?' Lucie forced herself to concentrate. 'But you have been away before, visiting us, and the servants have managed.'

'For a few days. But—this time I might be gone longer—unless you have changed your mind.' As Phillippa finished, she dropped her gaze from Lucie's face, as if fearing what she might see there.

'I have not changed my mind, Aunt! It is just—it is Tildy.' It would allow the young woman to try out the life Daimon proposed for her. But it might give Daimon false hopes. And what of the moral responsibility Lucie had towards Tildy? Should she leave her alone with a young man who was wooing her? 'You do not know what you ask,' she said.

'No. I suppose I do not.'

And how could she? Lucie told Phillippa about Daimon and Tildy.

Phillippa perked up at the tale, seemed her old self as she put hands to hips, shook her head. 'I see no problem. Put the question to Tildy—she is old enough to decide for herself.'

In the kitchen behind the hall, Tildy sat on a high stool and surveyed the tapestry she had spread across a trestle table. She tapped a toe in irritation and muttered to herself, occasionally using the breath to blow a stray wisp of hair from her face. From the rolled-up sleeves and askew cap Lucie guessed Tildy had had a struggle getting the piece down from the wall. She glanced up, noticed Lucie standing there, shook her head. 'It hurts to see such a beautiful thing torn like it was a rag. How could Daimon think his mistress did such a thing?' She lifted a corner. 'You have often spoken of the colours on this tapestry.'

Lucie had always thought it a cheerful tapestry, imagining the laughter of the three maidens as they made their garlands. 'Can you mend it properly? Enough so that it will not show in the shadows?'

Tildy screwed up her pretty face. 'I could replace the backing piece to hold it together, but over time it will fray. I cannot think what it will look like when Master Hugh brings his bride to the hall.'

Twenty years hence? Thirty? 'Perhaps I should take it back to the city, see whether there is a better way to mend it.'

'I would, Mistress. It is too pretty a thing to neglect.'

'I shall take it in the morning. My aunt has decided to return to

York with me, did you know?'

'I am glad of that. Her heart will be eased by the children.'

'But she is worried about leaving the hall without a mistress.'

'She has good folk here.'

'She hoped that you might stay and see to things.'

'Me? Stay here?' Tildy shook her head. 'But I cannot do that. Does she not understand that I am the children's nursemaid? When I stayed here before I was here for the children.'

'She knows. She asks the favour. I thought it was for you to decide.'

Tildy looked stricken. 'For me?'

'It is a reasonable request.'

Tildy stared down at the riven tapestry for a while, her toe still tapping. A lock of hair slipped from beneath her cap, curled over her chin. She blew at it to no avail. Taking off her cap, she tilted her head back, shook it, put back the cap, tied it beneath her chin, looked up at Lucie. 'What would you do?'

'In truth, I cannot say. I do not want you to feel you must do this for my aunt. Nor, if you wish to try your hand at running a household, should you feel responsible for Gwenllian and Hugh. Phillippa, Kate and I should be able to manage them until you return. You must look into your heart, Tildy.'

'It is a very large house, Mistress Lucie. A great undertaking for such as me.'

'I do not doubt you would manage well. But do you wish to?'

Tildy said nothing, but the tapping grew more insistent.

'You might also have time to become better acquainted with Daimon,' Lucie said. 'Or reacquainted.'

Tildy blushed. 'You know?'

'I know what I saw in the courtyard, what I see in both your eyes.' Lucie shook her head when Tildy would speak. 'I trust you, Tildy. And I want you to make the choice.'

'I might try running the household.'

'Talk to Dame Phillippa, then. She is eager to tell you what she would like you to do. Perhaps that will help you decide.'

• • •

After the evening meal, Phillippa called Tildy and Daimon to her. It was time for the final instructions regarding the manor while she was away. Lucie, who sat nearby with Brother Michaelo and Harold, noted how often Phillippa's conversation shifted from the matter at hand to memories of Sir Robert. At the moment, Phillippa was recounting Sir Robert's tales of the siege of Calais. Lucie smiled to hear how her father's role had expanded.

Suddenly the hall door burst open.

'Storm coming,' Phillippa said. Turning to Tildy, she began to advise her how to secure the hall in a windstorm.

But it was not a storm. A servant stumbled in, gasping, 'Armed horsemen. Six. At the gatehouse.'

'God have mercy,' Lucie cried. 'Daimon!'

The young steward had already jumped up, grabbed his sword belt. He struggled to buckle his belt as he strode to the doorway. Tildy rose to follow, but Lucie held her back. Already shouts rang out in the yard.

Phillippa, too, had risen with a cry, and shuffled towards the rear door of the hall. Brother Michaelo went after her.

'Come, Dame Phillippa,' he cried above the din of men's shouts without. 'You are best in here, by the fire. Burning brands are good weapons, if need be.'

'I must see to things,' Phillippa cried, trying to shrug out of his grasp.

Lucie sent Tildy off to gather the maidservants in the buttery. She noticed Harold, his sword drawn, standing near the hall door. 'You need not hold the door against them,' she said. 'We shall manage. Help Daimon.'

Harold nodded towards Michaelo and Phillippa. 'Your aunt is much distressed.'

'As she should be! Brother Michaelo will calm her.'

'Do you have a dagger?'

'We have a kitchen full of weapons. Go!'

'Bar the door behind me,' Harold said as he raised his sword and stepped out into the darkness.

As Lucie reached the door, she saw smoke beyond the courtyard. What was burning? The gatehouse? Two men struggled close to the door. Lucie pushed it to, barred it. Dear God in heaven, what if they had not been here this night? She watched Phillippa, still arguing with Brother Michaelo. Where did she think to go?

'It is the watchers,' Phillippa hissed. 'They *know.*'

Lucie met Michaelo's troubled gaze. 'The outlaws heard that Sir Robert was dead? It is possible. But what of our steward? Why would they attack an occupied house?'

Something thudded against the outer door. A man cried out. Tildy ran out from the buttery. 'That is Daimon!'

'The hall is not safe,' Michaelo said. 'Is there a cellar?'

'The maze,' Phillippa cried. 'We must go to the maze.'

'The kitchen maid saw horsemen near the maze,' Tildy said.

'The chapel,' Lucie said. 'Come, Aunt. Tildy, bring the others. Brother Michaelo, try to gain the yard, see whether Daimon needs help.' Taking her aunt firmly in hand, Lucie led the way to the chapel at the far end of the hall. Though her knees felt weak, she was determined to keep her aunt as safe as she might.

'For you, Sir Robert. I would do this for no other,' Michaelo muttered as he checked that his dagger was loose in its sheath, then took a torch from the wall and made for the hall door, which groaned against the bar. 'Holy Mary, Mother of God, have mercy on this sinner,' Michaelo whispered as he tried to unbar the door; but the pressure from the other side made it difficult to move. If he put the torch in the sconce beside the door and used both hands to work at the bar, he would be momentarily unarmed when whoever was pressing against it fell through. He cringed at the thought of the weight of the door and the body against him. His neck prickled with sweat. He reasoned with himself that he would have his dagger;

but that was a weapon of finesse, not force. Yet what choice did he have?

Michaelo put up the torch, put both hands to the bar, pushed it towards the door and tried to shove sideways. It did not move. He stepped back, rubbed his hands, took a deep breath, grabbed the bar, tried just shoving it sideways. It moved a few inches, then stuck. Now he put his whole body into pressing against the force being brought against the door. But it was suddenly lessened. The bolt slid easily. Taking a deep breath to quiet the violent hammering of his heart, Michaelo laid the bolt aside, grabbed the torch, opened the door. A body fell in. Michaelo thought he was about to choke on his heart. He forced himself to bring the torch near the body at his feet.

Daimon. Blood covered his head. Part of his tunic was scorched. Michaelo grabbed a shoulder of the young steward's tunic with his free hand and dragged him further into the hall. Then he knelt to him, checked for a pulse. *Deo gratias*. He lived. Even now Daimon tried to open his eyes, blinked at the bright light from the torch, muttered something unintelligible.

'Do not try to move,' Michaelo said. 'I must see to the door, then I will get help.'

He peered out of the door. The fighting seemed to have stopped. He paused with the door halfway shut. A sword glittered in the courtyard mud. Why leave a weapon for the outlaws? Michaelo made a dash for it. But he was too slow. Someone came up from behind, knocked him aside. Michaelo fell headlong, losing his grasp on the torch. He could just see booted feet dash past, a hand grab the torch, another hand the sword. The boots then continued on towards the stables.

Propping himself up on one arm, Michaelo looked round the courtyard. Finding himself alone, he dared to stand. Sweet Jesu, but his hip hurt. He hobbled back to the hall door, discovered it had closed behind him. He was certain Daimon had not managed that. He pushed. Pushed harder. He could not believe it. Barred from within. He pounded on the door, shouting, 'Mistress Wilton! Tildy! It is Brother Michaelo. Let me in!' He put his ear to the door, heard nothing. Perhaps they were too busy tending Daimon. He prayed that was so. Still, why did they not respond?

He turned round, leaned against the door, took a deep breath, let his eyes become more accustomed to the dark. Clouds of smoke hung over the gatehouse. He must not go that way. Round the back? See whether the rear door to the hall had been barred?

Lucie and Tildy had managed to get Daimon into the chapel just before the strangers rushed through the hall door. Before Lucie closed the chapel door she saw three figures enter the hall below, one carrying a lantern not quite shuttered.

'They will burn the house round us!' a maidservant whimpered.

'They have killed him,' Tildy moaned, bending over Daimon.

Lucie shushed them as she leaned against the door, trying to hear where the three had gone. But the walls were too thick.

'Let me go to them,' Phillippa whispered at Lucie's side. 'I shall give them what they want.'

'Help Tildy with Daimon.'

'But—'

Lucie crossed her arms, positioned herself in front of the chapel door. 'See to Daimon.'

As Michaelo came round the back of the house he heard a horse whinny. Flattening himself against the wall, he searched the darkness. But he could not see anyone. So he waited. A line of light appeared, widened, illuminated a man with three horses. Two men came from the house, hurried to join him. Without a word to one another, they all mounted and rode off.

Michaelo crossed himself, hurried towards the door. When he reached it, it was closed. He tried it, found it opened easily. Torchlight welcomed him. He hurried across the hall and up to the chapel, found all the women safely within. And Daimon, breathing, but just barely.

In a little while, Harold and the menservants came in, all of them sooty, sweating, most of them with minor wounds, all chattering at once.

Michaelo told them about the horsemen at the rear.

Harold proposed a search of the woods.

Lucie agreed that it would help everyone feel more secure, though she doubted the men would have been such fools as to linger.

She frowned as she turned round to Michaelo, drew him aside. Michaelo smelled the young steward's blood on her. Her gown and her scarf were stained with it. He hoped she did not wish him to help with Daimon. He was no good as a nurse.

'I saw three men enter the hall,' Lucie said. 'But you mentioned only two.'

'You fear one may yet be in the house?'

'Perhaps.'

Michaelo had not considered that. The three men had not hesitated for another before riding off. Three men. Of course. 'The one waiting with the horses—he was one of them. He must have slipped out earlier.'

Lucie did not look convinced. 'I shall take a few servants and search the house.'

'I shall accompany you.'

'I would have you watch Phillippa. And—when you go on to Bishopthorpe, would you carry a letter to His Grace for me?'

Now here was a service he would gladly provide. 'I shall write it for you if you wish.'

'I can write.' The cold voice of pride.

'So, too, can His Grace. As most men who employ secretaries. But I have a fine hand. It is the only skill in which I excel.'

Lucie smiled. 'Forgive me. I thought you doubted my ability. Shall we meet tomorrow morning?'

'I shall have my ink and points at the ready.' He was most curious what she might have to say to Archbishop Thoresby.

Michaelo, Phillippa and Tildy remained in the chapel, tending Daimon, while Lucie took a few servants to search the house. The hall door had held up well. Some silver plate had been taken from the hall, and a tapestry—the torn one, which Tildy had rolled up and tucked into the cabinet with the silver plate. Poor Phillippa. First the tear, now this. The thieves must have thought the roll might contain something of value—the tapestry itself might fetch a good price, but for the tear. Lucie went next to the treasury, a small, windowless room within the buttery, where the manor accounts and the money box were kept in a large chest. The door was ajar. She stood very still, listening for any tell-tale sounds. None came. They entered the buttery, then the treasury. The lock had been pried off the chest. The money box was gone, and the accounts, which were usually neatly stacked on a shelf above the chest, were in disarray, as if the thieves had hoped to discover more treasure among them. She would sort them out later. For now, she wished to see the rest of the house. What pricked at the back of her mind as she continued was that the treasury was a room only members of the household would know about. The servants, of course, knew of it because one must go through the buttery to reach the room. But guests of the household would have no knowledge of it, and strangers would have taken a while to find it. The thieves had been in the house a very short time. And the shuttered lantern—they had needed little light to find their way. Which meant they either had a colleague in the household, or one of them (or more) had once lived or worked here. Michaelo had asked whether she feared one of the thieves might yet be in the house. She did. But how might she find that person if he was part of the staff?

It was long after midnight when Harold's search party returned. A horse and several lambs were missing, the fire in the gatehouse was under control, but the roof was gone—an assessment of the rest of the damage to the building must wait until daylight. They had found no strangers on the property, but as a precaution a night watch had been organised.

Lucie thanked the men and sent them off to the kitchen for ale.

Harold stayed. 'You have shadows beneath your eyes,' he said to Lucie. 'What can I do to help hasten you to rest?'

'Help Daimon into the hall. Tildy and I made up a pallet for him near the fire.' As Harold turned away Lucie saw a rent in his leggings, a burned edge on his tunic. And he walked stiffly, as if weary to the bone. 'Harold,' she called softly. He turned. 'God bless you for all you have done this night,' she said. He smiled wearily, turned back to the task at hand. She watched him help Daimon to his feet. The poor young man was too dizzy to manage. Harold scooped him up and carried him to the pallet in the hall. The muscle-heavy Daimon seemed no burden to Harold.

'He is strong,' Tildy said at Lucie's side.

Lucie already had other things on her mind. She told Tildy her suspicion, that the outlaws might have an accomplice in the household. 'Keep your own counsel. Warn Daimon, too.'

'You think they might be back?'

'I do not know. Why would thieves take such risk for a horse, two lambs, some silver plate, a torn tapestry and a modest amount of money?'

'They took the tapestry?'

'It was near the plate.'

Tildy grinned. 'Well, I should like to see their faces when they see the tear.'

Her sleeve and skirt stained with her love's blood, her shoulders rounded with weariness—Tildy was a strong young woman to find humour in anything this night. Lucie appreciated it, but she could not smile, for she felt too keenly that they were still in danger. 'I am tired. And so must you be. See to Daimon, then get some sleep. You must be both lady of the manor and steward tomorrow.'

'You still mean to ride to York in the morning?'

'I do. Would you rather return with me?' It was Tildy's to choose. Lucie would not force her to remain here if she was frightened.

'No. I am needed here. I should see to Daimon, get him settled.'

Lucie watched the young woman hurry away. With her tender nursing the young steward would recover soon, Lucie thought. But how safe was Tildy in this house? Though Daimon had made sense when they asked him questions, he could not protect her. He said that when he lifted his bandaged head his stomach felt queer, which was worrisome but not surprising with a head injury. Besides that wound he had a swollen shoulder where his left arm had been pulled out of joint, a deep cut on his left palm and some slight burns. If Archbishop Thoresby granted her request, the two might be safe here. But what if he did not?

But at the moment she must get her aunt to bed. The poor woman sat with chin on chest, snoring softly. When Lucie waked her, Phillippa clutched her sleeve. 'How is he? Would you like me to sit with him?'

'Tildy is with Daimon now.'

Phillippa looked confused. 'Adam the steward's son? He is unwell?'

'Who did you think I sat with, Aunt?'

'Nicholas. You have not been up with him? Is no one with him?'

Michaelo glanced up from his prayers, gave Lucie a sympathetic look.

Phillippa had come to help Lucie nurse her first husband in his final illness. 'Nicholas is long dead, Aunt. You are at Freythorpe Hadden. Daimon is your steward.'

'Of course he is. I knew that,' Phillippa snapped. She fussed with her crooked, wrinkled wimple.

'Let us go to bed, Aunt. We have much to do tomorrow. Tildy will take care of Daimon tonight.'

'She is a good girl, Tildy.'

Phillippa's calm smile bothered Lucie more than her confusion. Her aunt had been in charge of this house for so many years—it was unnatural for her to smile so after the events of the evening.

As they crossed the hall, Tildy was leaning over Daimon's pallet, spreading more covers over him.

'I shall be down here with Dame Phillippa tonight, Tildy. I can hear if you call.'

Tildy nodded, but did not look up from her charge.

Lucie woke towards dawn, surprised that she had fallen asleep. Phillippa was not in her bed. Hurriedly dressing, Lucie ran out into the hall. Tildy dozed in a chair beside Daimon. Michaelo slept on a pallet just out of the light of the fire. Two menservants slept nearby. Harold must be on watch. Lucie checked the chapel. Empty. Where could her aunt be? When Lucie was small her aunt had told her to run into the maze if a stranger frightened her. They would lose themselves among the tall yews, and she would have time to run out the other way. She had spoken of the maze last night. Lucie hurried out into the pale dawn. The smell of damp ashes reminded her of the ruined gatehouse. She paused, cocking her ear. Slowly she walked towards the maze, still listening. As she drew near the entrance, she heard voices from within. Or beyond. She held her breath. As a child she used to stand here, just so, listening for her mother. She felt a chill. The voices grew louder.

'I promise you, Dame Phillippa,' Harold was saying. 'It will be our secret. But you must rest now. The early morning air is not good for you.'

Slowly Harold and Phillippa emerged from the maze, her hand resting on his arm. The sight of her aunt did not comfort Lucie. Her headdress was askew and torn. Her thin white hair fell round her face in greasy strands. Her eyes were large and dark, like those of a cat just in from the night's hunt. Smudges of dirt on her cheeks and nose matched her crooked, muddy hem. This was not the Phillippa who brought Lucie up.

'Aunt Phillippa! What has happened?'

'I fell in the maze,' Phillippa said, glancing up at Harold.

He nodded. 'I heard her cry out.'

'Why were you in the maze?' Lucie asked.

'I wanted to see if it is still possible to go through the proper way.'

'Why would it not be? Just last summer you taught Gwenllian how to find her way through it.'

'I forgot.'

How much of her forgetfulness was an act, Lucie wondered as she followed the two into the hall. She was thankful Phillippa wished to lie down. Lucie needed a moment to close her eyes and calm her heart.

6

THE CAPTAIN'S TALE

Owen and Jared climbed out of the valley in which St David's nestled, a valley so deep that the bell tower of the cathedral was invisible from the sea—indeed from all but the highest hills surrounding the city. They walked slowly, pausing here and there, hoping to trip up clumsy pursuers. Iolo, Sam, Edmund and Tom were scattered about, two ahead, two behind, watching for a ripple behind the bait. At the rocky crest of the ascent Owen felt invigorated by a sharp, salt-laden wind. Gulls shrieked above, waves crashed against the rocks below. Gradually, as the two descended towards the harbour, the rumble and creak of several ships at anchor in the high tide off Porth Clais, the port of St David's, joined the harmony.

What Owen most needed was to talk to Martin Wirthir, find out what he knew about Cynog, how involved the mason had been in the Lawgoch efforts. When last Owen needed to find Martin Wirthir he had climbed Clegyr Boia, a mound just beyond St David's walls. Martin had a hiding place within the ruins of the ancient fort atop the mound. Owen doubted that the Fleming would be there now. His friend's best defence was invisibility and he rarely stayed in one place for long; but he kept a watch on Clegyr Boia so that he might know when someone sought him there. And who it was who sought him. But if Rokelyn's guards were shadowing Owen, he might lead them to a man they would delight in capturing. It would not make Owen's life easier, either. How likely was it that Rokelyn would believe Owen and Martin were merely friends, not political cohorts?

So Owen was testing Rokelyn's word, seeing whether the archdeacon would have him followed to Porth Clais. Then he would know whether he might seek out Martin Wirthir.

Captain Siencyn was not on the waterfront. In fact, it was quiet for such a clear morning. Some fishermen far out at the westernmost edge of the inlet sat on the shingle working on their nets, two children played nearby under the gaze of an old man who avoided Owen's eye. Not far away, a woman stood quietly, looking out to sea. She wore a heavy cloak, the hood thrown back. Her hair was tightly braided about her head. 'That is Glynis,' Jared said. 'She is rumoured to be the mistress of Piers the Mariner.'

'God go with you, Mistress,' Owen said in Welsh, hoping that might put her at ease. He had to speak loudly to be heard above the roar of the sea. 'Would you know where I might find Captain Siencyn?'

The woman turned round, nodded up the rock face. At first Owen saw nothing, then his eye made out a stone building tucked into a ledge.

'The path begins just behind you,' said the woman. She did not wait for his thanks but, picking up her skirts, hurried away towards the fishermen.

'Seems we have sprouted horns,' said Jared. 'The folk were warmer a few days past.'

'Before I arrived.'

'Aye,' Jared said absently. He was staring up the cliff. 'That cottage? Is that where she pointed us?' He did not understand Welsh.

'It is.' Owen studied the steep, winding path that led to it. Ever since losing the sight in his left eye he had disliked walking narrow ledges. His accuracy in judging depths and distances had improved in ten years, but the doubt remained. When would not quite perfect not be good enough? Why was God so sorely testing him?

'Captain?' Jared called down, already halfway up.

Owen began the ascent. The path was not as precarious as it looked from below. It was well worn, with deeply indented footholds. He avoided looking down and, within moments was on a ledge on which scraggly tufts of grass valiantly stood up against the salty breeze. The cottage seemed a tentative structure, three walls of loosely piled rocks enclosing the hillside, a sod roof sagging above them. Smoke drifted out of the cottage's low door and numerous chinks in the rocks.

Jared bent, peered in the door. 'Captain Siencyn,' he called.

'Who wants me?' a man grumbled in reply.

Jared stepped inside. Owen followed.

The room within was faintly lit by a smoky fire and a lantern near the door. Blinking against the smoke and the sudden dimness after the bright daylight without, Owen felt he was a target for anyone whose eyes were adjusted to the gloom. He gradually picked out a large man seated in the middle of the room, bootless feet propped up on a stone so close to the fire it was a wonder his stockings were not scorched. To one side of him lay a large cat, to the other side the remnants of a meal. Behind him stood an incongruous wood-framed, cloth-draped bed. How had he brought it up that path, Owen wondered. Captain Siencyn slowly raised his head, nodded lazily. The firelight gave his heavy features a menacing look. The frown he cast towards Jared did nothing to soften the effect. Then suddenly he grinned, causing a dramatic transformation. He looked almost boyish.

'Jared, lad. You have saved me the bother of a journey up, over and down.' He spoke English, with no Welsh accent. With his Flemish name he was likely from the area round Haverfordwest.

'Captain Siencyn, this is Captain Owen Archer,' said Jared, stepping aside.

'Is it?' Siencyn thrust his head forward, squinted up at Owen. 'The patch, aye, they did tell me that about you.' He shifted his feet from the stone, hooked one foot round a bench nearby, dragged it towards the fire. 'Sit. I have something to tell you.'

Owen shifted the angle of the short bench so it might still be close to his host, but not so close to the smoky fire. Jared withdrew to the doorway.

Siencyn shook his head at Jared, tucked his feet back up to warm. 'How soon do we sail?' Owen asked, bringing Siencyn's attention back to him.

'I shall not be sailing,' said Siencyn. 'You must find another ship.'

'You want more money,' Owen guessed.

The man shook his head. 'It has naught to do with money. I shall not be sailing for a time.' He stuck out his chin as if daring Owen to protest.

'Is this about your brother?' Owen asked.

Siencyn's feet hit the floor. 'Why do you ask about my brother?'

'He is accused of murder. It is the talk of the city.'

Siencyn sniffed. 'I am not my brother's keeper.'

'I am glad to hear that. Perhaps we can still come to an agreement.'

'Who are you working for?'

'You agreed to carry us.'

'Why should I sail with someone who will not answer my questions?'

'Archdeacon Rokelyn wants to know why Cynog was executed. But I would rather depart for England.'

Siencyn grunted. 'Those beady-eyed churchmen. I thought you looked like a man would be no fonder of them than I am. Aye, they have locked Piers away. For want of a scapegoat.'

'You say your brother is innocent?'

Siencyn smirked. 'Not a word oft used to describe my brother. But I cannot think why he would hang a man, much less that mason.'

'Then why did they choose your brother as a scapegoat?'

'He is a fool for a woman, that is why. But this time a greater fool than usual. He was seen in the dead man's room a day or two before the hanging.'

'With Cynog?'

Siencyn snorted, causing the cat to raise its head. 'Piers was searching Cynog's room for proof his lady had been with the mason. He would hardly invite Cynog to accompany him.' Siencyn petted the cat, calming it.

Owen noticed that the man's hand trembled slightly.

'Cynog was your brother's rival?' Owen asked.

'He sees all men as such.'

'But he searched Cynog's room.'

'And how many others has he searched without being caught?'

Siencyn's behaviour struck Owen as inconsistent. Hostile, then co-operative, specific then vague. He slurred the occasional word to give the impression of being in his cups, but his eyes were sharp and his breathing steady. The hand was most likely nerves. 'So your brother was caught in Cynog's room. What happened then?'

'He went off and drank himself into a stupor is what happened then. While the black eye and the bloody nose turned lovely colours. He is subtle, my brother.'

'Did he prove her untrue?'

'Nay. And he looked so pitiful she forgave his distrust with a coo and a kiss.'

'Someone did not forgive him. Someone must have told the archdeacon about your brother's trespass.'

'Aye. They say, too, that the murderer tied the noose to the tree with a sailor's knot, and thus is Piers proved guilty. We are almost surrounded by water here. Is my brother the only sailing man about? Pah.'

'If Piers did not murder Cynog, who did? Does he know? Does he suspect another?'

Siencyn shook his head. 'He cannot save himself with that, more's the pity.'

'Enemies? Someone who wants him to suffer?'

'That would be too complicated for simple folk.'

Owen abandoned that thread. 'Do you have a plan to free Piers?'

'I might. Meanwhile, I shall not make it worse for him. Rokelyn has forbidden you to leave before you discover Cynog's murderer. To help you depart would endanger Piers.'

'You pretended you did not know for whom I was working.'

'It is wise in such times to test a man's honesty.'

'Such times?'

'Now who is playing the fool? Owain Lawgoch is gathering an army of unhappy Welshmen, financed by the King of France. Any one of you might be traitors to King Edward.'

'And not you?'

'King Edward of England welcomed my countrymen to this fair land. Why should I betray him?'

'Men have their own reasons for supporting such causes.'

'Treason is punishable by death. To me that is reason enough to avoid it.' Siencyn squinted at Owen. 'But mayhap, being Welsh, you see it otherwise.'

'You tire of my questions,' Owen said, rising. 'Send for me if you change your mind.'

'About treason?' Siencyn asked with a smirk.

Owen did not intend to be provoked. 'About sailing,' he said flatly.

Siencyn laughed. 'Fare thee well, Captain Archer.'

Jared had the good sense to keep his thoughts to himself as they descended to the beach.

Owen had made a mess of that discussion, allowing Siencyn to control it. And more disappointment followed. He had hoped to find Glynis before she conferred with Siencyn, but she was nowhere to be seen and it seemed no one in Porth Clais knew where she was. Some even denied that she had been on the beach earlier.

'I would wager it is not Piers for whom they are lying,' Owen muttered as they slogged back up the hill towards St David's.

Edmund joined them, looking equally disheartened.

'So what did you see?' Owen asked, expecting nothing.

'A vicar played shadow for a time, but returned to the city when you disappeared into the captain's hut.'

'Good.' Some luck at last.

Edmund scratched his head. 'Good? I thought you would worry.'

'Rokelyn will know that I am hard at work. Did you recognise the curious vicar?'

'Simon, secretary to Archdeacon Baldwin,' said Iolo, who had joined them so silently all three spun round, drawing their daggers. He grinned. 'I did not think that such bad news.'

Jared cursed him.

Owen paused at the top of the cliff, looking down into the valley of St David's, remembering the argument he had overheard the previous evening. 'Why does Archdeacon Baldwin care where I go?'

'It may have nothing to do with the archdeacon,' Iolo said. 'Father Simon is the self-appointed Summoner of St David's. Bishop Houghton has not bothered to oust him.'

Meaning he watched over the morals of clergy and laity alike. And hence Rokelyn called him a weasel.

Edmund laughed. 'So he thought to catch you in a tryst with a fair maiden, Captain.'

'I should be a fool to think that.' Owen regretted his words as soon as he spoke them. Edmund bowed his head and looked away. An apology might only make it worse. They had reached Patrick's Gate. 'Just Father Simon?' Owen said. 'No other shadows?'

Iolo and Edmund shook their heads.

'I am off to talk to Piers the Mariner,' said Owen. 'What have you learned about him?'

'You were right about Rokelyn's servant,' said Iolo. 'Eager to help a countryman. He says Piers was put off a ship for thieving. He swears he was blamed for another's crime, but no one will hire him. Except his brother.'

'And now he has been wrongly accused again? He must think himself ill used, indeed.'

'We have our man, eh?' Edmund looked hopeful. They all wished to be on their way.

'That is not the point,' Owen said, gently this time. 'Archdeacon Rokelyn wants to know on whose orders Cynog was executed. Find Tom and Sam. See whether any others followed me.'

Piers the Mariner was not in Bishop Houghton's official gaol—that was in the dungeon of Llawhaden Castle, a hard day's ride from St David's. Piers was confined in a windowless room in the undercroft of the east wing of the bishop's palace. Not a dungeon, then, but a dark, damp, unpleasant place all the same. He looked much like his brother but slighter and shaggier, the latter no doubt the result of his imprisonment. He sat cross-legged in the corner, flipping a spoon from one hand to the other. An oil lamp sat on the floor beside him.

'I like to see the rats coming,' he grunted in greeting. In English.

Owen greeted him in Welsh, explained that he wished to help Piers if he was innocent. Piers cursed, again in English.

'You do not speak Welsh?' Owen asked, still in his own tongue.

'Is that why I am here? Because I prefer to speak English? For pity's sake, I know you can speak English. I have heard of you, you know. You were to take ship home with my brother.'

Owen leaned against the door, judging it the cleanest surface in the cell, crossed his arms.

'Getting comfortable?' Piers growled. 'Shall I send for refreshments?'

Detecting the smell of ale in the noisome mix of sweat, damp, urine and rat, Owen said, 'You have had some refreshment already, eh?'

'Father Simon is generous with drink, if naught else.'

'I thought perhaps your wayward lady had been here.'

'Wayward? Is she?' Piers tried to sound indifferent, but failed.

Owen side-stepped the question. 'You searched Cynog's room.'

'And for that I shall be remembered.' Piers's laugh was hollow.

'Why did you suspect Glynis had been with Cynog?'

'He hated me for taking her away. He was a desperate man.'

Here was news. 'Cynog was Glynis's lover?'

'Surely he told you about it the night you bared your soul to him?'

Owen felt a shower of needle pricks across his blind eye. 'When?'

Piers looked amused. 'So you did not know that he had bragged about getting drunk with you, hearing all about your life? I can see that you did not. Is it an unpleasant surprise? That the city knows of your dissatisfaction with Archbishop Thoresby? Your beautiful wife? How tedious it is to work in her apothecary? How—'

'Quiet!' Owen shouted. 'I did not come here to be goaded by the likes of you.'

'Why did you come?'

'To find out whether Archdeacon Rokelyn has unjustly accused you of Cynog's murder. Why did you expect to find something in Cynog's room?'

'Someone had seen him with Glynis.'

'Who discovered you?'

'Would that I knew. My dagger might have put a stop to all this.' Piers jabbed the air with the spoon.

'Then how did you know you were seen?'

Owen thought Piers hesitated, but so briefly he could not be certain.

'The next day it was all the gossip.'

'What did you hope to find?'

'Her scent, of course.'

'Who told you that Glynis had been with him?'

'I cannot remember.'

'Surely—'

'In a tavern one listens with his eyes on his cup, Captain. Someone spoke of it, they all began taunting me. I could use a draught now. You might have loosened my tongue with a tankard.'

'Is that what Father Simon did? Loosened your tongue?'

'No. He delighted to tell me that as no one has come forward on my behalf I am to be hanged.' Piers's voice hushed as he spoke the last three words.

'And what did you say to that?'

'I asked him about a trial by my peers. He smiled at my request.'

'But you said no more? His threat did not bring a confession? Or a suggestion where he might find proof of your innocence?'

'I had no cause to harm Cynog. If Glynis meant to return to him, so be it.'

'You may say those things and yet be guilty.'

'No one wishes to look further. But there is one who will come forward for me.'

'Who might that be?'

'You will see. All will see.'

'But you will not say who it is?'

'I am a man of honour.'

Owen straightened. 'You have nothing else to say on your behalf?'

'No.'

'God go with you, then.'

'The Lord has thought little about me of late.'

Neither was Owen thinking about Piers as he walked through the bishop's wing into the great hall of the palace. He was thinking of Cynog. Had he so betrayed Owen? Had he gossiped about their conversation? How else would Piers know such detail? Owen had thought Cynog an honourable man. Had he been wrong about him?

7

CHAOS

Sleep eluded Lucie after her aunt's dawn adventure. And the longer she lay beside her aunt, staring at the candle left burning to calm them both, the more she worried. At last she gave up, thinking she would do more good relieving Tildy so she might rest. As Lucie reached for her clothes she noticed the bloodstains on her gown and scarf. She turned the scarf round and tried to tuck in the stained part; the gown she covered with an apron. She would save the clean clothes for travelling.

The hall was quiet, lit only by the fire and a small lamp on the table beside Daimon's pallet. People were still abed. Tildy sat close to the young steward, quietly talking to him, telling him of the damage, what had been stolen. 'He begged to hear,' she explained with a guilty grimace as Lucie joined them.

'Of course you would wish to know,' Lucie said to Daimon. 'I know you take pride in your role here. Now Tildy must get some rest, eh?'

Daimon agreed.

Though Tildy stumbled with weariness as she rose, she departed reluctantly. 'You will not let me sleep the whole day?'

'I cannot do without you that long,' Lucie assured her.

Daimon did not seem so well this morning as he had last night. He had a fever, though not an alarming one. The wound on his hand had swelled in the night and it did not smell clean. Lucie spent a good while with him, opening the wound to let it drain, packing it with a paste of woad that Phillippa kept on hand for reducing swelling.

And while Lucie worked, she asked Daimon about folk who had left the manor, or been recently chastised.

'No one has been treated so badly here that they should turn against us.' Daimon's voice was weak.

Lucie felt guilty about making him talk, but whom else might she trust? 'You cannot be sure you know another's heart, Daimon. Tell me about those who might be unhappy.'

The list, once Daimon understood that any slight might cause a person to turn on their master, was quite long. Two grooms who could not meet Sir Robert's standards; the young son of Nan the cook and his sweetheart, a kitchen maid, whose pranks had become spiteful and dangerous; a thatcher who believed he had been cheated; several minor servants who had not met Phillippa's high standards.

'The thatcher would not know of the treasury,' Lucie said.

'Servants talk. He flirted with all the women.'

'Are any of these people still here?'

'The kitchen maid. One of the grooms. The thatcher still works in the area.'

'What about Nan's son?'

'No one knows for certain. If cook knows, she will not say.'

'I do not recall her having a son.'

'None of us knew of him until he showed up. Mistress Wilton, if you are right, is Matilda safe here? I cannot protect her.'

'I shall get help until you are well, Daimon. I owe that to you.' She told him of her plan. 'All you need do is rest and recover.'

'Did you ask Matilda to stay with me?'

'Dame Phillippa asked her to manage the house while she is away. Tildy agreed. It was her choice.'

'She planned to stay before I was injured?'

'Yes. She did not tell you?'

'No.'

'Be good to her, Daimon.'

'If I have the chance.'

Brother Michaelo entered the hall with one of his saddlebags. A servant set up a small table beneath one of the great windows on the south side of the hall, then proceeded to clean it under Michaelo's supervision.

'I must leave you a while,' Lucie said to Daimon. 'But I shall be here in the hall if you need me.'

He settled back against the pillows, closed his eyes. There was a slight smile on his face.

Michaelo had paper and ink ready. 'You need not compose the letter, Mistress Wilton. If you simply tell me what you wish to accomplish...'

Lucie nodded, but did not begin until there were no servants nearby. When she explained her goal, she saw from the widening of the monk's eyes that he found it an extravagant request. But he bent to the task.

Lucie began to rise.

'I pray you, stay a little,' Michaelo said. 'I shall have questions.'

As Lucie sat quietly watching Michaelo's bowed head, listening to the slow scratching of his quill, Harold entered the hall, his tabard and leggings covered with muddy ashes. He bowed to her, moved off in the direction of the kitchen.

Michaelo raised his head. 'Their familiarity with the house. How did you note that?'

She explained.

He nodded. 'I have what I need.' He bowed over the letter once more. In a short while he asked her to read it and sign it. She did so, pleased with his tact, the grace of his words.

She was sitting by the fire, arranging pots and bowls of medicines on a tray, when Harold returned, pink-skinned from scrubbing, his hair slicked back, his muddy tabard traded for a loose linen shirt. 'Do I look less like one who cavorts with the pigs?'

Lucie was not ready for the feelings his appearance aroused in her, the glint of golden hair on his tanned neck, how it curled damply at the nape. 'You look—clean. God bless you for all you have done.'

'I could do no less.' His eyes held hers for a moment, those terribly blue eyes, and Lucie felt herself grow warm under his gaze. It was but a moment. Then he nodded towards where Daimon lay.

'How is he this morning?'

'Not as well as I had hoped.'

Lucie started to rise, tray in hand. Harold rose to help her. His hands touched hers briefly, their eyes met, then he drew the tray from her.

'Where shall I put it?'

Indicating a small table near Daimon, Lucie began to move away, wishing to break the tension between them that was beginning to choke her.

Harold joined her, falling into step beside her as she moved towards the buttery. 'Forgive me for overstepping my bounds, but considering Daimon's condition, might I suggest that I stay to organise the manor guard until he is recovered?'

And miss a ride through the countryside with me? The very fact that Lucie had thought that inclined her to say yes, stay. Stay away from me. But that was no way to make such a decision. She had already resolved how to protect the manor. 'There is no need.' She did not think it necessary to tell him her plan.

'As you wish.' He sounded wounded.

And what if Thoresby refused? She turned to Harold as they reached the door to the buttery. 'You have been a great help. And I thank you for your offer. I may yet have need of you.'

'You have only to ask.'

She touched the back of her hand to her cheek as she watched him walk away, felt the blush still there. How foolish she must look.

She lit a straw from the spirit lamp in the buttery to light a lamp in the treasury. The small room looked the same as it had last night. No one had tidied it. Lucie bent to the task of putting the account books in order. She shortly discovered one was missing. Lighting a second lamp, she searched the floor, behind the chest. From outside the hall came a loud rumble. Someone screamed. She heard people running.

Picking up her skirts, Lucie blew out the lamps.

'It is the gatehouse,' Michaelo told her as she hurried past him through the hall and out of the door. 'God help us, part of the upper storey has caved in.'

It was worse than that. On one side of the archway the outer wall had cracked beneath the burned roof and the crack was widening, the wattle and daub wall tilting crazily inward. Two men were trying to push a top-heavy cart away from it, but as the wall shivered and groaned they abandoned the cart and began to run. With a great shudder a large section of the wall fell into the yard. Debris rained down on the cart, shifting its precarious balance. It toppled sideways, sending the chairs, barrels, a bed frame and household items sliding towards Jenny, the gatekeeper's wife, who was struggling to carry her small boy and drag a sack out of the way. Lucie ran out into the yard, shouting a warning, but Jenny was too far away to hear her over all the din. Then suddenly, blessedly, Harold appeared from the far side of the yard, by the stables, and scooped up mother and child just in time, kicking the sack aside. Lucie hurried to join him at the stables, side-stepping a rolling barrel. She took the boy from Jenny's arms as Harold set the young mother down on her feet. She collapsed against him, sobbing.

By now the yard was abuzz with servants and tenants running about, catching up what they could of Jenny and Walter's household, tripping over each other as they raced for hooks and poles to tear down the tottering wall Across the yard, Phillippa stood in the doorway of the hall, wringing her hands.

Lucie carried the boy across and handed him to her aunt. 'Take him inside. I'll bring Jenny.'

'My bed!' Jenny sobbed as she stumbled across the yard in Lucie's grasp. Lucie guided her inside, murmuring reassurances that Jenny would have a new bed, a much better bed.

The little boy, wailing in Phillippa's impatient arms, threw out his arms towards his mother. She rushed to her son, pulled him from Phillippa's arms and settled down on a bench by the fire to nurse.

'Ungrateful woman,' Phillippa muttered.

Lucie wished she could tidy her aunt, but there was no time. The servants needed calming, direction. 'There are bound to be injuries, Aunt. You will need your medicines, clean rags, warm water.'

Phillippa shuffled towards the kitchen.

Lucie turned to Daimon, who was sitting up trying to catch someone's attention.

'What has happened?'

She told him. 'Jenny, Walter and their boy are safe. Rest, Daimon. We need you whole.'

In late afternoon, Lucie sat with Daimon, grateful for the quiet moment. She had sent Tildy, who found it impossible to rest, out to manage the preparation of a cottage for Jenny and Walter. Daimon had suggested one, unoccupied since the previous summer when the elderly woman who had lived there died of pestilence. They would not move for several days, after the dangerous vapours from the plague had been dispelled by a juniper fire and then the cottage aired out.

Lucie's quiet moment was truly just that, a moment. She was mixing a tisane for Daimon when he looked over her shoulder and closed his eyes with a sigh.

'What is it. A pain?' Lucie asked.

'Ma. I hoped she would not hear that I was injured.'

Lucie had forgotten about Daimon's mother. After Daimon's father's death, his mother had moved to a cottage at a distance from the manor house. Lucie had not thought to send word to Winifred of her son's injuries.

'Mistress Wilton,' Winifred said in her gentle voice, bowing her head slightly, her crisp white wimple rustling with the movement. 'God bless you for the care you have given my son.' She was a tiny woman, with pale skin and large, dark eyes. A servant carried her wool and spinning wheel.

'He was wounded defending the manor,' said Lucie. 'It—'

'As was his duty.' Winifred crouched beside her son, fussed with the bandage on his forehead. Glancing up at Lucie with an accusing frown she pronounced it damp.

'Ma,' Daimon moaned, 'Mistress Wilton knows what she is doing.'

'I have packed the wound to bring down the swelling,' Lucie said. 'Would you like some time alone?' She rose from her seat, offering it to Winifred, who slid up on to it. As she smoothed out the skirt of her grey gown she thanked Lucie and went back to examining her son.

Lucie thought to use the time to find something to eat and headed for the buttery. Some bread, cheese and ale would suit her.

Sarah, the kitchen maid, was in the room, hanging fresh loaves in a wicker cage out of the reach of mice. She seemed in a hurry to complete her task when Lucie arrived. It was Sarah who had enjoyed cook's son's pranks. She was a large, lumbering young woman, perpetually sweating and wheezing. Her saving graces were an infectious laugh and long-fingered hands that seemed to belong to another body. Not much with which to capture a man's heart. What had Nan's son, Joseph, seen in her? Daimon said he had been handsome, though not a young man. Sarah's presence in the buttery reminded Lucie that both Sarah and Joseph would have been aware of the treasury.

'Do not hurry on my account,' Lucie said. 'Cook managed to bake this morning?'

'She said we must eat,' Sarah mumbled.

'Does her son Joseph look like cook?' Lucie asked.

Sarah's ruddy cheeks darkened and she ducked her head behind one of the cages. 'He is dark like her, Mistress.'

'How long ago was he sent away?'

'He was not sent away. He went off to be a soldier.' She was inching towards the door.

'Have you seen him since?'

Sarah shook her head as she reached behind her for the latch and freedom. Sweat darkened the scarf on her head.

'You have no cause to be frightened,' Lucie said as she moved towards the door, forcing Sarah into the corner. 'Tell me about Joseph.'

Sarah shook her head. 'I am not to speak of him. Cook made me swear.'

'I am your mistress, Sarah. And Cook's.'

Lucie persisted, patiently asking questions, until the young woman began to talk. Joseph had been brought up by Nan's cousin, a tavern keeper, who trained the young man as a groom. But the lad could not take criticism from his betters. Saddle straps were tampered with, horses were fed purges as they departed the stable. Japes, Joseph called them. He had been ordered off the premises by his cousin. He had come to Freythorpe, thinking to become a groom at the manor. But he soon discovered that only Sarah laughed at his japes. Adam, the steward, had made it clear he would not entrust Joseph with the horses, having made it his business to find out why the man had left the tavern.

'Why do you suppose you are not to speak of him?'

'I don't know.'

'Did he aim any of his japes at Walter the gatekeeper?' It had occurred to Lucie that Walter might have been the target of the damage to the gatehouse.

Sarah was shaking her head.

'He had no problem with Walter?'

'No, Mistress. His mother, Adam the steward, the other grooms—he had his fun with them, no others.'

His mother, the steward and the poor lads who worked alongside him. Lucie stepped away from the door. 'You may go now. And do not fret, Sarah. I shall not mention this to Cook.'

As Lucie stepped back into the hall, she heard Winifred thanking Tildy for sitting with her son. Not the time for Lucie to appear. She slipped out of the rear door and into the kitchen garden. Brother Michaelo perched at the edge of the bench for which Lucie was headed, breathing hard. He had a bucket of water at his feet.

'I must wash off the dust and ashes,' he explained as Lucie joined him. He had soot on his tonsure and smelled of damp ashes.

'You have been helping with the gatehouse?'

'I have. Though how much help I have been I cannot say.'

His modesty was becoming. 'I am grateful for all you have done, Brother Michaelo. My father was blessed in his friends.'

He bowed his head.

'Have you seen Harold?'

'He is still out in the yard, helping clear the debris.' Michaelo began to rise, then changed his mind. 'Forgive me if I seem to pry, Mistress Wilton, but what do you mean to do? Will you leave as you had planned?'

'I cannot stay. My children, my work are in the city. I pray the servants and tenants understand that I am not fleeing the trouble. I would lief stay until everything is put right, but how can I do that?'

'Your people understand. But might I suggest—you could ask Harold to return after he escorts you to the city. He has worked hard, side by side with the men, and they appear to trust him. I can find no fault in the decisions he has made or the manner in which he has proceeded.'

'You have changed your mind about him.'

'I was uncertain about him before. God has given me the opportunity to judge him by his deeds. It is the best way to know a man. And now I shall hold my peace. I merely thought—'

'I thank you for your advice, Brother Michaelo. I shall speak to Harold.'

Michaelo looked relieved. 'And for my part, I shall urge His Grace to send at least two well-armed men at once.'

Brother Michaelo took his leave the next morning with gratitude and misgivings. The roofless gatehouse, charred and jagged, cast a gloomy pall over the courtyard. For the inhabitants of Freythorpe Hadden it would colour all their days until it was repaired or torn down. An inescapable reminder of the horror of two nights past and of yesterday, when the upper storey had given way. Who would not give thanks to God for calling him away? Was his relief in leaving the cause of his misgivings? A sense of guilt? Or was it the image of Sir Robert that kept coming to mind, his hand on Michaelo's head, asking him to keep Mistress Wilton in his prayers? Keeping her in his prayers was easy. But should he be doing more? He carried the letter to the archbishop, asking for protection, that was something more. And who else might be trusted to convince Archbishop Thoresby of the danger manifest in the attack? But what of leaving Mistress Wilton in the hands of Harold Galfrey? Could one man see them safely to York? Once she was in the city, Michaelo had no doubt she would be safe, but he prayed outlaws would not waylay the three travellers on the road.

He added a prayer for himself. Travelling alone was foolhardy in the best of times.

After two days of sunny, mild weather, the sky had dulled and there was a chill to the breeze that threatened rain. Lucie rubbed her hands together for warmth as she waited in the stable for Ralph, the groom her father had disciplined. He had yet to saddle her mount. At last he appeared, buffing a buckle with a soft cloth and humming to himself. When he saw Lucie he straightened up and assured her that her horse would be saddled at once.

She had resolved to speak to him, as she had to Sarah, hoping she might tell by his reactions to her questions whether he harboured ill feelings towards her family. Or Walter's.

She nodded to the buckle. 'Sir Robert would have been pleased by that bit of polishing.'

'Oh, aye, the master liked a shine to his saddle and bridle, God rest his soul.'

'You miss him, do you?'

'I do, mistress.'

'You would not always have said so.'

Ralph ducked his head. 'You have heard. Aye, at first he found fault with me at every turn. I ran away. He sent Adam the steward after me. Gave me a good whipping. Then he asked if I cared to learn how to do things right. They do say not many masters would have bothered about me.'

Lucie believed him.

'I am sorry about the trouble, Mistress,' he said.

'God bless you, Ralph.' He seemed content. Not a man with cause to strike out at her family.

As the small party rode out of the yard at Freythorpe, Lucie turned back again and again to stare at the crippled gatehouse. She had asked Brother Michaelo to pray for her, that God might reveal to her the sin for which she was so punished, and all her innocent tenants with her. Outlaws were not God's sergeants, he had assured her. They did not attack at God's command. Then why had this been visited upon her in the midst of all her other trials?

Perhaps because she sensed Lucie's distress, Phillippa had risen quietly, packed, dressed sensibly and, after a few last instructions for Tildy, climbed on to the seat of the cart to await her companions. She sat straight and tall, keeping her devils at bay. When Lucie would climb up beside her, she shook her head. 'You prefer the back of a horse. So would I if my old bones would permit it. Ride. I promise to keep my head and the donkey's.'

Lucie had felt Harold's eyes upon her as the groom helped her mount. Did he worry about her as she did Phillippa? An unpleasant thought.

But the gatehouse haunted her and he was right when he said as he rode up beside her, 'You must look forward, Mistress Wilton. The gatehouse can be rebuilt. Daimon will recover. And the sheriff might prove his worth and recover what you lost.'

The blue eyes and warm smile were not enough to cheer her. But she found it comforting to think of Harold overseeing the repairs and told him so. God had not completely abandoned her.

They rode most of the way side by side, in companionable silence.

Despite everything, it was a happy homecoming for Lucie. The garden rang with the children's joyful shrieks when they saw her and their Great-aunt Phillippa. Jasper declared he had missed her.

While Lucie told a wide-eyed Jasper of the troubles of the past few days, Harold crossed the street to Roger Moreton's house to discuss his return to Freythorpe Hadden. Roger came hurrying back with Harold in tow, not content with loaning Harold, but offering to hire a stonemason to rebuild the gatehouse—at Roger's expense.

'I know an excellent mason. A stone gatehouse is what you need. Let it be my gift to you and Owen.'

Lucie refused. She could not possibly accept such a gift. But she would be glad of his company when she gave her report to the sheriff on the morrow.

After Roger had departed, Phillippa tsked and flicked at invisible dust on the table until Lucie asked what ailed her.

'I thought you bold to ride so companionably with the steward Harold. But now I see that is nothing to how you behave with his master.'

Lucie sent Jasper off to the shop to make up an unguent for Harold, who had a painful blister on his leg, a burn that had been irritated by the ride. When the young man was out the door, Lucie turned to her aunt. 'To say such things in front of Jasper. How could you?'

'He is old enough to hear such things.'

'What? Untruths? Your imaginings? Did you think to ask me first how I felt about either man?'

'It is plain how you feel. A neighbour does not offer such gifts.'

'When Roger Moreton's wife was ill, Tildy and I took turns sitting with her. I saw how bad it was and sent for Magda. Roger was beside himself, he could not think what to do. He remembers, Aunt.' Lucie realised she was too angry, almost spitting out her words, and turned away, trying to calm herself. 'You have opened up a wound between Jasper and me that has just been healed with great effort,' she said softly. 'I cannot think why you would wish to do such a thing.'

Phillippa did not reply at once. Lucie heard her dust off the bench, fuss with her skirt, sit down. 'Kate neglects this room. The air is stale, the benches dusty and beneath—look at the cobwebs.'

Lucie turned to her aunt, but already the faraway look was back. It seemed futile to argue with her, but sweet heaven, how much more could she endure? People were kind to Lucie in her husband's absence and she was to turn them away? She escaped to the shop. Jasper was just wrapping up the unguent.

'Are you too tired to take a message to Magda Digby?' Lucie asked. The Riverwoman lived on a small tidal island upriver from St Mary's Abbey. Jasper assured her he was never too tired to visit Magda, even if the tide were in and he had to row. 'Tell her of the attack and Daimon's wounds. Ask her if she would journey to him. If so, I shall come to her tomorrow to tell her what I have done for him.' Jasper took up the unguent for Harold and walked happily out into the busy street.

8

INTO THE WOOD

On a morning of mists and the damp smell of earth, Owen set out for the cathedral. Rokelyn had sent a message recommending Ranulf de Hutton as the mason to complete Sir Robert's tomb. Owen wished to speak with him before he agreed.

The masons' lodge sat at the north end of the cathedral, just beyond the area plotted out for the cloisters and St Mary's college. Ranulf was not there, just two journeymen preparing stones for the cloister. Their chatter ceased as Owen approached. They nodded in greeting, but remained quiet and unsmiling, clearly uncomfortable with his presence.

'Master Hutton you will find in the nave,' one said to his question, 'repairing an ornament near Bishop Gower's tomb.'

Owen thanked them and left them in peace. The community was too close for work such as his. Too aware of his mission. And God help him, perhaps too aware of Owen's petty complaints. Why had Cynog gossiped about him?

Owen's boots whispered on the brown and ivory tiles as he entered the cathedral, moving to one side of the line of pilgrims progressing to St David's shrine. The tiles were beautiful, as artfully made and set as those in the fine Cistercian abbeys of Fountains and Rievaulx in Yorkshire.

In the nave, near the choir, the mason stood on a short scaffolding that held two lamps on either side of the stonework on which he was working. He was pressed close to the wall, running his fingers along the surface of some plainly carved moulding, his head to one side. His hands were wide and flat-fingered, missing a joint of the forefinger on his left hand.

'Built on a swamp, this church,' the mason said when he noticed Owen down below. 'Damp and settling, always replacing pieces.'

Owen could just barely make out one of the seams in the stone, though he could tell the boundaries of the section Ranulf examined.

The mason turned to Owen as he dusted off his hands. Cynog had been a slender man of middle years, with an expressive face and eyes that always seemed to be opened wide with wonder. He had had fine-boned, delicate hands with the long, tapered fingers of a musician. Ranulf was bandy-legged and pot-bellied, with huge ears that stuck out from his cap and looked chapped from the chill damp in the cathedral. 'I should not complain. It is good work and plenty, with never a rush. But I sometimes wonder who was the daft one to set it here.'

'I thought the story was God told St David to set it here,' said Owen.

'Aye, well, so they say. The good Lord was thinking of the masons, I suppose. We shall never want for work.' Ranulf scratched at his cap. 'But you did not come here to discuss the site, eh?' He climbed down from the scaffolding, revealing himself to be a head shorter than Owen. He took off his cap and scratched his oily hair with the stub of the damaged finger.

'Not as inconvenient as your scar, Captain Archer,' he said when he saw the direction of Owen's gaze. 'It is just part of a finger gone.'

'Forgive me.' Owen was embarrassed. He himself hated folks staring at his scar.

'And no, it does not hurt my work.' Ranulf hugged himself and shivered dramatically. 'God's blood it is cold in here. If we are to talk, let us step outside, where the lads are mixing mortar. They have a fire that will thaw my fingers and toes. I am a pleasant man when warm.'

But as it turned out he was pleasant only when talking about the tomb. He did not wish to veer from that subject, though about the tomb he was quite eager.

'I met Sir Robert, I did.' He squinted up at Owen and shook his head. 'You are surprised. A mason and a knight, what have we in common?' He rubbed his hands over the fire. 'Fine chin and cheekbones. Nice, long, delicate nose. I can make something of that.' He smiled as if already admiring the fruits of his labours.

'How did you come to meet Sir Robert?'

'He watched me work on some ceiling bosses. Admired my work. You see? I should have been your choice from the beginning. *He* would have chosen me.'

Owen liked him.

'And the tomb would have been finished by now,' Ranulf added with a self-satisfied sniff.

'About Cynog—'

Ranulf silenced him with a frown and shake of his head. 'I shall not speak of him. He is dead. Leave him in peace.'

'I merely wondered—'

Ranulf shook his head again. 'Nothing of Cynog. Look you, Captain, Archdeacon Rokelyn does not care about Cynog. The archdeacon's ambition is served by this investigation, not Cynog's memory. He wishes to stage a grand capture, one of the traitors, mayhap. Then Bishop Houghton will remember it when he is raised to his next position and will be pleased to carry the archdeacon with him. Let Cynog rest in peace.'

'Some feel a murdered man does not rest in peace until his murderer be known.'

'You have Piers. I can think of no one more likely to be guilty.'

'Then tell me. Why did Piers do it? Is *he* a traitor?'

Ranulf stamped his feet, shook his arms for warmth. 'I know nothing. And I shall talk no more about the dead.'

Owen did not wish to push Ranulf past his patience. He asked the mason a few more questions about his work, then declared himself pleased with Rokelyn's recommendation. With a shake of hands Ranulf agreed to begin work on the morrow. Should he have any problems, he would leave messages for Owen with the porter at the palace.

'Would you grant me one favour concerning Cynog?' Owen asked.

Ranulf muttered a curse.

'If you would just tell me how to find his parents.'

The mason frowned. 'To what purpose?'

'To hear from them any cause they can imagine for their son's murder.'

'You will go alone?'

'With one of my men, that is all.'

Ranulf pondered, seemingly talking to himself. At last he said, 'I can see little harm in it.' He described to Owen a farmhouse not too distant from the city, easily a day's ride there and back, with an early start. 'Though by foot would be kinder. Horses do not fare well on the rocky heights.'

Owen thanked him.

'You will tell his parents that we pray for them?' Cynog called after him.

Owen nodded.

And now where to go? It was too late to start for the farm of Cynog's parents—Owen must leave that for the next day. He still hesitated about going to Clegyr Boia to find Martin. He crossed Llechllafar while he considered his next move. But God decided for him. Among the pilgrims thronging at the south entrance of the cathedral stood a man about whom Owen was increasingly curious—Father Simon. The tall, fair-haired vicar stood apart from the others, watching Owen approach. He was a handsome man.

'God go with you, Master Summoner,' Owen said as he reached him.

Father Simon's fair brows joined in confusion. 'Summoner? We have none in St David's.'

'I pray you, forgive me. I had understood you act in that capacity here.'

The vicar blushed and his pale eyes narrowed as he backed farther away from the crowd of pilgrims. 'I believe you mean to insult me, Captain, but I am at a loss as to the cause. How have I offended you?'

'Yesterday you followed me to Porth Clais. Today you bullied Piers the Mariner after plying him with ale.'

'This offends you?' Simon spread his arms and smiled crookedly. 'Very well, yesterday I was concerned that you should not attempt to slip away. I knew that Archdeacon Rokelyn had ordered you to stay.'

'I am ever more confused. Are you not the secretary to Archdeacon Baldwin rather than Archdeacon Rokelyn?'

The smile disappeared. 'What do you want with me, Captain?'

'On whose authority did you interrogate Piers?'

'On my own.' Simon bristled as he said it. 'The mariner is an abomination in our holy city. As is the demon who ordered the execution.'

'Indeed. Which is why Archdeacon Rokelyn wishes me to investigate. There is no need for you to do so.'

'I wish merely to speed you on your way.'

'I thank you for that. You can assist me by seeing to your own work and leaving me to mine,' Owen said. 'Piers might have been more forthcoming with me had I been his first visitor today.'

'You flatter yourself.'

Archdeacon Baldwin appeared in the doorway of the cathedral, two servants preceding him to wave the pilgrims aside. 'Am I to be kept waiting all morning?' Baldwin demanded of Simon. He glanced at Owen, his expression softening. '*Benedicte*, Captain Archer. You are well?'

Owen bowed to the archdeacon. 'I am, Father. *Benedicte*. I did not realise I kept Father Simon from his duties.'

'One would be hard pressed to do that, Captain,' Baldwin said, lifting his eyes to heaven and shaking his head.

Simon flushed and averted his eyes.

'Come, Simon.' As the two clerics withdrew into the candlelit cathedral, the pilgrims flowed forward into the open doorway.

Owen turned down the path to Patrick's Gate—it seemed safe now to seek out Martin. He thought of Simon's embarrassment. He scorned the vicar's self-important piety, but how was Owen any better, sniffing out murderers, spending his days asking questions no one cared to answer?

Would that Owen were Iolo's age and free. To serve Owain Lawgoch—fight for a just cause, support a man of old, noble lineage—he had spoken the truth when he told Iolo that is what he would do. He could be useful to Lawgoch. For as much as he disliked being privy to Archbishop Thoresby's machinations, they had taught him much about the court and the Duke of Lancaster's vast household. But Lucie, Gwenllian, Hugh—how could he desert them? Was it possible they would come here, that Lucie would understand his need to feel he had chosen his own path?

Without the gate he headed up along the city walls until they bent towards the north-west gate, then struck off through the brush towards the hill on which the Irish Chief Boia had built his fort. Long ruined, its crumbling foundations and overgrown cellars lured lovers and others who did not wish to be seen. Owen climbed the hill, found a high place he might sit for a while, alerting Martin's watcher.

Was it possible he might change his life? That God had brought him here, at this time, to show him the task for which he had been in training all his life? Had God led him here? Or had he chosen the wrong fork somewhere along the way? Should he have chosen John of Gaunt, who succeeded Henry of Grosmont as Duke of Lancaster? Should he have remained Captain of Archers after his blinding? It had been his own choice to leave that life, thinking himself untrustworthy. Had that been a coward's act?

A seagull swooped down to study him as he sat. A raven arrived to declare the gull a trespasser.

Owen sat staring out into the distance, wondering how one read God's purpose.

With the permission of the Archdeacon of St David's, Owen and Iolo rode out early the following morning. Rokelyn had not tried to hide his disappointment that Owen still had no answers for him.

'This is a small community. You have had time to talk to

everyone by now.'

'If they would but talk. They all know what I am about. I approach, they drop their eyes and become mutes.'

'This does not happen in York?'

'York is much, much larger. But it is never easy.'

'And you believe his parents might talk to you?'

'If my son had been murdered, I would co-operate with anyone trying to find his murderer.'

Rokelyn had not looked happy. 'They are doubtless simple folk, Cynog's parents. Not given to confiding in strangers.'

'I believe they will trust me.'

Chin in hand, Rokelyn considered. 'Then go,' he said after a long silence. 'And may the Lord watch over you. Come straight to me on your return.'

Edmund, Tom, Jared and Sam stayed in St David's, keeping their ears pricked. They knew the route Owen and Iolo were taking to Cynog's parents and when they should reasonably return. There had been some muttering about the choice of Iolo, until Owen told them Cynog's folk spoke only Welsh.

Tom sat in the courtyard of the bishop's palace, watching the high-born pilgrims assemble for the daily rounds of shrines and wells. Some were dressed in sombre-coloured but elegant attire, others in rough pilgrim's robes. Many spoke Welsh. He tried to catch the few words he had picked up during this journey, but the language was too slippery. Jared sat beside him, slowly working a nail out of the sole of one of his boots. A movement on the steps leading to the bishop's east wing caught Tom's attention. Someone visiting the prisoner? A scowling, rough-looking man was speaking to Father Simon. The stranger was nodding, nodding, Father Simon tilting his head, as if he did not quite believe him. Suddenly an explosion of movement from the man made Father Simon back down a step. The guard approached them. Father Simon waved him back, bowed slightly to the stranger, then proceeded up the steps. The other stood for a moment, chin on chest, then, head up, he shaded his eyes, surveying the courtyard.

Tom poked Jared to get his attention. 'Who is he?'

Jared cursed as his boot slid and the nail nicked him. 'Look what you have done.' He held up a finger. 'Bleeding!'

'I see nothing but dirt.' The stranger had descended the steps and was elbowing his way through the crowd towards their perch near the stables. 'Do you know this man bearing down on us?' Tom asked.

Jared stuck his grimy finger in his mouth, glanced up. 'Captain Siencyn. I doubt he is for us.'

But Siencyn came directly to Jared. 'I must see your captain, lad. You must lead me to him.'

'Captain Archer has left the city for the day.'

'Why this day? Why must he go this day?'

'As good as any other. I shall tell him you wish to speak to him.'

Siencyn muttered a curse and began to depart, but turned suddenly, his scowl fierce. 'See you remember, lad.'

'He looked worried,' Tom said, watching the man push his way back towards the gatehouse. 'I wonder what he discovered in the gaol? Or learned from Father Simon?'

'The Summoner?'

'Aye. They were talking.'

'Simon is just nosy. More like the captain is not cheered by his brother. I cannot think Piers is jolly at present.'

Owen and Iolo travelled due east from St David's, up into higher, forested land. Despite Ranulf's warning about horses on the steepest parts, Owen had chosen to ride. At least the animals could carry some food and cloaks in case the weather turned. And, in case of injury, one of them.

'You expect trouble,' Iolo had said as they led the horses from the palace stables.

'I do.'

Even so, as they rode away from the city and into a grove of oaks at the foot of a gentle hill, Owen found himself humming under his breath. It was good to escape the eyes of St David's. He studied Iolo as they rode in the open country. There was a tension in the chiselled face that never eased, even in sleep. Owen would think it merely a trick of the eye but for the suddenness with which Iolo would move. And yet even a cat sometimes relaxed. It was as if he was ever ready to attack. He persisted in his determination to return to York with Owen. What would Lucie think of him?

In a short while they began to climb again, this time across a rocky outcrop over which they chose to lead their horses. They both felt uneasy, guarding their backs. When they had crossed over to the forest cover once more, they paused by a stream.

Iolo pulled off his cap, rubbed his bald spot while his horse drank. His light-brown hair was damp where the cap had covered it. He was sweating though it was chilly up in these hills. 'I once fell asleep watching for a fox at my uncle's farm,' Iolo said. 'The fox woke me, slipping past me so quickly I did not see him—he stank of death. For a long while after that any change in the scent of a room would wake me.' He dropped to his knees, cupped his hands and drank deeply, then dunked his head and shook himself like a dog.

Owen knelt, splashed some of the cool water on his face. 'Are you saying that you smell trouble?'

'I cannot be certain. I may be smelling my own fear. Or yours.' Iolo grunted as he rose, gathered his reins. 'God did not give us knowledge of the fox, we must learn about it.'

'God is ever testing us.'

Iolo mounted. 'And we dare not complain, for fear of hell's eternal fire.'

Owen, too, mounted. 'Your life does not seem one for complaint.'

'Of late, no.'

They rode forward into the trees.

Though the track was still wide enough for a modest cart, the trees, leafed out now in mid-May, shadowed the way. The distance between glints of sunlight grew. As the branches drooped lower and lower, snagging their hats, the two dismounted once more.

Iolo looked round warily.

Owen did, too. He sensed eyes on them. The feeling was far stronger than it had been earlier.

Iolo raised his hand, warning Owen to stay still, then slowly crouched down so he would not be a target above his horse's back. Owen did likewise.

'How much farther until we can ride again?' Iolo whispered.

'I am not certain.'

'Retreat?'

'No.'

Iolo nodded. He was with him.

They crouched there for a long while, listening. But they heard nothing. At last they rose, continued on, leading their horses.

Owen was just about to suggest they pause again, listen, when he felt a presence behind him. He drew his knife and turned, flung up his left arm to deflect his attacker's weapon, but his return thrust struck air. Someone called to the horses in Welsh. Owen's assailant slipped back into the shadows. Go after him? Iolo shouted. Owen spun round. The horses were gone. Iolo and a bare-legged man wrestled on the path, trying to reach a knife Iolo must have knocked from his adversary's grasp. Owen grabbed it, only to have it caught from behind by his attacker returned. The man yanked too hard. Owen shouted at the pain and swung round with murder on his mind. But there were two against him now and his right arm, wounded and sprained, or worse, was not responding quickly. Owen felt a sharp, hot pain in his side as he went down.

As quickly as the men had attacked, they vanished. Someone cried out, at a distance. Owen hoped he had maimed one of them. But he doubted it.

He rolled over, felt his right side below his ribs. Sticky with blood, as was his right arm. But the pain was worst from higher on his arm. He prayed it was not broken.

Iolo moaned.

'You are wounded?'

Iolo did not reply.

Owen sat up, cursing at the pain.

Iolo lay on the path. 'My foot or my ankle—something down there is on fire. And no horses.' He propped himself up on his elbows.

Owen rose, pressing his right arm to his side to try to stanch the blood from the wound above his waist and keep the arm still. He eased himself down beside Iolo. 'They might have killed us.'

'Your arm is injured?'

'And a wound in my side—but not so bad I cannot walk.' Owen put his hand on Iolo's right ankle. 'This one?'

'No, the other.'

When Owen touched the ankle Iolo jerked.

'If they meant to slow us down, they succeeded,' Iolo muttered. 'How am I to walk on that?'

9

THE HIGH SHERIFF

The archbishop's manor at Bishopthorpe bustled with spring activities. Men crawled about the gutters like spiders, making repairs. A glazier and his assistant worked at one of the hall windows. Several servants crept through the rose garden, adding new crushed rock to the paths. Another team of workers were planting seedlings in the kitchen garden.

John Thoresby had come outside to warm his stiff joints in the sunshine. He had not expected so much activity. All the chores had been ordered by him, it was true, to be begun when the weather calmed. But that they should all be attacked at once was bothersome when he was in residence. It was time Owen Archer returned from Wales and resumed his duties as steward of Bishopthorpe. He approached the position with logic and courtesy. Thoresby suspected that the Bishop of St David's had discovered Archer's talents. Adam de Houghton was a grasping sort. One had only to look at how he wooed Lancaster, involving him in his pious scheme to collect the vicars into a college where they might be supervised. Houghton meant to be Lord Chancellor one of these days. Might he find joy in it. But he could not have Archer. Thoresby had sent a messenger to Wales, recalling his man in no uncertain terms, telling him how Alice Baker had stirred up trouble and assorted other items that would lure him home. The duke's request for Archer's help in recruiting archers for his French campaign had been reasonable and, in truth, how could Thoresby deny him when his purpose was the defence of the realm? But surely Archer had completed the task by now. It was not possible Friar Hewald had yet delivered the letter, but he was well on his way to Cydweli.

Thoresby grumbled at the annoying hammering overhead. Perhaps it was quiet down in the river gardens. He turned away from the house. As he passed the gardener's shed, he heard an odd, sucking sound. Simon the gardener had suffered several attacks of catarrh during the wet spring, the last one lingering and bringing on a fever that had everyone worried. Fearing the man might be taking ill again, Thoresby pushed open the door.

Simon looked up, a curse dying on his lips as he recognised the intruder. He was elbow deep in a pungent mud and dung bath, kneading it like dough. 'Your Grace!' He began to withdraw his arms, the mud noisily sucking at them. 'Stinking mud makes fragrant roses.'

'Do not stop, Simon.' Thoresby could imagine the man forgetting himself and touching his face with those disgusting hands. The odour was overpowering. The archbishop shielded his mouth and nose with his forearm. 'I merely wondered at the sound. I did not mean to disturb you.'

'Your Grace is always welcome,' Simon said. 'But I do not blame you for retreating. My good wife has never been reconciled with this muck. She will send me down to the river this evening to wash before I set foot in the house.'

'She will not heat up water for you?'

Simon chuckled. 'My good wife has many mouths to feed and clothe, and no more hours in the day than we do, eh?'

'No, of course not.' If they used some restraint they might not have such a clutch of children. 'May God watch over all of you,' Thoresby said as he withdrew.

Outside, as Thoresby gulped the fresh air, he heard a horse trotting into the yard. Yesterday a galloping horse had brought news of a band of outlaws attacking Freythorpe Hadden. Was there more ill news? A high hedge blocked his view. Curious, Thoresby retraced his steps to the top of the path. Brother Michaelo. His secretary returned at last. Excellent. No doubt he would wish to speak with

Thoresby at once, but the archbishop wished to enjoy the day. He resumed his quest for a quiet spot in the sun. Tonight was soon enough to speak with Michaelo.

After much thought, Lucie sent a note to Roger Moreton suggesting that Harold Galfrey accompany her to the High Sheriff the following day rather than Roger. Harold could bear witness to her tale, then be on his way back to the manor. Roger expressed disappointment in his reply, but agreed that Harold was the better choice. He would inform his steward of the appointment.

The evening was chilly enough for a fire in the hall, but the air still so sweet that Thoresby had the servants set up a table and chairs near an open casement. Brother Michaelo had not been seated long when he asked permission to move his chair closer to the fire, away from the evening air. Thoresby motioned to the servant behind him to make it so. He did not doubt his secretary's complaint. What flesh had he left to warm him? Indeed, Thoresby's former secretary, Jehannes, now Archdeacon of York, thought Brother Michaelo much affected by his journey into Wales. Jehannes had dined with the archbishop the previous day.

'During his brief stay in York I found him much subdued, spending most of his time in prayer,' Jehannes had said.

But Thoresby noted that Michaelo still fussed with his carefully tailored sleeves, ensuring that they lay neatly on the arms of the chair. Gaunt he was, and mourning the death of Sir Robert D'Arby he seemed to be. But Thoresby did not see a holy man before him.

'You took your time returning,' the archbishop said.

Brother Michaelo glanced over at the servant, down at the flagon of wine, the cups. 'I should be honoured to wait on both of us, Your Grace.' He cocked an eyebrow towards the servant.

Intriguing. He must have something to say he did not wish the servants to hear. Thoresby waved the man out of the room.

'I accompanied Mistress Wilton to Freythorpe Hadden, to speak to Dame Phillippa about Sir Robert's last days.' Michaelo paused with a questioning look, as if belatedly asking permission.

Thoresby motioned for him to continue.

'We encountered difficulties,' Michaelo began, and proceeded to tell Thoresby about the outlaws at Freythorpe Hadden. No wonder Michaelo looked exhausted. 'Mistress Wilton intends to report it to the High Sheriff,' the monk concluded.

'Tell Chamont?' said Thoresby. 'Ha! Precious little he will do. If he is even in residence at York Castle.'

Brother Michaelo handed him a letter. 'From Mistress Wilton.'

Thoresby read quickly, disturbed by how well the thieves knew the hall. He was glad she had the sense to return to York. A few retainers was a sound request. This he could certainly do for the mother of his godchildren. 'I shall send some men at once,' he said, laying the letter aside. 'Is she safe even in York?'

Michaelo frowned at the question. 'I had assumed so, Your Grace. But if you doubt it…Perhaps we should have a talk with the bailiff.' He rose to pour wine.

'Bailiffs react after the damage is done. I need Archer here.'

'I am certain that Mistress Wilton feels the same, Your Grace.'

Sarcasm? Thoresby glanced up at his secretary as he handed him a cup of wine. His eyes were cast down, his expression unreadable. What did it matter? Thoresby set the cup on the table, rose to stand by the window. How sweet was the evening air; how transient was such a moment. He stood there a while, breathing, thinking. Michaelo's tale and Lucie's letter troubled him. It did not sound like the usual outlawry. He turned, found Michaelo pouring himself another cup of wine.

'What troubles me is the gatehouse,' Thoresby said.

Michaelo glanced up with a puzzled expression.

'With Sir Robert's death, Mistress Wilton now owns the manor and after her it goes to Hugh. There is no doubt about that, I suppose? Did Sir Robert mention any problems? Relations who might claim the property? Old enemies?'

'None, Your Grace.' Michaelo drew a cloth from his sleeve, dabbed his high forehead. 'But I had not thought to ask.' His face was lined with worry.

Thoresby waved away his concern. 'In faith, it is not the sort of thing one asks a dying friend.' He had an uncomfortable suspicion about Michaelo's concern for the family of Sir Robert D'Arby. 'You are most changed in regard to Sir Robert.'

'I had the greatest respect and admiration for him.'

'You have rarely shown such affection for the aged.' Handsome young men or men who might further his ambitions, yes.

Michaelo shot from his chair, indignation staining his cheeks. 'Your Grace! I have not broken my vow. And to think such a thing about Sir Robert!'

'Resume your seat, Michaelo. I did not mean to offend you—though you cannot find it strange I should wonder occasionally. The flesh is not insensitive, however one may struggle against the devil. But just then I merely wondered what you had hoped to gain by your devotion.' He sighed as the monk hovered overhead, aflutter with indignation. 'Sit!'

Michaelo sank back down.

'An ill-considered topic. Forgive me.' Michaelo said nothing. 'Are we at peace?' Thoresby asked. 'Can we continue?'

Michaelo lifted his head slightly, let it drop back down, chin on chest.

Thoresby took it for an unenthusiastic, melodramatic nod. Some things had not changed. 'I shall send Alfred and Gilbert to Freythorpe Hadden. Archer has taught them to think, which is helpful in this sort of circumstance, though inconvenient in others.'

Michaelo raised his head. 'Do you wish me to go to them?'

'No. I shall send one of the servants with the message. We have letters to write. To the sheriff and to Archer. I have already sent for the captain, but this tale should spur him on.'

Michaelo relaxed. 'You have sent for the captain, Your Grace?'

'Can you think of a worse time for him to be away from his family?'

'He hoped to be on his way home by now.'

'Excellent. He should be here.'

Michaelo tilted his head, as if considering. 'That is kind of you.'

'Kindness has nothing to do with it.' Thoresby moved ahead. 'What of this Harold Galfrey? You say he has been a steward. Of such extensive lands? Freythorpe Hadden is a great responsibility. The steward must play far more roles than Archer plays as my steward. Is this man competent?'

'I know little about him, Your Grace. A respected merchant of York, Roger Moreton, hired him as his steward, on the recommendation of John Gisburne.'

'Gisburne. His recommendation carries no weight with me. Quite the opposite, truth be told.'

'I have heard the rumours regarding Gisburne. But Mistress Wilton trusts Master Moreton's opinion. He truly is well respected.'

'Perhaps he is, but if he takes Gisburne's recommendation, he is likely to be a fool when it comes to hiring men. It does not sound to me as if Mistress Wilton asked sufficient questions. I must enquire about Harold Galfrey.'

Michaelo looked pained.

'What is it?'

'It was *I* who urged Mistress Wilton to consider Galfrey as temporary steward, Your Grace. It is *I* who asks too few questions.'

'A pretty courtesy, Michaelo. Let us eat, then see to the letters.'

The morning brought chaos to Lucie's house. Gwenllian feared that Lucie meant to disappear for another few days and clung to her skirts when she would leave the house for her appointment with the High Sheriff. Phillippa chided Lucie for not taking a switch to the child. Jasper belatedly announced that the guild master had called while Lucie was away, wishing to discuss Alice Baker's accusations.

He wished to see Lucie as soon as possible. Harold arrived at the door while Lucie sat in the kitchen trying to get Jasper to repeat everything the guild master had said. Phillippa said that the boy was merely trying to protect her from gossip. Jasper insisted that he was not keeping anything from her, he just could not remember all that Guild Master Thorpe had said. Harold took Gwenllian out into the garden.

When at last Lucie joined them there, Gwenllian was merrily teasing Crowder with a string on which she had tied a sprig of catmint. Harold lounged on a bench, trying to do a cat's cradle. He looked rested and cheerful. Lucie tried not to notice the warmth in his startling blue eyes as she sank down beside him. 'I think I shall go mad before sunset,' she said.

'I have seen the baker's wife and heard the gossip,' said Harold. 'No one believes you are in the wrong. They all know Alice Baker thinks herself an alchemist.'

'What matters is what the guild believes. There are members who think I never should have been accepted, and for certain do not deserve the honour of "master". It is not enough for them that being a woman I am left out of the ceremonies, the meetings...' And why was she confiding in her steward? Lucie stood up, shook out her skirt. 'Shall we attend the High Sheriff?' She was halfway to the house when she realised Harold had not followed her. She turned back, found him standing by the bench, his hands behind his back, watching her with an uncertain air. Lucie retraced her steps. 'What is it?'

Looking uncomfortable, not meeting her eye, he said, 'I pray I do not offend you, but I have asked Master Moreton to carry a letter to the High Sheriff from me. He awaits word that you agree.'

Did Harold wish to avoid her? She felt her face grow hot and was glad he did not see. Could he tell she had dressed with care, for him? That she had looked forward to the walk across the city, with him? 'Why?' she asked, her voice an inappropriate whisper.

Now he met her eyes. 'I wish to leave at once for Freythorpe Hadden. I am uneasy...I woke with a feeling that I should return as soon as I could.'

Lucie searched his face for dissimulation. He looked sincere, which chilled her. 'What do you fear has happened in our absence?'

'I pray nothing more has happened, but that I am belatedly realising the danger we faced. I had little time to think about it until last night. And then—' He raked his hand through his hair. 'I thought of what might have been, do you see? If the gatekeeper and his family had been in the gatehouse when the outlaws set the fire.'

'Where were Walter and his family?'

'In the kitchen, having their evening meal.'

'God watched over them.'

'Think how those left behind feel today. Every noise must be investigated with pounding heart.'

'You must go, of course. I—' Lucie touched his hand, moved by his concern. 'I thank you.'

He put his other hand over hers, pressed it, stepped closer, lifted her hand and kissed it, all the while looking deep into her eyes.

The warmth that infused Lucie's body with Harold's kiss warned her to step back, remember where she was, who she was. She withdrew her hand.

'And that is the other reason I should depart quickly,' Harold said. 'Forgive me.' He turned towards Gwenllian, calling to her.

The child came rushing over. Harold scooped her into the air and twirled her about, making her dark curls dance. She hugged him as he lowered her to the ground.

'I shall be off, my little love. Your mother has ordered me to ride off in defence of her castle.'

'What castle?'

'Freythorpe Hadden. It is as large as a castle.'

Gwenllian looked disappointed. 'Will you be back?'

'Of course I will!'

Lucie pulled Gwenllian close, hugging her as she watched Harold leave the garden, reminding herself that the man was no match for Owen.

• • •

Roger Moreton appeared moments later, dressed in the livery of his guild—to impress the High Sheriff with his standing, Lucie guessed. In the end, he might be of more help to her than Harold would have been. Perhaps more important, she did not have to watch her behaviour towards Roger.

'You do not mind the change in plans?' Roger asked, obviously reading something in Lucie's expression.

'Not at all.' With one last hug and a kiss, Lucie let go of Gwenllian, who skipped away to search for Crowder. Lucie rose, smiling. 'It is good of you to leave your work to escort me.'

'I am glad to do it.' He drew a letter from his scrip. 'Harold wrote down what he had noted, things you did not see. He hoped that it would be of use.'

'Then we are well prepared. Shall we depart?'

They said little as they passed through the crowds in Thursday Market, down Feasegate, across Coney and over Ousegate into Nessgate. Lucie worried about Phillippa—she had seemed lucid earlier, but just now she had been pacing the hall, muttering to herself, oblivious of Lucie's or Roger's presence. Had this deterioration worsened with the shock of recent events, or had she been this distracted all winter? She had received no clear picture from the servants.

'It sounds as if Harold was of great service to you,' Roger said, glancing over at Lucie with an odd expression. Worry? Could he read her mind?

'He was indeed. God bless you for proposing him.'

'Um.'

What was he thinking? Could he tell how she felt? How Harold felt? She must know. 'You are far away.'

'Forgive me, I am—' Roger stopped in the middle of Nessgate. 'I hope you are not offended, but I took it upon myself to have a word with Camden Thorpe about Alice Baker's accusations.'

His admission was so far from what Lucie had feared that she was silent a moment, absorbing it. Anger quickly replaced concern. 'You spoke to my guild master?' Two men walking past glanced over. Lucie realised how loud she had been and lowered her voice. 'What right had you? Do you think me a child who cannot speak for herself?'

Roger glanced round, anxious about the scene he had created. 'Perhaps we should continue walking.'

'No. Not until you explain yourself.'

'You are angry. Camden said you would be. He advised me to say nothing to you and promised to say nothing himself. But I wished you to know. I regret interfering. It was not right. I beg your forgiveness.'

'What possessed you to defend me to my guild master? What could you possibly say? Are you an apothecary, have you acquired the knowledge to argue my innocence?'

'I merely thought a word from a fellow merchant—'

'A word?' Lucie could not believe his naïveté.

Roger hung his head. 'He thought it as inappropriate as you do.'

'Do you intend to do the same with the High Sheriff?'

'I swear I shall hold my tongue.'

What must the guild master think about her relationship with Roger? Dear heaven, the man was a fool. But looking at his chagrin, Lucie reined in her anger. 'You meant to be a good friend, I know. But you have made things even more difficult for me.'

'I told you—he knows that you knew nothing about my going to see him.'

Lucie shook her head. She did not have the energy to argue. 'You are certain you can hold your tongue at this meeting?'

'I swear. I shall wait without if you prefer.'

'That should not be necessary.' Her anger was fading. Alice Baker had caused Lucie's trouble with the guild, not Roger. 'But I shall never forgive you if you break your vow.'

Looking relieved, Roger bowed, crooking his arm for her to grasp. 'Castlegate flooded in the rains. It will be slippery.'

They said little to one another as they made their way down the muddy street to York Castle. Lucie wondered whether all castles were so crowded. Here were housed numerous officers of the King, including the Master of the Mint, the two Keepers of the Exchange, the two custodians of the King's Merchant Seal in York, the Keeper of the Foss-fishpond, the Keeper of Galtres Forest and the High Sheriff, who was the sheriff of the county. It also housed a gaol. She always felt under scrutiny for some unknown wrong when she entered the bailey. She tried to ignore the bustle about her, attempting to order her thoughts. But she gave up as Roger steered her through a crowd watching a flogging, past armed guards surrounding several carts being unloaded at the Exchequer, through the smoke from the mint furnaces, to the sheriff's hall, which had once belonged to the Templars. At the door, Lucie withdrew her hand from Roger's arm and fussed with her veil. She wished to make a good impression on John Chamont, the High Sheriff, so that he would see she was not whining about a mere theft of baubles.

Chamont's clerk listened to her brief account with a solemn face, which heartened her, then showed her in to the High Sheriff's chamber.

The moment Lucie stepped inside, she knew she was wasting her time. John Chamont sat behind a large, exquisitely carved table on which a young boy and a puppy rolled about. An elegantly dressed woman, in silks and velvets and a gossamer veil, sat in the corner behind the High Sheriff, fussing with a servant about something. Mistress Chamont, Lucie guessed.

The clerk announced Lucie and Roger. Mistress Chamont hissed an order. The servant scooped up the boy in one arm, the puppy in the other, and hurried past the clerk and the visitors out of the room. Mistress Chamont then rose, nodded towards Lucie and Roger, and followed the departed servant with a slow, regal stride.

John Chamont frowned at the door, then at Lucie. 'Mistress Wilton, Apothecary?' He beckoned his clerk to his side. The clerk hurried over. After much whispering back and forth, he stepped back and Chamont looked up. 'Ah.' He nodded in Lucie's direction. 'Outlaws at Freythorpe Hadden.' He expressed his sympathy. 'His Grace the Archbishop has written to me of this, expressing his concern. You are fortunate in your friends.'

'I came to tell you what I know. And the man who is assisting me with my steward's responsibilities has provided information that may be of help.' She handed him Harold's letter, which he passed to the clerk behind him.

'We shall let you know if the outlaws are apprehended,' Chamont said with a benign smile.

The clerk bowed to the High Sheriff, then came round the table towards Lucie and Roger.

'You do not wish to hear my report?'

'My clerk will take your statement.' The High Sheriff waved his clerk to the door, smoothed his elegant houppelande as he rose from his chair.

'This is the extent of your duty?' she burst out. 'To receive letters and make empty assurances?'

'Mistress Wilton, what more can I promise you? I do not think you need fear another attack. Such thieves rarely return.'

Roger stepped forward, his face red with anger. 'If you will pardon me, sir, simple thieves rarely do such damage.' Lucie had never heard such a chill in his voice.

Chamont did not notice. 'Most unfortunate. But an accident, I am sure. The fire was meant to frighten you and did more damage than intended.'

'Are such fires common?' Lucie asked.

Chamont wagged his head. 'Barns are often set alight to create confusion. The point is, your losses might have been far worse. Your maids were not raped, your steward will recover. Others have not been so fortunate.'

'Fortunate,' Lucie repeated in disbelief.

The High Sheriff suddenly focused on her, his eyes surprisingly intense and not at all cordial. 'You make me wonder, Mistress Wilton. You pursue this as if you fear a particular enemy is behind the attack on Freythorpe Hadden. Is that so? Are you in trouble of some sort?'

His turnabout caught her unprepared, as she guessed it was meant to do. 'I know of no enemies.' Surely Alice Baker would not go to such lengths.

He looked for a moment as if he doubted her reply, but said, 'Then there is nothing to fear, for one surely knows one's enemies.'

Lucie had seen his sharpness, knew he was not that simple. It was merely a convenient assurance.

'As for the goods.' Chamont shook his head. 'Silver and gold plate, jewels, costly silks, livestock, tapestries from all over the shire. How many men would I need to recover all those treasures? Of course, if I apprehend the outlaws—I am quite certain it is all the work of a small band of men—I may indeed discover their hoard. And if I do, you shall know at once. I promise you, Mistress Wilton.'

'I am much consoled,' Lucie said. She saw little point in courtesy. Polite or rude, it mattered not to Chamont.

As if agreeing, the High Sheriff bowed to her.

Lucie and Roger withdrew. As they stepped out into the castle yard, Roger suggested a walk down to St George's Field, where the Foss and the Ouse converged.

Lucie, feeling oppressed both by the experience and the unpleasant steam from the mint furnaces, the press of the crowd round yet another flogging, welcomed a walk in the air. The rivers did not always smell pleasant downstream of the city, carrying the city waste and that of the tanners and butchers, but sometimes at their confluence the air was fresher. And the wide open sky would surely lift her spirits.

'When such a man accepts the title of High Sheriff,' Roger said, 'he thinks only of the prestige, not the responsibility.'

'I should like to be quiet, Roger,' Lucie said.

'Of course. But—you are not angry that I spoke?'

Lucie pressed his arm. 'Not at all. Your anger may not have stirred him, but I appreciated it.' As they passed the mills, and the field on which Owen trained the local men in archery, Lucie considered the High Sheriff's question about enemies. Was it possible that Sir Robert had enemies about whom she knew nothing? Or Owen? Surely in Owen's work for the archbishop he had angered people. But how was one to discover such an enemy? The river made her think of Magda Digby. The Riverwoman had agreed to go to Freythorpe Hadden. Now Lucie had another purpose for seeing her.

But first she must deal with Camden Thorpe and Alice Baker's accusations.

They stood at the edge of the fields, as if on the prow of a boat, except that the water flowed past them in the wrong direction. The breeze from the river was cool and damp, the sun hot above, the soil damp below. Lucie felt caught between winter and summer. She closed her eyes, lifted her face to the sun.

'You look content,' said Roger.

'God's grace is in this moment,' said Lucie. 'I pray it is a sign that I shall soon understand what has happened.'

Guild Master Camden Thorpe had a substantial stone house on St Saviourgate. Lucie and Owen knew the family well—Gwenllian was named for Mistress Thorpe, her godmother. Camden's warehouses sat to one side of the house and in between was a small courtyard in which Gwen Thorpe managed to coax several trees to grow. She had also trained ivy up the facing walls of the warehouses. It was a lovely setting.

Lucie had parted from Roger at Thursday Market, preferring to face her guild master alone.

A servant opened the door and, recognising Lucie, ran to fetch her mistress before Lucie could ask for Camden.

A large, handsome woman bustled to the door, one of her youngest children toddling after her. 'God bless you, Lucie, you must forgive Mary. It would not occur to her that this is not a time you would come to sit and chat with me. It is Camden you are wanting, of course. He is in the warehouse just across the yard.' She put a hand on Lucie's. 'Your father's passing is a great loss. God grant him peace. I shall attend the Requiem tomorrow.'

It was a mark of their friendship that Mistress Thorpe would take time out from her household—she had many children and a full staff, as well as two of her husband's apprentices and several servants who worked in the warehouses to feed. And as a guild master and alderman, Master Thorpe must needs entertain frequently.

'It will be a comfort to have you there,' Lucie said.

'Go on, then, tell him what a fool Alice Baker is. We all know it. Then if you have time, stop back here for some cakes for my godchild and her little brother.'

Gwen's friendly manner had taken the edge off Lucie's mood. As she crossed the yard to the warehouses she felt less as if she were meeting with an adversary.

Her good mood faded as she heard Camden's voice raised in anger. Two servants huddled over a cask and the smell of wine permeated the vast room. She began to back away, thinking it might go easier for her if she caught him in a better mood. But Camden noticed one of the servants looking up at her and turned to see who had witnessed his outburst.

'Mistress Wilton!' Camden smiled as he strode towards her. 'What must you think of me? My temper was justified, I assure you. But I would not have you think me a scold.' He was a bear-like man with bushy brows and a hawk-like nose.

'I apologise for interrupting at such a time. But Jasper just told me this morning about your calling at the house.'

'Not at all. Come, let us withdraw from this clumsy pair and escape the sad perfume of spilled wine.' He led her to a small room separated from the larger area with wood screens. The odour of the wine was not so strong here, but still the smell prevailed. Camden motioned for Lucie to sit on the one high-backed seat in the room. He settled on a bench, took a moment to calm himself, rubbing his forehead, pulling on his chin—an old habit from the days when he had had a beard. 'It is my own fault, I fear. Impatient is what I am. My apprentices would have managed it without mishap. But I had to ask those two to shift the cask.'

'Is it a great loss?' Lucie asked.

'Do you know, that is not the cause of my grief? It is the quality. A fine French wine I was saving for my Celia's wedding. Dear Lord but I am an old fool.'

He was not so old and no fool at all, but Lucie understood how much more of a loss it was than merely the wine. A fond father who wished to make his eldest daughter's wedding day perfect in a way he knew how. And the wedding was only a month hence.

'There is no time to replace it?'

Camden pulled on his chin. 'I shall get another fine French wine. In fact, I have others. But this one…' He shook his head, then suddenly sat upright and slapped his thighs. 'Enough of my moaning. You will be wanting to hear my thoughts about Alice Baker's accusations.' He dropped his eyes, regarding the floor for a moment. He was a heavy breather, being a man of great size.

Lucie listened to his measured breaths, wondering whether they were faster or slower than usual. She felt as if she were back in the convent, awaiting a punishment for some ill-conceived prank. 'I believe I know what happened,' she offered in much too small a voice.

Camden glanced up through his brows. 'So do I. So does the rest of the city. Alice Baker thinks that if a pinch is enough to cure most folk, a shovelful is what she needs. She believes she is a delicate creature, beset by devils in every organ and joint. Oh, aye, I know Mistress Baker.'

'That is possible, but the jaundice cannot be explained by one large dose of anything,' said Lucie. 'She mixed the wrong items.' She told him Magda Digby's theory and the remedy that she had recommended. 'But I cannot stand over her and force her to obey me.' She heard the defensiveness in her voice.

So did Camden, who motioned for her to calm down. 'I accuse you of nothing. I merely wished to be apprised of the details so that I might know how to defend you if anyone does attempt to accuse you.'

'No one has?'

'There has been some gossip among members, but primarily those who live without the city and do not know Mistress Baker. And, of course, there has been much discussion of her colour.' His eyes twinkled. 'In truth, it is not such a bad hue.'

Lucie bit her lip, fearing a rush of tears. 'I cannot tell you how

114

relieved I am.'

'I see it in your eyes, my friend. Come, let us go and have some refreshment with Gwen. I grow nauseated by the scent of that precious wine.'

On her way home, Lucie stopped in St Saviour Church. She knelt before the Blessed Mother, put her head in her hands and in the dim candlelight at last felt private enough to let the tears come. Tears of relief, mourning, fear and remorse—it did not matter. She felt purged when at last she rose and gathered the parcel of cakes for the children.

10

MATH AND ENID

A short-legged cattle dog barked at Owen and Iolo as they hobbled up to a large stone farmhouse. Owen tried to remember what William de Hutton had told him about the farm of Cynog's parents—did this look like what he had described? Or did Owen just hope it did? They had not walked far, but he felt as if he was dragging Iolo, not simply supporting him. Owen's hip was wet with the blood from the wound in his own side, and his arm was on fire.

A woman came out of the house, wiping her hands on a cloth. She shielded her eyes against the sun to see who approached, then hurried towards them. The dog followed, making wide circles round the two men as she barked. Owen's head pounded.

'I told Math I heard shouts in the wood,' the woman said in Welsh. 'Both of you injured!'

'We were attacked by three men,' said Owen. 'On our way from St David's to the family of Cynog, the mason.'

'And what did you want with them?'

'I wish to find out who killed their son.'

'Come.' She shooed the dog away, led them into the house and over to a large boxed bed.

Iolo sank down on to it.

Owen sat on the edge. 'If I lie down, I think I shall never rise from there.'

'Then I shall see to you while you sit by the fire,' the woman said. 'Your friend. He is very quiet.'

'I do not want to curse in front of you.' Iolo's voice was hoarse.

Owen forced himself up, placed a stool so that he might sit and lean his head against the wall. He thought he might close his eye while the woman tended Iolo. He woke when she touched his sleeve.

'You must slip your arm out of this.' She helped Owen shrug out of his leather and linen. He winced as the cloth pulled away from the wounds on his forearm and his side, but lifting the right arm brought the greatest pain, even with the woman's help. A broken arm would make him worthless with a bow—for the second time in his life. He searched for something to distract him. 'Do you know Cynog's folk?' Owen asked.

'I am Cynog's mother,' the woman said softly. 'God bless you for caring how my son died.'

'He was a good and gifted man.'

She traced a long scar on Owen's shoulder. 'By your scars I see this is not the worst wound you have suffered.'

After so long without a woman Owen found her touch disturbing. 'What of my arm? Is it broken?'

She ran her hands down his upper arm, pressing here and there, moving it slightly. 'It is swollen, but I feel no bones out of place.' Her face was lit from below by the fire, shadowed from above by the white cloth wrapped round her hair. Owen saw no lines—a smooth, pleasant face. She did not look old enough to be Cynog's mother. She put his soiled clothes aside, brought a lamp closer to examine his wounds. 'Not deep.' She felt along his arm once more. 'To have your arm twisted in the wrong way can be as painful as a break, I know. I shall clean the wounds, wrap them in cloth, then tie the arm against you to keep it still. That will help the healing.' She rocked back on her heels, rose, rummaged in a large chest by the bed.

'Iolo sleeps?' Owen asked when she returned with strips of cloth.

'He does.' She was quiet a moment, soaking one of the cloths in water. 'Iolo,' she said as she smeared an oily unguent on another cloth. 'And how are you called?'

'Owen.'

'I am Enid. My husband is Math. I am sorry, but you must lift your arm so I might clean the wound in your side.'

Owen held his breath as he tried lifting his arm sideways. He could not hold it there. Enid dragged over the one chair with a back and helped him raise his arm to rest on it. Her touch was gentle.

'How did you know my son?'

'Cynog was making a tomb for my wife's father. For St David's.'

Enid smiled sadly. 'My son had spoken of it. Very proud, he was, to carve the tomb of a man blessed with a vision from St Non. Did he complete it?'

'No.'

Enid said nothing for a while, her breathing uneven, as if she wept.

Were it not for his wounds, Owen would have drawn her into his arms. God watched over him. He would not insult this gentle woman so, and in her husband's house. And where was the husband? Owen could not tell the time of day in the dark, smoky farmhouse. 'How long did I sleep?'

'Not long. I wrapped Iolo's ankle, gave him a drink to ease the pain. Hold this to the wound.' Owen held the cloth with unguent to his wound while Enid secured it with a long strip round his waist. 'It is fortunate you are slender.' She tucked in the end. She helped him lower his arm, pushed the chair away. They said little to one another while she cleaned and bandaged the arm, then bound it to his side. When all was done, she helped him into a rough wool shirt. 'I must wash yours.'

'I pray you, I can do that when I return to St David's.'

'Do you have horses?'

'We did. Our attackers led them off.'

'Then your shirt will be ruined if not washed long before you return to St David's. It will be a time before your friend can walk so far.'

'I have friends in the city who know I should be back by midday tomorrow. They will come for us.'

'Unless your attackers lie in wait for them, too.'

Owen had thought of that.

Enid had moved to the fire, where she stirred something in a large pot. Owen, smelling herbs and pottage, realised he was hungry.

'Did you know the men who fell upon you in the forest?' she asked.

'No.'

A man entered the house, white-haired, deep lines round his mouth and eyes. 'Math, my husband,' Enid said.

Math brought the chair over to Owen, sat down with a weary sigh. 'What had Cynog done, that someone should hang him and try to kill his friend?' He looked much older than his wife, certainly old enough to be Cynog's father, and his eyes were much the same as his son's.

'Do not weary him,' Enid said.

'I came here with the hope that you could name his enemies,' said Owen.

Math shook his head. 'We knew of none. We were so pleased when he apprenticed in St David's. Our only son, so near to us. Now I wish he had gone away. Better alive and far away...' He bowed his head over his folded hands, which were knotted and swollen. 'To be hanged—it is a dishonourable way to die. As if he were a criminal. My son was an honest man, a man of peace.'

Owen let the silence linger a while. 'Did he come here often?'

'I do not know what is often,' Math said in the voice of one who is weary of thinking.

'For a time he had come monthly,' Enid said. 'I thought I had Glynis to thank, a woman's counselling. But even after she tore his heart from him he came every month, the day after the full moon.'

'She did not deserve him,' Math said.

'He was killed two nights before a visit,' Enid said softly.

'I am sorry to ask you to remember all this,' Owen said.

Math bent down to scratch the dog, who had settled at his feet. 'It is not as if we ever cease thinking of our son, Captain Archer.'

Owen felt chastised, though he understood it had been kindly meant. 'Why did Cynog come after the full moon?'

Enid shook her head. 'We never spoke of it.'

'Did he ever bring Glynis with him? Or anyone?'

'Glynis.' Enid hissed the name. 'We never met her. Nor any of his friends. Do you believe someone killed him to prevent his coming here?'

'You speak nonsense.' Math rubbed the swollen joints of his right hand. 'Why would someone care about a mason seeing his parents?'

'Do you believe it had to do with his visits?' Owen asked Enid.

'I believe it has to do with that man folk call the redeemer,' she said.

'Wife!'

'Owain Lawgoch? Cynog spoke of him?'

'There was a time when he did.' Enid ignored her husband's scowl. 'But of late he had talked only of his work. And how Glynis had betrayed him. He loved her with all his soul.' She looked away, choking on her words.

'He felt too much, that lad,' Math said. 'When I drowned the billy goats he would not speak to me for days.' He shook his head, remembering. 'Passion. Reckless passion. That is what he felt for that woman.'

'How do you know?'

'It is how he spoke of her.' Math faced Owen with his tired eyes. '"I cannot live without her," he said. It is sinful to think such things.'

The journey might be the key. Something done, someone met along the way, in the bright moonlight? 'When the weather turned to rain, no moon to be seen, did he still come?'

'He did,' said Enid.

'And had no trouble in the wood? Never arrived injured?' Owen asked.

'Why should anyone wait for wayfarers near our farm?' Math shook his head. 'Few people come this way.'

'Then what were three armed men doing in the wood today?'

'They must have followed you and Iolo,' said Enid. 'Come now, you must eat something and then rest.'

• • •

The small sturdy dog who fancied herself a guard lay beside Owen with her short legs curled up, enjoying the warmth from the ash-covered fire. Enid and Math lay on pallets across from Owen. Iolo still slept in the boxed bed in the far corner. Rain tapped softly on the roof and dripped in jarring rhythms from two unseen spots overhead. The pale light from the chinks in the door suggested daybreak. Pain consumed Owen. His wounds were only the visible injuries. The bruises had gradually made themselves known. Deep aches that made every move an unpleasant reminder of the ambush. That he could still drowse was a tribute to how exhausted he had been even before this latest misadventure. Owen was drifting back to sleep when the dog lifted her head, ears pricked, eyes on the door, and began to growl.

11

RUMOURS

The nave of York Minster was bright with candles and echoed with the voices of the chapter singing the Requiem in the choir. Lucie had not expected so many people to attend the Mass. Her father had made more friends in the city than she had known. Phillippa nervously regarded the crowd, asking Lucie to identify those she did not recognise or could not see with her fading eyesight.

'Do not worry,' Lucie murmured, patting the hand that clasped her upper arm. 'I have not invited all these people back to the house afterwards.'

'No strangers,' Phillippa said.

'Of course not. Why should I invite strangers?'

Phillippa glanced away and muttered something to herself.

Lucie prayed that the mood would pass. Phillippa flickered in and out of states of clear-headedness and confusion.

Bess and Tom Merchet, proprietors of the York Tavern next to Lucie's shop, had both noted Dame Phillippa's unpredictable moods. Tom had said they would all come to that in the end. Bess countered with, 'You must put her to work.' Work was Bess's solution for all odd behaviour, as if a person needed idleness in which to grow peculiar.

But idleness was not Phillippa's problem. Lucie wished it were. When Phillippa was clear-headed, she busied herself meddling in the household. She criticised Kate's cooking, her child handling and her cleaning; told Lucie that she was not strict enough with the children, yet spoilt Gwenllian and Hugh when Lucie disciplined them; urged changes to the children's diet to 'make them thrive'; took Lucie to task for the amount of time she spent in the apothecary. When she was confused, she sat, fidgeting and muttering to herself, or wandered slowly and aimlessly from room to room.

Lucie regretted bringing her aunt to the city. And not merely because she disturbed the household. Her fear of strangers fed Lucie's own worries. She had thought much about the High Sheriff's question regarding enemies. How could she know who might resent the family because of something her father had done during his military career, or because of Owen's investigations? She was frightened for the manor and for her family. She would much rather face an Alice Baker, who accused openly, than an invisible, unknown enemy—how could she protect her family against such a person?

Lucie tried to hold back a yawn, but her jaw popped with tension. Worry kept her wakeful—not simply about Phillippa, but about the manor, and Owen. And in truth she took some of her aunt's criticism to heart. Always in the back of her mind was the fear that because of the apothecary she spent too little time with the children, though she knew of no mothers who had the luxury to spend all the time they wished with their little ones. The previous night, as Lucie had tucked the children in, she felt a clenching in her stomach—she dreaded the long dark hours spent lying as still as possible so as not to wake Phillippa, or listening to her aunt fidget and mutter in her sleep. Lucie tried not to strain to understand her aunt's words, too jumbled to make sense, moans that chilled her. She wished she might bring Gwenllian and Hugh into her room and move Phillippa, have her share Jasper's room, but then the poor lad would be wakened by her. Besides, Lucie would doubtless still lie awake most nights. Her mind was too full.

Rustling drew her from her thoughts and she found herself still kneeling when everyone around her was on their feet. Rising, she bowed her head and turned her mind to prayers for her father's soul.

After the Mass, Brother Michaelo asked Lucie if they might speak a moment. She saw now the depth of his emotion, the eyes red and swollen from weeping.

It was not about Sir Robert that Michaelo wished to speak. He carried an invitation from Archbishop Thoresby to dine with him at Archdeacon Jehannes's house the following evening. His Grace wished to offer his condolences and learn more about the situation at Freythorpe Hadden, to find out whether there was more that he could do. Michaelo cheered Lucie with the news that Thoresby had already sent two retainers to the manor and even more so with who they were—the two men Owen most trusted. That he had also sent a messenger to recall Owen made her heart quicken. She would be so grateful to have him home.

Lucie hurried back to the house to be ready to greet her guests. Many guild members attended the gathering, kind in their condolences, eager to hear of the attack on Freythorpe Hadden, curious about what she heard from Owen. Council members also came and some people she had invited because they were too influential to exclude, John Gisburne among them, whose attempt to speak kindly to Phillippa was rebuked in an embarrassing manner.

Dame Phillippa had stayed close to either Lucie or Jasper, asking them to identify people. As long as the guests spoke about Sir Robert, Phillippa answered graciously, thanked them, but mention of the trouble at Freythorpe Hadden silenced her and brought a hunted look to her face that disturbed people. By the time Gisburne expressed concern about the incident, Phillippa could no longer bear it and hurried from the room.

Lucie tried to deflect curious questions by asking about chantry priests and praising Archdeacon's Jehannes's eulogy. No one mentioned Alice Baker outright, though Lucie saw folk with heads together draw apart with guilty expressions as she approached. In loud voices so that all could hear, guild master Thorpe and his wife, Gwen, made sure to invite Lucie to dine with them within the next week. It was a kind show of support that Lucie much appreciated.

The questions about Owen began to bother her. Too many people's queries implied doubt that Owen would return. The first time someone asked 'he is certain to return soon?' she interpreted it as being intended as a statement. But after two or three such slips, she could no longer ignore it. Or was it merely her usual worry when Owen was away that coloured her perception?

She noted what looked to be a quiet argument between Alderman Bolton and John Gisburne. Feeling her own back bristling with gossip, she thought it time to show Gisburne some appreciation for having come. When Lucie saw him backing away from Bolton, downing his cup of ale as he did so, she moved towards him.

'Master Gisburne, I pray you, forgive my aunt's behaviour. She has not been well and I fear this gathering was ill-advised.'

Gisburne bowed to Lucie, pressed his bejewelled hands together as he rose. He was an elegant man. His houppelande was deep blue, his cap amber silk. 'You need not apologise, Mistress Wilton. My grandfather was much the same, God grant him rest.'

Lucie did not know Gisburne well, in fact, had never had cause to speak to him before, as he favoured another apothecary. She had expected him to be loud, not quiet and courteous. 'You might know that Harold Galfrey has been assisting my staff at Freythorpe Hadden.'

'Is he? But I thought he was house steward for Roger Moreton.'

'Master Moreton did not need him as yet—'

'How kind of Roger. You are fortunate in that friendship. My father and your uncle were good friends, did you know?'

'My uncle, Douglas Sutton?'

Gisburne nodded.

Lucie was all the sorrier about her aunt's behaviour towards the man. 'I do not remember my uncle.'

'Nor I my father. He was killed during the Scots raids into Yorkshire.'

Gwen Thorpe joined them, asking after Gisburne's wife, Beatrice. Lucie withdrew to see how Phillippa fared. Her aunt sat in the kitchen, dozing in a chair by the fire. Lucie slipped back out into the milling crowd and made a point of talking to Alderman Bolton, so he would not feel himself slighted.

After the guests departed, Lucie found herself at leisure for the rest of the afternoon. Jasper had gone to St Mary's Abbey, his usual escape when he needed consolation. Phillippa was napping upstairs with the help of a calming draught. Gwenllian and Hugh were also up in their cots. Kate needed no help cleaning up—Bess Merchet had sent over a kitchen maid to assist. Lucie judged it a good time to see Magda Digby.

The sun warmed Lucie and softened her mood. Her troubles seemed less frightening. It was true the attack might have been much worse. Except for Daimon, no one had serious injuries. Far more might have been lost had the thieves known where her mother's jewels were kept. Or her father's weapons. But about other problems she found no consolation in the sun. Phillippa's confusion and weakness might never mend. Lucie might never know Jasper's heart.

Magda stood over a block of dense wood chopping roots with a small axe. A scarf covered her hair and an apron her colourful dress.

'I am glad to find you well,' Lucie called to her.

Magda nodded, but went on with her work. Lucie settled on a bench that allowed her to lean against the old house and consider the dragon's head that glared at her upside down. Magda's roof was an old Viking ship overturned. Magda had once explained that the frightening visage had protected the mariners from sea monsters and she thought it wise to protect her island home in case such monsters ever ventured upriver. Worms had pitted the dragon's face, weather had etched lines in the paint. He looked as old as Magda now.

'Thou art fast becoming friends, eh?' Magda said as she brushed the chopped roots into a jar. She wiped the axe on her apron and joined Lucie on the bench.

'Freythorpe Hadden needs a dragon. But I must needs settle for a few of the archbishop's men.'

'He is generous.'

'So are you.'

'Magda had already planned to leave tomorrow for a farm near Freythorpe, to encourage a babe from its mother's womb. In a day or two she should come to Daimon at Freythorpe, as soon as the babe agrees. Though Magda doubts she can do more than thee for the lad.'

'I was not the best nurse,' Lucie said. 'Too much happened all at once. I worry there is something I missed. I sent Harold Galfrey off yesterday with medicines I did not have with me at the time, but even now I do not trust myself to think of everything.'

'This Harold is to be Moreton's steward?'

'Yes.' Lucie told Magda how helpful he had been.

'Is it true John Gisburne commended him to Moreton?'

'It is. Why?'

'Gisburne is a friend to outlaws, thou knowest that.'

'Rumours.'

Magda grunted.

'Truth? But Harold—' Lucie stopped. What precisely did she know of the man but his deeds? 'I do not believe it of him.'

'Good. Thou dost not need more trouble.'

'The High Sheriff asked me about enemies.'

'There are many who fear thy husband's eye, but to Magda's knowledge none so foolish as to taunt Bird-eye with such a deed.'

'He is away. They might feel confident.'

Magda squinted up at the sun. 'Hast thou news of him?'

'A question much repeated today.'

Rising abruptly, Magda walked to the edge of the rock on which her house was perched, then stood with hands clasped behind her back, facing the city. Lucie joined her. Sun danced on the shallow water, a dog barked somewhere in the hovels crowded against the walls, a church bell tolled, children shrieked as they played in the water upstream, a ferryman shouted. But Magda was silent.

'What is it?' Lucie asked.

'How dost thou answer the rumours about thy husband?'

'What rumours?'

Magda watched the arc of a seagull as it swept over the river before she turned to face Lucie. 'Thou hast not heard them?'

'No.'

'These questions—folk ask without explaining why?' Magda shook her head at Lucie's nod. 'Even Bess Merchet?'

'Tell me for pity's sake!'

'Owain Lawgoch, Owain of the Red Hand. Thou hast heard the tales?'

'Yes. What has he to do with Owen?'

'It is said that Bird-eye might see in the princeling a noble cause.'

'Who accuses my husband of treason?'

'Magda guesses none accuse, they wonder.'

'Who could think such a thing of Owen?'

'Though he is thy husband, he is yet a stranger from the west.'

Lucie's legs felt weak. She withdrew to the bench, trying to remember whether Bess had also asked without explaining. And what of Gwen and Camden Thorpe? Why had they said nothing of this? Dear God, what of Jasper? How would he receive such a rumour? Is this why His Grace the Archbishop invited her to dine? To question her about Owen's loyalty?

Magda sat, took one of Lucie's cold hands in her warm, strong grasp. 'Look at Magda.'

Reluctantly, Lucie raised her eyes.

'Magda did not wish to tell thee. So it must be with all thy friends. Some may believe thou knowest what folk say and choose to ignore it. Which is what thou must now do.'

But Lucie's thoughts had turned to Owen's letters. 'I must talk to Brother Michaelo.'

'Thou suspects some truth lies behind this?'

'I cannot believe Owen would betray his king. But in every letter he wrote of the harsh treatment his countrymen received from the Marcher lords and their men. He found it difficult to hold his tongue.'

'He mentioned this princeling?'

'No. He would not take such a risk. The letters might have fallen into the wrong hands. Did the thieves hear these rumours? Is that what gave them courage?'

'Thy father also had enemies, to be sure.'

'I may never know the truth of this.'

'No.'

Lucie returned to her garden, not ready to see people. Her

small rake was not on its hook in the shed. As she dug round on the shelves among old baskets, she came across her father's old felt hat. Tears pricked her eyes as she lifted it, turned it in her hands. Sweat and rain had darkened it, a hand print was still visible on the crown where Sir Robert had plucked it off his head with a soil-stained hand to wipe his brow. Lucie pressed the hat to her, said a prayer for her father's soul, then hung the hat on a nail, out of the way, but visible in the light from the open door.

She knelt by the apothecary roses that surrounded the grave of her first husband, Nicholas. This had been his favourite spot in the garden, though he had loved it all. In the growing season they would work out here before opening the shop, Nicholas patiently teaching her the correct way to prune each plant, how to fertilise it, how to tell when it was diseased, how to harvest it while still leaving enough of the plant to grow to another harvest. They had been happy, and he had always been there. Not like Owen. Though she felt for Owen a passion she had never felt for Nicholas, Lucie missed the companionship of her first marriage. A wave of sadness washed over her. She had been so eager to rush into Owen's arms after Nicholas died. But her first husband had been a good man, and gentle. She bent to her work, loosening the soil, beginning to weed.

Footsteps behind her caused her to glance up. It was Roger Moreton, who paused now, looking down at her with concern. Lucie dabbed at her eyes with the hem of the loose jacket she wore over her gown and rose to greet him. Unexpectedly, he gathered her in his arms, pressing her head to his shoulder. Lucie was caught off her guard, but remembering her agonies over Harold's kiss, she quickly drew away. 'Roger!'

Two red patches burned on his cheeks. 'I pray you, forgive me. I just—seeing you kneeling there weeping, over Nicholas's grave, I knew what you were feeling. I weep for Isabel, just so. And now your father gone, too. And Owen away...' Roger clasped his hands behind him and looked down at the path.

'Why not complete it. Owen away on a treasonous adventure? Owen away for ever?'

He met her eyes. 'You do not think I believe such rumours!'

'Why did you not tell me?'

'You did not know?'

'Magda told me.'

'Your friends have had a care not to tell you then.'

'How long?'

Roger frowned. 'A while, but it began merely with puzzlement that Brother Michaelo returned alone. Then after the news of your father's death became stale, they turned to the captain.'

Lucie noticed that his hair was damp with sweat, as if he had hurried to see her. 'But you did not tell me the reason for your visit,' she said. 'Is there some news?'

'No, no, I merely wished to see how you were.' He looked increasingly uncomfortable. 'I shall come another day.'

'Do you wish to discuss Harold Galfrey?'

Roger hesitated, then said, 'We shall discuss it another day.' And with that, he turned and hurried away from her. As he disappeared behind the hedge that led to the gate, he gave an exclamation.

Lucie could not see through the bushes, but she heard Bess Merchet's voice quite clearly. 'Such a hurry, Master Moreton. There are no dogs in this garden, surely. Is the devil nipping at your heels?'

Roger murmured something. Lucie heard the gate open and shut. 'Bess?'

With her usual decisive tread, Bess appeared at the head of the path and came marching down. She had changed into what she called her scrubbing gown, a simple fustian with no trim, and one of her old caps, sans ribbons. Lucie imagined a serving maid was being instructed on the fine points of cleaning the inn. Bess carried a jug.

'You look as if you are busy. What brings you back here?' Lucie asked.

Bess tucked a loose red tendril back into her cap, then held up the jug. 'Brandywine. I had a thought you might need comforting, suddenly alone, thinking about your father. But I see Roger Moreton had the same idea. A different sort of comfort.'

Lucie felt herself blushing, which was unfortunate when under Bess's scrutiny.

'I see,' Bess said, her eyes narrowed.

'What do you see?'

'He embraced you and you did not pull away. I certainly saw that.'

'He found me weeping and thought to comfort me. I did pull away. And he apologised.'

Bess looked doubtful. 'Quite a red face he had as he left. I imagine he knows I caught you.'

'You caught nothing, Bess. A friend comforting a friend. That is all that you saw.'

'I cannot understand you, Lucie Wilton. Wed to the handsomest man I have ever seen, who loves you dearly, and you dally with a merchant and a steward while he is away.'

'What?'

'Or was Jasper mistaken? Was it not Harold Galfrey but Roger Moreton who kissed your hand the other day?'

This was worse than Phillippa witnessing it, with Jasper already suspicious of Roger Moreton. Now Harold Galfrey, too? 'When did Jasper tell you this?'

Bess set the jug on the ground at her feet and rubbed her hands. 'This morning. While we moved things for your guests. He looked sad. I said he must be missing Sir Robert. But I could tell that was not all. With some prodding I had it from him.' Bess shook her head. 'Was it Harold?'

'Harold Galfrey kissed my hand, it is true.'

'What is this all about? Has Owen been gone too long?'

The question startled Lucie.

Bess nodded. 'I have always worried about you when Owen went on one of his adventures.'

'I love Owen. I would not be unfaithful to him.'

'But?'

'I feel so alone.'

Bess's irritation dissolved into sympathy. She picked up the jug, put an arm round Lucie. 'Listen to me, chiding you when you have been beset by one thing and another of late. It would try the patience of Job, and I cannot think whose steadfastness. Jasper will not be ruined by what he saw. Tell him you love Owen, that is all he wants to hear. Come now, be at peace. Come into the house and share a cup of good cheer.'

Brother Michaelo walked back to the archdeacon's house slowly, disturbed by what he had just heard. Archbishop Thoresby had suggested that Michaelo go to the Bedern, the area in which the cathedral clerics lived, and listen to the gossip. Getting the clerks to talk had been no problem—they all knew that he had accompanied Owen Archer and Sir Robert D'Arby to Wales, and it was of that journey they wanted news. How had Sir Robert died, where was he buried, who was to live at Freythorpe Hadden now, was Wales as wild as they said, were the French on the shores, why was the captain still there?

It was the questions about the captain that disturbed Michaelo. He needed to think how to tell His Grace in such a way that he did not reveal Sir Robert's similar worries about Owen. For Sir Robert had been concerned about his son-in-law. Owen's behaviour had begun to change as the company crossed the Severn river and entered the Welsh Marches. He had become increasingly defensive about the Welsh and angry about how the English treated them. He had also been in contact with an old friend, a Fleming who worked for King Charles of France and at the moment was assisting the cause of Owain Lawgoch. To Michaelo's mind there was little chance that Owen would desert his family to fight for a puppet of the French king. The captain had spent too much of his life fighting the French. But what of his anger about the English behaving as conquerors in Wales? Michaelo caught himself—he, too, was being influenced by the rumours and he had been with the captain in Wales so recently.

Lucie lingered at the table with Bess, grateful for the warmth in her stomach from the brandywine. But her companion did not look at ease. 'I should not keep you so long from your work,' said Lucie.

Her words seemed to wake Bess from a reverie. 'The dirt will still be there, if I know my maids.' The complaint was flat.

'What is wrong?'

Bess grimaced, poured a finger more brandywine in both cups, ignoring Lucie's protests. But Bess did not drink, rather she stared into her cup. 'I do not wish to give you more to fret about. But you should know what folk are saying.'

'About Owen? I know, Bess.'

She made a show of slumping with relief. 'Praise God, I did not wish to be the one to tell you. Who did?'

'Magda. I do not understand how anyone could think that of Owen.'

'If you ask me, no one believes any ill of Owen, they just enjoy the talk. When a body is gossiping, he is not thinking.' Bess rose, crossed over the floor quickly to the kitchen door and opened it. 'There you are, Kate. How was my new serving girl this morning? Was she a help to you?'

Lucie could not hear Kate's reply over the sounds of the children awakening up above.

'Bess, ask Kate to bring Gwenllian and Hugh down.'

Bess did so, then returned to the table as Kate hurried up to the solar.

'You thought she was listening?' Lucie asked.

Bess pressed the cork firmly into the jug, brushed off her skirt. 'Kate is honest and hard-working, I know, but she is not so bright as to realise how gossip might hurt you.' She rose as Gwenllian clattered down from the solar. Kate followed, Hugh in her arms. She looked worried as she handed him to Lucie.

'What is wrong?'

'You will want to go up, Mistress Lucie. Dame Phillippa is gathering her clothes. She says she is leaving.'

Holy Mary Mother of God, what was the woman thinking? Lucie handed Hugh to Bess and hurried up to her chamber where, indeed, Phillippa's clothes were roughly crammed into the small chest she had brought from Freythorpe. Phillippa paced and muttered to herself. She wore the small linen cap in which she slept, her grey hair hanging down her back in thin, tangled strands. Her shift was wrinkled from sleep, her legs and feet bare. The gown she had been wearing still hung on a hook on the wall.

'Aunt?' Lucie said softly, unsure whether Phillippa woke or slept. The valerian should still have effect, but Kate had said Phillippa spoke to her and someone had packed the chest. Lucie called to her aunt a little louder.

Now Phillippa noticed her, stopped, glanced at the chest, then back to Lucie. 'You were kind to ask me to stay, but I must go back to the manor.'

'Why? Tildy, Harold and all the servants are there. I have sent Magda to see to Daimon. What more can be done, Aunt?'

'I should be there.'

Lucie ached to see the once indomitable Phillippa like this. She put a soft wool shawl round her aunt's shoulders. 'Come and sit down. I shall comb your hair and help you dress.'

'And then we shall go?'

'We shall see.' There, beside the bed, Lucie found the reason for Phillippa's wakefulness. Her cup of tisane was still half full. Lucie lifted it, held it towards her aunt. 'Drink this. It will calm you.'

'You do not understand.'

'Then tell me.'

'I forget too much.'

'As you did this drink.'

Phillippa took the cup, drank down the honey-laced valerian.

'Why not nap a while until we are ready?' Lucie suggested. She eased her aunt back down on to the bed, covered her and slipped quietly from the room. She would unpack the chest later.

12

CYNOG'S SECRET

Owen heard a horse whinny. And another. Math and Enid had no horses. The dog rose and began to bark. Owen struggled to rise. Math jumped up, grabbed a knife and a pitchfork he had propped by the door.

'Where are my knives?' Iolo called out from the corner.

'Do not waste your strength unless I cry out,' Math said. 'Both of you. Enid, keep Ilar quiet.'

Enid grabbed the dog and muzzled her with a strip of cloth from the wound dressings.

The farmer pressed an ear to the door, listening. 'Horsemen. Not many.'

'One is bad enough if the wrong one,' Enid murmured.

Especially if he were the murderer of her son?

Math opened the door quietly, slipped out into the wet morning. A horse whinnied again. Math shouted.

Owen pushed through his pain and stood up. But Math appeared in the doorway before Owen reached it. The farmer laughed as he shook the rain from his hair.

'Friends?' Enid asked.

'Aye. Cynog's friend. The one-handed Fleming. And two others. They are seeing to their horses.'

'Praise God.' Enid let the bitch loose. Ilar rushed from the cottage, barking. 'I must add more to the pottage,' Enid said.

'You sic that stubby, yapping devil on a friend?' Iolo asked. He was sitting up, looking as if he had spent the night under a tavern table.

'She knows Martin,' Enid said. 'And she is no devil, but the best watch dog a farmer could ask for.'

'Martin Wirthir,' Owen said.

Math gave an enthusiastic nod. 'He says he has come to crown you king of fools.'

'I shall greet the kingmaker.' Owen hoped that walking about would ease the stiffness in his legs. His wounds slowed his impulsive pace, but they did not stop him. Outside, he lifted his face to the cool drizzle, breathed in the fresh air. The expansion of his ribs brought pain, but his lungs felt cleansed. He headed into the brush to relieve himself. When he returned to the yard, Martin Wirthir was walking out of the barn, his pack over his left shoulder, the dog trotting happily beside him. She gave one bark when she saw Owen. Martin paused, crouching to pet Ilar. It was ever jarring to see Martin after an absence. He could be Owen's brother, they looked so much alike, but that Martin's hair was slightly lighter and straighter. Like Owen, he carried a terrible scar, though not on his face. He was missing his right hand. At the moment he looked muddy and bedraggled.

'I see you have ridden hard this morning,' said Owen.

'Walked. We camped the other side of the forest.' Martin laughed as Ilar pulled at his pack. With his left hand he grabbed a stick and threw it far across the yard, sending the dog racing after it on her squat legs. 'Ilar believes she is a deerhound,' Martin said as he rose, brushing off his muddy knees. 'Not a bad toss for someone who could throw only with his right hand a few years ago, eh?' Now he looked closely at Owen. 'By St Sebastian, you are not looking much the archer this morning.'

'My bow would have been of little use in the forest,' Owen said. 'Did my men tell you where I was?'

'No.'

'Your own spies told you?'

The dog dropped the stick at Martin's feet, then dashed into the cottage. 'She has the good sense to go inside, out of the rain.' Martin hoisted his pack over his shoulder. 'So do I.' He bowed to Owen and walked away. At the cottage door Martin glanced back at

Owen, who was still eyeing the forest. 'There is no need for you to stand out here. My men are on watch.'

Owen followed, though it was not because of the rain. The Fleming usually travelled alone. For him to ride with companions and set a guard—something had him worried. The men who had attacked Owen?

Enid and Math welcomed Martin with much affection. Owen learned from their conversation that Martin had been the one to bring them the terrible news of Cynog's murder. They had not mentioned him last night when Owen questioned them.

Martin bent over Iolo's wounded foot. 'I thought you were a better fighter than this, my friend.'

'It was three against two, three men who knew the forest,' Iolo protested. 'They had the advantage of our surprise.'

Martin straightened. 'Can you ride?'

'Ride, aye. But mounting and dismounting…' Iolo shook his head at his leg.

'We can assist you.' Martin turned to Owen. 'And you?'

'Tomorrow,' Enid said, stepping between them.

'Today would be better,' Martin said.

'Tomorrow is foolish enough,' she said. 'He will open his side and bleed all the way to St David's.'

'He might suffer far worse if he curls up and naps until his trouble appears.'

Martin's unease had Owen's full attention. 'Shall we talk about this trouble?' he asked.

'First we eat,' Enid said. 'Then I shall leave the three of you alone.'

Owen grew impatient with her mothering. But Martin thanked her graciously.

Enid's good, thick pottage and sharp cider soon calmed Owen and made him more confident he could ride. But he wondered about Iolo. The horses must be led for much of the way to St David's. Through the forest he might bend low against his mount, but it would be dangerous for him to stay mounted on the steeper rock faces. Yet how could he walk? Owen asked whether Martin had a different route in mind.

Taking their cue, Enid and Math rose from the table and donned their cloaks to set about their chores. They were already behind in their morning schedule, Math said as he hurried Enid—who would linger—out of the door.

Martin leaned his elbows on the table, toying with a puddle of cider on the wood. 'Do you wish to return to St David's? Might it not be wiser to journey south, and then east, towards home?'

'The time is not right.'

Martin glanced up from his fidgeting to look Owen in the eye. 'I should have thought it precisely the time.'

'With my men yet in St David's, the tomb unfinished…' Martin's grim expression did not change. 'Math said you had come to crown me king of fools. What did he mean?'

'What do you have to gain by returning to the city? If you have paid the stonemason, he will complete the tomb. Why should he not? It will be a monument to his artistry as well as to Sir Robert's life.'

'And Cynog's murderer? Do I abandon the search for him?'

'What will you gain by finding him for the archdeacon? A ship? I can arrange passage for you.'

'I am not finished here.'

'How much time would you waste in St David's?'

'He makes sense,' said Iolo.

Owen thought it madness even to consider it. 'What of the rest of my men? How can I desert them in St David's?'

'They are unimportant,' Martin said lightly. 'Rokelyn will not detain them. They should have papers—you were not carrying the papers when you were attacked, were you? Are you emperor of fools?'

Such an argument could continue all the day. Owen wanted to know what he was running from. 'You think our attackers will return, and soon. Why? To finish their work? They had the chance to kill us yesterday. Who are they? What do they want of us?'

Martin threw up his arms. 'So many questions at once, my friend.' He leaned forward. 'It is not only your attackers who might return—what of Archdeacon Rokelyn? You know that I dare not show myself to any loyal to King Edward. I cannot stay here.'

'Ah. It is you who must move quickly.'

'Do I misunderstand you? Do you enjoy being the puppet of clerics?'

Owen hated it. But when he returned to York he would be under Thoresby's thumb. Was he any better than Rokelyn? Martin was right—Owen should leave now. Perhaps ride. He might go by way of Usk and see his sister once more. For the last time? How likely was it that they would ever meet again?

Martin was laughing. 'Your caution is wise. But come now. Let us away.'

Owen was tempted. But he had never abandoned his men. It was the act of a coward, a man without honour. 'I shall not desert my men.'

Martin looked away, the set of his jaw, his clenched hand expressing his frustration. 'Then let me show you something. We shall ride, we two.'

'What about our attackers?' Iolo asked.

'My men will stay here,' said Martin. 'They will help you take cover if trouble approaches.'

'What of you two?'

'They are more likely to be watching the track to St David's.' Martin rose. 'Come, Owen. I wish you to understand Cynog.'

When Iolo and the captain had not returned by morning, Tom, Edmund, Sam and Jared prepared to search for them. But they had been surrounded at the palace gatehouse and escorted to the house of the Archdeacon of St David's. Apparently Rokelyn believed this was a ruse, that they meant to escape.

Edmund had tried to reason with the man.

'This is not a discussion,' the archdeacon had said, his eyes cold. 'This young one, Thomas, will ride with my men.' Tom's knees had begun to shake. 'I prefer to keep you separated.' The archdeacon had looked down his nose when he spoke to them and his eyes never quite met theirs.

Edmund and Jared had been given the task of guarding Piers the Mariner in his cell. Sam was to sit in the palace gatehouse with the keeper. Tom rode out of Bonning's Gate with head bowed, hoping that no one along the way recognised him in the company of the archbishop's guards. It was a pointless effort, for the ones who counted already knew of Tom's humiliation—Sam, Edmund, Jared. And soon Iolo and, worst of all, Captain Archer would be the wiser. The captain would surely understand why Archdeacon Rokelyn chose Tom to accompany the guards. Not that Tom had understood at first. Edmund had explained it to Tom as he gathered his things.

'You are young, inexperienced,' said Edmund, 'they doubt you would have the stomach to lie to them.'

All through his journey in Captain Archer's company Tom's stomach had betrayed him. Twice he had turned green crossing choppy water. He had embarrassed himself during a training session at Cydweli Castle, retching after being punched in the stomach. He had stopped counting how many times he stumbled out of the hall to heave after too much drink. The other men laughed and told him he would grow into being a soldier. But Tom had his doubts. He had the will, but not the stomach. And now these guards thought he did not have the stomach to lie. He prayed to St Oswald for the courage to deceive them. He did not yet see in what way he might do it. They had known the captain's plan. Captain Archer had told Archdeacon Rokelyn where he was going—indeed, he had received the archdeacon's blessing.

Owen and Martin slowly rode out of the yard. Owen turned once, saw Enid still watching. He saluted her. She stood there, motionless. He guessed that she feared he was deserting the search for her son's murderer.

'Her son's murder has tested her trust,' Martin said.

'You watch me too closely. I did not invite you into my thoughts. Even the Lord God gives us the courtesy of pretending He needs to hear our confession through His priests.'

Martin stared straight ahead.

The track they followed was overgrown and rocky, seemingly chosen to follow the most difficult terrain. Not so bad that they had to dismount, but the horses moved as slowly as the men might have done on foot—had not Owen been injured. His wounds stung more and more as he jounced on the horse. His shoulder ached as he shifted his body to balance in the saddle. He prayed they did not have far to go, else he could not imagine being in any condition to ride again tomorrow.

Halfway up a track that climbed a barren, stony height they dipped into a small depression carved out by a stream, shaded by a few young trees. Two paths led off at different angles. Martin signalled a halt and dismounted.

Owen dismounted with care.

Martin crouched on the bank of the stream, where it bent towards him, round a stone outcropping topped with gorse. In the bend was a mound of smooth stones—after heavy rains the water must come down from the highlands with force and speed, depositing some of the stones caught up in the torrent. At present the slow-flowing water left them dry. Martin seemed to be handling the smooth rocks idly, turning them over, then setting them back down on the mound. All white rocks.

'Do you read signs in the stones?' Owen guessed.

Martin bent to the stream, picked up a stone and handed it to Owen. Someone had chiselled out lines and angles.

'I have seen lettering like this—on wayside crosses. I cannot read it.'

'You are not meant to. Even one skilled in such lettering would find these a riddle.'

'Lawgoch has planted these?'

'Cynog,' said Martin. 'He carved them and put them in place.'

If ever there was a man Owen had misjudged, it was Cynog. 'What do they signify?'

'Directions. Safe paths.'

'For whom?'

'We shall talk when we return to the farmhouse.'

Owen stared down at the other white rocks in the stream. Cynog had spoken of Lawgoch to Math and Enid. If Cynog had been working for Lawgoch's cause, his murderer might well have been—as Rokelyn had surmised—a king's man, someone who wanted to make of Cynog an example for other traitors to the king. Someone who had come upon him carving the stones? A fellow mason? But why would such a man care so much about whether Cynog betrayed the king? Would the guild have decreed such an act? To protect their freedoms? Certainly the guilds in York felt strongly about the behaviour of their members.

Had Piers the Mariner searched Cynog's room for evidence of treason? Would a spy for the king have been so obvious? Even so, Edward was king here, no matter the feelings of the people. Someone would surely come forth to argue in Piers's defence if he were the king's man. But would anyone have understood what they saw, smooth rocks on which Cynog had carved some symbols? Was it not more likely someone had come upon him setting them out?

'Several of them have symbols,' Martin said as Owen continued to stare at the stones. 'Not all.'

Owen only now focused completely. 'How many learn these symbols?'

'Enough for someone to think it worth the effort.' Martin's dark eyes studied Owen. 'You see now the complications. Cynog was not the victim of a jealous lover.'

'I never believed he was.' But Owen had thought him an innocent.

'This is Englishman against Welshman,' said Martin. 'You are vulnerable. Neither side knows whether to trust you.'

'Do you think I do not realise that? I did not choose to become involved in this.'

'I could get you away from here. Back to Lucie and your good life in York.'

'You should want me to stay. Work for Lawgoch, as you do.'

Martin laughed. 'I work for King Charles. If he told me

tomorrow that I should slit Lawgoch's throat—well, I should much regret it, but I doubt I would hesitate.'

'You have met Owain?'

'Several times.'

'Tell me about him. Now, away from Enid and Math.'

Martin glanced at Owen, nodding. 'So. It is not your men who keep you here, it is Lawgoch.'

'Do you question my honour?'

'Not at all.' Martin looked around. 'We cannot talk here. It is too open.'

'Then elsewhere.'

Owen turned his back on Martin, led his horse to a rise in the ground, used it to help himself mount. When he was settled astride, he nodded to Martin, who still stood beside his horse, shaking his head.

Owen turned his horse down the trail towards the farmhouse. 'Come, Martin,' he called, 'lead the way.'

He heard the man mount.

Owen's side felt damp. The bandage meant to hold his arm and shoulder still had begun to unravel. But he had learned something at last.

Martin pressed ahead. In a while he turned off the trail, ducking beneath low branches. Owen thought he could hear rushing water. He followed, clutching his side as he leaned over his saddle. The trees thinned as the sound of the quick stream grew louder. Owen thought it a poor choice for their purpose—no one could hear them, true enough, but neither could they hear anyone approach. But Martin did not stop at the water; he crossed it, rode up a slope to a wooded hillock.

'Here we can watch all sides,' Martin said, dismounting.

Smoke rose from the farmhouse smoke hole. Geese squawked at the three who led their horses from the woods. A man peered out of the barn, withdrew.

'Come with me,' one of the guards ordered Tom. 'Search the barn,' he told his companion.

They were dismounting when a small dog came rushing from the barn, barking.

A woman emerged from the house, shouting something in Welsh. If it was an order for the dog to desist, it did not work. The man now strolled out of the barn. He was young, perhaps Tom's age, but with a patch of white hair over his right ear. He called in Welsh to the woman, who nodded and went back inside.

One of the guards was trying to shake the dog off his boot. The other kept muttering, 'What are they saying?' But neither seemed skilled in Welsh. Neither was Tom. But he did know how to befriend a dog. He squatted, called the dog to him. He did not want her injured by the one guard's increasingly angry kicks. As the dog trotted over to sniff Tom's hand, the two guards moved away. Tom scratched behind the bitch's ears, nodded to the man with the odd hair, who was approaching.

'Do you want to tell me who you are and what you want?' the man asked Tom. In English.

Tom introduced himself as Captain Archer's man, the others as guards from St David's.

The man nodded. 'I am Deri. Cynog's brother. Your captain was here yesterday. Was there something he forgot to ask?'

It seemed the captain and Iolo had left the farm early enough to have reached St David's before the curfew. Tom did not like that news—where were they? The guards had come over to hear the conversation.

'The woman speaks no English?' one of them asked Deri.

'My mam speaks only her own language,' Deri said. 'And my da. I was ruined when I went to sea.'

No wonder he had more confidence than Tom. He had already been to sea. And survived.

'So the captain is gone?'

'He is.'

'We would like to see for ourselves. The barn. The house.'

'Do as you will. I am sure my objection would make no difference to you,' said Deri.

The guards found nothing. But Tom did. In a basket shoved beneath a bench was a muddy, blood-soaked shirt with a familiar bit of mending on the neck. Tom had stitched up that tear for the captain. Back in the woods they had passed over an area where the mud had been churned up and the brush trampled. Had the captain been involved?

'The captain was injured?' Tom asked the woman, forgetting she spoke no English. But surely she would recognise the captain's name. 'Captain Archer's,' he said, holding the shirt out to her. She nodded, pushing it back towards him. Tom thought it meant she wanted him to take it.

He ran with it out to the man, Deri. The guards were talking to him. Tom thrust the bloody shirt in front of Deri's face. 'What happened to the captain?'

Deri wagged his head from side to side, as if so much blood were nothing. 'Ilar bit him,' he said. He nodded towards the dog, who was sitting quietly by his side.

One of the guards laughed.

Deri glanced over at him with a disgusted look, then turned his attention back to Tom. 'Mam cleaned up the captain, gave him one of my shirts.'

Tom did not believe it. The dog was friendly enough if approached in such wise. And the captain knew how to approach a guard dog. Deri grinned, shrugged. But the way he held Tom's gaze made the young man hold his tongue.

Owen sat down beneath the trees. Martin brought a wineskin from his saddle. Enid had filled it with a mixture of herbs and cider, for pain. Owen drank, but very little. He wanted to keep his wits about him.

Martin lowered himself beside Owen, but facing out in the opposite direction. 'What do you know of Yvain de Galles, the princeling who would redeem this country from the English?' He used Owain Lawgoch's French name.

'I know little,' said Owen.

'Yvain is a man of honour. The first time I met him was here, in Wales. His father had died two years earlier, but Yvain had just heard of it and that his lands had been confiscated. He had come from France to petition King Edward to restore his property.'

'Did he win it back?'

'Much of it. He then sold off some woods and was preparing to return to France with his money.'

Owen grunted. 'He wants the money. He is not the hero folk think him.'

'You are wrong. Even a hero needs money to live. When he returned to France he was joined by Ieuan Wyn, another Welshman. Perhaps you have heard of him?'

'You must be mistaken. Ieuan is Lancaster's constable at Beaufort and Nogent.'

Martin laughed. 'No more. Yvain and Ieuan joined Bertrand du Guesclin fighting in Castile—against your duke. Yvain is Llywelyn the Last's grandson, Ieuan is of the family of Llywelyn's seneschal. King Charles likes the echo of the past in their partnership—prince and seneschal once more. It is the sort of echo that the king puts much faith in. And Lancaster's loss. That is also pleasing to him.'

'How did Cynog know where to set the markers?'

'Has anyone in St David's mentioned Hywel?'

'No,' said Owen. 'Why should they? Who is he?'

'The stone markers, those are his doing,' said Martin. 'Your horses—he has them, I am certain.'

'A horse thief?'

'Not a common horse thief. He is what passes for a noble among your people,' Martin said. 'Wealthy, ambitious, generous to those who assist him, ruthless to those who oppose him. He claims to be Yvain's man, recruiting an army to support him when he lands. But Hywel is stealing money for his preparations that should come to me—for the prince. In fact, he fashions himself a prince. Soon he will forget that he meant to support Yvain and claim to be the Redeemer of Wales himself.'

'I should like to talk to Hywel.'

'You do not want to meet him. It is Yvain de Galles you wish to meet. Hywel is not of the same stuff. You may find yourself with a liege lord you would dislike as much as the Duke of Lancaster.'

'I should find it a pleasant change, to fight for my own people.'

'Yvain has allied himself with the French. You lost your eye fighting against them. He may have been in the field against you. Have you thought of that?'

'I asked to talk to Hywel, not to take up arms for Owain Lawgoch.'

Martin laughed. 'Oh, my friend, if you could see your face. You are already imagining heroic deeds that would free your countrymen. Enough of this. You must rest if you are to ride back to St David's in the morning.'

'Ride? You will loan us horses?'

'I would guess you could ride your own horses beyond the wood. I told you—Hywel will have them. My men Deri and Morgan will take you to him.'

'You will not accompany us?'

'I keep my distance from Hywel. We share no love for one another.'

'Then Deri and Morgan shall take me to him.'

Ilar announced their arrival, barking and scampering as if she thought they carried a bowl of meat for her. Deri and Morgan followed, and quickly told them of the visitors.

'Iolo heard their approach before we did. He hid himself well. There were three—two of the bishop's retainers and Tom, your man.' Deri nodded to Owen.

'Young Tom was with the archdeacon's guard?' Owen asked.

'Not willingly,' said Deri. 'He kept his mouth shut to help me in a lie.' He explained what had happened. 'They will ride back slowly, searching for you along the way. I think they expect to find you lying somewhere in the brush overcome by Ilar's vicious attack.'

Enid apologised for not thinking of the shirt. Math fumed about the archdeacon's sending out his men to search for Owen, but never a bother about his son.

'This is all about Cynog,' Owen said, trying to calm him.

'It is about Owain Lawgoch,' Enid said. 'I curse the day I ever heard his name.'

Archdeacon Rokelyn threw Owen's bloodstained shirt on to the table in front of Tom. 'I find your friends asleep on watch, and now this. Where is he? Where is Captain Archer?'

Tom opened and closed his mouth without a sound. He tried again. 'I do not know. As the others said, the captain and Iolo left in time to make it here by curfew last night.'

Rokelyn glanced at the two guards who had ridden with Tom. They nodded.

'Go then. You will find your friends by the palace stables. In one of the horse troughs.'

Hoping to escape quickly, Tom reached for the shirt.

'Leave it!' Rokelyn barked.

'But it is a good shirt,' Tom protested.

'If the captain returns, he may have it back,' the archdeacon said.

Sam awaited him outside the palace gatehouse. 'I have permission to return to the stables with you. Thanks be. I want no more of that man's temper.' He glanced over at the gatekeeper.

'Is it true that Edmund and Jared are in one of the horse troughs?'

'So I hear. They were found asleep on watch, stinking of ale.'

'It is not like them to do such a thing.'

'No,' Sam said, hurrying past the keeper. As soon as they were in the palace courtyard, Sam turned and demanded, 'Whose was the bloody shirt? Where is the captain?'

Tom told him what little he knew.

'Savaged by a dog? Captain Archer?' Sam shook his head.

'I for one do not believe it,' said Tom. 'But the man was relieved that I pretended I did so.'

'Then where is the captain?'

'I do not know. The horses were not there. Nor Iolo. That is all I know.'

The evening shadows chilled the stable yard. The troughs were deserted. Tom and Sam found their comrades snoring in a corner of the stables, blankets wrapped round them, their clothes draped over a line, drying. Someone had been kind.

Sam, whose mother was a midwife, knelt, smelled the breath of each.

He waved Tom over. 'Smell them.'

Tom knelt beside him. Sniffed. 'Bitter,' he said.

'Aye. They drank more than simple ale. A sleep draught, I think.'

Tom wished the captain were here. 'The captain would warn the men who guard Piers the Mariner now.'

'Aye, he would do that.'

'Then we must.'

Tom had a queasy feeling in his stomach as he ran across the yard, but he tried to ignore it. Sam led the way, taking the steps of the bishop's porch two at a time. The porter barred their way.

'Has the archdeacon ordered you in? I was not told if he has.'

'We need to warn the guards,' said Tom.

The porter shook his head. 'You must speak to the archdeacon.'

'That will take too much time, man!' Sam cried.

'I have my orders.' The porter stood firm.

13

PUZZLES

The old, rickety donkey cart wheezed and rumbled along the track. Magda Digby dozed in the sunlight on the seat beside Matthew the Tinker, smiling to herself each time he reached over to make sure she was not slipping off. It was always a pleasure when a patient still valued her after a particularly painful treatment, and his tooth, for all its rot, had been very stubborn about coming out. Magda snorted awake as Matthew brought the cart to a halt in front of a damaged gatehouse.

'We have arrived at Freythorpe Hadden,' said the tinker. 'They had a terrible fire in the gatehouse. Outlaws set it.'

The sun shone through holes in the roof and lit up a crumbling side. Several men climbed about with hooks, tearing down blackened thatch and sooty walls.

'Outlaws?' Magda wondered what they had thought to gain by such destruction. The stone manor house was intact. And the stone and timber stables.

'Mistress Wilton will be glad to hear they have begun repairs,' said Matthew.

A man emerged from the shadowy archway of the gatehouse, shaded his eyes to look their way, then turned and ran back towards the stables opposite the manor house.

Magda was not eager for trouble, but it boded well for Lucie's property that the approach of strangers had been noted. 'The borrowed steward set a watch, begins the repairs. Perhaps he is wise.' Magda wondered at how little Lucie had said about this. *Damage to the gatehouse*, she had said, and *my aunt's favourite tapestry stolen*. Some silver plate, some money. The gatehouse was not so precious to her as the tapestry. But such destruction must have made cold her heart. She did not like that Lucie had not wished to talk of it.

'I am not easy about being looked on as a dangerous intruder. But it is wise to set a watch,' said Matthew. 'The men might return.'

'In a creaky donkey cart?'

Magda's barking laugh startled the tinker into laughing also. 'Outlaws with a herald,' he muttered, wiping his eyes, then grabbing at his jaw as the pain returned.

'Magda begs thy pardon. She forgot thy tooth.'

'A good laugh is worth the pain,' Matthew said.

He was a wise man to know that. Magda climbed out of the cart, retrieved her pouch from the back. 'Thou hast been kind.' She squinted up at the tinker's swollen cheek. 'Without the rotted tooth the swelling will ease. Remember to let the brandywine Magda gave thee sit in thy mouth before swallowing it.'

Matthew nodded. 'God go with you, Riverwoman.'

'Thou art not selling thy wares at Freythorpe Hadden?'

'I do not bother folk who have had such troubles.'

'They must live.'

'I do not want trouble.' His eyes were on something behind Magda.

'Then be off,' Magda said.

She turned round. A fair-haired man approached, striding with authority. Two others followed close. 'Harold Galfrey?' Magda shouted over the noise of Matthew's cart loudly rumbling behind her.

The leading man nodded as he reached her. He squinted— against the sun, but Magda took him as a man who narrowed his eyes to hide his thoughts. 'Who are you? Why has the tinker left you here?' Harold demanded.

One of the men said, 'This is Magda Digby, the Riverwoman. She is a healer.'

Magda dusted off the pack she carried. 'Mistress Wilton worries about the wounded steward. Thou canst take Magda to him.'

'And the tinker?'

'Didst thou not see him depart?'

'He does not wish to barter here?'

'Magda took him out of his way. How fares Daimon?'

'Come within and you will see.'

Magda stepped into the hall. Tildy set down a pan she had been carrying and hurried to greet the newcomer, her face anxious. 'God bless you for coming, Mistress Digby.' The young woman's eyes were shadowed and red from lack of sleep. Her throat was tight as she spoke.

'He is not as thou wouldst wish, then?' Magda said.

'He sleeps most of the time and when he wakes he cannot speak clearly.'

'How long has he been so?'

'A day. Perhaps a little more. It has been gradual. He was doing well, then he began to fail.'

On a pallet near the hearth—for so it was a hearth and not a fire circle in this fine hall—lay the poor young man, sweating and restless. He tried his best to focus on Magda, blinking, shaking his head.

'Daimon, God has sent us Magda Digby,' Tildy said softly.

'Lucie Wilton sent Magda,' corrected the Riverwoman as she lifted the bandage wrapped round Daimon's head to examine the wound. 'Thou hast cleaned it well,' she said to Tildy, who hovered at her back. Magda lifted the wounded hand, unwrapped the bandage. 'Canst thou make a fist?' Magda asked Daimon. He did so slowly, weakly, wincing as he opened his hand once more. 'It will heal. Slowly. Tildy has done well.' She wrapped his hand once more, pulled down the blanket, gently felt round the young steward's swollen shoulder. 'Thou hast rubbed in the oil steeped with comfrey, gently but deeply?' Magda asked Tildy.

'I tried.'

'And he moaned or pulled away, worrying thee.' Magda smiled at her. 'Thou must be more confident.'

Magda leaned close, smelled Daimon's sweat. She covered him, took Tildy's elbow, steered her away from Daimon's pallet. 'Thou hast been too generous with the physicks.'

Tildy looked stricken. 'I have followed Mistress Wilton's instructions.'

Magda shook her head. 'His sweat stinks of the physicks. Thou mayest have followed in full measure and Daimon cannot take what others do. After Magda drinks something, eats something, she will tell thee what to give him and how much.' She put a finger to Tildy's lips as the young woman began to apologise for not serving her sooner. 'Thou art not Magda's servant. She can ask for what she needs.'

Tildy called for a servant and bustled her out to the kitchens, following close behind.

Magda settled into a high-backed chair by the fire, tucked a pillow behind her back that she had spied on a bench, and lifted her feet on to a stool she had dragged over for the purpose. She was beginning to nod when Tildy returned with stewed fruit, cheese and bread. A servant followed with a flagon of wine.

When the servant had gone, Tildy crouched down beside Magda, her pretty face knitted into a mask of worry. 'I watched Mistress Wilton carefully,' she whispered, 'and I am certain I have given Daimon the same amounts of the physicks.'

'Cease thy fretting. Mayhap his body endured it for a time.'

'Could too much of the physick kill him?'

The last two words were spoken so softly that Magda did not think she would have understood had she not been watching Tildy's lips.

'Aye, as is ever true, many a medicine is also a poison. But thou hast not killed him.'

'Not me. I am sure of it. But there is one here who might be pleased to be rid of Daimon.'

'An enemy?'

'A rival. What think you of Master Galfrey?'

'The borrowed steward? Thou shouldst call him Harold. He is not thy master.'

'But what did you think of him?'

The subject of their hushed conversation had just entered the hall. 'Magda thanks thee for the food,' she said loudly. 'Thou mightst bring a cup for Master Galfrey. Mistress Wilton will wish to hear his report when Magda returns.'

Tildy rose slowly, turned and greeted the steward by his given name.

Harold hesitated, then bowed to her. Turning to Magda, he said, 'I pray you pardon me for my earlier behaviour.'

Tildy, looking pale, took the opportunity to withdraw. Magda made note of her departure as she waved away Harold's apology. 'Thou art cautious, with reason.'

He made himself comfortable near her, looking quite at home.

'Thou hast begun the repairs on the gatehouse,' Magda noted. 'There was much damage?'

He nodded to the servant who brought another cup, rose to pour himself some wine, then held it up to Magda as if toasting. He took a drink, put the cup aside. 'I thought it best to begin repairs at once, while God blesses us with dry weather. All the roof must be replaced. And the crumbled wall rebuilt, the other walls patched. And most of the boards on the upper floor were damaged from either fire or water.'

'The rain will return before thou canst complete so much work.'

'We can do no more than try, and pray that God has pity on us.'

'Thou wouldst do better to find a way to protect thy work than to pray.'

Harold frowned, seemed about to say something, then threw his head back and laughed. Magda watched his movements as he took a long drink, emptying his cup. She noticed how closely he observed her and averted his eyes, then met hers with an expression much like that of a child who means to show an adult that he is not bothered by their criticism. And why would he not feel so after greeting her so boorishly? 'How is Daimon?' he asked abruptly.

Magda wagged her head from side to side. 'He will mend. Too much physick steals his wit and makes him sleep. Magda will see how he fares on less.'

'Poor Tildy. She loves him, you know.'

Magda studied the tanned face. The lines round his mouth said he frowned more often than he smiled. 'Magda did not suggest Tildy was to blame.'

'I did not mean to imply that she was. Merely that she suffers with him.' Harold stared into the fire, pressing his palms into his knees, as if soothing them.

'Do thy knees ail thee?'

'They ache. I am not accustomed to so much physical work. A steward sits, walks, rides. I cannot remember ever crawling about in damp ashes. But I had to see the extent of the damage'

'Thou art thorough. Magda will give thee something to ease the ache.'

'God bless you for that, Goodwife Digby. What of Daimon? You said he had too much physick, yet Tildy is not to blame.'

'One cup of wine can put some men to sleep. Physicks are the same.'

'Ah. He is a fortunate young man, to have Mistress Wilton send you to check on his care.' Harold rose. 'Will you be staying the night?'

'One or two nights. Until Daimon improves.'

'We shall all be the better for it. Forgive my abrupt departure, but I have much to do.'

'Before the rain. Aye.' Magda considered the man as he walked away. He was courteous enough to her, but he was the sort might be a stern steward. Mayhap that was the cause of Tildy's dislike. Or was there more to it?

As Lucie walked down Stonegate on her way to the Archdeacon of York's house she imagined eyes upon her, folk peering from behind the shutters, glancing at her as they walked by, all wondering whether she was the deserted wife of a traitor. Never had she felt so solitary in this city. Who were her friends, who her enemies? She also worried about Phillippa. If she were to begin fretting about

Freythorpe again this evening, would Kate have the sense to send for Bess to help calm her?

Lucie was plagued with misgivings about dining at the archdeacon's house. She hoped to speak with Michaelo. And she dreaded it. What if Owen had been drawn to Owain Lawgoch's scheme? What then? Would he resent his ties to York? His English wife? Was that possible? She needed him here, where his touch, his voice, would reveal his heart. But what if he did not return? She slowed as she reached Jehannes's house and almost turned back. But surely Brother Michaelo would have told her if he had any hint that Owen would not return. He seemed to respect her anew, as Sir Robert's daughter. It was enough to propel her forward.

Archdeacon Jehannes greeted Lucie warmly, welcoming her to his house. 'This is such a pleasure.' The broad smile that lit up his ever youthful face attested to his sincerity. 'You are so busy with the children and the shop, I cannot remember the last time you graced my home.'

Archbishop Thoresby rose from an ornate, throne-like chair that seemed out of place in the simply furnished room. His deep-set eyes looked sunken, his complexion pale.

'Your Grace,' Lucie said, curtsying.

Thoresby raised his hand and blessed her. She kissed his ring. His hand shook slightly. He was not young, nor had he been in the best of health the past year. His frailness made Lucie uneasy. If Owen had done anything to fuel the rumours, he would need a man of power to defend him. But if His Grace was ailing…

Jehannes motioned to a servant to bring her a cup of wine.

'How fare my godchildren?' Thoresby asked.

'Thriving. Missing their father.'

'If God hears my prayers Archer is on his way to York. Or will be very soon.'

'I am so grateful to you for sending a messenger.'

'I sent him before your troubles. So do not thank me. I want Archer back here, seeing to my business, not that of the Bishop of St David's.'

Lucie glanced round the room. 'Will Brother Michaelo be joining us?'

'He is fasting,' said Jehannes.

'He was much moved by your father's vision at St Non's holy well,' said Thoresby. 'It may yet redeem him.'

'You wished to speak with him?' Jehannes asked, always the solicitous and perceptive host.

'Yes. I had questions...' she trailed off, not wishing to explain, not wishing to lie. And should she disturb Michaelo during a fast?

Thoresby harrumphed. 'Is this about the rumours questioning Archer's allegiance? They are nonsense. I do not make such errors about whom I trust.'

Lucie felt Jehannes watching her. She had hoped to hide her anxiety fearing it revealed disloyal doubts about Owen. But it seemed these two knew her too well. 'Had one or two people with cause to be curious heard the rumour I might not be worried. But it has spread so quickly.'

'The merchants are worried about the French threat along the southern coast,' said Jehannes. 'The career of Owain Lawgoch is of concern to them.'

'But why should Owen be suspected?'

Thoresby made an impatient gesture. 'In faith, my gentle lady, you cannot believe this rumour began innocently. Someone expects to benefit from spreading it. You are right to worry about that.'

'Perhaps it would be best for you to speak with Brother Michaelo,' said Jehannes.

Thoresby agreed and called a servant to escort her to Michaelo.

The servant led Lucie to a door, then withdrew. Lucie was evidently to knock for herself. Michaelo responded to her timid tap with a curt, 'Come!' She took a deep breath and pushed open the door. It was a tiny, windowless room, lit by an oil lamp. The monk knelt on a *prie-dieu* set before a plain wooden cross, his head bowed. A leather scourge lay beside him. The room was otherwise bare.

'Brother Michaelo?'

His head jerked up, as if she had awakened him. 'Mistress

Wilton. *Benedicte.*' He rose stiffly.

'Forgive me for disturbing you.'

'You are welcome, Mistress Wilton.' Michaelo's face was haggard, but his eyes were peaceful. 'How might I be of assistance?'

'I had hoped— I do not wish to trouble you with more questions, but something has happened and you are the only one who might help me.'

'What is it?'

'I have heard rumours about my husband—' Her voice broke. 'I prayed you would not hear them.'

'I beg you, Brother Michaelo, tell me whether there is any truth in them.' Her legs shook from the effort to keep her voice steady.

'Come. Let us go out to the garden.'

The evening sky was still blue though the garden was in shadows, its colours softened to shades of grey. It was small, but a low stone wall invited them to sit.

The brief walk and the fresh air had helped Lucie regain her composure. 'Owen wrote that it was difficult, returning to his country. Painful.'

'It seemed so for him. But those emotions do not make him a traitor.'

'What is it you do not wish to tell me?'

Michaelo bowed to her. 'You are your father's daughter. He also saw through me.'

'As my father's daughter I ask you to be plain with me.'

'The captain complained,' Michaelo began, 'not about his people, but about how we English treat them. We allow them no dignity. We assume they are inferior, dull-witted, and yet we also call them treacherous.'

'My husband spoke openly about this?'

'His feelings were sometimes clear, though he spoke of it only to our party, Master Chaucer, Sir Robert…'

'How did my father receive it?'

'He worried about it. Reminded the captain of his duty.'

'Do you think my husband might be tempted by this Owain

Lawgoch?' Lucie whispered the question.

'Your husband is not a traitor,' said Michaelo firmly. 'He made certain of the garrison at Cydweli and he brought to justice a man who was traitor to our King.'

Lucie found comfort in that. 'He wrote that an old friend assisted him in his work. He said you might tell me who it was.'

Michaelo lowered his head.

Lucie felt her stomach clench. It was as she had feared—Owen did not name him in case the letters were read by the wrong person. 'Who was it?'

'Martin Wirthir.'

Lucie crossed herself. 'Thanks be to God.' Not someone who might speak treason, but a pirate. 'You have set my mind at ease.'

Michaelo made an odd sound in his throat and pressed his hands to his forehead. 'Wirthir is at present an agent of the French king. And he is in Wales collecting money for Owain Lawgoch.'

'Sweet heaven.'

'But to my knowledge they joined together solely for the sake of catching the murderer. Wirthir has no personal allegiance.'

'Are you sure of that?'

Michaelo turned to her. 'Mistress Wilton, your father walked in God's grace in St David's. When Sir Robert ceased worrying about the captain, so, too, did I. Hearing the rumours yesterday, I fell into doubt. But today, with much prayer and fasting, I see all more clearly. And I say the captain is no traitor. Your father knew he was not.'

By the light in the monk's eyes and the strength in his voice, Lucie was drawn to bow her head and ask for his blessing.

'My lady, I am not worthy of the honour you pay me.'

'Praying, fasting, scourging, your kindness to my father—what more could God ask of you?'

'I am uncertain whether I do this for God or for myself.' But he made the sign of the cross over her and blessed her.

When Lucie joined Thoresby and Jehannes they were standing by the table discussing plans for the Lammas Day Fair.

Thoresby studied her as she approached, his shadowed eyes

unreadable. 'You look solemn, Mistress Wilton. Michaelo was unable to reassure you?'

'He was most kind, Your Grace. And he seems convinced of my husband's innocence.'

'Excellent.'

Jehannes smiled, motioned to the servants to bring on the food. 'Come, my guests, let us fortify ourselves with my cook's stuffed chicken.'

Afterwards, Lucie had difficulty remembering the conversation at the table, so much of her consciousness being occupied going over and over her brief conversation with Michaelo. He was so confident that Sir Robert had seen into Owen's heart. Why was Lucie more uncertain than ever? Was it Martin Wirthir? He was a charming, persuasive man. Might he not convince Owen that his countrymen needed him? But Owen had never agreed with Martin's ethics. He would do nothing on only Martin's word. And, truly, Martin did not seem a man to commit to any cause. Was it Michaelo's description of the treatment of the Welsh that troubled her? How could any man bear it, much less Owen, who was not one to turn away, to run from that which angered him?

Thoresby had noted her preoccupation, drawn her out with questions about the raid on Freythorpe.

Late that night, when Lucie woke after a brief sleep, her thoughts returned to her conversation with the archbishop. He had not been impressed with her recounting of Harold's deeds after the raid. 'I am glad he was of assistance. But he might have a motive other than goodwill.' Thoresby had not suggested what that motive might be.

Lucie could think of none. She was tired of all the men taking her for such a fool. Even Jasper, young as he was. Why did they all mistrust those who gave her succour?

But what of Owen? How could she know his heart? His letters. She had read them quickly, looking for news of her father. Perhaps she might glean something from his letters. She rose, tiptoeing across the room, hoping not to wake Phillippa, who had rested peacefully through the evening and into the night.

'Lucie?' Phillippa sat up, clutching the bedclothes to her.

Lucie silently cursed, but went to Phillippa and smoothed the hair that had escaped her white cap. 'Go back to sleep. It is the middle of the night.'

'Why do you wake?'

Phillippa sounded calm. The sleep had helped.

'I ate too much, drank too much wine. I thought to reread Owen's letters. When I read his words, I can imagine his voice.'

Phillippa sat up straighter. 'Do you understand everything that you read?'

'I understand the words. But sometimes the meaning is hidden from me.'

'Do all who read understand the words?'

'If they read well, yes. Is there something you wish me to read for you?'

'No.'

'Then go back to sleep. It is the middle of the night.'

As Lucie began to rise, Phillippa touched her arm.

'There is something.' Her face was in shadow. There was little light coming from the window. But Lucie sensed her agitation. 'I must know what the parchment says. I must know if this is all because of my weakness.'

'What parchment?'

'My husband, John, called it his, but it had been entrusted to him. Not given to him to keep. He died so soon afterwards. So young. He was not a good man. And yet I loved him.' She dabbed her eyes with the bedclothes.

It was the most Phillippa had ever said to Lucie about her husband.

'Where is this parchment?'

'At the manor.'

'No one told you what it said?'

'I have never shown it to anyone but my brother, who said I need not know and need not worry. But I have worried. It was not drink that ruined my John, you know. That is what my brother thought, but that is not true. John was bitter. His family had lost their home in the Scots raids. And no one cared. Not the king, not the archbishop. No one.'

'What do you think is in the parchment?'

'John's father died of grief. All that he had left John, gone. So quickly. There was still land, but so much had burned. The livestock, the house, all gone.' Phillippa sighed. 'His mother died soon after. I do not remember how. Was she ill?'

'Aunt Phillippa, what of the parchment?'

Phillippa looked up at Lucie. Touched her chin. 'You are stronger than your mother. All will be well.' She lay back down.

'You wanted me to read something for you.'

'I do not know where it is.'

Lucie did not remember any mysterious parchment. Might it have been kept in the treasury? But she had recently searched that. As far as she could tell, the thieves had taken only money—and perhaps an account book. She had forgotten about that. She could not remember the years it had covered, but it was not a recent one. Could a parchment have been hidden in it?

'Where did you keep it?' Lucie asked.

'Many places,' Phillippa said sleepily. 'Too many places. I have brought this trouble on our house. I am too old to be of use.' She began to weep.

Lucie put her arm round her and stroked her forehead gently, as she did for her children when they woke in the night.

14

A SPY FOR THE REDEEMER

Tom and Sam were turned away at Archdeacon Rokelyn's door. At the palace gate they asked to speak with the captain of the guard. The gatekeeper said the captain might be found dining with his men. But he was not, and Tom and Sam did not know whom else to trust. Despondent, they shuffled down to the table set aside for pilgrims' retainers and ate their meal in silence. Afterwards, they returned to the stables. Exhausted by the day's long ride, Tom quickly fell asleep.

But his stomach woke him before dawn. The sleeping accommodations in the stable were far more crowded than in the great hall of the palace. Tom picked his way through the prostrate forms with care, his gut burning. He had a terrible thirst, too, but he dared not quench it before reaching the privy, for fear his stomach would explode. He carried a jug of water with him.

So it was that he sat on the privy flushing himself out for quite a while. Long enough to be joined by a guard who wished to gossip as he sat beside Tom. Most of the guard's chatter signified little to Tom, but one item caught his attention—Piers the Mariner had disappeared during the night. His guard had been found asleep outside Piers's cell, stinking of ale. Tom's privy companion had been awakened by his captain to search the stables.

Tom's stomach burned anew. The escape might have been prevented had the porter at the east wing permitted Tom and Sam to warn the guard last night. Why was God playing such games with them?

By the time Tom returned to his companions, Jared and Edmund were awake and complaining of thirst. Sam had wandered off to learn more about the search.

'I do not want the captain to see me like this,' Edmund groaned. His complexion was mottled like mouldy cheese.

'You need not worry,' Tom said, 'he is not in the city. Who did this to you?'

'Did what?' Jared's hair stood on end and his eyes were crusty.

'How could we know her ale would be so strong?' Edmund whined weakly as he pressed his temples. 'I did not think it possible to fell Jared with one tankard.'

'Whose ale?'

'Glynis. Piers's woman. She brought ale for him and shared some with us. She is a good woman.'

'Good at making fools of you,' Tom said.

'But he did not escape on our watch,' Edmund said.

'Aye,' Jared agreed. 'We might have been wrong to drink that woman's ale, but at least we did no harm.'

'I cannot believe you trusted her,' Tom said.

Jared had been examining his swollen finger, but now he rose to confront Tom, who backed away from the tall man, though not far. 'I would like to see you stand for half a day in a dark, damp cellar listening to water drip and feeling your joints stiffen, your nose grow numb. And then a pretty woman comes along with good ale and offers you a generous tankard of it. You would not say no to that.'

Tom thought he would, but he let it go. 'What was she doing down there?' he asked.

'Seeing her man,' Jared said. 'What else?'

'He was allowed visitors?' Tom thought that strange.

'We thought he must have been,' Edmund said. 'How else would she have appeared there, in the dungeon of the bishop's wing of the palace?'

Sam had quietly joined them. 'I have heard talk in the kitchen that the undercrofts are not watched closely unless the bishop is here.'

Jared looked at Sam. 'I had not heard that.'

'You prick your ears at the wrong gossip.'

'Why am I the goat this morning?'

'Calm yourself, Jared. No one called you a goat,' said Edmund, always even-humoured. 'We should go to the archdeacon. Tell him what she did.'

'He will not believe us,' Jared said.

'We tried last night, but he would not see us,' said Sam. 'Nor were we permitted to go down to the guard who had relieved you.'

'Have they found Piers?' Tom asked Sam.

'No. Not a sign of him anywhere.'

The four men rode out from the farm on three horses, Iolo and Deri sharing one, in early morning. Morgan led the way through the wood.

Owen did not know what he had expected, a lodge in the woods, a cottage, a hut. Not a colourful tent set up in the middle of a glade, opened to reveal a table and a man sitting at one end, his feet propped up on the edge. A half-dozen men stood before the tent, hands on swords and daggers, silently watching the four who approached. Apparently seeing no immediate threat, the man in the tent signalled to the others to hold off attack. Morgan and Deri each had an arm and shoulder occupied supporting Iolo, who had not the use of either hand. Only Owen might easily draw a weapon—but what was one against seven?

The man slid his feet off the table, stood and stepped out from the shadows of the tent. 'Captain Archer,' he said with a little bow, speaking Welsh, 'we have expected you.'

He was dressed in soft leather from head to toe, well-fitted leather that showed off a muscular build. His hair was a dark, curly halo round his head. His complexion was pale against the black hair, his eyes narrow and dark, his nose and mouth elegantly slender. Owen stood at least a head taller, but he guessed they would tip the scales alike. A man who made much of his hair and physique. Owen thought of a cat arching and fluffing his fur to impress a potential challenger. This must be Hywel. The other men had weathered faces, mud-splattered tunics and leggings.

'Bring the horse thieves to me,' Hywel shouted to the men on his left. His voice was as deep as his chest was broad. The three men disappeared round the back of the tent. Now Hywel turned to the newcomers. 'They were not to injure you or your man, Captain. Come, sit at my table, rest yourselves. You have suffered enough.'

'You would be Hywel?' Owen said.

The leather-clad man dipped his head in a gesture part bow, part nod. 'You are well informed.'

'Not as well as I thought I was.' Owen looked round for trouble as he entered the tent. A servant stood in the far corner. Otherwise the tent was empty but for the table, set with wine and cups. 'You did expect us,' Owen said, taking a seat facing the opening. A tournament tent, he guessed. Who was this Hywel to sit in such a tent, entertaining visitors? Morgan and Deri helped Iolo on to the nearest bench, then withdrew to stand warily in the doorway, arms crossed.

Hywel walked over, eyed them up and down. 'Wirthir's men.'

'They are,' said Owen.

'Serving the French king,' Hywel said.

'Nay,' Morgan protested, 'we serve Owain, rightful Prince of Wales.'

'Whom do you serve?' Owen asked Hywel.

The man bowed slightly. 'I, too, serve Owain Lawgoch. I am gathering an army to support my prince's coming.' He joined Owen and Iolo at the table, motioned to his servant to pour wine. 'Why is Wirthir not with you?' Hywel asked as he leaned back, cup in hand, and propped up his feet once more.

'I cannot answer for him,' Owen said. He had noted the men in the clearing. None seemed familiar. He had not seen much of his attackers, but one had been larger than any of these. 'You mentioned the men who attacked us and stole our horses. They were your men?'

'My horse thieves. Not my fighters.'

'They were not aware of the difference.'

'They will be taught.'

'You did not steal the horses of the archdeacon's men who followed us.'

'We had called enough attention to ourselves.'

'What else did you intend, besides stealing our horses? Was the attack a warning?'

'We wanted the horses. That is all. You are a worthy man from all accounts, Captain, but the prince has more need of the horses than you do.'

'That might have been true before the attack. Now we must needs ride.'

'For that I am sorry. Our people have suffered enough under the hands of the English. My prince would not thank me for the incident.'

'You could sell your fine leather garments and raise money for horseflesh.'

Hywel laughed. 'A leader of men must look the part.'

'We want our horses,' Iolo said.

'*Your* horses?' Hywel feigned puzzlement. 'I thought they were Bishop Houghton's, not the Duke of Lancaster's.'

Iolo growled.

'My companion is in pain, which makes him impatient with clever talk,' said Owen.

There was a stir at the tent entrance, men's voices, Morgan and Deri standing ground.

'Let my men pass,' Hywel ordered, dropping his feet, sitting straight.

Morgan and Deri stood aside as three men were pushed into the tent, hands bound behind them. One of them was almost as wide as he was tall.

'Here are your attackers,' said Hywel to Iolo. 'What would you have me do with them?'

Bruised and swollen faces, limping walks and the stench of fear—it was plain to Owen the men had already been beaten. Iolo must have thought so, too.

'There is no pleasure in watching you beat them,' said Iolo. 'I want the satisfaction of doing it myself.'

'With that injured foot, how would you lunge and parry? It is not in a man's nature to stand still for a beating. Would you like them held for you?' Hywel's tone was sincere.

Iolo turned his head in disgust.

Hywel shook his head, turned to Owen. 'What would *you* have me do?'

'We followed your orders,' one of the bound men said thickly.

Hywel showed no sign of having heard.

'Is this how you treat those who would serve you?' Owen asked.

'When they purposefully misunderstand orders,' said Hywel. 'In battle they would endanger their fellows. In truth, what would you have me do with them?'

'That is your decision. They are yours to discipline,' said Owen. 'For me, I would have your honesty. I would hear why you ordered the attack. Then I would like to hear what you know about Cynog's murder.'

'Take the thieves away,' Hywel said to his men. 'You and the others, return to your posts. Give the stolen horses to Wirthir's men. Go and attend your horses,' he said to Morgan and Deri.

The two began to protest. Owen nodded to them to go.

Hywel resumed his seat at the head of the table, propped up his feet once more. The servant refilled the cups. It was good wine, better than Owen had tasted since he dined with Bishop Houghton. He wondered whether this, too, had been stolen.

'It is true that they were not to injure you,' said Hywel. 'You were to walk back to St David's.'

'Why?'

'I do need the horses for the prince's infantry.'

'And?'

Hywel put down his cup, leaned his elbows on the table, hands steepled before him. 'A man like you—Welsh, English, you are dangerous.' His voice was hushed. 'The people trust you. They talk to you.'

'Oh, aye? Not of late.' Owen sat back, resisting the gesture to speak confidentially.'

Hywel nodded to himself. 'That is the archdeacon's fault, not your own. Glynis told me about you. You have been ill used by Adam Rokelyn.'

'When did you speak to Glynis?' Owen could not hide his interest.

Hywel ran his hands through his coarse hair, sat back, crossed his arms, studied Owen, then looked away as if deep in thought. Without turning back to Owen, he asked softly, 'What is your interest in Glynis?'

'I wished to speak with her.'

'Why?' Now Hywel returned Owen's gaze.

'It was you who mentioned her,' said Owen. 'Why now this riddling?'

'I feel responsible for her.'

'One of her lovers is accused of murdering the other. She might have much to say.'

'Does Rokelyn want her? Does he require two in the bishop's dungeon?'

Owen saw that they thought much alike, but Hywel did not see that. 'I am not your enemy,' Owen said.

'No? How do I know that?'

'I am looking for the murderer of one of your men.'

'Cynog?' Hywel sighed, shook his head sadly. 'God granted him a wondrous gift. They tell me he was carving a tomb for your wife's father.'

'Aye, he was.'

Hywel tilted his head back, gazed up at the top of the tent. 'Wirthir's recommendation?'

'You know much.'

'So does Wirthir.' He sat up suddenly. 'Now there is a man dangerous to the prince's cause.'

'You are mistaken. He is working for Owain Lawgoch.'

Hywel laughed. 'He is working for the French king. You know it, we all do. If King Charles turns on Owain Lawgoch, so will Wirthir.'

'Martin is not King Charles's man.'

'He is no one's, I know. Hence the danger. What he learns today about our cause he may use against us tomorrow.'

Owen could not deny that.

Hywel, ever restless, stood now with one foot on his chair, an elbow resting on his thigh. 'What about you, Captain Archer? Your work for the Duke of Lancaster is finished. Whom are you presently serving?'

'The Archdeacon of St David's, as you know. He has delayed my departure.'

'With Captain Siencyn, yes. Adam Rokelyn is enjoying his power, ordering you about. But do you wish to leave? Is this not your country, your people? Surely you do not prefer the English to us?'

'My family is in England.'

'So Cynog told me.'

'What are you suggesting?'

'Join me. For a while. You have been away so long, a few months longer would go unnoticed by most.'

'But the duke, the archbishop—'

Hywel held out a hand, silencing Owen. 'What I want is your help in preparing an army to support Owain, Prince of Wales. Train his archers. Teach his men what you have learned in service with the duke and the archbishop. Redeem yourself. Redeem your people.'

'Is my wife to worry that I have deserted her? I will not do that to her.'

'Would your wife deny you this? Spy for your people, train archers for them, not the English who despise us.'

Owen fought to sound indifferent. 'I know nothing of you, little enough about Owain. Yvain de Galles the French call him. Is he Welsh? Or is he now a Gaul?'

'Many Welshmen find respect fighting in the free companies across the Channel. Owain will bring many of them with him. Trained soldiers.'

'Then you do not need me.'

'Come now, Owen Archer. The great bard Dafydd ap Gwilym has told me of your remarkable skill.'

'He saw one performance.'

'He is a fine judge of heroes, Captain. He has met his share. But you must of course take your time, consider my proposal. Meanwhile, in exchange for your horses—'

'We owe you nothing,' Iolo said.

Hywel feigned surprise. 'I have groomed them, fed them. I ask you to deliver a letter for me. A simple task. The recipient is a pilgrim at St David's.'

'You are not so far from the city,' said Owen. 'Surely you might deliver it?'

Hywel laughed. 'You suggest that a known commander of Owain's supporters should openly ride into St David's? The English consider me a traitor to their king. Houghton is lord in St David's and he is English.'

'One of your men might go.'

'It is such a small thing I ask of you.'

It was Owen's turn to laugh. 'At this moment I am in pain caused by your men. Iolo cannot walk. And you ask for a favour.' He shook his head as if disbelieving. In truth he was delaying.

Hywel dropped back down into the chair, folding his arms. 'If you deliver the letter, I shall find passage for you. To England.'

'You no longer wish to persuade me to stay?'

'A generous commander never lacks men. You may change your mind. Return with your wife and children. I shall be here.'

This was the way a commander should behave. Despite his own injuries, Owen admired the man.

'Well?' Hywel drew a small parchment from a pouch sitting on the table. 'As you see, it will not encumber you. Griffith of Anglesey would be most grateful. As would I.'

'If it is so small a thing to ask, why would you be so grateful you would arrange passage for me?'

Hywel chuckled. 'You catch me at every turn. I can see you make an excellent spy. A spy for Owain, Prince of Wales. What could be a more honourable use of your skills?'

Did the man know the questions in his heart? Owen hesitated.

What would that be like, to turn what he had learned in the service of the archbishop to such a purpose?

Hywel saw his hesitation. 'You asked how you might show you are not my enemy. Carry this letter.'

Owen said nothing.

'Glynis is well, by the way.'

'She came to you?' Owen asked.

Hywel nodded. 'She began to fear Piers the Mariner and his brother. With cause. I have no doubt that Piers hanged Cynog.'

'What cause had he to take the man's life? And in such wise?'

'Ask him.' Hywel held out the letter once more. 'Will you take it?'

'Why did Glynis fear him?'

'Is it not plain? He is a violent man, Captain. So is Siencyn.'

Iolo sighed loudly. 'If we tarry much longer, we shall miss the curfew at St David's. We cannot ride fast.'

Hywel still held out the letter.

'If you arrange passage, how should I hear of it?' Owen asked.

'I shall find a way to inform you. I give you my word.' Hywel placed the letter on the table by Owen's hands.

Owen nodded, tucked it into the top winding of the bandage beneath his tunic. 'Iolo will need assistance to his horse.'

Hywel called for his men.

'I hope to have the honour one day soon of introducing you to Owain Lawgoch,' Hywel said as Owen rose.

'We shall see.' Owen bowed to him and left the tent.

'Griffith of Anglesey,' Hywel called after him. 'A large man with a red beard.'

Owen heard, but did not acknowledge it. He expected Griffith would find him.

At the edge of the wood, Morgan and Deri took the extra horse and left Owen and Iolo. Until Wirthir's men were out of sight, Owen sat his horse silently. Then he dismounted, pulled the rolled parchment from his tunic. A simple seal, wax on a string. With some heat, easily resealed.

'You will read it?' Iolo asked from his saddle.

'I think it wise.' The parchment was filthy, often used. Owen slipped his dagger beneath the seal. The writing surface had been scraped so often it had a sheen. Was it the condition of the parchment, or was it the nonsense that it looked? Long, curving lines, squiggles, splotches. No words, no signature. 'He has fooled me. Why?'

'I thought it strange he gave it to you.'

'But what is his game?' Owen studied it, turning it this way and that, certain it must have a purpose. 'By the Rood, it is a map.'

Iolo grabbed it, turned it about in his hands, passed it back to Owen. 'A map of what?'

'Hywel's markers? Safe havens? Guard posts?'

'Where?'

Owen stared at the map. 'I cannot make it out. I hoped that you might, being from this part of the country.'

Iolo shook his head.

Owen was disappointed, but that seemed to be his lot of late. 'It goes to a man from Anglesey. Most like it is Anglesey. It has been cleverly done, an area small enough that eyes not meant to see it can find no telling boundaries, shorelines. Hywel knows what he is about. There is no doubt of that.' He tucked it beneath his tunic.

'It is a dangerous favour you do for Hywel, carrying this map to a stranger in the city.'

'Aye.'

'I am sorry I called you a shopkeeper.'

'Come. We must make Bonning's Gate before curfew.'

15

HIGH AND MIGHTIES

Lucie and Jasper worked quietly side by side in the shop storeroom, sewing up linen envelopes of calming herbs—lady's bedstraw, valerian, camomile, with lavender for a soothing scent, and others of healing herbs for abrasions—one with marshmallow root and comfrey, one with marigold flowers and woundwort. It was a good rainy morning activity, when they would not be tempted to open the door and invite disaster with an errant draft. Wind blew the rain against the waxed parchment window in an uneven rhythm, now hard, now soft; wind kept it thrumming. Every so often Lucie stole glances at her young apprentice, trying to read his thoughts, learn whether he was truly at peace with her, as he had said, or whether he was still ill at ease. She had talked to him about Owen—how she missed him, the rumours, her confidence that he would not betray his king. Jasper had been indignant, then apologetic, then angry, ready to go to battle to protect the honour of their house. But Jasper's quicksilver temper kept her wary.

Her fingers were clumsy this morning from lack of sleep. And worry. Dame Phillippa had awakened in a confused state, uncertain where she was, talking of events in Lucie's childhood as if they had occurred yesterday. Lucie feared she had erred in the amount of valerian she had given her aunt. An elderly woman, not so active as before, so thin, it was possible that what Lucie thought a cautious dose had been too much. And the matter of the lost parchment—this morning Phillippa shook her head and swore she knew of no such thing.

Someone entered the shop.

'Mistress Wilton?' a querulous voice called.

'*Deus juva me*, it is Alice Baker,' Lucie hissed.

Jasper set his work aside, wiped his hands on his apron. 'I shall go to her.'

Lucie felt childish hiding in the storeroom, but she had not been proud of her behaviour the last time she encountered Alice and was not ready for another verbal clash.

'Good day to you, Mistress Baker,' Jasper called out in a friendly voice as he walked through the beaded curtain into the shop.

'Good day to you, lad. Where is your mistress?'

'Mixing a physick.'

Lucie was glad Jasper had not lied. The woman would think nothing of pushing past him and through the curtain if determined to find Lucie.

'How can I serve you?' Jasper asked.

Lucie could not hear the reply. Alice must be muttering. A muttering Alice was not good. She made some of her cruellest comments in an undertone.

'It is the devil making you say such things,' Jasper said, his voice cracking with emotion. 'The captain is expected home any day!'

Lucie dropped her work, and as she walked deliberately into the shop she prayed for patience.

Alice Baker leaned on the counter, her head bent as if whispering to Jasper but watching for Lucie. Her wimple pinched her face at the jowls and temples, accentuating her perpetual frown. But the white wimple also revealed a more natural colouring than she had had of late.

'You are looking well, Mistress Baker,' Lucie said.

Alice's smile could not expand beneath the tight wimple. Or perhaps she had meant to sneer. 'Not well, but improving, thanks be to God. Jasper tells me the captain will soon be home. I thought I had heard otherwise. But I must have misunderstood.'

'Yes, he expects to be home within the month,' Lucie said. She did not dare risk a smile for fear she would just bare her teeth. Sweet *Jesu* but the woman was horrible.

Another customer entered the shop. Lucie nodded towards Celia, Camden Thorpe's eldest, turned back to Alice. 'Was Jasper able to assist you?'

Alice straightened, tossed her head as if to dismiss the young man, moved closer to Lucie. 'Roger Moreton is a good man, Lucie. You must not take advantage of him.'

Lucie thought she would burst, but she would not satisfy the woman with a response. By the time she caught her breath Alice Baker was halfway to the door. 'God go with you,' she managed.

'And with you,' Alice trilled.

'She is a horrible woman,' said Celia Thorpe.

Lucie sank down on to a stool and was about to ask Jasper to help the young woman, but one glance at his trembling hands and she sent him to the storeroom.

'You must not mind her,' Lucie said.

'Ma says it is women's problems,' Celia said, no doubt newly indoctrinated in such things, her wedding being a month hence. 'She says it is quite common for a woman's humours to ferment in her skull when her fluxes cease.'

God bless Celia's innocence. It made Lucie smile. 'Mistress Baker's youngest is but three years old, Celia. I do not know whether we might assume her fluxes have ceased. But it is a forgiving theory and I thank you for it.'

They proceeded to debate the merits of various oils and creams for the young woman's already perfect complexion.

Tension was high in the kitchen at Freythorpe Hadden.

Nan, the cook, had thrown up her hands when Tildy announced the arrival of the archbishop's retainers. 'Two more high and mighties with appetites. And to what end? Did *Master* Harold protect us from the thieves?' She did not approve of the temporary staff, neither Harold Galfrey nor Tildy. 'What is Mistress Lucie thinking, to crowd us when we have the gatekeeper and his family underfoot?' Nan kicked at a pile of twigs in the corner. 'Sarah, work on that broom out in the yard. It will be set aflame if you work it by the fire.' She picked up the bundle and shoved it at the maid.

'I cannot work on a broom out in the wind and rain,' Sarah complained. She turned to Tildy for direction.

'Work in the corner of the hall,' said Tildy, 'by my alcove.' She was sleeping in Dame Phillippa's bed, so as to be close to Daimon if he should wake. 'You will have light there and peace.'

Nan wagged a bony finger at Tildy. 'You will get naught from her, treating her like a baby.' Her thin lips were pinched and curled into sneering disapproval. 'You are a young fool.' She threw a pair of trout on to the cutting board. 'We shall have naught in the fish pond by the time the mistress returns,' she muttered.

Neither Nan's mood nor her tongue bothered Tildy a whit. She was too happy. Only Daimon's recovery could make her happier. The archbishop had sent two of his most trusted men to guard Freythorpe. She could sleep in peace tonight. And, even better, she knew Alfred and Gilbert, and they her. They would listen to her.

'They will eat with Goodwife Digby, Harold and me,' said Tildy.

'Lord Harold will have something to say about that, to be sure.'

'He understands his station.'

'You think so, do you? Humph!' A lock of greying hair slipped out of Nan's cap as she slit open the trout. An impatient swipe of her hand left a silvery trail on her cheek. 'Harold is none too happy about the new arrivals. I could see that.'

Nor should he be, Tildy thought.

'He thinks himself a fighting man,' Nan continued. She did love to hear herself talk. 'You have only to watch him walk.'

Tildy had noticed. 'He knows that Alfred and Gilbert are *trained* fighting men,' she said. 'And he knows we know. We witnessed the difference the night of the raid. If Alfred and Gilbert had been here then, the thieves would have suffered as they deserve.'

'And Daimon would not be lying abed, eh?' Nan wagged her knife at Tildy. 'No joy will come of your ambitions, my lady. Daimon's ma thinks he can do better than you.'

Tildy knew that. Winifred, though praising Tildy to her face, had gone behind her back to complain about Tildy's inexpert care to Mistress Wilton, and again to Magda. To both Winifred had claimed that Tildy was nursing Daimon only to win his heart. Nan was telling Tildy nothing new. 'I am here as housekeeper while Dame Phillippa is away and I am in charge of Daimon's care. I have no ambitions other than to do my best at both tasks.' Tildy lifted her chin and flicked her skirt as she prepared to leave.

Nan snorted. 'Shall we serve the best claret, my lady?'

She must always have the last word. Tildy could not be bothered to retort. She must rehearse her facts so that she left Alfred and Gilbert with no doubt she was right about Harold Galfrey. But how would she manage to catch them in private?

Magda glanced up from her ministrations as the young housekeeper entered the hall. She noted that Tildy's step was lighter, her face more relaxed than earlier. Mayhap she had found a confidante—though it could not be the sharp-tongued Nan. Magda had failed in the role of Tildy's confidante. Since the young woman's outburst about Harold Galfrey being Daimon's rival, she had withdrawn and said little to Magda except to ask directions about the young steward's care.

But mayhap the kitchen had naught to do with Tildy's mood. She plainly rejoiced at the arrival of the two whelps who would be warriors. That had been a tense welcome, Harold Galfrey clouding over as Tildy brightened. The borrowed steward had sniffed at the boisterous assurance of the archbishop's men. Magda shared his doubts. She smelled much subtlety in the raid on the manor and worried that the lads were too inexperienced to pursue anything but the obvious.

What would they make of the man who had come round asking for Harold Galfrey this morning? Magda had recognised him—Colby, he was called. He worked for John Gisburne. An odd choice for the would-be mayor of York. Colby was trouble, always had been. Harold said Colby had been sent by Gisburne to warn him that Joseph, cook's son, had been seen in York. He would cause trouble at Freythorpe if he could.

Mayhap he had already. But Magda thought it best to consider other possibilities. Would Alfred and Gilbert?

As soon as the shop was empty, Lucie returned to the storeroom to see whether Jasper had calmed. He was not there. What had Alice Baker whispered to him? Lucie opened the door to the garden, thinking to search for the lad, but the rain changed her mind. A soaking would not make it easy to continue the cloth envelopes. And how certain was she to find him for all that? She resumed her work, listening for any sounds in the shop. But it was a creak on the old stairs up to the solar that caught her attention. Kate slept up there, but she would not be there now. Suddenly Crowder was rubbing against her skirt. Lucie had a momentary suspicion—Kate and Jasper? Sweet heaven, she was thinking like Jasper himself, immediately pairing people off. There was also an alcove at the top of the steps, outside the solar, in which an old bench had provided a quiet place for Lucie to nurse her babies during busy times in the shop. Lucie put aside her work, gathered her skirts and crept up the steps, but as she reached halfway she realised anyone up there was unlikely to hear her approach. Crowder dashed ahead of her. A hard rain drummed on the new slate roof and the wind rattled the shutters.

And there Jasper knelt, in front of the bench in the alcove, his elbows on the bench, his head bent in prayer.

The sisters of Clementhorpe had taught Lucie that it was a sacrilege to interrupt another's devotions. But what could Alice Baker have said to lead him up here to pray?

Still Lucie hesitated at the top of the steps, debating what to do. Crowder solved the problem by butting his head against Jasper's thigh. The boy's immediate response was to lower his hands and reward the ginger tabby with a good rubbing.

'Jasper?'

He turned, saw Lucie, slid back to sit on the floor. The hunch of his shoulders, lowering of his head, told Lucie his earlier good mood was gone—but so too the heat with which he had left the shop.

'Were you praying for Alice Baker's soul?' Lucie tried.

He shook his head. Crowder settled on Jasper's lap.

'Were you praying for your soul?' Lucie asked.

Another shake. One hand rose to scratch the tabby beneath his chin.

'You would like me to leave you alone.'

At last a nod. Something about his posture on the floor, embracing the cat, reminded Lucie of what she had felt like at his age. She had been desperate for privacy. Life in a convent, she had thought. But perhaps at a certain age, solitude was simply necessary. She withdrew.

16

AMBIVALENCE

Rokelyn sent for Owen's men late in the day. He stood before them, hands behind his back, chin thrust forward, anger-hardened eyes moving slowly from man to man. Tom noticed a vein pulsing along the side of the archdeacon's hairless head.

'Who brought ale to the prisoner while you guarded?' Rokelyn demanded of Edmund and Jared.

The two exchanged a look. Edmund dropped his head.

'Glynis,' Jared said. 'Piers's mistress. She put a sleeping draught in it.'

'And Captain Siencyn spoke to two of you yesterday, did he not?' The eyes swept the four, rested on Tom.

What could Tom do but admit it? 'Aye, Father.'

The archdeacon grunted. 'Captain Archer is too clever for his own good. But he has underestimated me.'

'What has the captain to do with it?' Jared asked. For once, Tom admired his boldness.

'Father Simon tells me Glynis and the captain met in Porth Clais. You were there.' Rokelyn nodded at Jared.

'She told us where to find Captain Siencyn, that is all.'

'Come now. You had already met Siencyn.'

'I did not know where he lived,' Jared protested.

'Why would she poison them?' Sam sputtered.

'Captain Archer would not help Piers escape,' Edmund said, finding his voice at last. 'Not when he was working for you.'

'No?' The single syllable curled upwards. 'What if he believed if he did so Siencyn would sail?'

Tom had heard enough. 'The captain would not betray you unless he thought someone would suffer for your mistake.'

Edmund elbowed Tom as amusement lit Rokelyn's face.

'So if he believed I was wrong...'

'And if Piers had been in danger,' Tom said weakly.

From the doorway came a most welcome voice. 'Bless you, Tom, for thinking so well of me.'

It was Captain Archer. His right arm was bound to his side and he looked haggard. But he was back, praise God. Tom pulled a chair towards him.

'You are wounded?' Rokelyn came forward to see Owen. 'A dog did all that? Where is your other man?'

'Sitting outside the door. He cannot walk. We were attacked. We found refuge in a cottage and only now felt strong enough to continue. What is ado?'

'Piers the Mariner has slipped away,' Rokelyn said. 'You were not injured helping him, were you?'

The captain's jaw stiffened. Tom always knew to leave him alone at such a time. 'I have told you what happened,' Owen said softly. 'Now tell me. How did Piers slip out of that guarded cell?'

'Glynis,' Tom breathed.

The archdeacon silenced him with a nasty look.

The captain looked puzzled, closed his eye, tilted his head, as if thinking hard.

'Did you learn anything from Cynog's parents?' Rokelyn asked, clearly impatient for news.

The captain did not answer. Tom enjoyed the archdeacon's frustration.

'I do not understand,' the captain muttered.

'Understanding can come later,' said Rokelyn. 'For now I need your advice—where do we search for Piers and his lady love?'

Owen sighed wearily. 'I do not know. Perhaps Porth Clais. Perhaps inland. I do not know.' He closed his eye, touched his right side with his left hand, winced.

'Rest a while there,' Rokelyn said, seeming at last to notice the captain's state. 'I shall send for a physician. For your man also. My servant will bring you wine and some food, some water to wash with.'

At last a civil gesture.

'You are kind,' the captain said, leaning his head back against the chair. Bone weary, he looked, in pain and unhappy.

The servant hurried from the room, but returned almost at once. 'Captain Archer, a messenger from the Archbishop of York waits without.'

'Archbishop Thoresby?' Rokelyn said. 'He sent a messenger all this way?'

The captain opened his eye, closed it. 'Did you not know he has one of the longest reaches in the kingdom?'

Tom thought the captain's response lacked the appropriate respect for the Archbishop of York. But surely a wounded man could be excused some discourtesy.

Owen had never met Friar Hewald, but he saw his condition reflected in the alarm on the cleric's face.

'We await a physician.' Archdeacon Rokelyn wore his public smile. 'The captain and his man met with trouble outside the city.'

'God grant you quick healing, Captain,' said Friar Hewald. 'It will be a difficult journey if we move at the speed His Grace wishes—all the worse for your wounds. In faith, it cannot be helped. I have lost time looking for you. I had thought to find you in Cydweli. I despaired when I learned at the port that you had journeyed so far as St David's.'

His side burning, his shoulder throbbing, Owen had not the patience to listen to the friar's complaints. 'You have a letter from His Grace?'

'I do. And a ship, and letters to speed us along once we land in Gloucester.'

Owen received the news numbly. He was far more pleased by

the arrival of Master Edwin, the physician.

Archdeacon Rokelyn told his servant to lead Owen, Iolo and Master Edwin to the guest chamber.

'I shall be eager to hear how soon we may depart,' Friar Hewald said as Owen rose.

Rokelyn no longer smiled.

'I would read His Grace's letter before we talk more,' Owen said. The friar handed it over. Thoresby's seal. It seemed out of place in St David's.

Owen nodded to the friar, the archdeacon and left the room in the company of the physician, who called for clean cloths and water in a basin. Two servants helped Iolo cross the screens passage to the guest chamber.

'I pray you, attend Iolo first,' Owen said to Master Edwin.

'I am not a babe, to be pampered,' Iolo muttered. But once he had shooed away the servants, he leaned back against the pillows and allowed Master Edwin's assistant gingerly to cut away the thick bandage Enid had wrapped round the foot.

After the servants had helped Owen with his boots, they withdrew. Owen moved to a bench near a lamp, broke Thoresby's seal and read. Thoresby's letter touched his heart as the messenger had not. Owen wondered at Alice Baker's jaundice, cursed the woman for blaming Lucie. Abbot Campian of St Mary's said that Jasper spoke of taking vows. That meant the lad was unhappy. At his age, such a mood could be difficult. Owen hoped Lucie would see it as a passing trouble and not fret over it. But the most disturbing news was that outlaws had attacked several large farms outside York. This was the cause of Thoresby's insistence on his hasty return. Thoresby wanted Owen there, seeing to the defences at his manors. He also complained of much work to be done, a steward's work. Owen cared nothing for the archbishop's manors. But what of Freythorpe Hadden? Was the young Daimon capable of defending it? Phillippa was now there alone. What could Lucie do if she heard of trouble at the manor? Alice Baker, Jasper, outlaws. And Owen away for so long. It did not sound as if Brother Michaelo had yet returned when

Thoresby wrote the letter. Then Lucie would have the added burden of grief for her father.

Master Edwin was shaking his head over Iolo's swollen, blood-caked foot. Owen took the opportunity to shift the map from his tunic to Thoresby's letter, rolling up the map within. He tucked the letter in one of his boots.

He sat back, waiting his turn with the physician, disturbed by thoughts of York. He pushed them aside. He must think how to escape the watchful eye of the friar, for he had no doubt the man would fret over his every move until they were on board ship. But Griffith of Anglesey must be delivered of the map before Owen could think about York. He needed brandywine. A servant's soft shoes showed beneath the tapestry in the doorway. Gritting his teeth against the pain, Owen walked the few feet to the doorway and made his request.

The brandywine arrived as Edwin's assistant helped Owen with his tunic.

'Good,' said Master Edwin. 'Pour him a good draught. He will need it when we remove the bandages. This good man would benefit from one also.' He nodded to Iolo, who lay back against the pillows pale as the costly bed linen, his thin hair clinging to his damp temples.

Owen knew full well the cause of the physician's comment—he had bled much on his journey from Math and Enid's farm. The bandage did not part from his flesh easily. The wound must be stitched closed once more. Owen's side was on fire by the time the physician and his assistant departed.

'He has not Enid's gentle touch,' Iolo muttered when the tapestry fell back across the doorway.

'Nor her patience,' said Owen. 'Why did they not put the brandywine within reach?'

Iolo shouted for a servant. 'So what says the archbishop?'

'He commands me to return at once. There is much outlawry in the countryside and he worries about his lands.'

'And your family?'

Owen was quiet while the servant filled their cups and smoothed the bedding.

'The lad Jasper is unhappy,' Owen said when they were alone once more. 'He thinks to find joy with the brothers of St Mary's. An ignorant baker's wife accuses my wife of incompetence. Mostly I worry about Sir Robert's manor and the troubles in the countryside. My wife's aunt is assisted by a young steward of little experience.'

'Then you must hurry home.'

'First I must see the map into the right hands.'

'You will seek out Griffith of Anglesey, then, despite the archbishop's summons?'

'I cannot think Master Edwin will advise us to travel on the morrow.'

17

MISTRESS OF THE HALL

The clouds parted late that afternoon and the sun beat down on the rooftops of York and glistened on the damp gardens. The irises drew Lucie's eyes away from her stitching, and at last she pushed the linen herb sachets aside and slipped out of the apothecary workshop into the garden. The lacy camomile bowed beneath the weight of the raindrops and their own tiny buds. At the end of the rose beds stood Phillippa, her hair tidy in a white cap, an apron tied neatly at her waist. She used her cane to support her as she leaned over the lavenders to see something behind them. Lucie joined her.

'Peonies,' Lucie said. 'I planted them last spring. I had hoped for blossoms this year, but no matter. The older ones make up for these with a fine show and by the time I need their roots these young ones will be old enough to bloom.'

'What else is new since my last visit?' Phillippa asked. Quite lucidly. Without a hint of this morning's confusion.

Lucie pointed out her new acquisitions, though it was difficult to remember what Phillippa might have seen. Her aunt was rewardingly delighted, requesting cuttings and seeds. They paused at the rosemary hedge, where Lucie crouched to pull at a twining clover.

'You do not like clover?' Phillippa asked.

'I prefer it on tapestries. It grows in all the wrong places.'

'It has its uses, Lucie.' Phillippa bent awkwardly to lift some rosemary branches and observe the intruder. 'But it is crowding the rosemary, I agree. I seem to recall that Nicholas had a spell for clover, to keep it in its place.'

Lucie believed in weeding rather than casting spells, but she saw a way to turn the conversation down a helpful path. 'He did find a spell. It is in one of the manuscripts in his chest. We should go through them.'

'But I cannot read.'

'You would recognise the drawing.'

Phillippa had straightened. She leaned on her cane, gazing down absently at the rosemary. 'I should have learned to read.'

'So that you would understand the parchment you spoke of?'

Phillippa looked up, startled. 'What parchment?'

'Something your husband had. You spoke of it last night.'

Phillippa pressed her heart, suddenly pale.

Lucie reached for her aunt's arm, but Phillippa turned away.

'Aunt Phillippa—'

'Say nothing more now,' Phillippa said softly, taking a deep breath.

Lucie cursed herself. She was no good with her aunt, did not understand what helped, what threatened her fragile dignity. Perhaps a cup of wine would soothe her.

'Do not leave,' Phillippa said as Lucie began to walk away. 'I am relieved to have spoken of it. But I do not remember—oh Lucie, it is the cruellest curse, to be witless one day, lucid the next. It is as if I have been sleepwalking and everyone has witnessed my foolishness. All look at me with such pity—and fear that they, too, might come to this end if they live so long as I have. It is horrible. Horrible.' Her jaw was set in anger and frustration.

'I wish that I had a physick to help you,' Lucie said.

Phillippa shook her head. 'I have told you before, there is no cure for old age. Except death. So I do not waste my prayers.'

'I wish only to help.'

'I know. But I am such an old fool. Had I learned to read, or showed the parchment to you…' Phillippa sighed. 'But my father thought reading unnecessary. It did not seem so important when I was young. My brother could read a little, with effort. My husband could read—not well. But look at you, keeping your accounts. You used your reading to study medicine.' Phillippa shook her head in wonder.

This parchment. Lucie wondered how something that apparently meant so much to her aunt had been lost. 'How did you come to lose the parchment?'

'I hid it too well and too often. I have searched all the hiding places I can remember, but it is not there.'

'Why did you hide it?'

'Douglas was so secretive about it. He had me sew it into the tapestry—the one I brought to Freythorpe.'

'But that is the one the thieves stole!'

'No matter. I removed the parchment long ago.'

'How long ago?'

'When your mother came to the manor. I did not know that she would have so little interest in the housekeeping. I was worried she would discover it.'

'Then it was not you who tore the tapestry recently?'

Phillippa had not been aware of the tear, but could not say with any assurance when she had last made note of the tapestry. 'You see? My servants must have thought I ruined it and did not wish to speak of it. Sweet heaven, I have been too proud, not asking for help.'

Lucie thought her father would have noticed the damage to the tapestry. Had someone been in the hall, searching for the parchment, since Sir Robert departed in February? If so, they had known where to look. At least where it had once been hidden. But so long ago. 'Did you receive any visitors this past winter?' Lucie asked, but already knew that it was the servants she should be questioning. She must go to Freythorpe. But how could she leave the shop again so soon?

Daimon improved under Magda's care. Tildy delighted to see him coherent, sitting up for hours at a time and eager to be back on his feet soon. But his pallor and the shadows beneath his eyes reminded her that he had only begun to heal. Magda had cut his hair close to his head so that it was easier to apply her healing ointments. He looked like a tousled child with tufts of hair sticking up like bristles.

'You misjudged Harold Galfrey,' Daimon chided her after Magda explained that he could not tolerate the amount of physick Lucie had instructed Tildy to give him.

'I did not tell you of my suspicion,' Tildy said. 'Did Magda?'

'No one needed to. When you came upon Harold bending over me yesterday, I saw the look on your face, Matilda.'

If her fear had been so obvious to Daimon, had Harold also guessed? 'Do you think I should apologise to him?'

'No.'

How quickly died the smile, thought Tildy. 'What is this?'

'Something—perhaps nothing. There was a man today, he asked for Harold by name. And his voice, it took me back to that night. The attack.'

'Sweet heaven!'

Daimon tried to shake his head, stifled a curse. 'I cannot be certain. That night the voice was rougher—he was threatening, shouting. This morning the voice was pleasant. I did not see him—I could not move quickly enough. Let me sit at the table tonight. Perhaps we might talk of this visitor.'

'That is simple to arrange.' Tildy smiled encouragingly and lifted her tray of medicines.

Daimon touched her hand. 'I wish also to keep my eye upon my rivals.'

'Alfred and Gilbert? Rivals?'

'They have seen far more of the world than I have.'

What did that matter to Tildy, who seldom went farther than St George's Field in York? 'I have heard their boasts at the captain's table,' she reminded him. 'They are soldiers born and no proper husbands for anyone.' She blushed, realising what she had implied.

Daimon's eyes lit up. 'Is it possible that your fears for me mean you have had a change of heart about us?'

'My heart has been yours all along,' Tildy said. 'It is my head that warns against your suit.'

'Then you have not changed your answer?'

'Ask me again when you are well and strong.'

'I shall recover quickly in anticipation of that moment!'

Tildy escaped from those hopeful eyes as quickly as she might.

The table was set up by Daimon's pallet so that he might be propped up and comfortably join in the conversation. Tildy had told Magda what Daimon had said about Harold's visitor. The Riverwoman had seen the man.

'It was Colby, one of the mayor's servants. He has been in and out of trouble all his life. Magda and thee shall see what he wanted with the borrowed steward, eh?' She would bring up the incident at dinner.

Tildy was glad that she need not spend the evening seeking a clever time in which to introduce Colby's unexpected presence. Without that worry she found it quite merry and indulged in the fantasy of being the steward's wife, accustomed to such evenings. Alfred and Gilbert kept up a lively chatter about their adventures and Magda joined in with stories of her own travels. Even Harold relaxed and told a tale about his youth. Tildy almost liked him at that moment. Daimon said little, but laughed heartily and ate with a healthy appetite.

Tildy began to wonder whether Magda had forgotten. The old woman drank more than her share of the wine, then brandywine. How could she think clearly?

But Harold provided the opportunity. 'Is it true you leave on the morrow, Goodwife Digby?'

'Aye. Daimon is, as thou seest, stronger now. Magda did wonder what is the news from York. Was that not one of John Gisburne's servants came to see thee this morn?'

Tildy watched Harold closely. Brushing his light hair from his eyes, he seemed almost embarrassed as he glanced at Daimon,

Alfred, Gilbert, then back to the Riverwoman. 'Yes, it was. But he said nothing of the city.' Now he glanced at the two servants who waited by the hearth to be called to serve. He leaned close to those at the table. 'He wished to warn me that Cook's son, Joseph, was seen in the city, said he was on his way here.' He said it all too quietly for Daimon, who could not lean across the table, to hear. Tildy whispered the news to him.

'We shall discuss this later,' Alfred said.

The topic seemed to signal the end of the festivities. The men withdrew. Tildy asked Magda to watch her prepare Daimon's physicks to see that she was doing it correctly and to help make him comfortable for the night. The supper had drained him of his energy and he was glad to settle down.

'But I warn you,' he told them. 'Joseph is trouble. Tell Alfred and Gilbert to have a care.'

'Aye, Magda has heard much of the man and nothing good.'

'I shall tell them,' Tildy promised. As she looked down on Daimon, she thought that his cheeks and nose were pink. 'His humours are out of balance again,' she whispered to the Riverwoman.

She received a pat on the forearm for her observation. 'It is the wine, my child,' said the Riverwoman. 'It is all right. Thou must allow him a pleasure now and then.'

'I did not mean to deny him,' Tildy protested. Why was the old woman treating her like a child of a sudden?

The Riverwoman drew Tildy away from Daimon's bedside, guiding her towards the hall door. 'Thou hast also had much wine,' she said. 'More than is thy custom.'

Tildy disagreed.

'Magda knows,' the woman insisted. 'A breath of evening air will do thee good.'

Tildy tried to wriggle away, but the Riverwoman's grasp was as strong as her will. She held firm to Tildy's arm until they had slipped out into the cool evening.

It was a welcome feeling, the breeze, the air. Tildy took a deep breath and turned her gaze upwards, to the dome of stars that stretched to the horizon. It was a test of her courage, to look up at the night sky. She had been born and raised in York, had seldom been outside the walls of the city until the past summer, when she had stayed here on the manor with Gwenllian and Hugh. When she first walked out into the night the vast sky had frightened her. It was too large, too mysterious, a monster with a hundred hundred eyes. Gradually, with the gentle guidance of Magda's daughter Tola, who had accompanied them as wet-nurse to Hugh, Tildy learned to see the stars as familiar friends, tracing the constellations.

Tildy felt the Riverwoman's presence beside her. It was much like Tola's, quiet, reassuring. Why had Tildy been angry with Magda? She felt remorse at her anger with the old healer. She asked Magda now about Tola and her children, Nym and Emma. Tildy knew they had stayed with the Riverwoman throughout the autumn and the Christmas season, and many folks said that Tola showed a gift for healing. 'Will she stay to help you?'

'Nay. Tola returned to the moors,' said Magda. 'She is needed there.' There was a sadness in her voice.

'She will be a healer now, like you?'

'One day. Magda took a long while learning.'

They said nothing for a time, gazing at the stars.

Then Magda broke the silence. 'Go to the stables, talk to Alfred and Gilbert, tell them thy concerns.'

The two men had gone there to see that their horses were in good hands.

'I do not like to interrupt them,' Tildy said, suddenly shy of the two soldiers.

'Thou art mistress of the hall, Tildy. Thou shouldst make thy wishes known to those who serve thee.'

Served her. Tildy sighed. She was still uncertain about her status, neither servant nor the true mistress and yet in charge of so many servants. She wished Magda would stay a while longer, a wish she had expressed to the Riverwoman before and repeated now.

'Thou hast made no mistakes these two days. Daimon's will to heal is strong. Thou dost not need Magda.'

'I feel safe with you here.'

Magda's barking laugh startled Tildy. 'With Thoresby's dragon slayers and Harold the Good, what dost thou need with an old woman? Magda will be on her way in the morning, going to those who need her more than thou dost.'

Tildy hugged herself, suddenly feeling the evening chill.

'Daimon will continue to heal,' Magda reassured her.

'But what if it is your presence that is healing him, not the physicks?' Tildy asked it softly, uncertain whether she spoke blasphemy.

The Riverwoman surprised Tildy by gently touching her cheek. 'Thou art Daimon's best healer, my child. Dost thou not understand how much he loves thee?' Then, with a shake of her head, the old woman turned away from Tildy and walked slowly towards the kitchen.

Tildy did not move for a long while. Could it be that her own presence had helped Daimon? Could he love her that much? If so, his was not an idle love, a young man's whim that might prove fickle. Might Tildy have misjudged?

Loud laughter slowed Tildy as she reached the stables. A small lantern glowed dimly near the stalls. The horses whinnied as she passed. The laughter rang out again—it came from the grooms' quarters beyond the horses and the work area. As Tildy drew near, she hesitated, uncertain that it was proper for her to be here. But she was the housekeeper until Dame Phillippa returned.

If Dame Phillippa returned. What would happen if Mistress Wilton found her aunt too confused or infirm to return?

'You have cast a spell on these coins, you cheat!' Angry words, but there was laughter in Gilbert's voice.

'I know nothing of spells. You have the luck of Job is all.' Alfred sounded bored.

Tildy knocked.

Ralph, the groom, opened the door, made an embarrassed bow. 'Mistress Tildy!'

She stood on tiptoe to see beyond him, but to no avail. 'Oh, for pity's sake, Ralph, I merely wish to see what all the laughter is about.'

'Mistress—'

'We are playing cross and pile,' Gilbert called out. 'Alfred and Ralph find my losses comical. Come, Ralph, let the mistress pass. She is not going to apply the switch to two grown men.'

Ralph stepped aside.

Gilbert and Alfred nodded to Tildy from where they crouched on the packed earth floor. A quantity of coins were piled in front of Alfred, a few were lined up by Gilbert. The latter now lifted one of his last coins, flipped it, let it drop on the back of his left hand, which he quickly covered as Alfred called, 'Heads.'

Gilbert peeked at the coin. 'You saw it,' he muttered, tossing it on Alfred's pile. He rose, brushing off his hose.

'I am sorry for interrupting your game.' Tildy felt out of place. They were hardly in a mood to listen to her fears and concerns.

'Mistress, you have saved me my last few coins. How may I be of service?'

Alfred swept up both his coins and Gilbert's and dropped them in a leather pouch. 'Gilbert wearied of my good fortune,' he said. 'He would have soon been out of coins anyway.'

'So you took the remainder?' Tildy asked.

'To divide up evenly the next time,' Gilbert said. 'What would be the fun if one of us had all the coins?'

She felt stupid. Daimon never made her feel this way. These men teased too much. 'You are tired. We shall talk in the morning.'

Alfred shook his head, drew forth a stool for her to sit on. 'Come. Let us talk while we have a quiet moment. You will want to tell us what we face here.'

So she began, haltingly, to tell them her various concerns— Harold Galfrey's too quick assumption of authority and her now mostly discarded fear that he had given Daimon something to cloud his judgement, Nan's son's rumoured return, Mistress Wilton's belief that someone among the thieves knew the manor well.

Both Alfred and Gilbert raised eyebrows at her fears about Harold Galfrey, but they did not make light of them, agreeing that

Daimon's position as steward on this manor would appeal to any man with similar ambitions.

'Even so, Roger Moreton will have a grand household,' said Alfred. 'His steward will command respect.'

'Master Moreton owns land up beyond Easingwold as well,' said Gilbert. 'Still, he is not a knight, not of noble birth, as is Mistress Wilton. But would she have Galfrey as her steward, I wonder?'

'Joseph, cook's son, is the one who sounds like a man to watch,' said Alfred.

'I will speak to the kitchen maid in the morning,' said Tildy. 'Perhaps she has heard something of him.'

'Aye. The cook is not likely to tell us, eh?' said Gilbert.

Tildy smiled and felt encouraged to ask, 'This Colby, Master Gisburne's servant, what is he like?'

Alfred snorted. 'Spawn of the devil himself. Why Gisburne trusts him...' He spat in the corner.

Colby sounded not unlike Joseph, Tildy thought. 'Daimon says that Colby's voice is much like that of one of the attackers.'

Gilbert and Alfred exchanged a look.

'And I cannot help but wonder how Harold knows him,' Tildy added.

'Or why it should be Colby whom Gisburne chose to send,' Alfred said. He spat in the corner again.

Although she appreciated how seriously he was taking all this, Tildy liked Alfred a little less for his manners, or lack of them. But she had heard soldiers were like that. Their poor wives. 'Daimon mentioned a thatcher, also,' she said, and, in a bold stroke, dared to add, 'You might ask Ralph where he could be found.'

'We will.' Alfred grinned. 'It is a nice change, playing the captain.'

Gilbert nodded in agreement.

Tildy was quite pleased with herself.

Brother Michaelo dropped the lash and lay face down on the floor of the little chapel with his arms outstretched, as if nailed to a cross.

He fought to remain conscious. Sleep was no penance. His hands and feet were cold despite the season. The floor was cool against his bare, sweating chest. Was that too comforting? Should he roll over on his raw back? But that which was now on fire would be soothed by the cool floor. He remained where he was, fighting exhaustion. When had he last slept? Or eaten? He had no doubt Archdeacon Jehannes knew—Michaelo was certain the archdeacon's servants spied on him. So long as he did not tell the archbishop, it did not matter. Jehannes was not one to interfere. Michaelo forced himself to think on his many sins, so to mortify his spirit as he had mortified his flesh. His mind wandered through a litany of selfish acts, loveless liaisons, glib and thoughtless lies and, most horrible of all, the attempt to poison the aged infirmarian, Brother Wulfstan. Bile rose in his throat. He pushed himself to a kneeling posture and retched, though his belly was empty.

The door opened. Michaelo tried to cover himself with his habit, but his hands trembled so.

'Enough of this!' Archbishop Thoresby declared from the doorway.

Michaelo still fumbled with his habit. Thoresby snapped his fingers. A servant knelt, offered to help Michaelo dress.

'Leave me,' Michaelo said.

'He will not. Look at you, trembling on the floor half naked. What of your duties? I allowed you to go on pilgrimage and look how you return my favour. You look like a snivelling penitent. I will not have it!'

Michaelo began to curse, bit his tongue and gave himself up to the humiliation of being dressed by the young man. He held back a moan as the servant helped him to his feet. He leaned against the wall for support.

'You may go,' Thoresby barked.

Michaelo struggled upright, took a step.

'Not you, the servant.'

The door closed softly.

Michaelo lifted his eyes to the archbishop. 'Forgive me for my weakness, Your Grace.'

'Of what use are you to me in such a state?'

Thoresby's deep-set eyes were unreadable in the shadowy room, but Michaelo interpreted his tone as impatient, not angry. Perhaps he would be receptive to Michaelo's purpose. But did Michaelo have the strength to explain it all?

'I must do penance for my life, Your Grace.' He licked his lips. 'On pilgrimage I was shown my base self. I have told you, I dreamed of Brother Wulfstan. He showed me what I must do.'

'Some other time. I have a task for you. Several tasks. I have sent for Brother Henry. He will see to your back and give you something to help you sleep tonight—after you have taken some broth and honeyed milk. Tomorrow you will resume your duties. You must talk to Roger Moreton, find out how much he knows about Harold Galfrey.'

Michaelo held out a hand to the archbishop, begging to be heard. 'Your Grace, if I may—'

'You have inconvenienced me enough.' Thoresby opened the door, instructed the servant to assist Brother Michaelo to his chamber. 'Brother Henry will soon be here.'

Brother Henry, now infirmarian at St Mary's Abbey, trained by the holy man whom Michaelo would have poisoned. Perhaps this was God's purpose, to let Michaelo suffer at the hands of a young man who must consider him the devil made flesh.

The hall was quiet. Magda found herself dozing as she waited for Tildy to return from the stables. So she did not hear the conversation between Sarah, the kitchen maid, and Harold, only his parting remark, 'See you do it!' He was a man of many moods, Harold Galfrey, and as he strode out of the door of the hall he was angry.

18

A PATTERN OF EVIL

Owen was awakened by the sound of people rushing about, a continual buzz of talk, but hushed, as if something were very wrong. He sat up.

Iolo snorted and opened his eyes. 'I have never slept in such a bed. Why do the wealthy ever rise? What could be better than lying here?'

Why was Owen fretting? Why should he care what befell the household?

'Am I talking to myself?' Iolo demanded.

'One must make the money to keep the bed, and a dry roof overhead,' Owen said. 'It *is* a fine bed, though for such a one it smells damp. The servants do not air it enough.'

'How do you know about such things?' Iolo asked. 'Do you have such a bed?'

'I do. Lucie's father and aunt gave us a fine bed when we were wed.' Owen had to laugh at Iolo's incredulous expression. 'In faith, it is true.'

'No wonder you yearn for home.'

Owen turned away. He would not like Lucie to know the confusion in his heart at present. 'I do not think I yearn enough of late. Have you noted the noises without?'

'They would have us wake, I think.' Iolo struggled to sit up straighter. 'You would stay here, Captain? Is it Hywel?'

'His cause is an honourable one. All who join him fight for the right to be ruled by their own prince. When I fought in France I thought only of serving my lord the Duke of Lancaster, a worthy man, a God-fearing man. But in serving him I helped King Edward fight for a crown that was not his, for a kingdom that did not want him. That is what Hywel meant by redeeming myself. I would make peace with myself and God by fighting for my people. But how can I?' Owen felt the familiar shower of needles in his blind eye, warning him he said too much. 'But we must talk of other things. Glynis was with Hywel at some point. You heard him say it.'

Iolo, whose eyes had fired at Owen's words, took a moment to respond. 'Glynis. Aye. Because she feared Piers.'

'If that were true, why would Glynis help Piers escape?'

Iolo caught up. 'Ah. Someone lies.'

'Good sirs,' a voice called from behind the tapestry.

'I told you they meant to wake us,' Iolo said.

The archdeacon's Welsh-speaking servant entered with a tray bearing a pitcher of ale, some bread and cheese.

'What is ado?' Owen asked.

The man placed the tray on a table near the bed. He stood uncomfortably, as if he wished to flee.

'Tell me what is wrong,' Owen said.

'Piers the Mariner and Captain Siencyn. They were found this morning hanging from the topcastle of the captain's ship. Their throats cut. They say it is a terrible sight to see.'

'Dear Lord deliver us.' Owen crossed himself.

Iolo murmured, 'Amen,' as he did likewise. 'Both brothers. Now that is passing strange.'

'What of the ship's watchman?' Owen asked.

'Missing,' said the young man. 'The archdeacon wishes you to go down to the port, if you are able. He says he trusts only you at the moment. I was to tell you that.'

Owen poured the ale, passed a cup to Iolo. 'What more do you know?'

'Your men are without, Captain. I think they know much more.'

'Call them in.'

It was a crowd in the small room and the four, too excited to sit, occupied most of the floor. Owen stayed on the bed.

'You have heard?' Tom asked.

'I have. The archdeacon wants me to go down to Porth Clais.'

'Aye,' said Edmund. 'He told us to wake you if you did not come out soon.'

'Strange, when the coroner will record all the archdeacon might wish to know.' Owen set the bread and cheese between himself and Iolo. 'What of Glynis?'

'No one has seen her since yesterday morning, captain,' said Jared.

'Is the archdeacon here?'

'He went out a while ago,' said Edmund. 'Looking angry.'

'You will go down to Porth Clais?' Tom asked.

'As soon as I finish breaking my fast.' He nodded to Tom. 'You will come with me.'

Sunshine filled the valley of St David's. Tom's tale of Rokelyn's guards absorbed Owen as they walked to Porth Clais. Father Simon speaking to Siencyn. The captain anxious to speak to Owen. What had happened?

Grim-faced folk passed them, talking quietly among themselves as they came from the beach. In the past, Tom would have grown increasingly nervous as they approached the scene. But today he was calm, wrapped up in his efforts to give Owen every detail of his journey. The lad had grown up in such a short space. Was that a blessing or a curse? Owen looked at Tom as if for the first time, noting his pale effort to grow a beard along the line of his chin like Owen's own, the fingernails bitten to the quick, the nose that seemed always sunburned even in the worst weather. So young, and yet able quickly to step into a lie when it would help Owen. And hold that lie firmly all the while he was with the archdeacon's guards.

'When we get back to England, do you look forward to returning with your mates to Kenilworth?' Owen asked.

'I am hoping they choose me for France,' said Tom. 'I believe I am ready now.'

'Aye, you do seem so. And you will be a good soldier. You will rise in the duke's service, I think.'

Tom pulled himself up and smiled broadly. Owen thought it a pity the young man was so eager to lose his innocence. For until he faced the enemy and cut him down, he could not understand the life he had chosen. But it was not for Owen to tell him.

The waterfront was crowded with onlookers. Pilgrims, servants, vicars, mariners, they were all there, staring out to sea. Captain Siencyn's ship rode at anchor out well beyond low tide. It had been fitted with small forecastle and aftercastle, as had many merchant ships during Edward's war with France. But the topcastle was at present the centre of attention. Not notably grisly at this distance, though as the ship rocked on the sea the corpses' arms and legs seemed alive. None seemed so curious as to launch boats for closer looks, which was a blessing. It was unlikely anyone had disturbed the ship. And yet how else would they be certain who dangled out there?

But why in God's name were they yet hanging? 'Has the coroner not yet come?' Owen muttered, looking round.

'Now it is low tide it will be sloppy carrying the bodies across the mud,' said Tom.

'That is not our job. We are but to look. Still, I should go out to the ship.' Owen glanced at the young man, who had suffered seasickness on a crossing of the River Towy, to see his reaction.

But Tom just nodded. 'I believe I see Father Paul.'

Owen followed Tom's gaze, spotted the snow-white hair of the vicar who acted as coroner in the city. As the two approached Father Paul, he turned to them, bowed, crossed himself.

'Have you been out to it?' Owen asked.

'I have.' Father Paul shook his head. 'What man does to his fellow man. You would go out to the ship now?'

'Is that why you have not cut them down yet? So I might witness it?'

Father Paul's nod was more like a bow—a slow, sad gesture. 'Archdeacon Rokelyn wished it so. For myself, I would as lief have avoided turning this into a faire.' His bushy-browed eyes swept the crowd. 'You would think the two men had been strung up there for the city's amusement. I am glad you have come at last. I shall find the boatman.' Father Paul slowly walked down the shingle. He was not so old, but today he looked as though he felt all his years.

A loud voice drew Owen's eye to one side of the crowd. The speaker was a red-haired man dressed in a rough pilgrim's gown. He had large hands and long arms, or perhaps it was his expansive gestures that made them seem so. His performance held a small group in thrall. Owen moved closer to hear the tale. The pilgrim spoke in a hushed voice now, describing a spectral procession that foretold a man's death. When he raised his voice for the climax, the audience jumped in surprise. An excellent storyteller. Owen was about to back away when the man looked up, noticed him and waved.

'Captain Archer!' He excused himself from the others and came towards Owen with a grim look. 'A terrible thing, is it not?' In a whisper he said, 'Griffith of Anglesey.'

'Griffith,' Owen said in a normal tone. 'Well met.'

'What a thing to see after coming from the grieving parents of our friend Cynog. They are bearing it?'

Hywel must have men everywhere, to pass word so quickly. 'They asked me to carry this to you so you might hear in their own words.' Owen withdrew the map.

'How thoughtful. I am most grateful to you.' Griffith turned to look at the ship. 'There is a madman loose, I say.'

'It is surely not the mistress who did all that.'

Griffith snorted. 'No, not the work of one woman—or man. I must go now.' He bowed to Owen and returned to his audience.

Father Paul appeared at Owen's side. 'Come with me. If we go to the end of the shingle, we walk through less mud.'

'You will accompany us?'

'If you do not object. I should like to hear anything you might notice. Anything I might have missed.'

'I am honoured by your confidence in me.'

'False humility does not become a man,' said the priest. 'Bishop Houghton has told me of your broad experience.'

'And I might not therefore be humble?'

The priest shrugged. 'It is rare in a Welshman.'

Owen grew weary of English insults. Weary in general. He said nothing, focused on walking evenly in the dry sand mixed with stones, so his side would not be jarred. Tom stayed close to his right side, ready to steady him.

Father Paul seemed to understand the silence. 'Forgive me. I did not meant to insult you. It has been a difficult morning.'

Owen nodded, but still said nothing.

At the edge of the shingle, they stepped into the wet sand. The wind buffeted them as the sand sucked at their boots. Gulls circled about the mast of the ship, shrieking mourners. Owen climbed into the little boat, grateful for Tom's assistance. But there would be a rope ladder for boarding the ship. He wanted both hands for that. Owen took his dagger, pulled back his open tunic, cut the cloth that held his arm to his side.

'What are you doing?' Tom leaned towards him.

'Freeing my arm.' Fortunately, he had not accepted Iolo's offer to lace up the front of his tunic this morning. Now he shrugged it off his right shoulder. He had not counted on the wind, which blew the tunic wide. Tom grabbed it, held it so Owen could slip his injured arm into the sleeve. It was a painful process.

Father Paul shook his head. 'Does Archdeacon Rokelyn know the extent of your wounds?'

'Aye.'

'He was not thinking of your comfort when he asked you to come out to the ship.'

Owen could not help but laugh at that, despite his discomfort and his dislike of the coroner. 'No, my welfare was not in his thoughts, to be sure.' He leaned over to the boatman, a large, quiet man. 'Did you note anything unusual last night?' he asked in Welsh. 'Lights? Sounds?'

'I might have heard something. But I sleep sound. Always been blessed with that.'

'When did you hear something? Evening? Middle of the night?'

'Cannot tell you. Woke in the dark and heard a shout. But as I heard no more, I thought it a dream. Went back to sleep. God watches over an old mariner.'

'Did you know the watchman on the ship?'

'Old Eli? Everyone knows the sluggard.'

'It would be like him to flee in the face of trouble?'

'Oh, aye, there is no loyalty to the man. Like Rhiannon's ladies, he is, protects himself and the hell with the rest, especially his master. As you see. Forgive me, Father, but it is true.'

'I would cut down the bodies,' said Father Paul, still choosing to speak in English.

'Then you will come out with another crew,' said Owen. 'We have not the strength among us. I am here to observe, no more.'

The priest gave Owen a dark look, but did not argue.

'I have never been at sea as crew,' Owen said to the boatman. 'Would you board with us and search below? For anything not common on such a ship?'

The boatman glanced up at the topcastle, did not speak at once. 'Aye,' he said as he drew the boat alongside the ship, 'I will do that, Captain.'

The gulls were loud here and, as Owen climbed up the rope ladder, gritting his teeth for the pain in his shoulder, they grew louder, joined now by the creaks and groans of the vessel. Tom was right behind Owen, then the priest. The boatman came last. Without a word, he headed below.

Blood stained the deck near the mast. Here is where they must have slit the throats of the men hanging above. The stench of blood mingled with the ship's tarry odour, the salt air and the sour smell of low tide. The eyes had already been plucked from the corpses. The gulls' cries were more ominous to Owen after that. He looked away, walked around, searching for the weapon, more blood, anything that might have been left by the murderers. Bold men, they were, to bring their victims out here. Anyone might have witnessed the passage.

Father Paul stood beneath the mast, praying for the souls of the two men. Tom poked about in the coils of rope on deck. Owen found a bloody footprint in the forecastle, but it would be difficult to know whether that had been made by the murderers or Father Paul's earlier companions.

'Captain!' Tom was running towards him with something dangling from one hand. A blood-encrusted knife. 'I found it behind a coil of rope.'

'Well done. Perhaps someone on shore will recognise it.'

Tom glanced at it, then his clothes. 'What shall I do with it?'

'Wrap it in something. Go below—surely there is a torn bit of sail, a cloth. Wait.'

The boatman was coming up the ladder from below, grunting as he balanced something in one hand. Tom handed Owen the knife, went over to help the boatman. Recoiled.

'Come now, lad, take it, will you? I have one hand to climb with. Your captain was right not to try it.'

Owen had joined them. He took the bowl. At first he did not know what he beheld. Raw meat or poorly cooked. It had not been there long. It smelled of blood, not rot. 'Jesus, Mary and Joseph,' he whispered, suddenly understanding. Two tongues. He was fairly certain they were human tongues.

Tom had run to the side of the ship to be sick.

'They were in the captain's quarters,' said the boatman. 'There is little to see down below, though someone has gone through it, strewn the bits about.'

'Was there any paper? Parchment? How were these laid out?'

The boatman shrugged. 'The bowl was there, by itself, on the bunk.'

Father Paul closed his eyes at the sight of the tongues, crossed himself. 'We shall bury them with the men.'

Later, when they were back on the shingle, Father Paul thanked Owen for coming. 'You saw things that I did not, Captain. I grow too old for this task. I cannot help but think we might know the truth of the mason's hanging had you been here. God go with you, Captain.'

Owen began to walk down the shingle with Tom, thinking about the climb back to St David's, when a thought struck him. He had not spoken to Father Paul about Cynog's death, the condition of his body, the way he had been hanged. All he knew was second-hand. The coroner was one of the first people he should have consulted. What was happening to him? He retraced his steps, Tom belatedly noticing the change and hurrying to catch up. Father Paul was mounting the wagon to bless the corpses. Owen sat down on a piling.

'What is it?' Tom asked. 'Why are we waiting?'

'Return to the city, Tom. I must speak with Father Paul.'

The young man frowned. 'You move as a man in pain. There are shadows—'

'Leave me!' Owen ordered, too angry with himself to fuss with courtesy.

Tom gave a little bow and hurried away, almost tripping over himself in his haste.

Father Paul puzzled to see Owen beside the cart.

'I would know all you remember about Cynog's death,' said Owen.

'I did not mention it to give you more work—your injuries— you need rest.'

'I can think while resting, Father.'

'So you can.' The vicar frowned, raised a finger, asking for patience. 'You test my failing memory.'

Folk were moving off, now the bodies lay covered in the cart. The gulls were reclaiming the beach, busily hopping round the bits of debris, hoping for food.

'Yes,' the coroner said at last. 'I remember now. He was hanging by the neck, one arm dangling by his side, the other tied to another tree limb. The noose and the loop round his arm were tied with sailor's knots.'

'His arm was tied?'

The vicar lifted his right arm, held it straight out to one side, the hand limp. 'Thus. I thought to myself his murderer had set out to crucify him, then found it too difficult.' The old man dropped his arm, closed his eyes, crossed himself. 'He was a good man, Cynog.'

Owen wondered at this detail. 'How could there have been any question whether Cynog took his own life? How could he have tied his arm while hanging?'

'No one asked for details, save Archdeacon Rokelyn,' said Father Paul. 'And Father Simon.'

Him again. 'Why Simon?'

For the first time on this grim morning, Father Paul smiled a little. 'Simon wishes to know all our sins. I think of him as a dog, who sniffs at his fellow's bottom. To know him.'

Owen would not have compared the elegant Simon to a dog. Paul was evidently immune to his charm. 'So it is not ambition? Or that he is urged by another—his superior?'

'The former, yes, yes indeed, he is greedy for power. He does all so that Bishop Houghton will make note of him. Archdeacon Baldwin despairs at his secretary's behaviour.'

'What else did Simon ask about Cynog?'

'That I cannot remember, Captain. Forgive me. I pay him little heed.'

Owen thanked him and was heading away once more when Father Paul called out his name.

'A moment! I thought you might wish to know about this morning.'

Owen shook his head, not understanding.

'Father Simon came down to the beach. Unwell, he looked. Wished to hear all I knew of this horrible crime, which is little. More now that you found the knife and—the other.' Father Paul dabbed his brow with his sleeve. The sun had grown quite warm. 'I thought you would wish to know.'

'Father Simon seems a man to whom I should speak.'

Father Paul gave a little bow. 'I should appreciate any further thoughts.'

'You will have them, Father Paul. God go with you.'

'And with you, captain.'

The climb from Porth Clais exhausted Owen. He had lost much blood a few days ago and he paid for it now. His head and heart pounded, his legs felt uncertain. He regretted unbinding his arm, which he tried to keep bent close to his body. The stitches in his side burned like hot coals. He slowed his gait.

What he had seen on board was horrible, but he had seen worse, far worse on a battlefield. Still, in war a man expected to see such things. One became numb. Owen was no longer numb. In body or in spirit. Who might order such an execution? And have the men to carry it out?

Hywel. Owen did not like that conclusion. But he kept coming back to it. Glynis had been in Hywel's camp. He had men all about. But what connection had Hywel to Piers? Or Siencyn?

A sudden sharp stab of pain stopped Owen near the masons' lodge. He clutched his side, swore under his breath. He feared he was bleeding.

Ranulf de Hutton approached. 'You look to be in pain.' He offered an arm.

'You are kind.' Owen let Ranulf help him to a bench just within the lodge. Two men worked in there, chiselling a design in some blocks. They ignored Owen.

The mason offered Owen a cup of ale. He took a sip, waited to see how it would affect him. He glanced round the work area. 'What part of this was Cynog's work?'

Ranulf nodded to a wall of the cloister that was almost complete. 'And some of the decorated capstones that have been set aside. Better?'

'A little. I thank you.' The sharp pain in Owen's side had subsided. It had settled to a dull ache. He imagined Lucie's gentle hands, rubbing soothing lotions on to the scar. How old would the scar be by the time he reached York?

Owen pushed away the thoughts of home. An idea teased him. Cynog's hand had been tied. Why? A symbol of his treason in making the carvings for Hywel? Was Father Paul right? A crucifixion abandoned for a simpler hanging? But Cynog would have been cut down by the first passer-by. Had the murderer been frightened away that morning? Before his work was complete? Tied the hand to the branch in preparation for hacking it off? A hand cut off. Tongues cut out—because Siencyn and Piers might talk? Were the brothers working for Hywel as well? Perhaps Piers had not been Cynog's hangman. Then what king's man was punishing traitors with such quiet brutality?

Owen had no idea. It was beyond anything he might suspect of the archdeacons. Their purpose was to keep the peace, not create a reign of terror. Staring at the walls, he tried to imagine this already a cloister—a quiet place to reflect. But it was impossible with the masons working, mallets to chisels to stone.

'Captain Archer.'

Ranulf de Hutton still stood a few paces distant, his hands resting on his round stomach.

Owen turned. 'I thought you had gone.'

'The tomb is nearly complete. Would you care to see?'

A moment of peace in this grim morning. 'Aye, I would.'

Ranulf did not move. 'Beside the tomb is a pile of stones on which Cynog scratched ideas. I have followed my own memory with Sir Robert's features, but I used Cynog's idea for the pilgrim's hat and the helmet at his feet. I recommend that you look through the rubble, see if there is anything you wish me to add.' Ranulf's large ears had grown quite red, as if the speech were difficult for him.

Now he turned on his bandy legs and led Owen to the back of the masons' lodge. With a dramatic flourish, Ranulf removed a quilt of sacking.

The tomb was magnificent in its simplicity. Sir Robert's features were suggested by subtle angles, though his hair was perhaps thicker than it had been in life. And of course the eyes were lifeless, but his gentle smile was there, in the curve of the mouth, the crease in the left cheek. The symbols of his two lives, that of soldier and that of pilgrim, were well conceived.

'I am pleased with it,' said Owen. 'What more might I add?'

Ranulf pointed to what seemed a pile of rubble to one side of the lodge. 'My fellow worked hard, Captain. Perhaps you will see something fitting that I overlooked. Or something you might wish to take with you.'

'And if I find nothing? I can tell the archdeacon the tomb can be moved into place in the cathedral? Sir Robert can be placed in it?'

'Aye. A bit of polishing to do, but that is less intricate work. I can finish it by lamplight.'

Owen's side protested as he crouched to look at the stones. He chose to sit on the ground. What work Cynog had invested in these chalk sketches on slate. Some of the rubble was softer stone and this he had used to carve shallow lines. Faces, helmets, pilgrim hats, feet, hands. And then a stone that looked familiar. A map. He put this stone aside, along with one of Sir Robert's face that Owen thought to keep. He found another stone with curved lines and small, angular marks. A map such as the one he had handed Griffith, but clearer, with more detail. Had Cynog been so foolish as to leave evidence of his map work?

Ranulf crouched down beside him. Softly he said, 'I see you found the puzzling ones.'

'Do you know these were done by Cynog?'

'They do not seem his work, though it was he who hid them away among the discarded stones. Father Simon would come for him, Cynog would go to the pile, then leave with something concealed beneath his apron. Part of the wall he was repairing for Archdeacon Baldwin? Then why the secrecy? I was not going to speak. But after what was found this morning, I hated myself for my silence. I might have helped you prevent two more deaths. God's children, they were, no matter whether I liked them. And seeing your pain, that settled me. After all you have done to find Cynog's murderer.'

'How often did Simon come for Cynog?'

Ranulf thought a moment. 'I cannot put it so particularly, but more that Cynog's visits to his parents provoked much work on the wall. He worked on it for almost a year. Not so much of late. He begged the tomb. And then—' Ranulf looked away.

'I thank you for telling me.'

'I was jealous of him, you see. He had everything—fair of face and form, gifted, and this tomb. I followed him about, hoping to catch him at something wicked. I almost took the stones to Bishop

Houghton. But I had a feeling about them. I thank the Lord I said naught. I cannot have been the cause of his murder. But—might the others be alive if I had told you?'

'I am not that gifted in this work, Ranulf. I do not think so.'

Ranulf pulled off his cap and wiped his forehead, his eyes, nodding his thanks, his relief. 'You might look at the wall in the archdeacon's undercroft. Damp from the river. As I have said, God watches over the masons here. Take a lantern down there after the household leaves today. Better if Simon does not catch you.'

'Baldwin's household is leaving?'

'For Carmarthen. He is Archdeacon of Carmarthen, you understand.'

'I do.'

'Can I give you a hand up, Captain?' Ranulf spoke the last in a louder tone.

Owen appreciated the help. 'God bless you for everything, Ranulf,' he said when he was standing once more.

Ranulf handed Owen a sturdy cloth pouch, bent over, lifted the two stone maps and the face. He smiled as he handed Owen the latter. 'Faith, that is my piece.'

'I thought so. My wife will like to have it. God go with you, Ranulf.'

'And with you, Captain. May He watch over you.'

May He allow me to find Father Simon still in the city, Owen thought.

19

PENANCES

It had been a quiet day in the household and the shop, but the peace was shattered when Lucie sent Jasper up to fetch Phillippa for dinner. In little time he came clattering down the steps, knocking Gwenllian over in his haste. 'Dame Phillippa is gone! Her clothes, everything,' he gasped.

Lucie hurried upstairs. The bedclothes were smoothed, Phillippa's cloak was not on the hook, her walking stick was not propped beside it. Gwenllian began to wail in delayed indignation. Lucie looked round the room. Phillippa's chest was at the foot of the bed. Perhaps she had tucked her cloak and walking stick in there. Whispering a prayer, Lucie lifted the lid. Phillippa's second gown and her nightdress were neatly folded over her extra shoes, stockings, her brush and silvered glass. But the cloak and stick were missing.

Struggling to control her panic, Lucie slowly descended the steps. Kate was just disappearing into the kitchen with the children.

Jasper sat on the bottom step. Lucie gathered her skirts and joined him. 'I shall go mad,' she muttered. 'I shall, well and truly. Where can she be?'

'What can I do?' Jasper asked.

Lucie hugged him. 'You are my strength just by being here.'

Jasper patted her back awkwardly. 'Dame Phillippa cannot have gone far. Kate says she checked on her in mid-afternoon. She was sleeping then.'

Lucie straightened up. 'She wants to return to the manor, so she will be looking for transport. Roger Moreton's house? She knows we travelled in his cart. Or the York Tavern.' Had it been yesterday's conversation in the garden that had prompted this?

'Dame Phillippa was confused again this morning,' Jasper said. 'All know her state and no one will agree to take her anywhere. But why would she want to leave us?'

'Because I unpacked her things when she would go home.'

'Why does she want to go home?'

Lucie looked at the young man before her, smoothed back his hair. 'Go search for her, Jasper, that is what you can do. Then, when we have her safely at home, I promise to tell you. I do not know why I did not already—you might be able to help me think how to help her.'

Jasper rose. 'Master Moreton's, then Mistress Merchet's.' He hurried out.

Lucie went into the kitchen to ask Kate what she remembered about Phillippa's behaviour and to see whether Gwenllian had been hurt or just startled. Magda Digby, still wrapped in a long scarf and booted from her journey, was in the kitchen, Gwenllian on her lap, telling the child a tale of the Norsemen. She glanced up as Lucie entered, nodded, but did not falter in the tale. The little girl was leaning her head against Magda's shoulder, her eyelids heavy. Kate was cutting up bread to soak in warm milk for the children. Hugh sat at her feet playing quietly with a handful of twigs.

'She says Daimon is slow to mend,' Kate told Lucie.

'How is your sister?'

'The Riverwoman says Tildy is happy now Alfred and Gilbert are there.' Kate sighed at a knock on the hall door, wiping her hands on her apron.

'Stay here, take care of the little ones,' Lucie said. 'I shall see who it is.' Whoever it was, Lucie intended to send them on their way. She wanted to hear what Magda had to say.

But it was Roger Moreton on the doorstep, hatless and anxious. 'Jasper has told me,' he said breathlessly. 'What might I do to help?'

Lucie thanked God for her good friends. 'Jasper must be at the tavern. You might search with him. Do you think the guard at Micklegate Bar would remember whether Phillippa had passed through?'

'We cannot know without asking,' said Roger, already backing away. 'I shall offer Master Jasper my services.'

'God go with you, Roger,' Lucie called after him as he bustled down the side garden and out on to Davygate, where he turned left, towards St Helen's Square.

She found Magda sitting at the abandoned dinner table, unwrapping the long wool scarf from her head, neck, shoulders. At last she shook her head and patted her white braids. 'Better now. The children are having their meal. Thou shouldst calm thyself and think of other matters. Thou hast a good pair searching the city.'

Lucie took brandywine and two mazers out of a cupboard. Magda sat at the head of the table. Lucie slipped on to the bench that ran down the side. She rubbed her hands. 'Tell me how you found Daimon. And the household.'

Magda felt Lucie's hands. 'First pour thy brandywine and tell Magda why her old friend Dame Phillippa has wandered away from thy house.'

'I found her—'

'Warm thyself with the brandywine,' Magda ordered, pointing imperiously at the bottle.

When Lucie had complied, taking several fortifying sips, she told Magda about Phillippa's conviction that she was needed at Freythorpe and about the parchment that seemed so much on her mind.

'Douglas Sutton, aye. Phillippa mourned him, but the gods smiled on her when they took him so young.'

'Did you know him?'

'Magda did not need to. He was still in Phillippa's eyes. They were not happy eyes.'

Someone shouted in the street. Lucie's heart raced. She began to stand, felt Magda's strong hand on her forearm.

'If it is for thee, they will come to the door,' she said.

Of course they would. But how could Lucie sit still?

'What dost thou think will befall thy aunt? She is not a fool.'

'She is lame, confused...'

'Does she carry a money purse?'

'No.'

'Wear jewels? Fine rings?'

'No.'

'The thieves will ignore a poor crone. Magda knows.' Her deep blue eyes smiled.

Jasper and Roger clattered into the house. Roger stood at a distance, while Jasper rushed to Lucie, kissed her forehead. He smelled of fresh air and sweat.

'Bess had not seen her, nor the gatekeeper at Micklegate or Bootham, nor at the stables of masters Cobb or Wakefield.'

'Now the churches,' Magda said. 'Begin with the minster.'

'Why?' Jasper asked.

'Dost thou question the Riverwoman?'

'Go, Jasper,' Lucie said, her heart pounding. Pray God Magda was right. She pressed his hand.

He hugged her and loped across the room to Roger. 'Come, Master Moreton. We have many churches to search!'

Poor Roger looked weary, but he nodded to Lucie and Magda, and followed Jasper out of the door.

'Let us hope Magda has not sent them on a futile search.'

'Do you doubt what you said?' Lucie asked, fearing to have her hopes dashed.

'No. Now Magda must tell thee about Freythorpe.' She told Lucie about Daimon's response to the physicks, Harold's efficient work, Tildy's gentle rule over the household.

Lucie found Daimon's delicate humours distressing. Could she have forgotten that about him? For surely she had nursed him before. She pushed that aside, to think about later. 'Alfred and Gilbert have arrived?'

Magda made a face. 'Aye, two eager soldiers. Young Tildy is much relieved, but the borrowed steward wishes them gone.'

'Why?'

'He would be first knight. Their presence insults him.'

'That is silly.'

'He has some secret he keeps close to him. Hast thou observed him with servants?'

'What sort of secret?'

'He keeps it well. Didst thou observe him with servants?'

'I did. He was solicitous of Tildy. Showed respect to Daimon. Is he too lenient with the servants?'

Magda sniffed. Frowned out of the window. 'He showed a different face to thee, Magda thinks. He is a Janus, then. Mayhap that is why Tildy does not trust him.'

'She said nothing to me.'

Magda shook her head. 'It is a thing happens slowly—doubts, questions. She thinks he finds being steward of Freythorpe Hadden to his liking. But Daimon stands in the way.'

It took a moment for Lucie to catch the implication, which then outraged her. 'Has Tildy lost her wits! You have told her that Daimon's confusion was my fault. Harold is a good man. He would never poison a man to steal his post. He has no need.'

Despite her age, Magda had piercing eyes, which were now locked on Lucie's. 'How thou dost protest, Mistress Apothecary. Dost thou know Galfrey so well?'

'You know that I do not. But I judged him to be a good man. What has he done to deserve such suspicion?'

'Naught but that he is too comfortable.'

'Tildy is a foolish girl.'

'Nay. She is loyal to thee. It is far easier for her to believe a stranger could make such a mistake than that thou couldst.'

Lucie saw the truth in that. 'Forgive my temper.'

'Thou hast much on thy mind. A little temper is a good thing. But Magda is not finished. Dost thou know Colby, John Gisburne's servant?'

'The thief who is always pardoned?'

'Aye. He appeared at Freythorpe yesterday and asked for the borrowed steward. He told him that Nan's son Joseph was about.'

'It was good of John Gisburne to warn my steward.'

'Aye. Too good of him.'

'Why would you doubt it?'

'It seems a long way to send a servant with such information. Does Gisburne owe thee such a favour? Didst thou save his life?'

'No. You do have doubts about Harold.'

Magda wagged her head. 'Magda does not like Gisburne's interest in this.'

Neither did Lucie. John Gisburne had never been particularly friendly to the family. 'Perhaps he knows Harold Galfrey well. He did recommend him to Roger.'

Magda picked up her scarf, pushed herself away from the table. 'Magda must see whether her home has floated away.'

'I wish you would stay until Jasper returns.'

But Magda was already winding her scarf. 'It is best to reach Bootham Bar before the gatekeeper closes it.'

'God bless you for everything, Magda.'

'Magda enjoyed the hearth and the food. Nan curses the sod, but she graces the kitchen.'

Goodwife Constance opened Roger Moreton's door. She was a tiny woman, hardly more than a child in stature, though her face was lined with age. Her nose had apparently continued to grow after she stopped, for it would suit an amazon. Or an eagle. 'Oh, what will you think of the master. He is not at home. But come in, I pray you, and I shall see that you have wine to soothe you and a goodly chair in which to wait.'

Brother Michaelo bowed to her. 'Perhaps I am too early?'

'Not at all. I pray you, come in.'

Constance showed him into a large room with a brazier and several chairs of excellent design, large carved backs, embroidered cushions on the seats. Master Moreton had elegant taste.

'The master will return anon,' babbled the woman, 'for certain, he has not forgotten. It is only that Mistress Wilton's aged aunt is missing and they are worried about the poor woman. She is not as she once was. Master Moreton is helping Jasper de Melton in his search.'

'Dame Phillippa missing?' Michaelo crossed himself. Remembering her confusion at the manor, he understood their concern. 'I shall be patient.'

This, then, was to be Michaelo's penance—to sit here, waiting for a merchant, listening to this woman's chatter. He resigned himself to his punishment, though he would have preferred to be left alone to pray for Dame Phillippa.

Weary of waiting and needing a distraction, Lucie went into the kitchen to see the children. But Hugh was already asleep in Kate's lap and Gwenllian curled up on a bench in the corner with her favourite rag doll.

'I should put them to bed,' Kate whispered, 'but they are so peaceful where they are.'

'Let them rest. When you grow weary, or Jasper comes in, take them up to bed.'

Lucie tore some bread from the loaf on the table and went back out into the hall to pace as she chewed.

She was trying to focus on Magda's news, consider what she should do, but she could not keep her mind from worry about Phillippa. All that could be done was being done. But if any ill befell her aunt, Lucie could not bear it. It would be her fault. She should have understood how much Phillippa wished to return to the manor. Was she lying in a ditch? Sweet Jesu. An elderly neighbour had been found last week in a rain-swollen ditch by the edge of the road in the Forest of Galtres. It was said that her family had refused to escort her to the house of an old friend in Easingwold who lay dying. Folk already gossiped about Lucie. What would they say about this? Catastrophe loomed in the shadows.

When she heard someone fumbling with the latch on the hall

door, she ran with pounding heart to open it. God be thanked, it was Jasper and Dame Phillippa. Weeping with relief, Lucie hugged her aunt, guided her to a chair while chiding her for not telling anyone she was going out.

'I was praying,' Phillippa said, 'at many churches. Why did the lad bring me home?'

Lucie glanced up at Jasper.

'Kate has kept the pottage warm and there is a good loaf of bread. Bring some for you and Dame Phillippa.' Lucie turned back to her aunt. 'What is this about?'

'I mean to pray in every church in York that the Lord might hear my need and tell me where I hid the parchment.'

Phillippa began to wriggle out of her cloak. Lucie helped her.

'Why every church?'

'I cannot believe the Lord would ignore a prayer from every church in York.'

'How many did you manage?'

Phillippa closed her eyes and straightened a finger for each church as she recited, 'The minster, St Michael-le-Belfry, St Christopher's Chapel, St Helen's, St Martin's. Master Moreton and Jasper interrupted me there and insisted that I come along with them.'

This was not one of Phillippa's confused moods. Lucie had learned a valuable lesson this evening. She would not treat her aunt like a child again, simply forbidding, not discussing. 'Next time, please ask one of us to accompany you. I promise you we shall.'

Jasper placed a bowl of pottage and a chunk of the soft centre of the loaf before Phillippa, poured her a cup of wine and added some water.

'You are the best lad,' Phillippa said, patting his hand. 'I pray you forgive an old woman's fit of anger.'

Jasper hunched his shoulders. 'I do not like my plans interrupted either.' He slipped on to the bench beside her.

Lucie asked after Roger Moreton.

'He remembered a guest, who had already waited a good while,' said Jasper with a mouth full of bread.

'I shall go to his house with a basket of flowers tomorrow to thank him,' Lucie said. She would also ask him about Harold's relationship with John Gisburne. 'Wait for me down here,' she told Jasper. 'I shall see the children off to bed, and aunt, and then we shall have the talk I promised.'

Michaelo drank little wine. He was comfortable—Goodwife Constance had noted how he winced when he leaned back in the chair, thrown up her hands in horror that he had not told her he was suffering and offered elegantly embroidered cushions to ease him. But that was the trouble. Michaelo had slept well the previous night, thanks to Brother Henry's sleep draught, but one night's rest did not compensate for his long bout of penitential sleeplessness, and he feared that wine and a comfortable chair might undo him. The goodwife wished to hear all about Wales, so he kept himself awake by talking, giving her lengthy, detailed descriptions of the castles, palaces, great houses and abbeys in which he had stayed on his pilgrimage.

When Roger Moreton entered the hall, dishevelled and red of face, the goodwife rose reluctantly.

'Did you find the poor woman?' she asked.

'We did indeed.'

'God be praised. Will you be needing anything more than wine?'

'If we do, I shall call for you.' Roger waited until she was well away. Then he turned to Michaelo and apologised, telling him of his mission and its happy outcome. 'But I have kept you sitting here so long. You have my full attention.'

Indeed, Michaelo felt he had been more than patient even though he understood the circumstance. 'His Grace the Archbishop is concerned about the troubles at Freythorpe Hadden. As godfather to young Hugh, the future heir, and his sister, His Grace sees it as his duty in their father's absence to watch over the family. He therefore requests your assurance that Harold Galfrey is capable to serve as steward while the wounded steward recovers. He should like to see his letter of recommendation, hear anything else you might know about his former employment.'

Roger made a face. He truly was an unsophisticated sort. 'In faith, I did not see his letter. He was set upon by outlaws on his way to York. They stole his purse. But he served as steward for the Godwin manor near Kingston-upon-Hull.'

'How then did John Gisburne come to recommend Galfrey so highly, if he had no letter?'

The merchant looked embarrassed. 'I did not think to ask him.'

'Is there anything else you might tell me about him?'

'No. I feel quite foolish to confess it. But I put my faith in John Gisburne. He has ever been good to me.'

Deus juva me, Michaelo had accepted Mistress Wilton's reassurances. But had she known that Roger Moreton was so under the influence of John Gisburne? The man's taste in servants and retainers had been cause for more than a few rumours. Michaelo dreaded reporting all this to Thoresby.

The hall was quiet, only two oil lamps still burned, one at the bottom of the steps, one on the table. Lucie wondered whether Jasper had been too tired to wait for her to finish settling Phillippa for the night. She had been reluctant to drink her calming tisane. Lucie had spent a long while up there convincing her aunt that she would not sleep the sleep of the dead. In truth, the tisane was stronger than on previous nights, but Phillippa need not know that. Lucie did not wish her to wake confused and attempt another church.

Picking up the lamp at the bottom of the steps, Lucie held it high so that she might see more of the table. Now she saw Jasper's fair hair hanging over the bench on which he had been sitting. As she crept closer she saw that he lay on his side and had covered himself with a blanket. Sleeping, yes, but determined to talk to her. He had been a great help to her of late. Did she thank him enough?

She could never predict his behaviour these days. But why did that bother her so? Had she ever truly been able to predict him, or had he simply been more obedient earlier, more eager to do what he thought she wished than to follow his own heart.

'Jasper,' she whispered in his ear, was about to settle in the chair at the head of the table but found Crowder and Melisende curled up together. She moved to the bench across the table from Jasper.

With much rubbing of his eyes and shaking of his head, Jasper rose and wrapped the blanket round his shoulders.

'She is abed?' he asked.

'Safely, yes.' Lucie smiled at the question. 'You do not wish to go in search of her again this evening?'

He laughed. 'Tell me what this is about.'

Lucie told him all she knew of the missing parchment about which Phillippa was so concerned, and more. She confided in him her belief that the thieves had included someone who knew the house well, told him of Daimon's slow healing and Tildy's suspicion, of Colby's visit to the manor. She saw that he understood that he was being treated as a man.

Jasper listen with a grave face.

When Lucie was finished, she poured them both some wine, watered both cups. 'God has been trying me sorely,' she said. 'Forgive me if I have not listened to you as I might.'

'I could go to the manor to search for the parchment and check the account books.'

Ignoring her inclination to reject the offer, Lucie said, 'I shall consider it. We need to discuss it with Dame Phillippa, learn where she has hidden it in the past. Perhaps that will suggest where to look.'

'Or she might remember. What do you think it might be?'

'I wish I knew, my love. That might also help us know who attacked Freythorpe.'

'Will I be there, when you talk to her?'

'You will.'

They finished their wine in companionable silence, then climbed wearily up to their beds, the cats padding softly ahead of them.

20

THE MORALITY OF
HYWEL'S WAR

Owen hoisted the pouch of stones over his good shoulder and
trudged off along the new stonework of the cloister to the west
front of the cathedral, ordering his thoughts as he walked. Though
aware that Friar Hewald waited anxiously at Rokelyn's house, Owen
could not abandon Cynog, not now. He had pieced much together,
but there were gaps and contradictions for which he could not
account. He must settle for what he had—the imminent removal
of Archdeacon Baldwin's household forced his hand. He must
confront Baldwin and Simon to discover what they knew, or indeed
what part they had played in the three deaths.

Cynog's parents had said that at one time he had talked
much about Owain Lawgoch, but then grew quiet. Had he been
disillusioned? Had he given copies of Hywel's maps to Archdeacon
Baldwin? And Cynog's right hand—who was the executioner who
had been frightened away before completing his grim task? Owen
feared it was Hywel who had ordered the deed: he had beaten the
horse thieves for their mistake, he might well have a traitor mutilated
and executed. Did this serve his prince?

He still had too few facts to accuse anyone of Cynog's murder.
Piers the Mariner? Why? And why, then, was Piers executed, and
his brother as well? At first Owen had suspected that they had been
hiding something on the ship. But the tongues had turned his mind
to lies or betrayals. Was he wrong? Were the tongues leading him to

a false surmise? But surely such a grim deed had been meant as a message? Had served a purpose?

All three men had been executed. Rokelyn had been right about Cynog's death from the start. But what had Baldwin and Simon to do with it? And how was it that Rokelyn knew nothing of their involvement? Or did he? Was that why Owen must investigate, rather than someone in the city?

What else did Owen know? Glynis had put a sleeping draught in the ale she gave Edmund and Jared. But she had not helped Piers escape that day. It was later that night that she did so. Had she been frightened by something on her first attempt? Or had she learned something from Piers, betrayed him to Hywel, who then ordered her to deliver her lover to him?

As Owen crossed over Llechllafar, passing the pilgrims' entrance to the cathedral, he thought about Sir Robert's tomb. Cynog had been blessed with such a gift. Would Owain Lawgoch, rightful Prince of Wales, order the death of such a man? In war, perhaps. But this was not war. Yet.

The house of Archdeacon Baldwin sat apart from most of the others, across the River Alun from the palace, near Patrick's Gate. Several carts crowded the narrow lane. The pilgrims had to pick their way past them and a few servants stood guard over the contents.

One of them stepped forward to bar Owen's way.

Owen dropped the pouch to the ground, rubbed his left hand. 'I wish to speak with Archdeacon Baldwin and Father Simon.'

'What is your business with my master?'

'If you would tell him Captain Archer is here,' Owen said quietly, though he put all his irritation into the eye that glared at the servant.

The man withdrew to the house.

In a moment, he returned. 'The Archdeacon will see you, Captain.' He offered to carry the pouch.

Owen nodded. 'It is for the Archdeacon.' He did not glance

back, but he heard the man's curse as he lifted the pouch. It was not unreasonably heavy, merely a surprising load when one expected other than stones.

Owen followed Baldwin's loud voice—suited for sermons, not housework. The archdeacon was directing the packing of a chest in the hall.

'*Benedicte*, Captain Archer.' His dark hair was dusty, various pieces of cloth draped over one forearm, a pile of documents at his feet. 'As you see, I am about to depart. I hoped to make Llawhaden Castle by nightfall, but the incident on the beach has turned all fingers to thumbs among my household.'

The servant following with the pouch of stones set it down with a thud at Owen's feet. Baldwin looked down inquiringly.

'Would you permit me to look at the wall Cynog repaired in your undercroft?' Owen asked.

'What is in the pouch?'

Owen glanced at the servant bent over the chest. 'It would be better to talk in private.'

Baldwin followed his gaze. 'No, no. No time to let them be idle.'

'Perhaps we might talk in the undercroft? And then I would talk to Father Simon.'

Now Baldwin fixed his eyes on Owen. 'He is at the cathedral.'

'Could you send for him?'

'What is this about?'

Owen lifted the pouch of stones. 'Do you have a lantern?'

Baldwin dropped the cloths, told the servant to continue packing—the chest must be ready when he returned. At the hall entrance, the archdeacon shouted to one of the men guarding the carts to fetch Father Simon from the cathedral at once. Then he took a lantern from a hook and led the way through a door to a landing atop wooden steps that dropped down into darkness.

Baldwin opened up the shuttered lantern, closed the door behind them. 'Is this about the deaths?'

'The executions,' Owen said.

'You think I would order such heinous acts?'

'You might. If by such deeds you thought to ensure peace in this holy city.'

'Are you mad?' Baldwin held the light closer to Owen, almost blinding him.

'God's blood,' Owen growled, grabbing the lantern with his right hand. Painful, but worse if he stumbled after the fool blinded him in his one good eye with the light. 'The wall, Father.'

'We have peace in the city.'

'For how long? When Owain Lawgoch arrives with his Welsh and French army, do you think they will skirt round St David's and leave you in peace? And those within—how many Welshmen would rather die for the rightful Prince of Wales than for King Edward?'

'Are you one of them?'

'Show me the wall.'

'You think *I* am one of them. Or that Simon is.' Baldwin started for the door.

Owen barred the way, lantern in one hand, bag of stones in the other. Pain shot down his right side, but by the Rood he meant to see that wall before Father Simon arrived.

Baldwin nodded to the pouch. 'What is in there?'

'Stones. Come. Show me the wall.'

The archdeacon turned back to the landing. Owen shone the light down the steps.

Baldwin hesitated. 'Why should I trust you?'

'I am working for your fellow, Archdeacon Rokelyn,' Owen growled.

'Faith, I had forgotten that.' Baldwin shook his head and began the descent.

The stench of damp, mould and worse, and a chill that erased memory of the spring day without, enveloped Owen as he left the landing. He understood the archdeacon's hesitation. But once Baldwin was in motion he made short work of the stairs. Owen left the pouch on the bottom step and hurried after his guide, who navigated through piles of old furniture, barrels stacked atop one another, to a cleared area before the far wall.

It was a stone wall, like any other, bare of plaster, the stones exposed. Owen passed the light along its length. On the far left, dampness glistened on stained stones, to the right the stones were dry.

'As you see, a damp wall, too close to the river, partially rebuilt where the rats came through. What did you hope to find, Captain?' Baldwin's voice seemed muffled in this cluttered dungeon.

Owen moved closer to the repaired side, looking for some sign of loose or decorated stones, something to indicate where the maps were or had been. Where would Cynog have placed them? The ceiling was low—this was more a cellar than an undercroft. Owen could see the top stones. Simon was as tall as he, but not Cynog. Owen crouched down, ran the light across the lower stones. Nothing. 'Christ save us, it must be here.'

'Master Baldwin?' someone called from above. It was Father Simon.

'Simon!' Baldwin shouted. 'Come below.'

Pushing up from his crouch, Owen hurried to the steps to retrieve the stones. Baldwin, protesting the loss of light, followed. Pouch in hand, Owen considered what he should do. Father Simon bore an oil lamp, which gave off such a dim light he must move slowly. Even so, he was by now almost to the bottom.

Owen slipped off to the right, Baldwin following.

'Master?' Simon called.

Setting the lantern on a barrel, Owen lifted out the stones bearing maps and handed them to Baldwin. 'Do you recognise these?'

Baldwin held them towards the light, turned them about, studying them. 'Someone has defaced these? Why do you show them to me? What have they to do with Simon?'

'I have reason to believe Cynog used stones such as these in the repairs to your undercroft. They are not defaced, they carry messages.'

'Messages? In my cellar wall?' Baldwin managed a nervous laugh. 'You *are* mad.'

Owen sensed Simon behind him, grabbed the lantern and spun

round. Blinded, Simon dropped the oil lamp.

'For the love of God!' Baldwin cried, lunging towards a smoking pool of spilled oil.

A healthy fear of fire, but Owen saw there was no need. 'It is a small lamp,' he said, 'and an earthen floor.'

'But the barrels.' Baldwin made to stomp out the smoke.

Owen pulled him back. 'Save your boots. You are more at risk if the hem of your gown touches the smouldering oil.'

Simon bent down to retrieve the empty lamp, sat it on a barrel. 'Have you found what you sought, Captain?' he asked in a voice lacking all emotion.

'He claims—' Baldwin began.

'I have two of the stones,' Owen said.

'You cannot,' said Simon. 'I removed them this morning.'

'What is this?' Baldwin grabbed his secretary's arm. 'What do you know of this?'

Simon shook off the archdeacon's hand. 'Cynog came to me. I did not go to him. But neither did I turn him away.' He spoke to Owen.

'What is it?' Baldwin looked from one to the other. 'What have you done, Simon? What are these stones?'

'I ask only that Bishop Houghton judge me, not Archdeacon Rokelyn.'

Not the words of a man intending to run. Owen thought fresh air and light was worth the risk. 'Let us go up. We have much to talk about.'

The servant in the hall was dismissed. In the light, Owen saw the ravages of the day on Simon. Hollow-eyed, slack-mouthed, he was a man who had seen the enormity of what he had helped put in motion. He sat down on a bench, head bowed.

Baldwin stood over him. 'You meddling man. Tell me. Tell me all of it.'

Owen eased down into a chair. 'What did you do with the maps?'

'I meant them for Bishop Houghton. He has the forces to capture Hywel, save our holy city from civil war.'

'What are these maps?' Baldwin demanded.

'The way to Hywel's camps. Cynog carved markers based on

stone maps such as these and placed them in the countryside,' said Owen.

'And then scratched maps on stones for Father Simon?' Baldwin did not sound as if he believed it.

Simon shook his head. 'The maps were already on stones—they were delivered to Cynog that way—Lord Hywel must have thought it a clever ruse. After using them to set the markers, Cynog brought them to me under cover of working on the undercroft. I hid them in the wall until I could deliver them to Bishop Houghton.'

'Lord Hywel,' Baldwin murmured. 'I begin to understand. But you should have gone to Archdeacon Rokelyn.'

Simon sat silently, his eyes downcast, his hands limp in his lap.

'Cynog thus gave you the means to locate Owain Lawgoch's supporters,' Owen said. 'And it was for that, his betrayal of Hywel, that he was executed. Am I right?'

'I should not have agreed to it,' Simon whispered.

Baldwin sank down on to a chair with a look of horror. 'This is how you meant to protect us from bloodshed?'

'Cynog was angry,' said Simon. 'I should have guided him to prayer, not deceit.'

'You should have kept your own counsel,' Baldwin cried.

'I pray you,' Owen said to the archdeacon, 'let Simon speak. We must hear the truth of this.'

Baldwin put his head in his hands.

'What made Cynog so angry?' Owen asked.

Simon lifted anguished eyes to Owen, shook his head slowly, as if wondering how he came to be here. 'Why do you torment me with questions? You know the tale.'

'Tell me the tale.'

'Cynog loved Glynis. She told him she admired the men who were joining Hywel's cause. To win her admiration he approached Hywel, joined his men. And after a time Glynis withdrew her affections. At Hywel's command, she turned her eye to Piers the Mariner.'

'Why him?'

Simon's breathing was shallow, quick. 'Piers had boasted that he might join Hywel's army. His brother Siencyn encouraged him. Piers was not a man any captain wanted on his ship, even his brother. He used his fists rather than his wits.'

'And Piers executed Cynog,' Owen said.

'He did. He confessed to me that he did it to prove himself trustworthy to Hywel. It might have worked, had you not come along. People wanted to believe they had fought over Glynis, that Cynog had been winning her back.'

'A man does not hang a rival, Father.'

Simon stared down at his hands in silence.

'And what did Cynog do to win Hywel's trust?' Owen asked.

Simon took a deep breath. 'I do not know how he first won it. But, of late, Hywel sensed Cynog backing away and set him a new task—he was to find out what he could about you, so that Hywel might have something to use in persuading you to join his cause. Cynog was sorry for that. He meant to warn you when you returned.' He raised his eyes to Owen. 'And what was your test, captain? I cannot think you managed the execution of the brothers, not injured as you are. What did you do? Or is it my execution that will confirm your standing with the madman?'

Baldwin's head shot up.

Dear God, is that what he thought? Owen began to protest. But he was so close to understanding. This was not the moment to reassure Simon. 'Hywel had Piers executed because he confessed to you, is that not true?'

'His tongue cut out.' Simon covered his face with his hands.

'But Piers must have done far more than that,' Owen prodded.

The secretary said nothing.

'Piers named others in St David's who worked for Hywel,' Owen guessed.

'Yes,' Simon whispered.

'Why?'

Simon raised his head, his face defenceless. 'I told him that Archdeacon Baldwin meant to urge Rokelyn to send him on to the bishop's gaol at Llawhaden, to be tried as a traitor to the king. Unless he helped us.'

'I see why the archdeacon called you a meddling man.'

Simon did not deny it. 'All along, Piers believed that Hywel would save him. But help had not come.'

Foolish man. 'Piers had not understood he was to be a martyr for the Welsh cause.'

Simon shook his head. 'But Captain Siencyn guessed. And he explained it to Piers.'

'He did his brother no favour. From martyr to traitor—he merely hastened the execution. Did Siencyn not understand that traitors are executed in war?'

Simon looked at Owen as if he were mad. 'We are not at war.'

'*You* are not. Hywel is. So Captain Siencyn was executed for convincing his brother to betray Hywel?'

'He, too, betrayed him. It was from him that I learned much of what I know. Even some of the names. There were not many in the end. So. Are you here to execute me?'

'You would not dare!' Baldwin thundered.

Owen rose. 'I know little more than what I have heard here. I came not to execute you. I wished only to resolve Cynog's death and learn more about Hywel.'

'You tricked me,' Simon cried, rising.

'Not at all. I merely delayed correcting you.'

'How can you be so cruel?'

'How? You ask *me* that?'

'Now what will you do?' Baldwin demanded of Owen.

'I shall tell Archdeacon Rokelyn all I have learned.'

'That is it?' Baldwin asked. 'You want nothing of him?'

'I wanted only the truth. There is precious little of that to be had in this holy city.' Owen slung the now much lighter pouch over his shoulder. 'God go with you, Father Simon, Archdeacon.' He strode across the hall and through the doorway.

Outside, the sunshine caressed his face. Though beneath his tunic his shirt stuck to his bleeding side, he did not turn towards the city, but to Patrick's Gate. No one stopped him.

21

TROUBLING UNCERTAINTIES

Irises, some early roses, sprigs of rosemary and lavender. Lucie tied them with long grasses and took them to Roger Moreton. Goodwife Constance, exclaiming at the bouquet, stepped aside to allow Lucie in.

'I shall not take them until the master has seen the fruit of your garden,' the housekeeper said. She called to a servant, had him fetch Roger. 'Come into the hall, do.'

'It was good of Master Moreton to join the search for my Aunt Phillippa yesterday evening.'

'Poor Brother Michaelo sat here and told me of such wonders as he waited. He is a most patient man.'

'Brother Michaelo?'

'Goodwife Constance,' Roger said from the doorway. His tone sounded a warning to the woman, who could not seem to remember that all the city did not need to know the details of her master's life. Indeed, should not know some details.

The goodwife curtsied and left the room.

'Mistress Wilton.' Roger bowed to Lucie.

She held out the flowers, feeling a bit foolish now for the gesture.

But Roger was his usual gracious self, praising their beauty, assuring her that he needed no reward.

'Jasper did not require my assistance.'

'I felt better knowing he was not alone,' Lucie said. 'But I am sorry you were late to receive Brother Michaelo.'

'You are wondering about that.'

She was also worried about it, seeing Roger's smile fade. 'What is it?'

'See what friends we are, to read the other's face.'

Lucie imagined Jasper standing with her, hearing that. 'You need not tell me what you discussed. I do not mean to pry.'

'But it concerned you. His Grace the Archbishop wants to know more about Harold Galfrey. I fear I did not impress the archbishop's secretary with my confession that I knew little of the man. I intend to discuss him with John Gisburne.'

Lucie prayed she had not been foolish to trust Harold. She did not need more trouble. 'I shall be grateful to hear what Gisburne says. The Riverwoman is also concerned about Harold.'

Roger threw up his hands. 'Why does everyone suddenly distrust him?'

'I do not, Roger. I think Harold an excellent steward. Magda truly had all good things to say about what he has accomplished. But Gisburne's servant Colby went to Freythorpe to see Harold the other day. He asked for him by name. He warned Harold about Nan's son Joseph being close at hand. Would John Gisburne send that particular servant on such a mission?'

It was plain from his expression that Roger was puzzled. 'God forgive me for saying so, but it is not like John to trust Colby in such a thing, or indeed to be so thoughtful as to warn someone about a matter like this. I shall find out all I can. It is the least I can do.'

Roger was such a good-natured, well-intentioned man. But Lucie was belatedly realising that his trusting nature could be a liability. It seemed an odd quality in a successful merchant.

John Thoresby shifted his position on the stone seat. Old bones should not perch on cold stone. They would be down in the cold earth soon enough. The archbishop and Jehannes, Archdeacon of York, sat in the garden of the archbishop's palace near the minster. Thoresby had put his servants to work airing out the great house.

He grew weary of playing guest at Jehannes's house, but the roof repairs at Bishopthorpe continued. So he had compromised by opening his house in the city. The sun this morning was warm enough to heat Thoresby's head even through his hat, but the stone seat held the chill of the night and the morning dew. He would be sorry for this perch later. But he had wished to speak with Jehannes away from Brother Michaelo and yet be nearby if his secretary had any questions. Michaelo was occupied in the palace supervising the servants.

Thoresby disagreed with Archdeacon Jehannes regarding what to do about Brother Michaelo's sudden passion for penance. Jehannes believed it might be a sign of spiritual awakening and thus should be encouraged, or at least not discouraged. Thoresby had never had patience with the idea that self-inflicted beatings were the way to God. And with Michaelo it was particularly questionable.

'He is much changed, Your Grace,' Jehannes argued.

'Not for the better. The journey to Kingston-upon-Hull to inquire about Galfrey will be good for Michaelo.'

'Seeing to this house will surely be enough of a distraction. Another journey is cruel so soon after Michaelo's return from Wales.'

'He journeyed to Wales as a pilgrim. This will remind him he is a representative of the Archbishop of York and as such has duties that require him to have his wits about him.'

'Such devotion should be encouraged in him, sire. He is a monk.'

'Of course he is. But that never bothered him before.'

Thoresby saw Jehannes struggle to hide a smile. Good. The man had been distracted from his pious protest. Michaelo was off to the Godwin manor at Kingston-upon-Hull on the morrow and that was the end of it.

'Why are you disturbed about this man Galfrey?' Jehannes asked. 'Mistress Wilton's message mentioned that the manor was well guarded and that work had already begun on the repairs. The man may be unknown to you, but he sounds a worthy steward.'

'I merely wish to know. And Michaelo is idle. Three days, I should think. Another might ride there in one, return the next, but he will take a leisurely pace. Mark me.' Thoresby rose, his bones demanding a change. 'Let us see how the work progresses.'

It was early afternoon when Thoresby could at last sit in the hall of the palace and reacquaint himself with the atmosphere of the house. It was not so pleasant as Bishopthorpe, but it had a grandeur and a sense of the past that he had always found to his liking. He heard Brother Michaelo explaining the value of careful work to a servant who had disappointed him. Perhaps opening up the palace had been sufficient to pull Michaelo from his foolishness. Now if Archer were here, life might be pleasant once more. He would arrive soon enough, surely. And it must be soon. The palace roof was in terrible condition. Someone must speed the work along at Bishopthorpe, then move the workmen here.

Thoresby was considering Michaelo's ability to oversee that work when a servant announced Roger Moreton. The name was familiar. The face, however, was not—solid, flushed, handsome in a common sort of way. The man wore the livery of the Merchants' Guild. Wealth here, new wealth. But who was he to Thoresby? The archbishop rose, offered his ring to kiss. The man dropped to his knees, kissed the ring. Clean fingernails, excellent workmanship on the felt hat. Good boots.

'*Benedicte*, Master Moreton. How can we help you?'

'Your Grace. I should perhaps see Brother Michaelo. But he said last evening that it was Your Grace's concern about Mistress Wilton's property that led him to make inquiries about Harold Galfrey.'

Ah. So this was the neighbour with good intentions. 'It is my concern, as godfather to Mistress Wilton's and Captain Archer's two children. Do you have more information than you were able to offer last evening?'

'I have just come from John Gisburne's house, Your Grace.'

John Gisburne. A wealthy merchant of questionable character who had yet to pledge any funds towards the completion of the minster. 'Was Gisburne of any assistance to my inquiry? Do take a seat, my good man. I shall have a sore neck if I look up at you much longer.'

Roger Moreton glanced round, chose a comfortable chair, nodded to the hovering servant to place it closer. Thoresby approved. A man who knew his worth. Perhaps his judgement could be trusted in the choice of a steward.

'See what refreshment might be had,' Thoresby told the servant. 'And ask Brother Michaelo to join us.' The archbishop was curious about the man who had been such a friend to Mistress Wilton. A widower living next door to a handsome, wealthy woman of high esteem in the community, a woman wed to a man beneath her who was lingering far too long in Wales. Did Roger Moreton entertain hopes that Archer had indeed deserted his family as the rumours would have it? 'You have proved a good friend to Mistress Wilton,' Thoresby said.

Moreton frowned. 'My Christian duty, Your Grace.'

'The loan of your cart, your horse, your steward? That seems more than Christian duty from even the broadest of interpretations.'

A blush, but Moreton's eyes did not flicker. He was not a timid man. 'Mistress Wilton was a great help to me when my wife lay mortally ill.' He was quiet a moment. 'I have no need of my steward at present, Your Grace. But it is about him that I came.'

Brother Michaelo entered the room. Thoresby motioned him to a chair.

'The servants will bring refreshment, Your Grace, Master Moreton. They—' Michaelo pursed his lips, shook his head slightly. 'Forgive me. You do not want to hear of it.'

'Not at present,' Thoresby agreed. 'Master Moreton comes to us from a conversation with Master Gisburne regarding Harold Galfrey.'

Michaelo tucked his hands up his sleeves and leaned back to listen. Thoresby inclined his head towards Moreton. 'Now. If you would tell us what you learned about Galfrey.'

The merchant cleared his throat and turned his eyes to the floor. 'I do believe that Master Gisburne imposed upon our friendship when he urged me to see Harold Galfrey. Harold is apparently Gisburne's distant cousin and counted on this relationship when he arrived in York with no letters of introduction, those having been stolen.'

'You said apparently his cousin,' Thoresby noted. 'One either is or is not.'

'I chose the word intentionally, Your Grace. In fact, Gisburne had never met the man and Harold knew no one in the city, so Gisburne took him at his word.'

Thoresby did not like what he was hearing. 'Did he write to his relations to verify the man's claims?'

'No, he did not, Your Grace. But he said that had he any cause to doubt them he would so have written. When I mentioned Colby's visit to Freythorpe Hadden—'

Brother Michaelo sat forward. 'What visit?'

It appeared Michaelo knew this name, Colby. Moreton explained the visit, concluding with an interesting piece of information—Master Gisburne had been surprised to hear of the incident.

Master Moreton, it seemed, had learned how much he did not know. Thoresby thought the two untrustworthy servants were of interest.

'We must write another letter to the High Sheriff before you depart,' Thoresby said to Brother Michaelo.

'Are you leaving York again so soon?' Moreton asked pleasantly.

'He rides to Kingston-upon-Hull tomorrow, to the manor at which Harold Galfrey last served,' Thoresby said, not wishing Michaelo to emote at this particular moment.

Moreton looked keen. 'You head for the Godwins?'

Michaelo nodded.

'Might I accompany you?'

'Why should you wish to do so?' Michaelo asked. He had become quite a cautious man of late. Thoresby approved that change.

'I should have investigated the man's character before recommending him to Mistress Wilton.'

'But you did not,' Thoresby said.

Moreton flushed. The man deserved no delicacy. 'I wish to make some atonement.'

Apparently Michaelo pitied Moreton. 'I should welcome a companion,' he said gently. 'It is a long journey to make with only a servant.'

The discussion had become tiresome. Thoresby wished to withdraw to his parlour to consider what he might do to improve the palace, not arrange companions for his secretary. He rose. The two men also rose.

'If you can ride tomorrow, I have no objection to your accompanying my secretary. I shall leave you to make your arrangements. I thank you for your information, Master Moreton, and look forward to even more on your return.' Thoresby bowed himself out of the hall.

After Kate took Gwenllian and Hugh to bed, Lucie, Jasper and Phillippa sat round the small table in the kitchen near the fire. Though the day had been warm when Lucie took the flowers to Roger, the evening was chilly. Jasper sat slumped over the table, picking at a splinter on the edge. His hair hung over his eyes. Lucie knew the cause of his pout. Upon returning from his interview with Thoresby, Roger Moreton had offered them his donkey cart for the journey to Freythorpe, but asked that they wait until he returned with more information about Harold Galfrey.

'Be patient, Jasper. You will go to Freythorpe,' Lucie said. 'It is not Master Moreton's cart we await. I wish to know more about Harold Galfrey so I might advise you.'

Jasper said nothing. He had already voiced his certainty that Lucie and Roger would find reasons to keep him in York. No one considered him man enough to make the journey.

Phillippa, too, was glum. She wished to accompany Jasper to Freythorpe. Lucie had firmly refused. This was one request she could not grant Phillippa.

'But you would help us by telling us all you remember about the parchment,' Lucie had said. 'Anything you can recall about your husband's activities at that time, anything about that time at all.'

Dame Phillippa had been tidier and more coherent for the past few days. Lucie hoped that perhaps she had recovered from the shock of the raid on the manor and was more herself.

'At times the past is clearer to me than the present,' Phillippa had said. 'But I have tried to forget Douglas Sutton.'

It was Jasper who brought up the subject again.

'Why did you want to forget your husband?' Jasper asked. 'Was he a bad husband?'

'No, lad, he was as good a husband as he could be. And I loved him. And my baby, my Jeremy.' Tears fell on to Phillippa's knobbed and wrinkled hands.

Jeremy had been Lucie's cousin, never met. Dead before she was born.

Jasper put a hand over one of Phillippa's. 'I have some ideas about where you might have hidden the parchment.'

Looking up expectantly, Phillippa wiped her eyes with her free hand. 'Tell me. Perhaps they will help me remember.'

'It was once in the tapestry you brought from your home, so perhaps you moved it to another?'

Phillippa shook her head. 'I worried even then about the damp and someone tearing it. I would not have put it in another such place.'

'Beneath a chair seat?'

The old woman chuckled. 'Clever lad. I am not so clever.'

Lucie tiptoed away to see whether Kate needed her help. When she returned, Phillippa was talking of the Scots raids into Yorkshire three years after her marriage. Jasper sat transfixed, imagining himself fighting the Bruce, no doubt.

'The destruction was so horrible that many a lord with lands in the north and many a town paid the Bruce to go away,' said Phillippa, 'or to spare their lands. I cannot remember which lords, which towns. We had no such money—the Suttons had land, but they had fallen on hard times. I was at home, frightened for my family—I was with child during that terrible spring and summer. The rumours terrified me. Douglas was often away.'

'Fighting?' Jasper asked.

'He had fought with Archbishop Melton's forces at Myton-on-Swale. That was a massacre. Our men were not trained as soldiers. Clergy, most of them. The Scots had their way with them and it was bloody. But Douglas survived. I nursed his wounds. And then we were wed.'

'You wed him because he had been brave?' Jasper asked.

'My father allowed it because he had been brave,' said Phillippa. 'Before the battle I had been forbidden to see more of Douglas. My brother Robert had never liked him, neither had father.'

Lucie had never known her grandfather. She slipped back into her seat to hear the rest. But Phillippa's eyes were far away. Jasper gave Lucie a questioning look. She nodded and gestured for him to try again.

'Aunt Phillippa,' he said, 'did Douglas Sutton fight again after you were wed?'

She shook her head as she brought her gaze back to the present. 'I do not know, lad.'

'But you said he was often away.'

'On business.'

'And the parchment?'

'After being away for days, sometimes weeks, he would return weary and quiet. But never as quiet as the day he brought the parchment. He returned much sooner than I had expected. He said it was because he was worried about me, it was near my time and I had lost our first two babes. He asked me to stitch a back on to a tapestry that had been his mother's. I did not want to, but he said it was a good place to hide things from the invaders. So I stitched, leaving a space open at the top. I finished just before our baby was born. We christened him Jeremy, after the neighbour who was his godfather.

'While I lay with little Jeremy I heard someone come to the house, argue with John.' Phillippa rose from her chair, groping for her cane. Jasper rose and handed it to her. She glanced round, seemingly confused. 'My chest. Where is my chest?'

'Up in the bedchamber, Aunt,' said Lucie. 'Do you want Jasper to fetch it?'

Phillippa leaned on the cane with her right hand, her left hand pressed to her eyes. She shook her head. 'No,' she whispered. 'I burned the clothing long ago. I do not know why I thought of that.'

'Would you like something to calm you?' Lucie asked, putting an arm round Phillippa, who was shivering. 'Come back to the fire.'

Phillippa shook her head, pulled out of Lucie's grasp. 'When you know what I did you will not forgive me.'

Jasper pulled a chair near the fire, more comfortable than the bench by the table. 'Sit here, Aunt. Tell us. We must know everything if we are to protect the people at Freythorpe now.'

'You are right, lad. Mother in Heaven, you all suffer for my sin. I had forgotten so much—but that man—seeing him—'

'Who?' Lucie asked.

Phillippa did not seem to hear Lucie's questions as she let Jasper help her into the chair. Or perhaps she was lost in the memory. 'The sounds coming from the other room frightened me. Jeremy began to cry. I nursed him—oh, I have oft thought my fear curdled my milk and that is what killed my little one. Or his father's guilt.' She took a deep breath. 'Later Douglas came to see me. He had changed his clothes. I asked him why he had changed clothes in the middle of the day. He was pale, quiet, sat down beside me, took Jeremy's tiny hand in his, kissed the baby's forehead. Something was wrong, I knew. But he just sat there, his head bowed.

'I crept from bed the next morning, very early, and found Douglas out by the barn, burying his clothing, I thought. What a waste of good cloth. No matter what the stain, some of the cloth would be of use. I stepped closer. It was a body.' Phillippa lifted eyes dark with memory. 'He said the man had already been mortally injured. It was his partner, Henry Gisburne, he said. They had been attacked, Douglas had left him for dead. He had not known Henry could have been saved. And now, after walking all the way to our house, Henry had died.'

Lucie and Jasper crossed themselves.

'John Gisburne said his father and my uncle had been friends,' Lucie said.

Phillippa was not listening. '"Fetch the priest," I said. But Douglas said they would not believe he had not killed Henry. "What of his family?" I asked. Douglas said Henry had none. Had none, he said. So I—I returned to bed. A few days later he told me to sew up the opening in the tapestry. I could feel something in there. He made me swear never to speak of it until he brought it forth. I broke the vow once. I had a dream and begged him to tell me what was in the tapestry. "A letter that will be our salvation," he said. "When the time is right, someone will pay much for it." Henry was certain of it. Douglas died not long after of a fever. And Jeremy, too.'

No one spoke for a long while. Lucie studied her aunt's ravaged face and wondered how she had lived so long without speaking of this. How could she sit with Douglas Sutton night after night, day after day, and not ask what had happened?

'What of the chest in your bedchamber at Freythorpe?' Jasper asked.

Phillippa glanced over at him, confused.

'The parchment. Might you have hidden it in the chest?'

'Douglas hid his bloody clothes in there, not the parchment. You do not hate me, lad?'

'Your husband might have done nothing wrong,' said Jasper. 'The parchment might prove his innocence.'

'But what of Henry's family?' Lucie asked. 'Did they come to you? Do you think they know of the parchment?'

'Douglas said the parchment had been hidden in our home because henry had caught his wife looking at it.' Phillippa bowed her head. 'So many men went off to fight and never returned.' She pressed her fingertips to her eyelids. 'I met Mistress Gisburne once.' Her voice had dropped to a whisper. 'I said nothing. God forgive me.'

This was the sin that burned in Phillippa. But had it not been her husband's fault? 'Why did Douglas Sutton just bury his friend? The priest would know that many had crawled home to die.' Lucie remembered Phillippa's fears about the men who had been watching the manor. 'Do you think it was Henry Gisburne's family who watched the manor, Aunt Phillippa?'

'Henry's sons. I learned that he had sons. I had a son. But like your Martin he died before he walked.' Phillippa's voice fell into the flat tone of her confusion.

'Go to bed, Jasper,' Lucie said. 'We shall try again on the morrow.'

Wearily, Lucie helped Phillippa up to bed.

Long into the night Lucie sat by her chamber window, wondering about her uncle. And the Gisburnes. Had they any way of knowing Henry had died at Douglas Sutton's home? How much better for everyone if her uncle had sent Henry's body to his family. Unless, of course, he had murdered him. But why would he have done so? Perhaps Jasper was right. The parchment might hold the key to all of this.

22

WRETCHEDNESS

Owen was grateful to Archbishop Thoresby for this ship, for passage home. But he could not sleep the first night on board. He never could. Other men either hung over the side in wretchedness or slept the sleep of a babe in a cradle. Owen could not understand the latter. The tarry stench, the creaking, the rocking, the splash of the waves, the awareness of the depths below him, full of sea monsters and dead men, it was not a thing to make him sleep.

His thoughts wandered back to St David's the day of Sir Robert's entombment—the echoing cathedral, Sir Robert's shrouded form, the mingled scent of decay and dried lavender, rosemary, frankincense—a gift from Bishop Houghton—the lonely, frightening grinding sound of the stone closing over Sir Robert. Owen wondered whether God let the blessed gaze down upon the earth, whether they know at last it is truly over when they watch their burial.

Friar Hewald joined him. 'You are missing your friend?'

Owen shook his head. 'Thinking of Sir Robert's tomb. I wish my wife could see it.'

'Then I shall leave you to your memories.'

In truth, Owen would miss Iolo, who had chosen to join Hywel's forces. Despite the man's cruelty.

'Have we fared better under the English?' Iolo had asked.

'*You* have, Iolo.'

'Aye. Of late. But you know it is not true for all.'

'Hywel is not the answer.'

'He is what we have. You will tell no one?'

Owen should. He should warn both the Duke of Lancaster, whose household Iolo had observed closely so recently, and Bishop Houghton, who had sent Iolo to the duke.

But Owen would not betray the young man who had guarded his back. They were not so different. Had Hywel been a Christian knight, had Owen felt confident that he would improve the lot of the Welsh, the friar might be returning to England with only the duke's borrowed men, Tom, Sam, Edmund and Jared.

When Owen left Archdeacon Baldwin's house his anger had propelled him far along the coastline, ignoring his pain as he walked, almost ran, and cursed the meddling, ambitious clergy, cursed Hywel, who had made ugly a righteous cause, who would free the people of Wales only to enslave them himself. He was no better for the people of this land than King Edward. How could Owain Lawgoch have chosen such a commander?

Martin Wirthir had found him, appeared from the air as was his wont. And Owen had hoped in the moment between seeing him and asking the question that Martin would redeem the dream.

'Did Lawgoch choose Hywel?'

'He did, my friend. He is not a god, merely an earthly prince.'

Martin had provided food and shelter for two days, while Owen burned with fever. Then brought him to Patrick's Gate on the dawn of the third day.

Friar Hewald and Owen's men had been frantic, and desperate to get him away before any more danger might befall him, but Owen had insisted on Sir Robert's burial. Ranulf de Hutton had been there, weeping for the friend who had begun the task.

Now, as Owen sat looking out on the horrible deep, his anger rose again, its target this time himself. He had almost made the same mistake as Cynog. Or Glynis, perhaps. Hywel had seemed to him a harsh commander, but fighting a Godly cause. How easy it had been to discount that which he despised in Hywel for the higher purpose.

Now he carried a guilt he must keep ever secret from Lucie. She must never know. She would not understand. Of all that had happened on this journey, this was the decision, the turning point, that he most needed to confide to her. But he could not. He would not inflict that pain, sow that seed of doubt in his love. For he did love her. And his children. He had been so tempted by a chance to fight for his own people after all those years of fighting for King Edward. But God had saved him from himself. *Deo gratias.*

23

NOT AS THEY SEEM

Geese squawked in the courtyard at Freythorpe Hadden, chased by Walter the gatekeeper's young boy. The gatehouse was silent today, the men away for the day, cutting timber. Tildy moved her stool out of the sunlight. Mending was easier in half-light, where she did not squint.

'It is pleasant out here,' Daimon said. 'I thank you for your trouble.'

'And who deserves it more than you?' Tildy dropped her work, smiled at Daimon. She hoped the sun might revive him. She did not like his pallor, the shadows under his eyes. He had good reason to be so, trapped in the house all this while. He had insisted on walking across the hall and out to the chair, but two servants had walked with him and he had been grateful for their support when he stumbled. Tildy had set out a high-backed chair, a stool so he might prop up his legs, a blanket and some cushions. Once settled, he looked much cheered to be outside.

'A man is not meant to sit idle by the fire,' Daimon said.

They sat in a companionable silence for a time, until Hoge, the gardener, appeared. Taking off his sweat-stained hat, he bobbed his head towards Daimon and Tildy. 'Master. Mistress.' His dark hair was matted to his head on this warm day, his young face spotted with sunburn. He did not meet Tildy's or Daimon's eyes, but rather watched the ground. 'I would have my say to Master Galfrey, if he were about, but as he is not, I shall say to you. If you be not pleased with my work in the garden, you might make your complaint afore having others come behind my back.' He twisted his hat in hands stained green and brown by his work.

Tildy could see that the speech had cost him much anxiety. 'I am satisfied with your work, Hoge,' she said. 'I know nothing of others coming behind your back. Whence comes this complaint?'

'The maze, Mistress. All tilled up. I know not why you would wish me to do such a thing, encourage the mud on the paths, but you had only to ask.'

'Tilled the paths?' Daimon muttered. 'What nonsense is this? I pray you, go with him, Matilda, see what has happened.'

Hoge turned round and with his characteristic gait, caused by a poorly formed foot, led Tildy to the maze, where someone had, indeed, been digging up the paths. The gravel was mixed with the dirt.

'I do not understand,' said Tildy. 'Why would one do this?'

'I ask the same, Mistress. What does Master Galfrey know of the garden?'

'Do you know that he ordered this?'

'Nay. But who else? You have more sense, as does Master Daimon.' Hoge shook his head at the mess.

Tildy was pleased by his words, but disturbed by her second puzzle today. She could not think of a reason Harold might order this. He was too busy with the gatehouse. 'I suppose you might press it down well, then add more gravel,' she said.

'Aye, that is what is to be done, for certain, Mistress.'

But why had someone done such a thing? 'Is it so all the way to the heart of the maze, Hoge?'

'Aye, it is, and dug up well even beneath the benches. But the path the other side is not so much disturbed.'

Had someone been digging, not tilling? Tildy did not want to put thoughts in the man's head. 'Could you guide me through the maze so I might see?' She had been through the maze many times the past summer, with Gwenllian and Hugh. She thought she might notice if anything had been changed, but Hoge would be the more likely one to make note of anything. 'Show me all that is amiss.'

'It is muddy, Mistress. Are you certain you wish to walk it?'

249

'I am.'

She stepped with care and soon regretted her idea. But how else might she be able to describe this clearly to Alfred and Gilbert? They were away today, searching for the thatcher who Daimon thought might bear a grudge against the D'Arbys. The digging seemed rather shallow, though in some places the soil was quite churned up, with various textures visible. In the centre, where four stone benches flanked a flagstone area rather overgrown with thyme, one of the flagstones had been pried up and reset.

'Careless work, that,' Hoge said, shaking his head mournfully.

'Can you reset it properly?' Tildy asked.

'I can if it pleases you.'

'It would, Hoge.' Tildy looked round, saw nothing else amiss but the digging. 'What a great deal of pointless work.'

'Someone made sport of me, mayhap,' Hoge said.

'Why?'

He ducked his head and looked away. Tildy was mystified, but asked no more. 'Thank you for showing me this, Hoge. Please repair it when you have time. I shall tell the steward to loan you a good worker to assist you.'

'Thank you, Mistress.'

Tildy walked back to Daimon wishing he were not so frail. She would like to confide in him, but she did not wish to worry him.

She could not connect this incident to what she had witnessed early this morning. She had come across Nan with a basket of food. Seeing Tildy, the cook quickly covered the contents, said she was taking food to Walter the gatekeeper and his family, who had moved into the cottage the previous day. Later Tildy had learned that Walter's family had not yet moved.

She wondered whether Nan's son was about.

Late in the afternoon, after helping Daimon inside, Tildy went out to the stables to confide in Alfred and Gilbert. Unfortunately, Harold came in as they talked. Alfred and Gilbert nodded as Tildy described the churned-up garden path. Harold shook his head.

'A riddle, that, the garden path,' said Gilbert.

'A puzzling mischief it is,' Harold agreed. 'I shall have two men watch either entrance tonight. If the deed is not complete, we might just catch the culprit.'

'What of Nan's son, Joseph?' Tildy asked. 'Has anyone seen him?'

'Have you asked Nan about him?' Harold asked.

'She might not wish us to know,' said Tildy.

Harold grinned. 'She is too much for you.'

Alfred and Gilbert smiled.

Tildy wondered about trusting them. They seemed too friendly with Harold.

'I know that she is ill-tempered,' said Harold, 'but who here could replace her?'

I could, Tildy thought, and peace would reign. 'Thank you for setting a watch tonight,' she said to Harold. Then, turning to Gilbert and Alfred, she asked, 'What of Jenkyn the thatcher?'

Gilbert stretched out his legs and yawned as Alfred said, 'We found him easy enough. He is working on a roof nearby. He seems a courteous sort.'

'Jenkyn is a courteous sort, is he?' asked Tildy. 'That is not what some of the maidservants have told me.'

Alfred shrugged.

Tildy turned to Harold. 'Will you be talking to Jenkyn?'

Harold had two reactions to Tildy of late. He either frowned at her as if she had said something quite irritating, or he laughed at her. Now he frowned. 'And why would I be doing that? Surely he is too weary at day's end to come over and dig up the maze.' Now he grinned.

Tildy's right hand burned she wanted so to slap him.

Alfred and Gilbert also smiled.

24

GLOUCESTER

At the guest-house of the Benedictine Abbey of St Peter in Gloucester the hospitaller handed Owen a letter as the party arrived. It carried the seal of John Thoresby, Archbishop of York.

'Is the messenger yet here?'

'The messenger departed for Wells the next morning,' the monk said. 'That would be two days past.'

Two days. Thoresby would not send a second message unless something further had gone wrong. Was it possible the aldermen or the guild had paid heed to Alice Baker's complaint? Owen waved on the other men and the servants who carried their belongings. He would find his chamber after he had read Thoresby's letter.

'*Deus juva me*,' he whispered as he read. The manor attacked and Lucie there in the midst of it. Praise God that Thoresby was sending Alfred and Gilbert. The destruction of the gatehouse worried Owen the most—the violence, the danger. Roger Moreton's new steward had accompanied the party as protection.

'Much good he did,' Owen muttered.

'What is it?' Friar Hewald asked. Owen had not noticed him standing nearby.

'We must depart at once for York. Find the infirmarian to change my bandage.'

'You must rest the night. His Grace would not wish you to be deprived of sleep.'

'I care nothing for His Grace's wishes. Find the infirmarian!'

25

JOURNEYS

Melisende woke Lucie before dawn, plopping down beside her and using her for a support as she cleaned herself after her early morning hunt. The rhythmic movement lulled Lucie back into a drowse. Harold was no longer behind her closed eyes. A pity. His sun-warmed shoulders…Lucie opened her eyes, bemused by the vivid sensuousness of the memory. But in the dream she had feared him, feared what he was.

What if Tildy was right to distrust Harold? What if the Gisburnes had known of the parchment? Or suspected John Sutton of murder? Had Harold been placed at Freythorpe to exact revenge? But Gisburne had recommended Harold to Roger Moreton, not Lucie.

She hoped Roger would return this morning. She was itching to wake Phillippa and try to learn more. But broken sleep would not help her aunt's memory.

Lucie rose, irritating Melisende, who had just curled up tightly against her. Some gentle strokes and soft words calmed the cat. Melisende rose, stretched, sought out Phillippa's legs and settled in for another nap.

Hoping to find comfort in Owen's letters, Lucie picked up the box that held her correspondence and took it to a bench by a small window. She drew out his letters from Wales, opened the shutters just enough so that she might see but Phillippa would not have light in her eyes, then tucked her feet beneath her and unfolded the first, hoping to be calmed by imagining his voice.

The letters did not have the desired effect. By the third, Lucie had difficulty keeping her mind on the words. The rumours did not seem so unreasonable this morning. Lucie could well believe Owen might choose to fight for his former countrymen. In the end, what did a woman really know of her husband?

It had been more than four months since Owen's departure. A few nights past Gwenllian had waked, crying for her father. Did Owen dream of them? Did he wonder about them? What did he think about as he rode with his men?

Lucie guessed she was not the only wife who paced the floor wondering about her husband. Cecily Gra had given birth to a child conceived before her husband left for Brussels. The child was born and died before her father could hold her in his arms. Other merchants' wives suffered likewise. Some took lovers.

Which reminded Lucie of her dream. If they were to become lovers, would Harold be discreet? Could he be trusted? Pointless questions. In faith, tantalising as Harold was, Lucie did not burn for him as she had for Owen when they first lay together. She closed her eyes, thought of the scent of her husband. By the Rood she loved him, though she hated him for this long absence.

And if he did not return? Her stomach burned with the thought, as did her eyes. *Heavenly Mother, do not let him forget me.*

Enough of this. Lucie dressed, went down to the kitchen, where she found Kate already stirring the fire. She ate bread and cheese, drank enough ale to quench her thirst and headed for the apothecary in the cool early morning. Work warmed her, wearied her. Two customers and still no Jasper. Lucie could hear Gwenllian shrieking and giggling in the garden. Slipping out through the workroom, Lucie called to Kate, who came running, her cap flying away in the breeze.

'Have you seen Jasper this morning?'

'No, Mistress,' Kate panted. 'I thought he had gone early to the shop. He was not in the room when I went to the children.'

Could he have gone to Freythorpe? Would he do that? 'Bring the children to me. I shall watch them while you go to the Merchets and Roger Moreton's house. Ask if they have seen Jasper.'

'But Master Moreton—'

'Is away, yes, but his housekeeper will be there. Go!'

'Aye, Mistress.'

Calm yourself. Kate will return with no news and later Jasper will appear, explaining that he went to St Mary's Abbey. And if he had gone to Freythorpe? Perhaps everyone's suspicions were unfounded. But Lucie's heart did not believe that.

Hugh and Gwenllian wanted to linger in the workroom, where great stone jars, baskets and bags of dried herbs, stones and more exotic items sat on low shelves along one wall. Lucie shooed them into the shop.

But Kate returned too soon, her face all frowns.

Dear God, what am I to do?

'He has taken a horse from the Merchets' stables, Mistress!' Kate said. 'The groom believed you had sent him off to Freythorpe.'

'Holy Mother, protect him.' Lucie picked up Hugh and held him close. What should she do? How could she help Jasper now?

After Kate departed with the children, Lucie paced the shop. Bess came to apologise for the part her groom had played in Jasper's disappearance.

'At another time I would think naught of the lad riding off by himself,' Bess said. 'But with all the brigands on the roads, and after such a savage attack upon Freythorpe, I shall not feel at peace until he returns.'

'It is worse than that, Bess,' Lucie pulled her into the workroom and told her all that was on her mind.

'Dear Heaven. I shall send a servant with a message to the archbishop's retainers. They must go after the lad.'

'They are the archbishop's men. I cannot order them to help me.' Lucie hugged herself and fought hysteria.

'Then send a message to the archbishop, for pity's sake,' Bess urged.

At least Bess agreed with her about the need to muster help. Lucie had just gathered her pen and parchment when Alice Baker entered the shop.

'Mistress Wilton, I am in need of—'

Lucie interrupted her. 'There is an excellent apothecary in Stonegate, Mistress Baker.'

Alice Baker straightened, frowned. 'I do not care for him.'

'Perhaps you should try him again. For I shall no longer serve you.'

'You cannot refuse me.'

Keeping her voice low, Lucie said slowly, enunciating each word, 'Leave my shop.'

'I shall take this up with the mayor.'

Lucie kept her eyes focused on the paper, refusing to say more. She had said nothing she might regret Alice repeating. So far.

'Mistress Merchet, you have witnessed this,' Alice said in a shrill voice.

When would the woman leave?

'I have,' said Bess. 'And I approve. She should not give you the means to poison yourself.'

With a twitch of her skirts, Alice flounced out of the shop. The door closed loudly behind her.

At last Lucie glanced up.

Bess beamed at her. 'Well done!'

Lucie could not smile. 'I must go after him, Bess.'

'And what would you do?'

'He is but a boy.'

'That I know. And you are but one person, torn between your little ones, your ailing aunt, your apothecary and an apprentice who has gone off to help you. Alfred and Gilbert are at the manor. If Thoresby sends men after Jasper, the boy shall encounter help no matter which way he turns. I shall fetch one of my lads to carry your request to the archbishop. It will not be the groom who loaned Jasper the horse, I promise you.'

'It was not his fault.'

'He should know better.'

Lucie sat down and composed her letter to His Grace. By the

time she had finished, one of Bess's servants stood ready to hasten to the archbishop's palace.

Lucie had not long to wait for his reply. She had taken care of three customers when the young man returned.

'His Grace assures you that he is sending four men at once,' he said, giving a little bow.

'God have mercy, he is a good man,' Lucie whispered, crossing herself.

26

A CROWD

At the crossroads, Owen and Friar Hewald halted to say their farewells to Edmund, Sam, Tom and Jared, all Lancaster's men and headed for Kenilworth. Owen would be glad to be quit of them. All along the way they had exclaimed about his letter, the outlawry rife in the countryside, how expensive it would be to replace a gatehouse. He wished to be alone with his own thoughts. His own worries. What enemy had he made who sought revenge by attacking his family? If he had not waited for Gwen, had not been delayed by Cynog's death, might he have prevented it? Would his enemies have chosen to attack him instead?

Jared broke into Owen's anxious thoughts. 'There is no need for fare thee wells. We have resolved to accompany you.'

Sweet *Jesu*, Owen had dreaded this. 'I must make haste. And your duke awaits you.'

Edmund doffed his cap, bowed from the saddle. 'By your leave, Captain. The duke does not know of our arrival in Gloucester. He does not know to expect us.'

'So a week, it will matter naught to him,' Tom finished with a hopeful grin.

'If you would have us,' Sam said softly.

'You are good men, all,' declared Friar Hewald.

Owen could think of many arguments against them, but he had already wasted precious moments. 'Keep up with me,' he said, taking spurs to his horse.

27

AN UNNATURAL SLEEP

After breaking her fast, Tildy slipped into the buttery to fetch Daimon's morning medicine. She took advantage of the privacy to smooth her gown, tug at her cap and pinch her cheeks. The door creaked open.

'Oh!' Nan exclaimed, backing up and shutting the door.

What had she meant to do, that Tildy was such a disturbing surprise? Tildy puzzled over the cook's behaviour while mixing Daimon's physick. As she closed the jars, she noticed how little mandrake was left. Had there not been more of it last night? She used very little—Magda had said it would ward off evil spirits in the house and give Daimon peaceful dreams, but that it was dangerous in larger doses. Tildy had not used so much of it, surely. She hastened out into the hall, kicking the buttery door closed behind her.

Yesterday by this time Daimon had already been helped outside by one of the servants so he might relieve himself, and while he was gone Tildy had freshened his bed. It was no wonder he slept late today, after sitting out in the yard all the previous afternoon and getting agitated about the maze. But was that the true cause of his long sleep? Tildy stood near him now, noticing the dark blond stubble of his beard, wishing she might shave him. But there were small blisters on his face from the fires and she dare not risk a blade near them. Such a pity to hide any of his handsome face.

Tildy crouched beside Daimon and leaned close, whispering his name. When he did not respond, she bent closer and gently kissed him on the forehead. It was the merest brush of her lips, nothing too bold. But oh so sweet. Still he did not move, his eyelids did not flutter.

She sat back on her heels, perplexed. How could he sleep through that? Did he play with her?

Or had he been given the mandrake? Becoming alarmed, she reached for the flagon of watered wine she had brought him to wash down the ill-tasting physick, poured some into a cup, held it up to Daimon's mouth. No response.

She called his name, patted his cheek.

One of the servants came over, asking what was wrong. Tildy told her to get water and a cloth. She patted Daimon's cheek again. At last his eyelids fluttered, he gasped as if suddenly taking in much more air, flailed his arms.

'God's blood, I am awake. Give a man a chance!' Daimon cried.

'Has anyone been bringing you food but me?' Tildy asked.

He blinked at her in confusion for a moment, then gulped the wine. 'No,' he said at last. 'Why?'

'You were difficult to wake.'

'I am ever so. Did I say anything to offend you? My mother says I sometimes curse her.'

He did seem fine. She felt a bit foolish. 'You said nothing stronger than "God's blood".'

When Daimon was sitting up and had eaten a bit of bread soaked in milk, Tildy took the tray back into the buttery and gathered the jars. There was still the mandrake—someone had used it. Where could she hide the jars from Nan—who else might slip something into his food? She thought of the treasury. Lucie had entrusted the key to her. Only to her, Tildy had thought. But when she opened the door and took in the small lamp, she discovered a jumble of accounts books on the table. She had been in here the previous day. Everything had been tidy then. She straightened them. Noticed that there was more room on the shelf than yesterday. One book? Two? She searched the room, behind the chest, in the chest, beneath the chest and the table. Nothing.

That did it. She locked the treasury, locked the buttery and went back to Daimon.

Nan stormed over a while later. 'Someone has locked the buttery.'

'I did,' said Tildy.

'I cannot have that.'

'I cannot have it open,' Tildy said.

'Why?'

'If you have need of something from the buttery, send Sarah to me.'

'I shall never get anything done.'

Tildy said nothing more. Nan marched away.

'What is the trouble, Matilda?' Daimon asked. 'Why have you locked the buttery?'

'Things have gone missing, my love. Nothing for you to fret about. Rest now. You must be bored, sitting there.' She did not want him to go back to sleep. 'Is there something you might do to occupy yourself while sitting there?'

He brightened. 'Some wood and my whittling knife are in the stables.'

Tildy sent a servant off to collect them while she began the tidying of the hall. As she worked she daydreamed about Harold's departure and Phillippa's return. What would her status be then? Would they send her home? Would she stay to assist Dame Phillippa? Would she marry Daimon?

She peeked at Daimon, now humming as he picked up the pieces of wood, considering which to use. Had she been mistaken about the medicine? Had he truly just been that tired? But the jar of mandrake should be fuller.

As she turned back to her work, she noticed a blank space on the wall above one of Sir Robert's shields. Three swords should hang there. The brackets were still in place. She looked round, thinking the maid had taken them down for cleaning, though that was the groom's job. Perhaps Ralph had taken them—but he should not do that unless Tildy ordered it.

Nan's behaviour, the swords, the maze. Something was very wrong. This was not her imagination. Checking that Daimon was engrossed in his work, she hurried out to the stables. She would talk to Ralph, then Alfred and Gilbert, if they were still there.

Ralph knew nothing of the swords. Alfred and Gilbert agreed that perhaps another tour of the property was in order. They would leave now, look carefully at the surrounding houses and outbuildings.

In the yard, Tildy encountered Harold.

'Nan and Sarah tell me you have locked them out of the buttery,' Harold said, his eyes cold.

'I have.'

'Why?'

'Someone has searched the treasury behind it, removed some account books and I do not know what else. Too much of Daimon's medication is gone. So I locked the buttery.'

'You mean to stir up trouble. Why?'

'How can you say that? I am not the one causing trouble.'

'I heard Daimon protest that he was fine.'

'One of his powders is too low.'

'The treasury has a separate key.'

How did he know that? 'I—yes, I know that. But two locked doors are more difficult than one.'

'You suspect Nan or Sarah of all this? Stealing physicks and account books? Neither of them can read.'

'No. I do not know. But I mean to keep order. I am sorry to make them come to me. But that is how it shall be until—' Until what? Harold waited for her to continue. 'Until I see fit to unlock it.'

He grinned. It was no smile. 'What is your scheme, Mistress Tildy? To poison Daimon, take the money in the treasury and run away with some lover? Who might it be? Joseph, Nan's son? Eh?'

'You are mad!' How had he turned this around? 'I do not have time to stand here and listen to you. I do not *need* to stand here.' As Tildy moved, Harold grabbed her arm.

'You are a foolish woman, Mistress Tildy,' he said in a soft voice.

She yanked her arm away and ran from him back to the house.

• • •

Tildy kept herself busy tidying and fetching for Nan—who was getting her revenge for the locked buttery by discovering items she needed at once, one at a time.

Shortly after midday Tildy heard a shout at the gatehouse, then a horse enter the yard. Dreading more trouble, she glanced out of the hall door. 'Jasper!' she cried, running outside. Just the sight of him cheered her.

'What are you doing here, lad?' Harold asked, frowning as he walked out from the stables.

'Is anything wrong in York?' Tildy demanded. Jasper looked agitated.

'Mistress Wilton allowed you to come alone?' Harold inquired. 'In these times?'

Ralph came running from the stables to help Jasper dismount and take the horse.

'Mistress Wilton does not know I came,' Jasper said. 'I wanted to help her. She is occupied with Aunt Phillippa, who is much confused. She asked for a few things from the manor. I thought to fetch them—Mistress Wilton has enough to worry about.'

It was a breathless speech for Jasper. Tildy knew something was wrong. She ushered him into the hall. But Harold followed them. She needed to get Jasper to some place where they could talk.

Daimon called out, 'Jasper! It has been a long while since I have seen you. You are taller than I am, I trow.'

The young man crouched down, pretending to study Daimon's carving, but Tildy heard him ask Daimon how he was, truly, for the Riverwoman had been concerned. What did Jasper know, that he played the spy? Had Magda Digby spoken of Tildy's concerns? Mistress Wilton thought so highly of Harold Galfrey, which bothered Tildy. Mistress Wilton had always been a good judge of a man.

'Go with Matilda,' Daimon said quietly. 'Try to keep out of the man's way.' He raised his voice as Harold approached. 'I have been too long idle. See how I ruined this piece of wood?'

Jasper picked up the wood, turned it over thoughtfully. 'I could not do as well.'

'Alfred and Gilbert rode off earlier,' Harold said, 'but when they return and you have gathered what you came to fetch for Dame Phillippa I shall have them escort you back to York, Jasper. You should not be on the roads alone.'

'It might be dark by then,' said Jasper. 'Would it not be better to return tomorrow?'

'I do not want Mistress Wilton to worry about you.'

'Then we have no time to lose,' Tildy said, whisking Jasper off to the buttery. She grabbed the oil lamp that sat outside and closed the door carefully behind them.

Jasper glanced round the buttery, began to rummage among the baskets and jars.

'What are you looking for?'

'Aunt Phillippa keeps talking about a parchment. She thinks that is what someone is looking for. It had once been sewn inside the tapestry that was stolen.'

That is why it had been torn. How awful—someone had been searching the hall even before the attack. 'Where is the parchment now?'

'She cannot remember where she hid it.'

'How can that be? Something so important—'

Jasper shook his head. 'She is old, Tildy, and she hid it in many places.'

'Well, parchment or no, I think Harold is trying to poison Daimon.'

Jasper did not laugh.

'You think it is possible?' She saw that he hid something. 'Tell me.'

'No one knows much of him, Tildy,' he whispered, eyeing the door fearfully. 'He claims to have been robbed on the road to York, his papers, everything. John Gisburne knows little of him but that he claims to be a distant relation.'

'Dear God.'

'What is amiss here? I must know all if I am to help.'

Tildy wondered. Jasper was but a lad. But he was Lucie's

apprentice. Surely that meant she had confidence in him. Tildy told him everything—Nan and the food, the maze, the swords, the account book, the mandrake. 'I think someone is hiding on the manor—eating the food, arming himself with the weapons,' Tildy said. 'I think it is Joseph, Nan's son.'

'And the mandrake?'

'If Daimon is not being poisoned, I do not know who is. Nor why anyone wants the account books.'

She unlocked the treasury for Jasper, lit another candle.

But what was this? The treasury had been straightened and now the account books filled the shelf, as they had yesterday.

'Who has done this?' Tildy whispered. 'The books are all here.'

'At least one was missing when Mistress Wilton looked in here after the raid,' Jasper said. 'Could someone be searching the books for the parchment?'

'Should we?' Tildy asked.

'Which books have been missing?'

Tildy shook her head.

'Bring that lamp over. We shall check all of them.'

While they paged through the books, Jasper asked whether Alfred and Gilbert knew all Tildy had told him.

'Yes. They are out on the manor grounds now, looking round.'

'Come back to York with me, Tildy.'

'I cannot leave the house. It is my responsibility.'

'Then I shall just pretend to leave with Alfred and Gilbert.'

'No! You must go back to York.'

'I shall send one of them to the archbishop to request more men. We shall discover what is happening here. You must go on as if nothing is wrong.'

'That will be difficult.'

'The additional men could be here tomorrow, Tildy.' Jasper put the last book back, finding nothing.

'Come,' Tildy said, 'Harold will come to check on us if we linger here.'

She locked the treasury, then the buttery. Gilbert startled her, coming out of the gloom by Phillippa's screened bedchamber.

'Quietly, before I am discovered in the hall,' he said. 'I do not want Nan to hear. Joseph is hiding in an abandoned outbuilding with several other men I do not recognise. There is your problem. Not Harold.'

'You will not tell Harold about this!' Tildy said.

'We have not. But why should he not know?'

Tildy told him about Harold knowing the treasury key was not the same as that of the buttery.

'I have not trusted him from the beginning,' Jasper said. 'And now it seems very little is known about him. He has no proof he is who he says.'

Gilbert grunted at the news. 'This is a sorry muddle. How do you come to be here, Jasper?'

'I want to help.'

'We shall need to watch the outbuilding. You might do that while we talk to Jenkyn the thatcher again.'

'You will have no time to do that,' Tildy said. 'Harold wants you to escort Jasper to York.'

'I shall only pretend to go,' Jasper said, telling Gilbert his plan.

'What of you, Mistress Tildy?' Gilbert said.

She felt all atremble, but she must think. She closed her eyes. 'I shall try to go on as usual. But if things get bad, Daimon and I can flee to the chapel. There is but the one window, high up. And the outside door is barred with iron. That is why we hid there the night of the raid.'

Harold had found them. 'Well, Jasper, did you find what you needed?'

'I must just check Dame Phillippa's chamber,' Jasper said.

'Hurry back,' Tildy whispered as she left him.

28

BEDEVILLED

Would he tell Lucie of his temptation? Owen imagined her response. She would be hurt. Angry that he could even think to abandon his children. Doubt he had ever loved her. And how might he ever reassure her? Would his return be the proof? Might he not have returned for other reasons? Merely a sense of guilt? Cowardice? Sweet *Jesu*, he could not tell her. He was galloping across the countryside, mad with fear for her. But she would not know. She would not believe.

A ford swollen from spring rains required his attention. Owen watched Edmund and Sam cross, saw the spot with the heavy undertow, tried to guide his mount to face into the current. The horse faltered, stumbled, limped to the bank.

Owen dismounted, calmed the horse, examined the hoof on which the beast fell. A shoe was missing.

'I see smoke ahead,' Jared called out. 'We may find a farmer shoes his own horse.'

'None so rich along this road,' said the friar. 'But he will know the nearest smithy.'

'I shall ride on with the friar on one of your horses,' Owen told the others, who had returned to see to the matter.

Sam and Tom stayed with the lame horse.

And was it God's sign Owen must confess all to Lucie? Why else had this happened now, at that moment when he vowed to stay silent? *Dear God, help me in the telling. So she understands.*

29

ILL NEWS

After hours of pacing in the shop between customers, Lucie at last retreated to the house, hurrying through the garden as rain began to fall. The scent of rain on the dry earth after a warm spell was lovely, but not enough at the moment to make her pause.

Kate and the children were in the kitchen, working on a cake, the children adding fruits and nuts one by one as Kate mixed. 'I thought it best to keep them occupied,' she said quietly.

'Bless you, Kate.' Lucie was fortunate in both of the sisters, Kate and Tildy. 'Where is my aunt?'

'Going through your books about the garden. She says she is looking for a drawing you told her of, that marks a spell for clover. Then she was going to ask you to read of it.'

'She is clear-headed?'

'Aye. She says because you have given her nothing to calm her today.'

Lucie sighed. She wished it were that simple.

Phillippa sat at the table in the hall surrounded by Nicholas's books and even older ones that had been his father's. In their journals they had recorded all the new plants, seeds, specimens and all the lore of the apothecary garden that they had collected. Letters from many lands were tucked between the pages. At the moment, Phillippa sat with her hands in her lap, staring out of the window to the garden. A journal lay open before her on the table. Her wimple was tidy, her eyes alert as she turned and noticed Lucie.

'Do you know, I thought to keep myself occupied and out of

trouble.' She smiled and beckoned Lucie to join her.

The extent of Lucie's relief made her feel guilty. Her aunt's confusion had become just another one of her troubles. She slipped on to the bench beside Phillippa and looked at the cover of the journal that lay open. 'The notes for Nicholas's masterwork. This is the heart of the garden.'

'There are letters in many hands. I do not think I respected him sufficiently,' said Phillippa.

'You respected him enough to encourage our marriage.'

'But I ever thought you were better than he. What is blood, I wonder? Why do we respect it so? It is what we do with God's gifts that matters in the end.'

'All these thoughts from looking at the journals?'

'And thinking of my husband. A good family, excellent blood. Your grandfather relented and allowed our marriage because of Douglas's courage in battle. But he still could not manage his lands. He was worse than his father. And then the bitterness set in. "Why do others have and I have not?" he would say, never, "What might I do to improve the land?" I am so ashamed.' Phillippa shook her head. 'At the same time that your father-in-law, Paul Wilton, was working hard to become an apothecary, learning all this, Douglas and Henry offered themselves as couriers between the fearful people and the Bruce's men. They took advantage of people's needs. Paul Wilton's work was of more worth. And more lasting. I can see that afterwards Nicholas improved on what his father had done.'

'You cannot read these journals.'

'I can see the care that went into making each letter, Lucie, my love. These were good men, hard-working. God must have welcomed them with a choir of angels.'

'As a courier, was your Douglas not helping the people?'

Phillippa patted Lucie's hand. 'You do not understand. They skimmed off the top of the tribute they carried—a jewel here, a gold piece there.'

'I wonder at the Bruce's men, then. Did they not miss those things?'

'Douglas said it was expected that couriers did that. That was bad enough. It tortures me to wonder if he was also a murderer.'

'I doubt we shall ever know, Aunt Phillippa. But he did come home to you when you needed him.' She looked away, thinking of Owen, suddenly hot with anger.

'Come,' Phillippa said, 'let us search for clover.'

John Thoresby considered Brother Michaelo, wet and bedraggled, but worse than that, quite pale. That should not be, after but two days' journeying. Still, he had made the trip much more quickly than expected.

'Terrible news, Your Grace.'

'I can see that by the looks on both your faces. How is your back, Brother Michaelo?'

The monk shook his head slightly. 'Harold Galfrey was not steward.'

'I am not surprised. Go on with you. To your room. I shall send for Brother Henry.'

'There is no need, Your Grace.'

'I say that there is. Go. Take off the wet robes, get beneath enough covers to boil you. I shall send a servant up with a brazier, ale, something warm to eat.' He waved him off. 'Master Moreton can tell me all I need to know.'

He faced the other bedraggled traveller. 'I am certain my servants can find something for you to wear while they dry your clothes in the kitchen,' Thoresby said. He could not bear the odour of human and horse sweat, mud and wet clothing.

'If Your Grace will forgive me, I would rather hurry home, stop at Mistress Wilton's...'

'It is early evening. You may do that later. Your man is without?'

Moreton nodded. 'He awaits me.'

'He will be given a seat close to the fire and fed well. Come now, my servant will take you to the guest chamber.'

When Moreton was out of the hall, Thoresby rose slowly—the

return of the rain had made his joints ache—and made his way to Michaelo's chamber.

A servant was there, making a fire. Michaelo lay in bed, on his stomach.

'I do not need this fuss.'

'I think that you do. I am pleased to see you obeyed,' Thoresby said, withdrawing.

Moreton was already down in the hall when Thoresby returned, wearing a fustian tunic and leggings. He looked like a gardener.

'I am grateful for the dry clothing, Your Grace.' His teeth seemed to be clenching.

Thoresby nodded to the warmed wine on the table. A servant came forward and poured for both of them.

'Come, sit and tell me what you learned.'

'Harold Galfrey had no such surname when he worked for the Godwins, nor was he steward. He acted as sub-treasurer, a post he abused by acting a most helpful and agreeable courier but keeping much of the funds himself. His thefts were discovered, but he and Joseph, the groom, fled before he could be brought to justice. Joseph is the son of the cook at Freythorpe, a vengeful man who was sent away after causing trouble at both manors.'

It would be difficult to imagine a worse combination in the circumstances, save that one or both were murderers. 'You received this from a reliable source?'

'Mistress Godwin herself, Your Grace.' Moreton produced a sealed letter. 'She was good enough to dictate this to her secretary.'

Thoresby studied the seal. He would read it after he had sent Moreton on his way. No need to show the man how much light he needed and how far away he must hold a document these days. 'It would appear that Mistress Wilton is the victim of your good intentions.'

Moreton dropped his eyes. 'Yes, Your Grace.'

'And Jasper de Melton, who took it upon himself to ride to the manor.'

He looked up, dismay staining his cheeks. 'Alone?'

'I have sent men after him, but yes, alone.'

Moreton buried his head in his hands. Thoresby drummed his fingers on the arms of his chair, thinking what more he might do. The High Sheriff must be told of this development.

Lucie and Phillippa had their heads together looking through the books when a knock came at the hall door. Lucie rose to answer it, waved Kate back into the kitchen.

Her heart dropped to see Alfred, wet and muddy from riding through the rain, stinking of horse sweat.

'Mistress Wilton.'

'Come in, Alfred. We have some wine at the table.'

'I cannot, Mistress Wilton. I must hie to His Grace. But I wanted you to know that I had seen Jasper. He arrived at Freythorpe just after midday. He found nothing missing in the treasury. Harold Galfrey asked Gilbert and me to escort him home to you. I fear he used the courtesy to his own purpose.' He paused for air.

'Jasper is here?'

Alfred shook his head. 'He and Gilbert turned back as soon as they were out of sight of the manor. Jasper wished to slip back to Tildy, help her prove Harold is the source of the troubles. I rode on for more men. I met four of our fellows on the road just beyond the city, bound for Freythorpe Hadden.'

'You were good to come.'

'Being so near the city when I met the men, I thought to inform you that Jasper will be safe and tell His Grace what has happened.'

Lucie's stomach knotted. 'What has Harold done?'

Alfred told her how the maze path had been dug up, the treasury had been searched, swords were missing and Joseph was about, with additional men.

'Holy Mother of God,' Phillippa whispered. 'What is happening?'

'What of Tildy?' Lucie asked.

'She was going to lock herself in the chapel with Daimon.'

'You said swords, young man?' Phillippa asked.

Alfred nodded. 'Aye, three of Sir Robert's collection of swords no longer hang in the hall.'

Lucie noticed with an inward groan that Dame Phillippa had a faraway look. 'What is it, Aunt?'

'Something.' Phillippa shook her head. 'Gone. Something about the swords.'

Lucie prayed that she was not falling back into her confusion. She needed her clear-headed, for she had to be able to leave Phillippa and go to Freythorpe. 'Are you returning to the manor?' she asked Alfred.

'In the morning, aye. I am going now to speak to His Grace. It is raining hard. I would not venture back out on to the road tonight. Break my horse's leg in a puddle. Now I must hasten. God be with you, Mistress Wilton. Do not worry.'

'God watch over you, Alfred. I am grateful.'

Alfred left a trail of rainwater in his wake as he crossed the hall to Thoresby's comfortable chair by the fire. The archbishop was about to send him away, steaming and stinking as he was, but a closer inspection of the man's eyes made him ask instead, 'What has happened at Freythorpe Hadden?' As he listened, Thoresby shook his head in dismay. Worse and worse. And the lad not returned. 'You will stay here the night and in the morning you will tell your tale to the High Sheriff before you ride back to Freythorpe.'

'But Your Grace, if he is not there I shall never—'

'Fear not. Two of my men will be despatched this evening to inform the High Sheriff that the Archbishop of York commands his presence at his palace in the morning. I do not think John Chamont will keep you waiting.'

• • •

The rain came down heavily now. A puddle formed on the wood floor in the corner of the children's room. Gwenllian demanded to know where Jasper was. Lucie left that for Kate to answer. Someone was knocking on the door. As Lucie hurried down the steps she made a mental note that the tiles in the corner of the roof must need repair. She did not want to follow her fears about who this might be.

When Roger gave her his news about Harold, she gasped, feeling the air pushed from her. 'For what is God punishing me?' she said in a voice she did not recognise. 'What have I done?'

'You?' Roger rose, came to her side of the table and sat down beside her. 'Sweet friend, it is my fault. My horrible error. I cannot believe I did such a thing to you.'

'Tomorrow you will go with me to Freythorpe,' Lucie said angrily. 'We must confront Harold.'

'Whatever you wish.' His eyes were full of remorse.

'Lucie, are you awake?'

Lucie pulled herself into a sitting position. 'What is it, Aunt. Do you need something?'

'I have remembered! Sweet *Jesu*, I have remembered. When Robert brought those swords, he also brought a reliquary. The hand of St Paula—you remember—for me, a widow.'

'It is in the chapel, yes. He brought it back from the Holy Land.' He had thought to give it to Clementhorpe Nunnery, where Lucie lived, but gave them a jewelled cup instead, saving the relic for Phillippa. The sisters had been most disappointed.

'That is where I hid the parchment,' Phillippa said. 'In the reliquary. I knew none would open it. Robert forbade anyone to touch it.'

30

THE MAZE

Lucie and Roger rode out through Micklegate Bar into the grey, humid morning. The rain had stopped, but the clouds hugged the land and the river. The air smelled of rotting fish. The usually loquacious Roger was quiet this morning. Lucie had not slept and her thoughts shifted nervously from worry to worry.

What would Owen have done differently? He would not have hired Harold Galfrey, that is certain. But he could not have prevented the raid on the manor. How would he have dealt with it? What had she done wrong? She had not asked enough questions. Oft-times she had chided Owen for his distrust of everyone and everything until sufficiently known. Never again. Roger Moreton felt he was the culprit, but Lucie shared the blame. With Tildy and Daimon locked in the chapel—pray God they were there—the reliquary was safe. Unless Harold and Joseph had already found the parchment. What if they were already gone?

Halfway to Freythorpe they heard a rider pounding up from behind and moved to one side to let him pass. But he slowed, growled an oath. Alfred.

'You have departed at leisure,' Roger said.

'I met with John Chamont, the High Sheriff. He has agreed to send additional men today.' Alfred doffed his cap to Lucie. 'Faith, Mistress Wilton, you should not be on the road.'

'Do you think I can stay in the city when Jasper and Tildy are in danger? And my home?'

'But you will be—'

'In the way? I shall try not to be.'

'In danger, Mistress Wilton. Captain Archer would never forgive me if aught happened to you. I would fear for my life.'

'You are welcome to ride with us, or ride ahead, as you wish.'

Alfred fell in with them.

The three rode most of the way in silence, stopping only once to fortify themselves with meat pasties and ale, supplied by Bess Merchet.

'Jasper is growing into a fine young man,' Alfred said, breaking into Lucie's agitated thoughts. 'You must be proud of him.'

'I am. How was he when you saw him? Frightened?'

'I would say he seemed determined to do what needed to be done.'

Roger, long silent, had clearly been fuming. 'How could John Gisburne be so careless?' he cried suddenly. 'How could he recommend a man he knew so little?'

'Perhaps he knew more than he admits,' Lucie said.

'He would not use me like that. A liveried member of the guild.'

'If he has, he will have taken care you will never prove it,' said Alfred. 'Just as he has protected Colby from the bailiffs and sheriffs.'

'I shall bring it before the guild,' Roger declared.

In the early morning, Jasper had slipped into the hall to warn Tildy, who nodded in a chair beside Daimon, that Nan was carrying food to the outbuilding they had been watching.

'What have they waited for all night?'

'They said it was better to attack when they can see that no one escapes. Nan may see the archbishop's men surrounding the house. If there is fighting, you will be safe in the chapel. I shall come get you as soon as we can slip away.'

Tildy had waked Daimon and helped him to the chapel. But Harold had discovered the move and she was forced to lock them in before she could bring the medicines and some food. It was now mid-morning and she was so thirsty. She could not imagine how Daimon felt. Men needed far more food and drink than women. But he protested that being locked in the chapel with her was the greatest comfort.

Nan came to the door now and then, tempting them with offers of food and drink. Though they were hungry and Daimon in need of his medicines they did not open to her.

As Lucie and her companions neared the manor, she noticed a figure running across the fields, in the opposite direction. 'Alfred! What is happening?' Another running man appeared and a horseman following, leaning from his horse to grab the man.

'Dear God,' Lucie moaned.

'The rider is one of ours,' Alfred said. 'We must have attacked.' He loosed his sword.

'Why, for pity's sake, are they pursuing?' Roger cried. 'There are people in the hall who might be harmed.'

'You want these men caught, certainly?' Alfred asked.

Lucie did, most assuredly. But Roger was right, too.

'Is there any way we might get to the hall without watchers seeing us?' Roger asked her.

How could they know what was watched? In the name of heaven, how was she to think clearly? They must try to remain concealed. 'I could lead you through the woods into the orchard behind the hall and from there to the maze, through the maze, and then it is but a short run to the hall.'

Alfred perked up. 'You might just do that, aye. I shall ride up to the house, try to keep attention on myself. But you must not endanger yourself by approaching the house.'

'I mean to find Jasper, Tildy and Daimon,' said Lucie. 'Beyond that I do not care.'

• • •

At first the noise had been so far off, Tildy could not be certain what she heard.

But Daimon sat up, his eyes fearful. 'Men shouting.'

'Where?' Tildy whispered. She did not want Harold at the chapel door again. He had frightened her a while ago, pounding at the door. He had said she had imagined all this, that they would starve in here and she was depriving Daimon of his medicine, a warm fire, because she was mad.

Daimon had taken her hand. 'He is wrong, Matilda. He wants to get in here. Mayhap this is the one place he has yet to search.'

How had he known what she had been thinking?

Now there were noises in the household, someone running, Nan shouting something. Tildy went to the door, pressed an ear against it.

'The archbishop's men have attacked,' Nan was saying. 'What do they want with my son? What has he done? Why is Ralph hiding the mistress's apprentice in the stables?'

'Go back to the kitchen, woman.' It was Harold Galfrey's voice, but different now, angry.

Footsteps approached the door. Tildy backed away with a horrible feeling that Harold could see through the heavy wood. But it had held so far. She did not know why Sir Robert had put a bolt on this side of the door, but she thanked God for it. She returned to Daimon, knelt beside him.

'What is that smell?' Daimon asked.

She smelled it, too. She glanced over, saw smoke beneath the door. Daimon pulled himself from the chair, caught her shoulder.

'We must open the door, Matilda.'

A man stood just outside, sword ready. Tildy screamed as the small fire caught her skirt.

Lucie had lost Roger somewhere. They had heard a rustling behind them. He had waved her on. Now she stood just within the tall hedges of the maze, peering back, praying that he would soon follow. All along she had feared to see one of the running men, or a body—Jasper's body. She pushed the idea away as often as it came to her, fearful lest even the thought would make the deed.

Something, now, in the orchard. Gone. A bird, mayhap.

What was that? A shout, from the direction of the house, another higher scream. Footsteps. Several pairs. Somewhere close. A quickly muffled cry. The hair at her neck prickled. Surely that had been Jasper's voice. From the sheath on her girdle Lucie drew a dagger, one Owen had given her when first they wed, for protection if she should ever be surprised in the shop. She had never used it.

A pair of pigeons took flight above her. She could not be certain, but she thought they had flown from somewhere in the centre of the maze. The footsteps were closer, then a shout and the sound of a struggle.

'What do you want from us?' Jasper cried.

Lucie gathered her skirts, and, holding the dagger in her fist, made her way swiftly, quietly to the centre of the maze as the sounds of a struggle grew loud, then suddenly stopped.

Harold sat on one of the stone benches with his back towards Lucie, wrestling to control someone thrashing on the stones beneath him. He was breathing hard. He leaned forward. Lucie crept closer, trying to see whether it was Jasper who lay on the ground. She recognised his shoes.

'Where is it?' Harold hissed, his bent right arm jerking.

Jasper coughed and struggled, gasping for air. Harold was choking him.

Lucie ran towards them. Hearing her approach, Harold turned awkwardly on the bench, but she plunged the knife into his back before he knew what was happening. He shrieked in agony. She pulled out the knife, slashed at his upraised arm. He knocked the knife from her hand as he fell sideways. Jasper had pulled himself up on to the bench. He bent double, struggling for air. There was blood in his hair.

'Jasper!'

Suddenly Harold scooped up Lucie's bloody knife and rose

beside her. How could the man move? Jasper struggled up behind him. And then Lucie was falling to one side, twisting as someone ran past her. Her head hit the flagstones.

Had she fainted? She tasted blood in her mouth. Someone moaned by her side.

'Lucie? My love. Lucie!'

Sweet heaven, Owen had returned in time. Lucie opened her eyes, closed them as the world spun and her stomach protested. Strong arms helped her up, held her as she retched.

'I shall never forgive myself.'

It was Roger, not Owen.

'Mistress Lucie.' Jasper circled her with his arms.

'Your head. You are alive?'

'I am.'

'Harold?'

Jasper lowered his head towards a still form on the path.

'I killed him,' Lucie whispered.

Lucie had been put to bed in Phillippa's chamber in the solar. But she could not sleep. Horses in the yard below stomped and whinnied. Men shouted. She felt removed from it all, as if floating above them, listening to them from high in the air—a not unpleasant feeling.

Save that her head throbbed, her left hip ached, as did her left hand. She must have fallen on that side. Remembering blood in her mouth, she explored with her tongue. A tooth felt wobbly, the inside of her cheek was cut. She dozed.

She heard men's voices Down below, so many of them. Or was she dreaming? Was Owen among them? Why did he not come up? Her head had been bandaged. Something cool eased the pain.

Tildy tiptoed in. 'Can you sip some steeped herbs, Mistress Lucie?'

As Tildy bent down, Lucie remembered someone talking of fire. She touched Tildy's face. She was unscarred. 'Nan told me your gown had caught fire.'

'Aye. Nan saved me. Threw a bucket of water, then tore off my gown. I have blisters on my legs, but that is the worst of it.'

Lucie's jaw ached when she spoke, and her head. But she had questions. 'Then Nan was not one of the thieves?'

'No, though she had been feeding them.'

'Jasper? How is he?'

'He has a nasty cut on his head, atop it, not to the side like yours. And a badly bruised neck. A black eye. Naught else that a young man would fuss about. And even those he counts nothing. But we have him resting in Sir Robert's chamber.'

'And Harold Galfrey?' Lucie whispered.

'He is dead and I say may he burn in hellfire. Now let me help you sit up a moment.'

May he burn in hellfire. How easily Tildy said that. And what of Lucie? She had done the deed. Harold had murdered no one— she had.

Tildy tucked pillows behind Lucie's head. 'We have sent for the Riverwoman.'

She helped Lucie drink—mandrake, poppy. Tildy meant for her to sleep. Lucie turned her head away.

'You must rest, Mistress Lucie.'

'Horses, men, who is here?'

Tildy stood back a moment, shaking her head.

'Answer my questions, then I shall drink it all, I promise you.' Lucie rested her head against the pillows.

Tildy tsked, but sat on the edge of the bed. 'The archbishop's men, six of them, and a dozen from York Castle. The High Sheriff sent them.'

'Not Owen?'

Tildy looked down. 'No. Not the captain.'

'The fire in the chapel.'

'Just without the door. Nothing lost.'

'The reliquary. Would you bring it to me?'

'Master Moreton has seen the parchment. He said to tell you.'

Lucie's eyes grew heavy. 'And Daimon?' The words were difficult to shape, her tongue thickening. Too much poppy.

'Ash from the fire hurt his eyes, but Mistress Winifred showed me how to make a soothing wash. Are you asleep?'

'Soon,' Lucie murmured, unable to lift her heavy lids.

When Lucie woke, Jasper sat at the foot of the bed, watching her with concern. His hair was damp, combed back. His face looked gaunt. His neck was wrapped in cloth. In a corner of the room, Magda bent over a brazier, stirring something.

'Are you in pain?' Lucie asked.

'No,' Jasper whispered. 'But the Riverwoman said my neck must be protected when we ride to the city.'

'Thou shouldst not try to speak,' Magda said, turning from her work. 'And thee, Mistress Apothecary? Art thou in pain?'

'I want to see the parchment.' Lucie eased up, pushing her pillows behind her.

Jasper handed her a folded letter, the seal broken. Here it was at last. Her head pounded. *I killed him. Does it matter whether or not he was guilty? I have killed a man.* She lay back against the pillows and closed her eyes.

Magda leaned over her, put a damp cloth on her forehead, redolent with herbs. 'Lie still a while. Magda would strengthen thee for the journey to the city. The charred wood is not good for thy humours. Healing is difficult in such a house.'

Jasper took the parchment from Lucie. 'This is a letter to Robert the Bruce,' he said, 'from Alderman Bolton's father, offering a bejewelled cup if he would spare their lands.'

'That is it? It cannot be the cause of all this suffering.' Lucie's heart pounded. He was killing Jasper. She must remember that. He had been choking Jasper. *Sweet Mother in Heaven, intercede for me, tell your Son you would have done the same.*

31

BENEATH THE LINDEN

Weary and winded, Owen and his company dismounted at Micklegate Bar late in the afternoon. Steam rose from wet cobbles as afternoon showers gave way to sunshine. Folk stared at them and no wonder—five liveried men and a friar, all filthy from days of riding, soaked this afternoon, now steaming.

Inside the Bar, Micklegate was crowded with merchants and country folk departing after a market day. The pillories at Holy Trinity were full as usual. As the street sloped down towards the bridge, York Minster seemed to rise over the city. Owen smelled the fishmongers well before he reached Ouse Bridge. Crossing over, they encountered an overturned cart blocking part of Coney Street. They had to squeeze past to the music of curses and shouts as children ran off with the spilt hay.

Would Lucie be in the shop? Or the house? What would Owen say to her? Were the children well?

They rounded the corner into St Helen's Square. From the York Tavern, Owen heard Bess Merchet shouting to one of her servants. 'Quickly now! Careful!' And there was Lucie's apothecary. Owen hesitated, the prodigal son uncertain of his welcome.

Friar Hewald put a hand on Owen's shoulder. 'We should leave you to your family. The porter said His Grace is at his palace in the city. We shall go there, let him know of your arrival. I shall send word where we are couched for the night.'

'Aye.'

Jared took Owen's reins. As Owen moved his pack from the

horse, Jared said, 'I look forward to meeting your fair lady.'

'Aye. God go with you.'

The others touched their caps to him as they moved on, guiding the horses up Stonegate.

Pausing at the shop door, Owen remembered the first time he had entered the apothecary, how he had stood near the door watching Lucie with a customer, wondering at the confidence of this apothecary's daughter, as he thought her. He must behave as ever, no words or gestures revealing his uncertainty. She would find out all soon enough. He pushed at the door. Shut. Locked. Holy Mother of God. He hurried round the corner to the front of the house, pushed open the door.

'Da!' Gwenllian was in his arms before he could see her properly.

'My love, my love.' He smelled her hair, kissed her cheek. Hugh sat on the floor nearby, gazing up at him with confusion and a little fear. Four months and forgotten.

'Captain!' Kate lifted his pack from the floor. 'You will want to see Mistress Lucie. She is above, resting quiet. Jasper, too.'

'Hush, girl, let him catch his breath. I thank God you have returned safe and whole.'

'Aunt Phillippa. What are you doing here?' And why are you leaning on a stick?

Lucie sat up in bed. Was she yet dreaming? Or had she heard Owen's voice?

'Sit up so quickly and thy head shall punish thee,' Magda warned. 'Two days since thou wast injured.'

'Is Owen below?'

'Aye, Bird-eye is here. Magda must see to Jasper. Thou must see to thy husband.'

'I cannot think how I must look.'

'Thou lookst lovely, as ever. Magda made thy bandage with her many-coloured cloth. Not a rag.' She picked up a tray and slipped from the room before Lucie could ask for her silvered glass.

And then he was there, in the doorway, travel-stained, weary, so handsome. She stood up and was in his arms before either said a word. He flinched when she slipped her arms round him. A fleeting motion. Then gently he lifted her chin for a kiss. And still it was too soon that he stepped back.

He shook his head as he gazed on her. 'You threw yourself into danger,' he said sharply.

'Who told you?'

'Dame Phillippa. How could you? If anything happened to you, what of the children?'

'Me? Four months and more you have been away, with no thought for your children, it is rumoured you will not return at all, and you chide me for trying to help Jasper and Tildy? Who else would, I ask you?'

Owen sat down on the bed, staring at her. 'There were rumours?'

That was what stung? The rumours? What had happened to him? Was it possible he no longer loved her?

'What were the rumours?' he asked.

'The merchants are full of Owain Lawgoch. Worried lest he disrupt shipping. They say all Welshmen will fight with him. That you would stay in Wales to do so.'

He closed his eye, bowed his head.

She caught her breath. 'You were tempted.'

'Aye. For a time.'

So nearly lost. 'Why did you return?'

He lifted his head. Dear God but he looked weary. 'Because I cannot live without you.'

'You are injured.'

'Aye.'

'Fighting for that man?'

'No. Seeking a murderer.'

'Even there, in Wales?'

'In a holy city. The victim was the mason who had begun your father's tomb.' Owen took a stone from his pack, handed it to her.

All with his left hand, she noted. 'This is the work of Ranulf de Hutton, who completed it.'

A face had been carved in the stone. 'Father,' Lucie whispered. 'It is so like him.' She began to weep.

Owen held her to him. She buried her face in his broad shoulder.

In the early morning, Owen walked through the wakening city. A mist hung over the streets. He felt better than he had last night, for certain, with Magda's comforting bandage on his wound and his arm supported by another of her cloths tied round his neck. He could use the arm if he must, but he thought merely to talk with Joseph and Jenkyn where they sat in chains in the castle gaol, awaiting hanging.

To his surprise, Lucie had encouraged this mission. She would know all of it that she might. And then be done with it. She would not be done with it, though. He recognised the haunted look in her eyes. Archdeacon Jehannes must speak to her, shrive her.

The gaol was not as clean as the one in St David's, nor as dry. The men sat on filthy straw mattresses.

'Where are the others?' Owen asked the gaoler.

'Up above. These are the two to watch. The others are just greedy fools.'

'Captain Archer,' one of the men said. He had dirty bandages on a leg and a hand. 'I never thought to see you.'

'That is Joseph, Captain,' the gaoler said. 'T'other is Jenkyn, a thatcher.' He withdrew, but just to the doorway.

'You never thought to live so long as to meet me?' Owen asked.

'A Welshman. I thought you would be fighting with the prince of your people.'

Owen shook his head. 'It is you I have to thank for that rumour?'

'It so pleased Alice Baker. I could not have found a better gossip.'

Owen liked the feel of his knuckles against the man's jaw. Neat, quick, just enough. Not to kill him. Why waste a hanging?

'Forgive me,' Owen said to the gaoler, who had turned the other way, feigning ignorance. He was not bad with his left fist.

'Now, Jenkyn, as your friend is nursing his jaw, you can tell me all about this plan gone wrong.'

The two men blamed it all on Harold Galfrey, claimed he had thought to make money selling the letter to Alderman Bolton. Joseph had heard that once Phillippa had hidden something in the tapestry and often she paused to touch it, he had seen that. Long ago he had stolen the treasury key and had it copied by a discreet smithy. Galfrey had seen his opportunity when asked to accompany Lucie. He arranged the attack, with enough damage caused and the steward injured, that Lucie would have need of him. But they could not say how Galfrey had learned of the letter, or why he was so confident Bolton would buy it. Owen detected a larger presence behind the plan. Galfrey's acquaintance with Lucie had depended on Roger Moreton and his friend Gisburne.

'And what of Colby, Gisburne's servant?' Thoresby asked. 'He is involved. I know that Gisburne is involved.'

He had summoned Lucie and Owen, Dame Phillippa, Jasper, Brother Michaelo and Roger Moreton to the palace. Not Alfred and the other retainers—they need not know Phillippa and Douglas Sutton's roles. Owen had not wished to come, but Lucie reminded him of the extent of Thoresby's help.

And so Owen sat there, in the palace hall, watching with growing discomfort the familiarity between Roger Moreton and Lucie, how frequently they spoke to one another and on each other's behalf.

'What will be done with the letter?' Lucie asked. 'It is proof of treason against King Edward. Robert the Bruce was his greatest enemy.'

Thoresby picked it up, studied the seal, his deep-set eyes unreadable. 'Treason indeed. And cowardice. Many in the North sought to save themselves in such wise. I should think it best burned.'

'But what of Alderman Bolton?' asked Roger. 'Would it not be a kindness to deliver it up to him?'

'Mistress Wilton and Mistress Sutton have surely suffered enough from your advice, Master Moreton,' Thoresby said.

'He has done all he could to make recompense,' Lucie countered. How could she be so forgiving? God's blood, what was she about?

Thoresby greeted her comment with a slight shrug. 'Still, of what use would it be? Neither the king nor Bolton have need of it. Robert the Bruce is long dead, Bolton is respected in the city. And we shall not mention it, any of us, ever, shall we? So the secret is safe.'

'And what of Gisburne?' asked Owen. 'You say there is no proof. What of those who saw Colby at Freythorpe?'

'He might have been there for the purpose he states,' said Michaelo. 'To warn the household that Joseph was about.'

'But Henry Gisburne knew of the letter,' Phillippa said timidly. 'And his wife.'

'Do we wish to make this public knowledge, Mistress Sutton?' Thoresby asked. 'Have you not suffered enough?' He said it kindly, gently.

'I—' Phillippa glanced at Lucie, seemingly confused.

Lucie took her aunt's hand, pressed it. 'Let them rest in peace, Aunt.'

Dame Phillippa's eyes turned to a space beside Owen. Her lips moved, but he could not understand, she spoke so softly.

Lucie rose. 'Your Grace, my aunt grows tired. I should take her home.'

Owen rose. 'Shall I come?' He did not yet understand these fits the old woman had.

Lucie gave him a little smile, shook her head. 'No need.' She led the frail Phillippa from the room.

Owen glanced over at Roger Moreton, saw the concern on his face. He did not like it.

• • •

Tom Merchet brought out a special ale for Owen's farewell drink with Jared, Edmund, Sam and Tom.

'We shall be off to France soon, I trow,' young Tom said proudly.

They spoke of past adventures, plied Owen for tales of his time in France. It was a long, boisterous evening. The men went stumbling off to their lodgings in the minster close when Tom could keep the tavern open no longer. Curfew was curfew, even for the duke's men. Owen lingered, helping his friend lock the doors.

In the kitchen, Tom poured cups of ale for both of them and sat down with a sigh. 'I grow old, my friend. The evenings seem to stretch on too long of late.'

Bess appeared. 'Is this men's business, or am I invited?'

'You are most welcome, gentle Bess,' Owen said and realised he had drunk more than he had thought.

Bess chuckled as she poured herself a cup of brandywine. Settling beside Tom, she nuzzled his neck with her nose.

'Now, that is a lovely sight,' said Owen.

'I am sure such awaits you at home and more,' said Bess with a wink.

'I do not like the way Roger Moreton looks at Lucie,' Owen burst out. He had meant to lead up to this. His mind was a muddle.

'He was a good friend to your family in your absence,' Tom said. 'You would complain of it?'

'In my absence. That is the point, is it not?'

Bess sniffed. 'Tom is right. Be grateful for such a good neighbour. Though he has much to answer for with Harold Galfrey.'

'Aye. And what of this Harold Galfrey? How was Lucie fooled by him?'

Bess downed her drink and rose. 'I am to bed. Do not stay too long.' She pecked Tom on the head and withdrew.

'What did I say?' Owen asked.

Tom shook his head. 'I do not try to understand her. There were rumours about Lucie and Roger—better you hear it from me.'

'And no wonder, the way he looks at her. And you should have heard her today, defending him, forgiving him all.'

'She is a gentle woman, a good wife and true,' Tom said. 'Alice

Baker is behind the rumours, all of them.' He chuckled. 'Bess has brought charges against her, as a scold. Is that not grand?' He slapped his thigh. 'Alice will be ordered to make a public apology, a confession of her mischief.'

Owen did not laugh. He feared that as the rumours about him held some truth, so did those about Lucie. Though not about the jaundice. 'I do not know what to think of all this,' he muttered.

'Think nothing of it. Forget it.'

'I shall never leave her alone again. I swear it.'

'You are drunk, my friend. But it is a good beginning. Now go home to your wife.'

Lucie waited for him in the hall, sitting by an open shutter, watching the garden. As always, she had tripped over her temper. Not that Owen had not provoked it. And his confession—that he had thought to fight for Lawgoch. She must not think of that.

She wished to make amends, have a proper homecoming. But the later it grew, the more she wondered whether he was ready to settle back into his life. It grew chilly. She wore only her shift. She should have brought a blanket. Where was he? Had he not missed her at all?

She rose when she heard the door and called to him.

He stepped into the hall. 'What is it? Why do you wake?'

'I waited for you. It is such a night. We have not sat out in the garden at night in so long.'

'I had too much to drink,' he muttered.

'You will miss the four of them? Do they remind you of your old comrades—Bertold, Lief, Gaspare, Ned?'

'No, never them. These were but lads, not true soldiers. But they will be. After France.'

He grew melancholy. That would not do.

'Come out to the garden, my love.'

'Am I?' He swayed ever so slightly as he stood there in the moonlight.

'The cool air will clear your head. Come.' She took his arm.

'Am I your love?' he demanded as he followed her, stumbling over one of the children's toys.

Lucie steadied him. 'Of course you are. How can you doubt it?'

Out in the garden, she led him to a bench beneath the linden, his favourite spot.

'What of Roger Moreton?' he demanded as he sat.

Sweet Heaven, not that! Hold your temper. Say nothing.

Lucie took his head in her hands, kissed him hard.

'Why do you not answer?'

She kissed him again. 'Is that not an answer?'

She slipped his linen shirt from his belt, explored his chest—what was not bandaged—with her hands. He began to fumble with the lace to her shift. She untied it for him, stood to let it drop on the grass beside the path.

'Lucie,' he whispered.

She shivered as he ran his hands over her body.

'I dreamed of you,' he whispered.

'And I you, my love. Come.' She coaxed him down on to the grass. He was not so drunk after all.

EPILOGUE

'Such a coarse, common woman,' Brother Michaelo was saying, 'why folk paid heed to her imaginings I cannot think.'

John Thoresby smiled to hear of Alice Baker's humbling. 'She has deserved the brand of scold for many a year, I have no doubt. I am glad of the alewife's action.'

'Which reminds me, we must order a barrel of her husband's fine ale. The duke's men consumed the last of what we had.'

A servant knocked, peered round the door. 'Your Grace, Master Gisburne has arrived.'

Ah. Thoresby had invited John Gisburne to the palace, luring him with its planned refurbishment.

Michaelo smiled. 'I have my pen and paper ready.'

He was to walk behind them, making note of those items Gisburne agreed to procure.

'Then let us proceed.' Thoresby drained his cup and rose, shaking out the wrinkles in his formal robes. The city grew unpleasant, too humid for his tastes. He would leave for Bishopthorpe in the morning.

Gisburne bowed low, sweeping a bejewelled hand to his heart, then kissed Thoresby's ring. He smelled of lavender and roses. What a fussy man. But better than smelling of sweat.

The three strolled through the palace, Gisburne keeping up a steady commentary—what was needed, how he might acquire it for the archbishop, Michaelo making notes. Thoresby had known the man was a merchant in the broadest sense, with his hand in many commodities. But he had not been aware of quite how far Gisburne cast his net. Still, Thoresby recognised the nervous chatter of someone hoping to control the conversation.

When they had completed the tour, Thoresby invited Gisburne into the hall for some wine. Michaelo withdrew.

'My purpose in inviting you was not only business. Or rather, not merely the matter of refurbishing this palace,' Thoresby began. 'I have learned of your father's partnership with Douglas Sutton.' He drew the long-lost letter from beneath a pile of documents on the table beside him, enjoyed watching dread sour his guest's expression.

Gisburne tried to keep his eyes away from the document, frowning in false confusion. His attempt at dissimulation was pitiable.

'Your father, it seems, was not a soldier, but a courier,' Thoresby continued. 'And not always a trustworthy one. This is a letter entrusted to him by Alderman Bolton's family along with a jewelled cup. They thought to buy protection from Robert the Bruce. But as you see, the letter did not reach the Scots.'

Gisburne said nothing, though his jaw had dropped.

'I understand you were most accommodating to the thief Harold Galfrey.'

'Of what are you accusing me?' Gisburne asked.

'It is said you would be mayor. You, who could not hold on to the office of bailiff. Alderman Bolton's support is what you hoped to buy, is it not?'

Gisburne suddenly grabbed for the parchment.

Thoresby moved it out of his reach. This was more like it. 'From whom did you learn of the letter? Your mother?'

Gisburne glowered. 'I admit nothing.'

'Many men wrote such letters at the time. Even churchmen. Abbots. But people have forgotten that. One of these days you will be caught in your web of deceit, Gisburne.' Thoresby stared at the merchant a good, long while. 'But for now, you are a wealthy man with a great sin on your conscience. And I am an old one, with a tomb to build. This is the matter I wish to discuss. If you are generous enough, I might even see my way to allowing you to present Bolton with the letter.' He smiled as a medley of emotions flickered across the merchant's face. He had him where he wanted him.

AUTHOR'S NOTE

When I set out to tell a York story while Owen was yet in Wales I did not think what a burden I was placing on Lucie's shoulders. But I quickly realised that she would feel she had to protect Freythorpe Hadden without neglecting her apothecary, her reputation, her children, her ailing aunt and her home in the city. She did all this by employing a network of assistants. Unfortunately, not all proved trustworthy.

Still, I found the political situation in Wales and Owen's response to it too intriguing to hurry him home. Alas for Lucie.

Hywel is a fictional character, born from my understanding of the type of tyrant who often begins with the best intentions but falls victim to his own ambitious and violent nature. Owain Lawgoch, however, is a historic figure, as are Archdeacons Rokelyn and Baldwin, Bishop Houghton, and John Gisburne.

I provided some background regarding Owain Lawgoch in the notes for *A Gift of Sanctuary*. As Martin Wirthir tells Owen in this book, Owain Lawgoch returned to Wales to claim his inheritance after his father's death, then returned to France, where it is believed he joined the free companies (bands of mercenaries of mixed nationalities). In French chronicles he is known as Yvain de Galles, a hero, respected by the great commander Bertrand du Guesclin. But Owain's place in Welsh tradition is based not on his exploits, but on what the people hoped he would do. In Welsh tradition as well as the traditions of many cultures, there is a legendary redeemer-hero, who E.R. Henken defines as 'one who has never really died, but who, either in sleep or in a distant land, awaits the time when his people will need him, when he will return and restore the land to its former glory.' (*National Hero*, p. 23). Over the centuries eight such heroes have been believed to be the redeemer of Wales: Hiriell, Cynan, Cadwaladr, Arthur, Owain (oddly generic, never specified), Owain Lawgoch, Owain Glyndwr and Henry Tudor (p. 25). I was fortunate to have Owain Lawgoch fall in the period I am chronicling through Owen Archer. The coming of the hero was the subject of many songs and poems. The bards prepared the people for Lawgoch; many men readied themselves with horses and arms in preparation for the coming battle. Owain did set off for Wales in December, 1370, commanding French ships, but a storm forced him back at Guernsey. It was a costly and futile expedition. Perhaps that is why King Charles kept Owain occupied in France for the next eight years. In 1378, while Owain commanded the siege of Mortagne on the Gironde estuary, he was approached by a man bringing news from Wales and offering his service. The man, John Lamb, became Owain's chamberlain, one of his most trusted men. One morning, when the two sat alone watching the castle under siege, Lamb stabbed Owain through the heart. Lamb received 100 francs from the English government in appreciation for his murder of 'a rebel and enemy of the King in France.' There is no clear evidence that Lamb acted on orders from the English government. In the *Anonimalle Chronicle* of St Mary's Abbey, York, in an entry under 1378, it says: 'At this time was killed a great enemy of England called Uwayn of the Red Hand and he was of Wales, the heritage of which he demanded of the crown of England and he was the chief warrior, after the Marshal of France, at the siege of the castle of Mortagne'. Interestingly, A.D. Carr suggests that the 'order for his elimination must have come from a very high level and the name of John of Gaunt [Duke of Lancaster], [then] the regent for the young Richard II, comes to mind...' (*Owen of Wales*, p. 57).

We do not know much about the various archdeacons in St David's at the time, but I used their actual names. Bishop Houghton became Lord Chancellor of England in 1377, probably thanks to the influence of John of Gaunt. He died in 1389 and was buried in the chapel of his college of St Mary in St David's—unfortunately his tomb no longer exists. Nor does the stained glass that tradition has it depicted a story about Houghton that I heard in St David's. It is said that the bishop was excommunicated by Pope Clement VI, and that Houghton excommunicated the pope in return. The story as given is chronologically impossible, but if the anti-pope Clement VII (1378-94) is intended, it is possible, though not probable. Still, a good story.

That the outlaws who attack Freythorpe Hadden have been hired by a wealthy man is in keeping with the times. Consider the case of Bishop Thomas de Lisle, who was accused of supporting 'a number of criminals, including his own brother, his cousins, manorial officials, and even beneficed priests...' They were often indicted for 'crimes ranging from petty theft and extortion to kidnapping, arson, assault, and murder...[his] men were said to have looted and burned people's houses, breaking and entering at night while the occupants were asleep' (*Criminal Churchmen*, introduction). Although John Gisburne's activities in *A Spy for the Redeemer* are fictional, he was accused later in his career of harbouring criminals, some of whom were accused of a murder in 1372. As mayor of York in 1371 and again in 1381, he will return as a prominent character in future adventures of Owen Archer.

For further reading about Owain Lawgoch, see *Owen of Wales: The End of the House of Gwynedd* by A. D. Carr (University of Wales Press 1991) and 'Owain Lawgoch—Yeuain De Galles: Some Facts and Suggestions' by Edward Owen in *Transactions of the Honourable Society of Cymmrododorion*, Session 1899-1900, pp. 6-105. For the redeemer-hero, see *National Redeemer: Owain Glyndwr in Welsh Tradition* by Elissa P. Henken (University of Wales Press, 1996). For further reading about the merchant class and its clashes in York, see *Medieval Merchants: York, Beverley and Hull in the Later Middle Ages* by Jenny Kermode (Cambridge University Press 1998) and 'The Risings in York, Beverley and Scarborough, 1380-1381' by R. B. Dobson in *The English Rising of 1381*, eds. R. H. Hilton and T. H. Aston (Cambridge University Press 1984) pp. 112-142. For Bishop De Lisle, see *Criminal Churchmen in the Age of Edward III* by John

Aberth (Penn State University Press, 1996). May McKisack notes Robert the Bruce's harrowing of Yorkshire in *The Fourteenth Century 1307-1399* (Oxford Clarendon Press 1959), p. 75. A more extended discussion of the Bruce's strategy can be found in *The Wars of the Bruces: Scotland, England and Ireland, 1306-1328* by Colm McNamee (Tuckwell Press 1997).

THE OWEN ARCHER SERIES

THE APOTHECARY ROSE

In the year of our Lord 1363, two suspicious deaths in the infirmary of St. Mary's Abbey catch the attention of the powerful John Thoresby, Lord Chancellor of England and Archbishop of York. One victim is a pilgrim, while the second is Thoresby's ne'er-do-well ward, both apparently poisoned by a physic supplied by Master Apothecary Nicholas Wilton. In the wake of these deaths, the archbishop dispatches one-eyed spy Owen Archer to York to find the murderer. Under the guise of a disillusioned soldier keen to make a fresh start, Owen insinuates himself into Wilton's apothecary as an apprentice. But he finds Wilton bedridden, with the shop being run by his lovely, enigmatic young wife, Lucie. As Owen unravels a tangled history of scandal and tragedy, he discovers at its center a desperate, forbidden love twisted over time into obsession. And the woman he has come to love is his prime suspect.

Lovingly detailed, beautifully written, *The Apothecary Rose* is a captivating and suspenseful tale of life, love, and death in medieval England.

THE LADY CHAPEL

Perfect for fans of both Ellis Peters and CJ Sansom, *The Lady Chapel* is a vivid and immersive portrait of court intrigue and a testament to the power of the medieval guilds.

Summer in the year of our Lord 1365. On the night after the Corpus Christi procession, a man is brutally murdered on the steps of York Minster. The next morning his severed hand is found in a room at the York Tavern—a room hastily vacated by a fellow guild member who had quarreled with the victim.

Archbishop Thoresby calls on Owen Archer to investigate. As Owen tracks the fleeing merchant, he uncovers a conspiracy involving a powerful company of traders, but his only witness is a young boy who has gone into hiding, and his only suspect is a mysterious cloaked woman. When Owen discovers a link between the traders and a powerful coterie in the royal court, he brings his apothecary wife Lucie into the race to find the boy before he is silenced forever by the murderers.

THE NUN'S TALE

Based on an enigmatic entry in the records of Clementhorpe Nunnery, this authentic, gripping mystery conjures a 14th century ripe with forbidden passions and political intrigue.

When young nun Joanna Calverley dies of a fever in the town of Beverley in the summer of 1365, she is buried quickly for fear of the plague. But a year later, Archbishop Thoresby learns of a woman who has arrived in York claiming to be the resurrected nun, talking of relic-trading and miracles. And death seems to ride in her wake.

The archbishop sends Owen Archer to retrace the woman's journey, an investigation that leads him across the north from Leeds to Beverley to Scarborough. Along the way he encounters Geoffrey Chaucer, a spy for the king of England, who believes there is a connection between the nun's troubles, renegade mercenaries, and the powerful Percy family. Back in York, however, Owen's wife Lucie, pregnant with their first child, has won the confidence of the mysterious nun and realizes that there are secrets hidden in the woman's seemingly mad ramblings...

THE KING'S BISHOP

From the marshy Thames to the misty Yorkshire moors, murder stalks Welsh soldier-sleuth Owen Archer and one of his oldest friends.

On a snowy morning in 1367, Sir William of Wyndesore's page is found in the icy moat of Windsor Castle, and some whisper that the murderer was Ned Townley—a former comrade-in-arms of Owen Archer. Burdened with a reputation as a notoriously jealous lover, Ned cannot hope to clear his name; even Mary, his ladylove, is unsure of the truth. Hoping to put Ned out of harm's way while solving the murder, Owen places his friend in charge of a mission to Rievaulx Abbey at the edge of the moors. But when the travelers receive news of Mary's drowning, Ned vanishes into the wild.

Riding out in search of his old friend, Owen does not know whether he will be Ned's savior or executioner. With his one good eye, Owen sees more than most, but now he must find a way to penetrate the curtains of power that surround the Church and England's royal court and discover the truth of Ned's innocence or guilt...

THE RIDDLE OF ST. LEONARD'S

In the year of our Lord 1369 the much-loved Queen Philippa lies dying in Windsor Castle, the harvest has failed, and the pestilence has returned. In York, the atmosphere of fear and superstition is heightened by a series of thefts and violent deaths at St. Leonard's Hospita, as well as rumors that these crimes are connected to the hospital's dwindling funds. The Master of St. Leonard's, Sir Richard Ravenser, hurries north from the queen's deathbed to summon Owen Archer, soldier-spy, to investigate the scandal before it ruins him.

While his wife Lucie faces the plague-panicked townsfolk at the apothecary, Owen encounters a seemingly random series of clues: a riddle posed by one of the victims at the hospital, a lay sister with a scandalous past, the kidnapping of a child from the hospital orphanage, and a case of arson. The answer to the riddle of St. Leonard's lies in the past, and as Owen's family is caught up in the sweep of the pestilence, he must abandon them to race across the countryside to save the next victim.

A GIFT OF SANCTUARY

Under the pretense of escorting his father-in-law and the archbishop's secretary on a pilgrimage to the sacred city of St. David's in Wales, Owen Archer and Geoffrey Chaucer, in truth, are carrying out a mission for the Duke of Lancaster. England and France are at war, and the southern coast of Wales is vulnerable to invasion—Owen and Geoffrey are to recruit archers for the duke's army and inspect his Welsh fortifications on the coast, while quietly investigating whether the duke's steward at Cydweli Castle is involved in a French plot to incite rebellion in Wales.

But trouble precedes them in the cathedral city of St. David's. On Whitesands Beach beyond the city a young man is beaten and left for dead, then spirited away by a Welsh bard. Shortly afterward a corpse clothed in the livery of the Duke of Lancaster is left at the city gate, his shoes filled with white sand. Meanwhile, at Cydweli Castle, a chain of events begun by the theft of money from the castle's exchequer ends in a violent death and the disappearance of the steward's beautiful young wife. Owen and Geoffrey begin to see connections linking the troubles in city and castle, and learn they must unravel the complex story of betrayed love and political ambition to prevent more deaths. But in the course of his investigations in the land of his birth, Owen is haunted by doubts about his own loyalties...

THE GUILT OF INNOCENTS

Winter in the year of our Lord 1372. A river pilot falls into the icy waters of the River Ouse during a skirmish between dockworkers and the boys of the minster school, which include Owen Archer's adopted son Jasper. But what began as a confrontation to return a boy's stolen scrip becomes a murder investigation as the rescuers find the pilot dying of wounds inflicted before his plunge into the river. When another body is fished from the river upstream and Owen discovers that the boy Jasper sought to help has disappeared, Owen Archer convinces the archbishop that he must go in search of the boy. His lost scrip seems to hold the key to the double tragedy, but his disappearance leaves troubling questions: did he flee in fear? Or was he abducted?

On the cusp of this new mystery, Owen accepts Jasper's offer to accompany him to the boy's home in the countryside, where they learn that a valuable cross has gone missing. A devastating fire and another drowning force Owen to make impossible choices, endangering not only himself, but the two innocents he fights to protect. The bond between fathers and sons proves strong, even between those not linked by blood.

A VIGIL OF SPIES

Archbishop Thoresby of York, the second most powerful cleric in England, lies dying in his bed. The end of his life is seen by the great families of the North as a chance to promote one of their own as his successor, and Thoresby himself announces he will leave the matter to the dean and chapter of York. On the eve of this decision, the dying archbishop agrees to a visit from Joan, Princess of Wales, wife of the Black Prince, heir to the throne of England. Thoresby's captain of the guard, Owen Archer, has no doubt that trouble will follow.

As soon as the company rides into the palace yard he is proved right: they arrive burdened with the body of one of their party, and Owen finds evidence that the man's death was no accident. Within days of this discovery, a courier carrying an urgent message for the archbishop is found hanging in the woods. With guards surrounding the property, it is clear that the murderer walks among the palace guests. The powerful Percy and Neville families are well represented in the entourage, including a woman who remembers an afternoon tryst with Owen as much, much more. Even the princess' son is suspect. As Owen races to unmask the guilty and rid the palace of the royal party, his final wish for his lord is that he might die in peace.

THE MARGARET KERR SERIES

A TRUST BETRAYED

In the spring of 1297 the English army controls lowland Scotland and Margaret Kerr's husband Roger Sinclair is missing. He'd headed to Dundee in autumn, writing to Margaret with a promise to be home for Christmas, but it's past Easter. Is he caught up in the swelling rebellion against the English? Is he even alive? When his cousin, Jack, is murdered on the streets of Edinburgh, Roger's last known location, Margaret coerces her brother Andrew, a priest, to escort her to the city.

She finds Edinburgh scarred by war—houses burnt, walls stained with blood, shops shuttered—and the townsfolk simmering with resentment, harboring secrets. Even her uncle, innkeeper Murdoch Kerr, meets her questions with silence. Are his secrets the keys to Roger's disappearance? What terrible sin torments her brother? Is it her husband she glimpses in the rain, scarred, haunted? Desperate, Margaret makes alliances that risk both her own life and that of her brother in her search for answers. She learns that war twists love and loyalties, and that, until tested, we cannot know our own hearts, much less those of our loved ones.

THE FIRE IN THE FLINT

Scots are gathering in Murdoch Kerr's Edinburgh tavern, plotting to drive out the English forces. Margaret takes her place there as innkeeper, collecting information to pass on to William Wallace—until murder gives the English an excuse to shutter the tavern. The dead man was a witness to the intruders who raided chests belonging to Margaret's husband and her father, the latest in a string of violent raids on Margaret's family, but no one knows the identity of the raiders or what they're searching for.

Margaret's uncle urges her to escape Edinburgh, but as she flees north with her husband Roger, Margaret grows suspicious about his sudden wish to speak with her mother, Christiana, who is a soothsayer. Margaret once innocently shared with Roger one of Christiana's visions, of "the true king of Scotland" riding into Edinburgh. Now she begins to wonder if their trip is part of a mission engineered by the English crown...

A CRUEL COURTSHIP

In late summer 1297, Margaret Kerr heads to the town of Stirling at the request of William Wallace's man James Comyn. Her mission is to discover the fate of a young spy who had infiltrated the English garrison at Stirling Castle, but on the journey Margaret is haunted by dreams—or are they visions?—of danger.

He who holds Stirling Castle holds Scotland—and a bloody battle for the castle is imminent. But as the Scots prepare to cast off the English yoke, Margaret's flashes of the future allow her to glimpse what is to come—and show her that she can trust no one, not even her closest friends.

A Cruel Courtship is a harrowing account of the days before the bloody battle of Stirling Bridge, and the story of a young woman's awakening.

9 781682 301074